SCATHING REVIEWER

SCATHING REVIEWER

BOOK ONE

BananaDragon

Podium

Published in 2025 by Podium Publishing
www.podiumentertainment.com

Podium

SCATHING REVIEWER

CHAPTER ONE

I'm Peijin."

That was how I usually introduced myself, and people, trying to be nice, would respond by saying, "What a pretty name. You must be very ambitious."

Yes, exactly. To be precise, my name directly translated to "full of gemstones and fine jade," and it was associated with determination and the essence of humanitarian ideals.

However, my parents must have named their beloved daughter while ignoring the fact my name also insinuated tragedy, disappointment, and cynicism—all of which were deeply felt when I failed the National College Entrance Examination and was sentenced to a shameful job.

Now the glow from my laptop screen illuminated my pale face in my otherwise-dark apartment. I sat on an old swivel chair and rested my head atop my bent knees.

My short black hair was brushed out of my face and tucked behind my ears; my bangs were wrapped around a Velcro hair roller stuck on top of my head. I saw a notification pop up in the corner of my screen and opened up the web novel site, reading the new comment under chapter 3,649—my most recently uploaded chapter.

Fourteen-year-old me thought a good pen name would save me from my doomed fate, even if it was just for a stupid web novel I was writing. I had bitterly and pridefully settled on JiaLi1825, which meant "good, beautiful girl." Two things that I wasn't.

Ten years later, my lonely and unremarkable life could be summed up as such: Liu Peijin, twenty-four, single, pest control.

I kept updating the web novel daily, though, and I supposed that was where all my ambition was going. Everyone loved a clichéd, mass-produced web novel. A classic, depressed but resourceful male protagonist with a lousy job, no prospects, a scummy apartment . . . Wait.

"Dammit, my life sucks," I said while lightly banging my head against my messy desk.

Qiu Feiyu was my very handsome and very generic protagonist, but I had poured my heart into writing about him. Sometimes it felt like I was writing this entire story for him . . . or maybe for the stranger who'd inspired him. Teleported to a world dominated by divinities, demons, and ghosts within a gaming system, Feiyu had to cleverly escape dangerous challenges.

Even in the first chapter, Feiyu had to intelligently navigate and survive a challenge that would kill more than half the population in a flash. Things weren't necessarily easy for him, and I took joy in that. Not that I was a sadist or anything.

Although I had started out writing for my own fulfillment, projecting myself onto these characters, I later wrote basic tropes specifically for readers. My numbers went up for the infinite dungeon grind, blue boxes, Demon Kings, goblins—I wrote it all.

Except for anything romantic. I was single, after all.

Hey, people liked what they were familiar with. But at some point, I didn't. If a part of me had ever been proud of my work, it was now long, long gone. I could hardly recognize my own story at this point. It was a monstrous conglomeration of what I thought people wanted to read.

Thanks to my childhood self's good saving habits, my web novel generated enough funds to get through each month. And *Surviving My First Run* had been successful, garnering around nine million total views.

But the greedy web novel contract I'd signed meant I wasn't making as much money as I should have been. My Paytron account still accumulated enough, though, and as a reward for supporting me, I even let users buy their way into the storyline as characters.

Apparently, however, I drove away some readers with my allegedly "confrontational" personality. I wouldn't really call myself confrontational—maybe "reactive" was a better word. Fourteen-year-old me was incredibly defensive, but I swore I'd grown since then. At least a bit.

I looked at my computer. The newest comment glared at me from my screen.

MolaMola: Thank you for the chapter!
I'm a bit confused . . . isn't Feiyu on his first run?
He shouldn't have any buffs from previous
regressions that wouldn't exist.

> **JiaLi1825**: It doesn't really matter.
> Feiyu got the staff from a divinity anyway.
> **MolaMola**: Just wanted to point out a
> consistency issue if you cared enough to fix it.
> **JiaLi1825**: I definitely care, it's just not
> that relevant to the plot. Past regression or
> not, he would've attained the staff somehow . . .
> **MolaMola**: It's a minor issue.
> No need to get so defensive.
> **JiaLi1825**: I'm not being defensive.
> **MolaMola**: You should still fix it.

I stared at the message; my brows furrowed in annoyance. Okay, sure, I wasn't the greatest at writing a tightly knit plot, but it always got on my nerves when commenters were dismissive about my efforts.

Had I been too defensive, though? I knew I wasn't the best at talking to people, since I spent most of my time alone . . . I pulled my chair closer to my computer to go ahead with making the edit. MolaMola was right. It really wasn't that big of a change, and despite what people said about me, I wanted to avoid confrontation. I'd make the edit, respond to MolaMola with a brief thanks for their comment, and—

> **MolaMola**: Hello? I've been a longtime reader.
> Trust me, I know the ins and outs of this story, lol.

Never mind.

I deleted the comment thread. If MolaMola cared so much about a story, they could just write their own. Now this interaction would be on my mind all night.

I stood up, kicked my chair in, and haphazardly walked through my tiny, cluttered apartment to scrounge for a meal. After saying a half-hearted prayer, I used long black chopsticks to stir steamed white rice with some marinated pork before going back to my bedroom. To me, this was a fancy meal. Normally, I just ate a bowl of ramen with one boiled egg.

My small mailbox for private messages had a new little red notification, and I clicked on it apprehensively. Realizing it was MolaMola, I let out a frustrated groan but continued reading.

> **MolaMola**: I didn't mean to offend you.
> I simply had a question about the content, but there
> was no need to act so rudely about my feedback.

> You forget who your readers are and how they've
> brought you to this point. You're going to regret deleting
> my messages, Jia Li. Tomorrow, 1 p.m. I have a surprise for you.

My chest tightened, and my face flushed from a mix of embarrassment and annoyance. Was I really that bad at talking to people? I glared at my computer screen for a moment longer before reporting MolaMola and blocking them. Seriously, who'd go out of their way to threaten someone who had so generously written a story for an entire decade? What a narcissist. And their username was stupid.

This was my mundane, unfulfilling life. Everything was the same—even on the night before the apocalypse.

For those reading this now, congrats: You survived the apocalypse. But please don't come looking for me. I'm sorry this was the best ending I could write, but it was the only way to save you.

"What a complete dump." I surveyed the infested house before me, which was teeming with cockroaches and bedbugs. I was totally prepared in white protective gear with my black bob tied up in a short ponytail. "I don't understand how people live like this, let alone let it get this bad."

Fat brown cockroaches hissed, some darting away when I awkwardly shifted through the room. It was the day after I'd received MolaMola's message, and I was going about my day as normal.

Yang wrapped the dirtied white couch with a clear plastic wrap to trap the insects and then stood up, brushing off his suit. He wore a plastic suit that matched mine, large goggles over his eyes. They were fogging up now as sweat collected on the interior.

"Don't be so judgmental, Peijin," Yang said. "A lot of them struggle with their mental health."

I let out an exaggerated sigh before I helped him clean up. "If only I hadn't flunked that stupid college test . . ."

"I don't know, I find it rewarding to help them," Yang said with a small smile, and I could see large beads of sweat sliding down his forehead. He was working much harder than I was. "We're helping them get their lives back in order, you know? I'd hope someone would do the same for me."

I looked at him, my eyes narrowing in suspicion at his words. We'd been co-workers for a while, and seeing him smile up close, I could understand why people in our office found him to be the most attractive one there. He had light brown hair and deep coffee-brown eyes that caught and reflected light perfectly, making his irises almost orange. Even as he wiped the sweat from his forehead with his gloved forearm, he looked as if he were glowing.

I scrunched my nose. Since I was young, I held sky-high ambitions for myself. I'd fallen terribly short from them, which was probably why I acted like a bitter old woman. But even though Yang was in the same position as me, he acted nothing like me, and I knew that he would do great things, while I continued to lag behind.

Yang was a completely different person than me, and we ended up at this job for just as different reasons. I hated how perfect he was, but I didn't hate Yang.

"I don't get how people like you are real, or how you even survived this long." I felt a crawling sensation and slapped my leg, exhaling to calm my heart. I looked down and saw a puncture in the leg of my suit and a crushed cockroach on the inside. "Shit . . ."

Yang peeked over, his face twisting into a teasing grin. "It's fine. You brought the steamer, right?"

We always needed to bring a steamer to kill all the bugs that might be on our clothing, jammed in the soles of our shoes, or hiding in furniture.

"Weren't you supposed to pack it?" I asked.

"You've always packed it, Peijin."

I shot him a crushed look.

Yang's expression turned considerate. "Let me drive back to the office to pick one up. My suit is fine, so it's unlikely I'll bring any bugs with me."

Damn his kindness.

"I don't want you getting in trouble," I insisted. "Let's just finish up. When we get back to the office, I'll ask for a steamer and deal with the consequences."

"Are you sure?"

"Confident."

He tilted his head curiously. "I thought you only had one more warning until you got fired."

"Did you really have to bring that up?!"

Yang gave another toothy grin as he went to lift the couch into the van. "Don't worry about it. Rookie mistake. I'll head back and vouch for you if needed."

I didn't know how he could put up with me or how he could remain this calm, but I was glad I made the error with him there and not someone else.

We lifted the couch into the back of the van and flicked off any visible bugs from the protective layer of plastic before unsuiting. I thought back to my cluttered, dirty apartment; just a few bedbugs on my shoes could become a complete disaster. My face flushed as I remembered the earlier conversation where I had judged the client's home.

Moving into the driver's seat of the van, I groaned, gripping the steering wheel and pressing my forehead against it. "Why is my life so bad?"

"Maybe because you failed your college entrance exam?"

"Shut up."

Yang typed the directions back to the office into my phone and set it on the dashboard for me. "We'll get there by 1:17 p.m. At worst, there might be a few loose bedbugs, but I think most are contained by the wrap." He grinned and lifted a finger to point at the aux. "Do you mind if I listen to my podcast?"

"You listen to podcasts? That's really weird," I said. "You're preparing for that senior citizen life already."

He shot me a mortified expression while I laughed, pulling onto the freeway. "It's just that American politics are so fascinating. I want to move there in the future. It's much different than China."

It was thrilling to watch Yang speak—he was diligent and a good person, and when he spoke, his glowing eyes focused on just you, and it made you feel like the only person in the world.

"I'm trying to learn English," I replied in a feeble attempt to look cool, tilting my chin up a bit while keeping my eyes on the road to avoid his stare.

"Oh really? Are you watching shows in English or taking any private lessons?"

"I read English novels and plays."

Yang's expression lit up with excitement. "Which ones?"

I paused, trying and failing to elaborate on the lie. Well, it wasn't like I was *completely* lying—I definitely read novels, just not in English. But I wasn't going to list off trashy web novels; that would be completely embarrassing in front of someone as studious as Yang. So, suddenly, *The Potentate* by BananaDragon became Shakespeare.

"I'm reading . . . Shakespeare."

From the passenger seat, Yang gasped in awe. "Really? Wow, that's impressive. You should help me with my English. Which play are you reading?"

"Umm . . . *Merchant in Venice.*"

"That's so niche! You must really be an expert." Yang's face broke out in a bright smile as he continued. "I'm reading Fitzgerald right now, and it's so difficult. Do you have any advice?"

Shit.

"Just read a lot. You'll get there, since you're very smart."

I laughed awkwardly before turning my focus back to the road, embarrassed and a bit ashamed. A notification suddenly pinged on my phone, blocking the map's directions.

Yang was quick to react. "Let me switch it back to the map." He went to tap on my phone but paused. "MolaMola sent you a message and a file. They said, 'Thanks for writing *Surviving My First Run.* As promised, here's the surprise.'"

My eyes widened, and I looked at the time: 12:59 p.m. They couldn't even time it right. Hadn't I blocked them? They shouldn't have been able to send me any messages.

"Oh, I have no idea what they're talking about," I said, playing it off as I rubbed the back of my neck.

"Do you write web novels? Isn't *Surviving My First Run* super famous? I always see the ads in the train station." He turned to me, looking amazed.

"What are you talking about? I've never heard of it." I pursed my lips, swallowing and continuing to stare down the freeway.

My phone pinged again, and Yang peeked at it. "They sent another message—"

Before he could read it, I snatched my phone and read the notification, slowing the car.

Why hide it if you wrote it?

My blood ran cold, and I could feel my throat thickening from anxiety and anticipation. Was this person some freaky stalker?

That was the moment when the phone screen and the van around me seemed to vanish. A glowing blue screen appeared before me, with a message in bright white text.

Your free trial on Planet-2099 has ended.

. . . What?

The van returned, and I looked back at the road, careful of the cars around me. The blue screen stayed there, but I could see through the interface to the cars beyond. By the shocked expression on Yang's face, I could tell he saw it, too. He must have had his own screen; his vision was locked on a seemingly empty space above his lap.

I glanced at the time on my phone. It was 1 p.m. On the dot.

A blinding flash of light and a massive explosion on the freeway a few cars ahead sent debris, vehicles, and massive chunks of concrete and asphalt flying into the air. Car windows cracked from the force of the explosion, and a deafening boom rang out.

I gripped the wheel and swerved into the emergency lane, trying to avoid the ensuing chaos. Yang cried out and grabbed my arm to stabilize himself. Cars crashed and reversed, their drivers and passengers surprised by the eruption and trying to escape.

A small dragon, barely longer than my forearm, appeared from the bright blue blast, floating in the air a few feet above the cars. After unfurling itself, it moved its limbs awkwardly, like a newborn giraffe learning how to stand, and each eye blinked independently before they eventually synced up. My jaw dropped as I stared at the creature.

"¡™£¢∞§¶•ao"

The dragon seemed to speak in a foreign language—no, a completely *new* language—before it opened a glowing blue interface, fidgeting with buttons and scratching its head.

One of the Four Auspicious Beasts of China would appear on the freeway, and for the first time, it would open its eyes and find humanity. In their craze and panic, humans would come to recognize it as the Azure Dragon.

I knew this. I knew this setting perfectly as that sentence popped into my mind—that sentence that I had written. This was the opening scene to *Surviving My First Run*.

My heart was beating out of my chest, and my head spun. I stopped the car at once, unable to piece together any coherent thoughts.

There was no way any of this was real, right? I mean, seriously, my web novel becoming reality? I must have been hallucinating, or maybe I died in some freak car accident and was sent to a hellish afterlife.

> **Your free trial on Planet-2099 has ended.**

The blue screen was still in front of me. There was a white *X* in one corner. Did this interface operate the same as it did in *Surviving My First Run*? Without hesitating, I easily controlled the screen, moving it with my hand—or just by thinking about it. I closed it with a mental command.

Yang's voice snapped me out of my flurry of thoughts.

"Peijin? What is this?" Yang seemed to shrink in front of me as he tugged on my sleeve, shaking.

I gave him a reassuring squeeze while trying to calm myself down, too. "Don't say a word. I need you to trust me on this."

A booming voice sounded, exuding an air of wicked power and confidence. Yet the words were those of a rookie.

"Hello? Hello? Can you hear me now? Sorry about that. You guys have a lot of dialects, and I got confused. I've never seen this specific planet before. My boss just assigned it to me this morning."

The dragon's voice was heard by everyone within the vicinity. He looked around and saw all the bewildered glances from people exiting their cars, and he let out an evil, cackling laugh.

"China is open for the apocalypse!"

> **The first arc has begun.**
> **Now commencing Chapter #1—Prerequisite.**

CHAPTER TWO

The small dragon lifted a clawed hand to its snout, loudly clearing its throat.

"You humans have been living such meaningless lives, waking up every day without knowing your purpose. Isn't it unfair to rot away while taking up so much valuable space?"

That wasn't entirely untrue, but I took great offense. Had I really written something like that? I guess fourteen-year-old me would be incredibly disappointed we ended up in pest control.

"Finally, you will join our beloved entertainment industry. You'll now live to entertain our glorious gods. What an honor! It's time you all did something wort—"

"Can you get out of the fucking way? Some of us are trying to get to work!" a man in a suit shouted, honking his horn and blaring his headlights.

The small dragon looked rather taken aback by the man's disregard. He tried to restart his speech, but a young boy cut off the dragon.

"Mommy, is that a talking lizard?" He pointed at the dragon, his head sticking out from the back-seat window of a small sedan.

"Huh? No!" the dragon exclaimed in anger, though it was contrasted by his small, almost-adorable blue body. "I am one of the Four Auspicious Beasts!"

He let out his most vicious roar, and a minuscule flame equivalent to a cigarette lighter puffed from its open mouth, small rows of jagged white teeth lining his bright red gums.

People shouted jeering but curious remarks from all over the road.

"Huh? So, does that make you the Azure Dragon?"

"Don't belittle our culture like that! That thing is way too cute to be the Azure Dragon!"

"Hey, it kind of looks like one if I really squint."

"This must be a hologram advertisement for that web novel. I read the first few chapters, and this is exactly how it started," a woman chimed in, getting out of her car and standing in front of the dragon.

She'd read my novel. Did that make me a celebrity?

More people exited their vehicles, infuriated by the disturbance. Those who swerved or got into accidents were now yelling at the dragon, raising enraged fists into the air.

"Get this advertisement out of the way. I heard the author was total scum, but who knew they'd go as far as to block a freeway during the middle of a workday."

Never mind. I was definitely not a celebrity.

Channel #IS-2948 is now open.
Observers have been invited to watch Channel #IS-2948.

The blue notifications popped up back-to-back. My face twisted in confusion—what the hell were "observers"?

In *Surviving My First Run*, gods, demons, and ghosts would watch these broadcasts as a form of entertainment, betting their money—known as stars— on the humans and deriving entertainment from both their suffering and victory.

Karmic restraint was the system that kept them in check—it was the law of equivalent exchange. If a god abused their power to influence a challenge, for example a god possessing disciples, they would face severe physical repercussions in the form of karma. It could only be offset if they gave up an equivalent amount of their spiritual energy—which was earned by increasing their number of believers, or through other means like contracts, dungeons, and challenges.

But observers? They definitely didn't exist in *Surviving My First Run*. But other than that, everything was identical to my novel.

I tapped a finger on the glowing notification in hopes of revealing more details about the observers, but the interface rejected my request with a small vibration.

"A web novel?" The dragon gawked. "This is the real deal. Don't mock me! Do you know how many planets I've streamed?! I'm about to be promoted!"

Yang shook me, forcing me back into this newfound reality. "They're not talking about you, are they?"

"Of course not."

This bickering dragon was really killing my hard-earned author reputation.

As if on cue, the dragon was finally fed up with the crowd's shouting. "I told you—don't mock me!"

He roared, his body growing larger as it started evolving. Sharp rows of dagger-like scales tore through his flesh. The flock of people in front of him seemed to freeze before their heads and bodies compressed into a ball. I could hear their bones snapping and crunching before a wet gushing sound erupted and sent a mist of red blood flying all over the freeway.

Yang and I both screamed, and I clasped my hands over his gaping mouth, accidentally poking his eye. He screamed again while I repeatedly apologized, panicked.

Little blue flames filtered up through the ground and began scavenging the dead bodies, pocketing their eyes, teeth, and jewelry. These flames were the weakest ghosts, human souls that were lost in the afterlife. They danced around before vanishing back into the pits of the underworld.

This was insane. Utterly impossible. Still, on the off chance this was real, there was no one in the universe more qualified and knowledgeable than me. After all, this was my world, and it was following the rules I'd laid out.

"Isn't this fun?" The dragon cackled, opening his arms to the sky to speak to the gods. "Come. Come and watch my show! You'll never see a story like this!" He must have received spiritual energy from the gods if he could kill humans so easily without facing karmic backlash.

People shrieked, scrambling back into their cars and attempting to drive away—but they imploded. With loud *pops*, car windows were suddenly splattered with blood that dripped out from underneath the doors and onto the light gray pavement, coloring the freeway a dark red.

At least two hundred of the people in front of me were now dead.

"W-where is the Liberation Army or the police?" a woman cried, screaming as she collapsed onto the ground, staring at the unfolding scene.

A man wearing rectangular-rimmed glasses shouted back as he stared at his phone, "The government has already been hit! Apparently, these creatures are showing up globally!"

"Where'd you read that?"

"My mother-in-law posted it on WeChat!"

"Then of course it's not true! The government is coming to save us, I'm sure of it!"

Of course there was no government coming to save us.

There was no government at all anymore.

Nobody was immune to the system in *Surviving My First Run*. Not the rich, not the powerful, and not even the gods. I'd written it that way to demonstrate the high stakes and indiscriminate slaughter—no one's old life could save them here.

Besides, what fourteen-year-old wanted to deal with the government?

So far, the scenes were playing out as I'd written them. Even the dialogue followed a similar trajectory. There were some unknown factors, like the observers, but for now, I knew I could rely on my knowledge.

I ignored the ensuing panic, pocketed my phone, and turned to the new blue window that had popped up in front of me and skimmed its text. Whoever MolaMola was, they'd need to wait until the first arc was complete.

CHAPTER #1—PREREQUISITE
Difficulty: F
**Task: Survive the ensuing onslaught of monsters, beasts, and insects.
Half of the remaining human population must die within the given
time frame. If more than half of the population survives, automatic
death will occur until the quota is met. Killing monsters, beasts,
insects, or humans will provide exemption from automatic death.**
Time: 20 minutes
Reward: 100 stars per slain entity
Failure: Death

This was, verbatim, what I had written ten years ago in *Surviving My First Run*. Reading the rules now, it seemed so cruel. This was the cutthroat world I had created, and it was now the world everyone had to try to survive in.

I scanned the freeway as the timer began to tick down, preparing to drive off before I suddenly felt something beneath my foot.

Looking down, I spotted the cockroach crawling out from under me. Its countless legs were spasming in the air as it rolled over onto its back. It proceeded to grow at a rapid speed, its wings fluttering.

[Observer Chat]
Socrates: It looks like Jia Li is in a bad spot. Maybe this is her karma lol

My blood ran cold when I heard my pen name mentioned. Socrates? That's right—I knew Socrates.

Socrates was one of the readers I blocked.

"Dammit!" I cursed, another realization dawning on me. If insects had infested the car in this chapter, they'd soon become gigantic, man-eating beasts.

"P-Peijin, this isn't real, right? Can't we try to talk to the dragon? It might let us go," Yang pleaded, fully unaware of the situation that was playing out.

"Do you want to argue about American politics with it?"

"Well, no, but—"

I shot Yang an annoyed look before I glanced out the window, checking for the dragon. I could see it in the distance, managing countless blue interfaces and excitedly commentating on the chaos.

In *Surviving My First Run*, the Four Auspicious Beasts, which included the Azure Dragon, streamed the suffering of humans for the gods to enjoy. They typically couldn't interfere with challenges without facing immense system backlash—the only exception was the first challenge on a new planet. The dragon, however, already exerted the extent of its influence in the slaughter of the civilians. For now, it wasn't a concern.

I frantically slapped at the bugs. My hand made a dull sound as I stomped on the car floor and smacked my leg, crushing a pregnant cockroach beneath my palm. A gross fluid oozed between my slim fingers, but I was too preoccupied by the blue notifications blocking my view to react.

> **You are exempt from automatic death.**
> **You have killed an entity.**
> **You have received 100 stars.**
> **You have killed an entity.**
> **You have received 100 stars.**
> **You have killed an entity.**
> **You have received 100 stars.**

The sudden influx of money and blue screens sent a thrill through me. I shut off the notifications with a mental command. There must have been at least forty eggs from that single roach. Even in such a perilous situation, my heart was beating with joy. Had I always been this kind of person?

Without warning, the entire truck lurched forward before tipping dangerously to one side. A sharp, grating buzzing could be heard from the back of the vehicle as the metal trunk *thunk*ed loudly and became marked by deep protrusions.

Yang yelped as he reached up and grabbed the ceiling of the truck, trying to balance himself. My gaze darted to the back seat, from where I grabbed multiple cans of the strongest bug spray before hopping out.

"Yang, help me kill the bugs in the back before they get bigger!"

If we didn't handle the bug infestation now, the situation would escalate, and I wouldn't even survive the first chapter.

I really should've quit my job.

I flung open the trunk door and covered my mouth using the inside of my shoulder, bracing myself with the open can of bug spray in my outstretched arm.

A horrific sight greeted me; cockroaches as large as my leg tumbled out of the trunk, their hooked brown arms flailing and mandibles snapping open and shut. Enlarged bedbugs crawled all over the walls as they spilled out and flailed on the ground before finally rolling over. I shook the can and sprayed wildly.

Large cockroach antennae brushed against my bare skin, causing me to shiver in horror.

I choked on the overwhelming smell of pesticides despite trying to hold my breath. A cockroach lunged from the trunk, wings flapping as it moved to clamp its horrific jaws onto my arm. I smashed the bottom of the can against its back, throwing it onto the ground and ferociously stomping its head in.

"Yang, where the hell are you?" I cried out, taking steps back as the bugs continued their assault. They were growing larger and more aggressive by the second, and I could feel the spray can's weight lightening in my hand.

In an instant, thousands of small blue portals opened all over the freeway, and grotesque green creatures stumbled out of them. With pointed noses and ugly, contorted skin, they clunkily waddled around, small wooden sticks or rocks in their wrinkled hands. Goblins.

These creatures had always existed in various universes and on other planets. The system had merely brought them all together.

Panic swelled in my chest at how overwhelming all this was, but I turned my focus back to the cockroaches, struggling to keep my composure.

A cockroach bashed into me, sending me flying into the rocky and boiling hot pavement that tore up the soft skin on my elbows, leaving them red and raw. My weakening arms struggled to throw the cockroach off. Its jaws snapped just in front of my face, menacing and deadly.

Even in my own fabricated world, I was the exact same person. Still a disappointment. Still a failure.

Well, at least I had given it my best shot.

I shut my eyes, preparing to feel the cockroach dig its vile mandibles into my flesh. Suddenly, the cockroach was launched off me, and my eyes flew open in surprise. Yang stood above me, holding a large spray bottle in one hand and a crowbar in the other. His chest heaved with each labored breath, but he sprayed down some bugs while bashing larger ones with the crowbar.

"Took you long enough," I said in a snarky tone.

You have received your first review!
<u>REVIEW:</u> ★ ★ ☆ ☆ ☆
Very deus ex machina. Liu Peijin shouldn't have survived,
although I was very entertained by her struggle while it lasted.

Were observers leaving . . . ratings and reviews?
Are you kidding me?

[Observers Chat]

Socrates: Boooo, this is boring to watch. I don't understand why you're struggling, Jia Li, when you created this world.
Nipon23: lmao imagine how much of a loser she must have been before. i finally found another observer who knows that this girl is JiaLi1825.
Socrates: Did you get blocked before, too? For what?
Nipon23: i commented "TYFTC" instead of "thank you for the chapter"
Socrates: She was THAT petty??? She blocked me even though I was a big Paytron supporter :(Rude.
Nipon23: i was one too. maybe only subscribers recognize her idk
Socrates: Well, it's not like she had many. Not a lot of people would pay for content if they were getting blocked 80% of the time lol

Great, there were more. Were the people I blocked seriously the only observers?

My face flushed in embarrassment at their comments, and I nervously met Yang's eyes, unaware if he could see the observers' notifications. Based on his still-glowing expression, I realized they could only be seen by me—at least for now.

I let out a shaky sigh of relief as I stood up, continuing to crush loose insects. The mixture in Yang's hands was a combination of soap and water. Since cockroaches and bedbugs breathed through the holes in their skin, this solution would suffocate them. Surprisingly, soapy water was much more effective than some insecticides.

> **You have enough stars to purchase from the Azure Dragon store! Would you like to access the tutorial?**

I flicked the notification away with my eyes, watching as Yang killed more insects. For someone who was so frightened just moments ago, he was adapting to the situation much faster than I'd anticipated.

Yang froze for a moment as if a screen popped up in his vision. I figured he must have just gotten the notification for the store as his fingers danced across an invisible interface. His thumb was rubbing against the tip of his index finger anxiously.

Once we had killed all the bugs in the van and dragged the couch out from the trunk, I hopped back into the driver's seat.

> **Total: 2,430 stars**

Yang turned to face me, noticing the blood dribbling from my skinned arms and onto my white seat. "Peijin, you're injured," he said in a strange tone before popping open the glove compartment and sifting through the miscellaneous items inside.

I didn't know whether to laugh or cry. Scraped elbows were the last thing to worry about. "It's fine. We need to get out of here first."

"And where would we go? Everything is in shambles," Yang replied, his voice pitched higher from his anxiety. His brows were knit together, and worry was clearly written in the wrinkles at the corners of his eyes.

The Azure Dragon was still hovering in the air while the horde of goblins waddled beneath him. They curiously explored the scene, tapping on car doors and banging their makeshift weapons together.

I ignored Yang's question and slammed on the gas, weaving our white truck between the parked cars and wreckage. If I had really teleported into my web novel, the next thing I had to do was catch up with the main characters before they could split off.

But the last person I'd want to run into would be Qiu Feiyu, my protagonist.

Yang trembled anxiously but nodded at my resolve, chewing on his lower lip. "Why aren't the . . . goblins outside doing anything?" He stumbled on the word "goblins," as if he couldn't quite believe the reality before us. "Can't we just kill them for more stars?"

"Don't touch them. If you do, then . . ." I trailed off, realizing I seemed way too assertive and knowledgeable.

Although the goblins were mostly passive creatures, the moment one was attacked, they would all band together to kill the assailant. This challenge was intentionally set up so people would be inclined to kill the meek goblins—to then be slaughtered themselves.

If I shared that with Yang, he would know that I truly was the author of this world, though he was probably smart enough to have put it together by this point. Still, I didn't want that to happen.

"This is just like one of those apocalypse survival games," I said. "So, let's just make it through the first round."

Time left: 13 minutes, 13 seconds
Percent killed: 14%

I doubled back, staring at the blue window. Fourteen percent? That couldn't be possible . . . It shouldn't have been that rapid of a decline. No one had even touched the goblins yet. I shrugged off my thoughts to focus on my goal.

Ah, there it was. The blue Toyota and the androgynous man standing beside it. He stuck out like a sore thumb; his waist-length brown hair was tied up in a high ponytail, and although he wore normal clothing, one could see the white bandages wrapped around his forearm.

A phone was pressed against his ear as he called the police and shouted at others to remain calm. In ushering seniors and crying children to the side of the road, he made his overwhelming desire to protect them obvious to any onlookers.

I swerved the car and parked, blocking two whole lanes—yet just before I could get out, the freeway rumbled as parading footsteps and a deafening roar sounded, sending spit flying everywhere.

I glanced up to see a black bear the size of a small house charging straight toward my van.

CHAPTER THREE

Besides the human realm, or Planet-2099 in this case, there were three main realms: the heavenly realm for divinities, the demon realm for powerful beasts that had rejected divine status, and the ghost realm for humans who had fallen from grace and become resentful spirits. All of them invested in humans—who became known as disciples—to make themselves more famous.

According to my stellar and very original worldbuilding from *Surviving My First Run*, these three realms had always existed but only became accessible to Planet-2099 at the start of the web novel.

Of course, there were anomalies, given transmigrators, reincarnation, et cetera, et cetera, but I avoided most of the complexities by avidly banning any form of time manipulation or regression from my novel. Call it lazy writing, but I considered it caring for my mental health.

Jun Wei, however, transcended this system of gods and disciples.

He had no knowledge of this fact. He was just the man standing beside his blue Toyota, watching as the bear stormed toward my truck. He had no clue he would rise to the top five most powerful beings on this planet.

Yang thrust his arm across my chest and forced me back into my seat as he leaned over, blaring the car horn and flashing the headlights at the bear.

I exhaled in surprise before squeezing my eyes shut in anticipation of a sudden attack, but I realized the sound had upset the bear, causing it to let out a roar before scrambling backward.

"Black bears hate noise," Yang said into my ear, his hand still firmly pressed on the car horn. The bear growled before standing on its hind legs, bringing up an arm to shield its face before turning to another way, in search of an easier meal.

Once the bear retreated, Yang let out a tense breath and turned to face me. "You all right?"

A complicated emotion passed through me, and I pushed his arm off. "I was thinking of doing that. You just beat me to it."

He withdrew his arm, like he had been burned by red coals, as realization set in. "Ah, sorry," he said in a nervous tone, waving his hands in front of his face.

Yang opened his mouth to say more, but I moved my hand in front of my lips in a gesture to shush him. The goblins were casually wandering the streets, not yet attacking the frightened people, but that wouldn't last long.

A sudden knock sounded from the car window, causing me to jolt before I saw Wei's face. I rolled down the window just a sliver to hear what he had to say.

"Ma'am, are you all right? Please don't panic—I'm sure officers will be here soon."

Aw, he was so cute!

Wait, did he just call me "ma'am"?

Did I look that old?

[Observers Chat]
Socrates: "Ma'am"? That was cruel, even if it's Jia Li.

One of my eyes twitched as I heard a gentle laugh from Yang. Clearing my throat, I responded, "Thank you" with an incredibly pressed smile and annoyed tone. "Do you mind if we join you? What's your name?"

"My family name is Jun, and my given name is Wei," he said. "Please feel free to join. I've already called the police."

Wei's eyes lingered on me for a moment before he spoke up, seeming rather flustered. "Is something wrong?"

"Huh? Oh," I mumbled. I had zoned out, and my hand had moved as if about to push up Wei's sleeve to look at his bandages. "My name is Liu Peijin."

"What a nice name," Wei said. "You must be very ambitious."

Before I could respond, a blue flash appeared beside us, causing both of us to turn away from the burning light. From it, the Azure Dragon emerged.

The Azure Dragon gave a little wave toward me with its small, clawed hand. "You seem to have adapted pretty fast."

"Move your broadcast somewhere else. I'm kind of in the middle of something, if you haven't noticed," I replied in a snarky tone, waving my hand back and forth as if shooing an annoying fly.

"Aren't you a bit too cocky this early on?" he snapped. "Do you wanna die?!"

The Azure Dragon initially served as a moderator and streamer, bringing entertainment to the gods through the demise of countless planets; however, it seemed as if observers, or my past commenters, had joined the market.

How thrilling.

"You haven't done anything to me since the chapter began, so I doubt you're allowed to. Besides, I'm bringing in a lot of viewers, right? I'm already receiving notifications."

The Azure Dragon gave me a stunned look as he continued to float on his tail in the air. After all, what I said was true. What did interest me, though, was that there were thousands—if not millions—of moderators when counting the Vermillion Birds, White Tigers, and Black Tortoises.

If what Socrates and Nipon23 discussed was true, then not all observers automatically knew I was Jia Li. What set them apart must have been their Paytron status. And if that was the case, I could boost my ratings and reviews by catering to the other observers. If all observers found out I was Jia Li, I would immediately be review-bombed, though I wasn't sure what that entailed. Given that I created this system, though, I'd probably face something catastrophic and blow up into flames or some nonsense.

More importantly, I wanted to be adored just as much as the next person. This was my chance to reinvent myself.

The Azure Dragon opened its long snout to respond, but a desperate cry sounded farther down the freeway, and my attention shifted.

Right, the real challenge was going to start soon. The timer was ticking down, and people were panicking. In testing times like these, people became the real monsters.

10 minutes, 39 seconds
Percent killed: 20%

A woman stumbled out of her car, wielding what I assumed was her son's metal baseball bat. He was waiting in the car, his face pressed up against the window. Dozens of goblins had climbed all over the vehicle, poking and tugging at the various parts, and they stared at him curiously.

"I—I can't take it anymore! I don't want to die!" Tears streamed down the woman's face, and she raised her arms in the air before slicing the bat down on the head of a curious goblin that had been peering inside her car. Its skull cracked in half as the goblin collapsed onto the ground, convulsing as she struck it again.

More and more people joined the woman in attacking the goblins, tearing off their small limbs as they cried out in pain, trying to scatter away. They let out pitiful, vulnerable cries, but they continued to be massacred. Even some of the elders and children who Wei had escorted to safety began to attack the goblins in fear.

A ghastly, animalistic scream rang out among the crowd. It was beginning. The Azure Dragon's face lit up with excitement, and he darted into the chaos, eagerly recording it.

The woman who'd attacked the goblins first was suddenly swarmed by all nearby goblins. They grabbed her hair and pummeled her to the ground. Already holding a sharp skewer from when it had spawned, a goblin stood above her face as she let out bloodcurdling cries. He lifted the skewer and pierced it through her eye and into the soft flesh of her brain, killing her instantly. She fell limp, and her eye oozed out onto the hot pavement and sizzled.

More goblins attacked, swarming people who had assaulted or killed goblins. Wei stumbled forward to protect the children who were now being cornered, but I quickly unbuckled my seatbelt and pushed open the van door, stepping out. I gripped his hand and pulled him back toward the van.

"You can't change their fate! If you do, the goblins will kill you next. You can't save the kids and avoid the goblins!" I shouted, my fingers pressing so tightly into his exposed arm that I left white finger-shaped imprints.

Time left: 8 minutes, 38 seconds
Percent killed: 32%

Wei turned to me, fierce determination set on his face as he tore his non-bandaged arm from my grasp. "I can do both!" Whipping his head around, he sprang forward to help.

A small knowing smile spread across my lips as I signaled for Yang, who was still in the passenger seat, to follow me. As long as I could paint Wei as someone who fought for justice, then he and a certain god would forge one of the most powerful bonds in *Surviving My First Run*.

Wei reached down and picked up a child who was being assaulted by the goblins and dashed toward his car. Once he made it to the vehicle, he threw open a passenger door and placed her in the back seat. I watched as he ran back to try to reach an older man who had fallen while trying to run from the chanting goblins that were surrounding him.

Suddenly, a young girl wearing a university uniform lunged at the elderly man and bashed her fists into his face, goring him and assisting the goblins. She panted, her fists drenched in blood, with deep purple bruises already forming, and the goblins clamored around her, cheering. The goblins almost appeared to be performing a ritual as they banged sticks and rocks together.

He Yue.

She was a truly despicable character, and it was easy to see how she became a Wrath—a Demon Queen of the highest rank. Cruel, calculating, and menacingly intelligent, she approached this new world in a purely pragmatic manner.

But she didn't appear this early in the story. So, I concluded that not only could my worldbuilding diverge from the original story, but I could also change the plot by using my characters.

"No!" Wei cried, rushing to tend to the elderly man. But it was far too late—he lay dead on the pavement, his body nearly unrecognizable.

Yue cackled as she stood up, blood dripping down her arms in thick black streaks. Glittering blue particles exploded from her feet, creating a halo of light around her.

Lifting a long, slender finger, she pointed at a parked car—the same car that Wei had just left a child in—and watched as the goblins raided it, smashing windows and attacking the girl.

I scowled. I hated Yue the most out of every character I'd created. She adapted too fast, far too fast, as if she had been waiting for this very situation.

Just like me, I realized.

"How dare you!" Wei shouted, his fists balled, trembling with rage. "How could you ever kill another person!"

Yue's head swiveled over to face him in a nonchalant manner as she gave a thin, wide smile. "Just trying to get some more stars."

Wei looked at her with shock and disgust. Despite Yue's twisted expression and willingness to kill, Wei clenched his fists and approached her.

It was like watching two parts of myself fight each other. Had I not known anything about this world, who was to say I wouldn't have taken a similar route to Yue? Even now, my actions were guided by a form of author manipulation; I had a desired conclusion for Wei, and I was manipulating him to reach my goal.

My eyes shifted to Wei's arm, where the bandages took on a mind of their own, unraveling with a menacing air. Now was my time to jump in.

"Hey, Yue!" I shouted, walking toward her and cracking my knuckles before shaking out my hand.

She whipped her head around and stared at me with insane eyes. She let out a scoff as she turned her body toward me and spat on the ground. The goblins eagerly awaited her orders, waving their arms in the air and singing.

"Using my first name? You're entitled. Who are you?"

"Doesn't matter."

I said a few words to myself in my head: *Invest five hundred stars into Strength and one thousand into Physique.*

Strength level 1 → level 5
Physique level 1 → level 10

I could instantly feel a rush of energy throughout my body, and I was completely thrilled by it. Crafting the perfect body suddenly became a possibility.

Time left: 6 minutes, 59 seconds
Percent killed: 38%
531 observers are following you with immense interest!

Yue's eyes trailed to the pest control van behind me, reading the company logo. "So, you're in pest control too? That's pathetic."

"I'm a fortune teller, actually."

She tilted her chin up, mock-impressed. "Really? Then go ahead and predict the future. What's about to happen?"

"I'm about to beat the shit out of you."

CHAPTER FOUR

Yue stared at me for a moment before doubling over laughing. She clutched her sides, and her shoulders shook. She stumbled, trying to stop, before she was able to stand upright with a wicked grin. Stealing a short blade from one of the goblins, she lunged forward and slashed the blade with vicious speed at my throat.

"Peijin!" Yang shouted, rushing to me.

With the strength from my heightened physique, I grabbed her wrist and bent it backward, wrestling with her for the blade.

Yue bent her arm and closed the distance between the two of us, pulling my hair and smashing her fist into my face.

My hair covered my delighted smirk. Her punch didn't hurt—it didn't even leave a mark.

Unaware, Yue pulled her hand out of my grasp and swung again at my face, landing a firm punch. I remained unharmed, but I stumbled back and touched my face.

"Ha, so you're all talk," Yue said. Her words were laced with malice.

She flipped the blade in her hands and swung frantically, but I pulled back just before she could deal any damage.

Catching sight of my cocky smirk, Yue got messy with her swings. Finally, I let her get close enough.

Her blade struck my throat with astounding force, but it simply clattered against my skin. Yue froze before readjusting her grip on the knife and driving it into my stomach. The blade snapped in half. I stared down at Yue, smug.

When Yue looked up at me, her brows were furrowed, and her eyes were black with rage. "What are you?"

I gave a confident shrug. "Just a pest control worker," I replied before balling my hand and slamming my fist into her liver. I watched her fly back and slam into a car. She let out a surprised yelp as she bounced off the now-totaled car and skidded across the asphalt.

> **954 observers are following you with immense interest!**
> **4 major gods are watching you closely!**

I couldn't help but enjoy messing with my own creation. I was rapidly adjusting to this reality—I could never prefer pest control to a world where I could finally leave my monotonous life.

Our fight was the most exciting action in the area. The Azure Dragon gasped at the sight of me hovering over Yue and covered his snout with his stubby hands. I could practically see the dollar signs in his eyes. "Do I really have a fortune teller in my channel? This will be so good for business!"

I glared at the greedy Azure Dragon and then looked back to the freeway, watching the horde of goblins sprint toward me for attacking their "ruler." With a simple sweep of my foot, they dissolved into speckled black ash that dissipated into the air. More of them charged, only to meet the same fate, and others ran toward Yue, crying out as they struggled to lift her back onto her feet. I leisurely walked closer to Yue.

The freeway was filled with more dead bodies as people kept fighting and losing against the violent horde. Blood and gore littered the streets, painting the initially dusty gray and cracked asphalt with deep red. I shook out my fist in the air, rubbed my knuckles, and waited for Yue's retaliation.

> **[Observers Chat]**
> **Socrates**: This is the action I wanted to see. Keep this up, and maybe I'll leave you a good review. We all know you need it.

"Am I a pest control worker *and* street performer now?" I grumbled before I looked up at the sky. Stars were the system's currency, but stars in the sky represented gods who were watching the broadcasts. It was difficult to see the stars in the afternoon sky, but a few were present above, twinkling down on me, so at least some were showing an interest.

> **[Observers Chat]**
> **Socrates**: Wooooow, that was the first time you responded to me. I almost thought these messages weren't getting through. I'll send more now, though :)

> **Time left: 4 minutes, 39 seconds**
> **Percent killed: 44%**

Yue coughed up blood and wiped the side of her mouth with her raw, battered hands. She tried to stand with the help of the goblins, but her legs gave out beneath her, and she fell onto her knees, gasping for breath. Her long black hair fell over her face.

"Yue," I said in a firm voice, kneeling beside her, "I want you to team up with me."

Yue was, unfortunately, part of the main cast, but more importantly, she'd become one of the strongest characters in *Surviving My First Run* by taking the Demon Bull King as her sponsor to receive his spiritual and financial backing. As one of the only beings to ever rival Sun Wukong, the greatest Chinese divinity, the Demon Bull King was a truly formidable god.

Wei looked over, admiration peeking through his surprise. He nudged Yang's arm while Yang was trying to wipe the bug guts from his hands.

Wei was too far away to be in earshot, but he was receptive to my actions. He was easy to please, like a dumb dog.

Yue snickered and tilted her head back, eyeing me as I stared at her busted lip and the blood smeared on her face. "I don't really have a choice, do I?"

"No, not really."

She sat up and reached for my hand, and I shot her a cheeky, pleased smile.

Yue's hand slammed into my gut with unexpected force, and I fell back onto the ground, mostly from the surprise.

"These observers and stars do come in handy, huh?" Yue dusted herself off, readjusted her school skirt, and hovered over me. Her fists were balled at her sides, ready to pummel me into the asphalt.

How could she possibly have enough stars to level up her strength like that? I groaned, getting up rather quickly. She should have, what, maybe five hundred or six hundred stars? That wasn't enough to overpower my Physique level.

The Azure Dragon gawked as he narrowed in the broadcast to my fight with Yue.

"Seems like a lot is going on here, too! Feel free to donate some more stars to my broadcast so I can bring you better content!" The Azure Dragon batted his bright red eyes at an invisible camera just above Yue and me.

> **[Observers Chat]**
> **Nipon23:** Sorry not sorry Jia Li

> **You have received a new review!**
> **NIPON23 REVIEW: ★ ☆ ☆ ☆ ☆**
> **He Yue needs to win this fight. Liu Peijin is beyond incompetent.**

Seriously? This guy again? What an ass. As an observer, he had read *Surviving My First Run* and knew I was better than Qui Feiyu at this point in the story.

If these insulting observer ratings had an impact on my progression, I was completely fucked.

I checked the blue screen to see how the chapter was progressing.

Percent killed: 51%

It looked like the goblins had done their job of killing the majority of the population . . . This was unsettling; the numbers had climbed a lot faster than I'd expected.

I returned my focus to Yue. She must not have invested many stars into Physique, given her labored breathing and the sweat on her brow.

I didn't want to use this many stars for the Prerequisite arc, but I knew I had to.

2,000 stars used.
Strength level 5 → level 15

"Sorry, Yue, I don't think you understand what's happening." I lowered my hands to my sides, trying to avoid coming off as intimidating. "Your fortune ends here."

Yue's fists started glowing with ominous black and purple flames that flickered up her arms. She looked down in amazement, a chaotic grin lighting up her face. "Did you predict this, then?"

Yue's fist threw me backward and hurled me straight into the fence on the side of the freeway. My body crashed straight through the metal railing before I hit the ground like a starfish, groaning in pain.

---

638 observers have turned away!
8 gods are doubting your ability!
1 major god has turned away!
Many demons are pleased by your failure!

I'd underestimated Yue. She'd already unlocked her Demonic Fire skill. Now my Physique was too low. Yue was advancing faster than she had in *Surviving My First Run* from my toying with her, which meant I could force my characters to grow faster than their original trajectory.

I smiled at the thought, struggling to stay conscious.

1,000 stars used.
Physique level 10 → level 15

Wei sprinted over to me, lifting me up and slapping my cheek to keep me awake. He armed himself with metal rubble from the cars and stood before me, holding Yue back.

> **You have unlocked Hindsight.**
> **Hindsight activated!**

". . . and this seems to be a very embarrassing play on behalf of our . . . fortune teller," the Azure Dragon commentated.

At once, my perception of the entire world changed; I saw the entire world play out in blue frames like movie stills where countless possible shots overlapped one another. Yue's hands continued to glow with the demonic flames. White text surrounded her and described every possible move in detail.

The amount of information was overwhelming, but my mind comprehended it with surprising ease. With every breath Yue took, the flames shifted to show possibilities in blips of red and purple frames. Above her, a strange, ominous green creature with pointed ears and a squished face now lurked, glaring at me with glowing white eyes. My Hindsight allowed me to see him.

> **Demon King of Resourceful Goblins feels great animosity toward you!**

The Demon King of Resourceful Goblins. That bastard was mad at me for killing all those goblins, and now he was controlling Yue's movements to kill me.

> **[Observers Chat]**
> **Socrates:** You just lost a bunch of observers and gods from that hit, Jia Li. And right before you have to pick a sponsor :(

Yang was still fussing over me. I grabbed his shoulder and gently pushed him to the side. "I'm fine, Yang. I'm just fucking pissed now."

Yue faced me, angling her chin up with both of her arms now blazing with demonic fire. Admittedly, I hadn't quite seen this coming; even though the skill was the same as in *Surviving My First Run*, she wasn't supposed to activate it until the second arc. These observers were seriously throwing off my entire story.

Just like they had before the apocalypse.

"Come back for more, Peijin?" When Yue said my name, it sounded like an insult. She must have picked up my name earlier from Yang's shouting.

I spat out blood onto the freeway, creating a thick splatter. "Yeah, yeah, whatever." My hands were raised in front of me and gestured for her to make the first move. "I'm not here to fight you."

Yue stared at me, dumbfounded, before she burst out laughing, borderline cackling like a hyena. "Ha! You're really something, Peijin."

"I'm not talking about you, you narcissist. I'm talking about the demon you signed a contract with."

There was no way the Goblin King could be influencing this chapter so heavily unless he had taken a deal with Yue in which they both had to sacrifice something to offset karmic restraints.

As soon as Yue moved, the blue frames highlighted the most likely possibility before vanishing, forcing me to synthesize all the information in seconds.

Yue's fist barely missed my right cheek as I dodged, sidestepping at the very last moment. I let out a sigh of relief—maybe I'd be able to keep a sliver of dignity despite the Azure Dragon's convoluted broadcasting.

I sucked in a sharp breath, then shouted over the sounds of chaos. "These aren't your movements! You let the Goblin King control your body to kill me, didn't you?"

A flaming fist narrowly missed the top of my head before I ducked, jumping to the side and regaining my footing. Yue's jaw was clenched, her brows furrowed in rage, but she continued to throw violent punches one after another.

"What's wrong, Yue? Cat got your tongue?" I smirked, lightly jumping back and forth between my two feet. Growing more comfortable with the Hindsight skill, I danced around her in a mocking manner.

You have received a new review!
REGUS3 REVIEW: ★ ★ ★ ★ ☆
Liu Peijin is very quick to understand her opponents, and she pieces together complex deals or relationships with seeming ease. She's not as cool or good as Qiu Feiyu, though.

I glared at the notification. *Just make it a five, god dammit! Forget about Feiyu!*

Just then, a flow of energy coursed through my body. Ha, I got it now. In a way, observers were like believers. The positive reviews gave the recipient more spiritual energy, heightening mana and potential skill power.

Yue let out a frustrated cry as she battered me with her fists, but I easily blocked every single move with my forearms. Each burst of her demonic flames would leave the top-most surface of my skin charred black, but thanks to my Physique level, the soot easily dusted off.

My leg smashed into her side, launching her into the pavement again. Her body crunched, leaving a human-shaped indent in the ground before she skidded a few feet farther. Yue drooped, unconscious, as she lay on the crusted asphalt with spit dripping from her open mouth.

> **Time left: 2 minutes, 19 seconds**
> **Percent killed: 54%**

At this assault on their leader, dozens of goblins shrieked and charged at me, furiously wielding their sticks and stones. A clever few even picked up shards of glass and attempted to slash my legs.

With a light kick to my side, an entire row of them faded to black ash as they dwindled in number.

I let out an exhausted sigh, my shoulders slumping. I struggled to calm my racing heart while clearing through the countless blue notifications that had been blocking my view. The skill Hindsight toggled off by itself to conserve my energy, and my vision returned to normal.

"Peijin! Are you all right?" Wei asked, stepping toward me.

"Of course I am," I replied. I signaled for him and Yang to step back, and I opened the Azure Dragon Store and began browsing.

The Azure Dragon Store was the most convenient place to purchase many goods. A big limitation, though, was the tier system. To access the better items, one had to buy into a higher tier by paying an expensive membership fee. The tiers ranged from silver—the default—to gold, platinum, titanium, and black.

But some of the best items could only be won through the challenges, and my current strategy was to save as many stars as possible in case I had an emergency that required me to make a large purchase or massively upgrade my stats.

If Yue had made a deal to be possessed by the Goblin King, then an exorcism potion would do the trick . . . except that cost a couple thousand stars.

Yellow sparks flitted in my peripheral vision, and I snapped my head toward them. Blue sparks signified the system was working—yellow sparks were from karmic restraint acting on an unfair action.

The Azure Dragon let out strange chirping and clicking sounds of utter excitement.

Yue's unconscious body was being lifted into the air like she was a doll. The movement began rigid but grew more fluid.

> **Time left: 1 minute, 36 seconds**
> **Percent killed: 55%**

Judging by the yellow sparks, Yue must have agreed to let the Goblin King aid her movements in her earlier fight with me in return for the support of the goblins. But she must not have agreed to total control, even when she was unconscious.

My eyes widened in surprise, and I let out a small huff. This strong of a reaction from a god this early on? What a total loser the Goblin King was.

Hindsight activated!

White puppet strings became visible, connecting all of Yue's limbs to the massive but blurry figure of the Goblin King hovering above her. He expertly moved his hands forward, and Yue's body launched right at me.

This time, without being hindered by Yue's control, the Goblin King expertly maneuvered Yue. Even if he was a low-ranking god, he was still a god, and Yue was far more of a threat now. Her fist flew at me, and I lifted both my forearms, barely blocking it.

The blow knocked the wind out of me. I skidded back, digging my heels into the ground. I could see Wei and Yang panicking, but I shook my head, signaling them to keep out of it.

Yue's leg lifted into the air and connected with my hip. I let out a small grunt but stabilized myself, increasing the distance between us. It was a good thing I'd updated my Physique level earlier.

I faced Yue, her head lolling back and forth but her body alert and ready to dash at me again. The karmic sparks were beginning to eat away at her body, punishing the physical form of Yue in response to the Goblin King's abuse of his power. Her skin was burning with every spark, and pieces of raw flesh were visible on her ankles and shin.

Though I hated Yue, I hated the gods more. The fact that the Goblin King would go this far and use Yue's body as a tool—it made me livid.

I wouldn't be able to get close enough to make her drink the exorcism potion anymore. I picked off a sturdy knife left behind by one of the goblins and fiddled with it. It wasn't the strongest, but it would do for what I wanted to test.

Yue charged at me. I let her get close enough to swing for my chest, then I ducked out of the way. I grabbed onto her shoulders and pushed her down, striking above her head at the puppet strings that connected her to the Goblin King.

The small knife shattered like glass on impact. The strings didn't even move.

Yue whipped around and grabbed the side of my head, smashing me into the pavement. I let out a sputtered grunt, struggling beneath her grip and trying to wriggle out from beneath her.

My frustration with the Goblin King only grew with each passing moment. Since he was fighting with her body, I didn't want to strike Yue. Any drastic move would undoubtedly hurt Yue more than him. What a bastard.

I had to rise to the top of this system and tear down the gods with my own hands. There was no question of it now.

Unable to hold back any longer, Wei rushed forward, and Yang followed suit. Yang used the crowbar to hit the nearby goblins. Blue sparks glimmered at Yang's feet while he leveled up his Strength and Physique levels to avoid getting swarmed.

Wei reached beneath Yue's arms, tugging her off me. But she overpowered him. Her elbow raised high in the air before she attempted to strike it into his ribs.

Time left: 39 seconds
Percent killed: 56%

I gasped for air and struggled to my feet. I caught Yang's eyes—he gave a curt nod, defending Wei and me from any of the goblins and letting us focus on Yue.

I nodded back, understanding his role. Just like at work, Yang immediately picked up on the role he needed to adopt in any given scenario. Usually, I was countless steps behind him, but this time, he stepped back to give me the spotlight.

Blue sparks erupted from my hand before the exorcism potion and a thin but incredibly sharp needle appeared. The needle had to be sharp and hard enough to ensure it wouldn't snap when it met resistance.

Yue landed a blow on Wei, and he was thrown back, bouncing off the asphalt and tearing open his arms and legs. His breath was heavy, and his limbs were bloodied—he didn't have enough coins to level up the way Yang and I had. His eyes locked on Yue; he was utterly enraged as he got up.

He handled the blow far better than any other human of his level could have. What a formidable asset he was—one I had to get my hands on.

I uncapped the needle and filled it with the small but powerful exorcism potion—powerful enough for a god this pathetic, at least.

Time left: 18 seconds
Percent killed: 56%

Thanks to the opening Wei had created, I was able to run forward with the bottle in my hand. Then Yue whipped around and prepared to block me.

I grabbed onto her button-up shirt and pulled her toward me. With my other hand, I tried to force the potion down her throat.

She instantly blocked me, digging her nails into my wrist. Through Hindsight, I could see the Goblin King's figure inflate with pride, mocking my stupidity.

Yue twisted my wrist until the bottle crashed to the ground and erupted into pieces. The potion spilled out, spreading into a thin puddle.

I released Yue's collar and revealed the syringe. I jabbed it into her neck, injecting her.

With a rancid puff of smoke, the goblin demon's energy burst out of Yue's mouth with a cry before exploding into yellow sparks.

You have unlocked Editor's Pen.

A god influencing such an early chapter would undoubtedly be subjected to the horrific punishments of karmic restraints. After all, karma was all-powerful. The Goblin King would face consequences from the system for such heavy interference.

Yue herself was beaten up. The yellow sparks had left the skin on her ankles and shins raw.

"Peijin, be careful," Wei said. He stood up, wobbling and clutching his arm in pain.

"Is it broken?" I asked.

Yang brushed past and supported Wei with his own body. "I'll take a look. You take care of Yue," he said to me.

My feet crunched on the broken glass as I picked up Yue, wrapped my jacket around the waistband of her skirt, and threw her over my shoulder.

[Observers Chat]

BMelv: How are you gonna be a whole demon and lose to a human this early on?? Mad embarrassing

CannedWorms: LOL you know the Goblin King is getting absolutely demolished in the demon realm right now

MoldyBlanket: Either way Liu Peijin pulled that off really well. You could see her think through the system

Socrates: Eh. I mean, is Peijin that impressive, or is the Goblin King just weak?

Nipon23: BOOOO tomato tomato

I made it back to the pest control van and let out a heavy sigh, sinking against its battered side. This had become much more convoluted than I was hoping for.

I could hear the dragon's relentless yapping in the background, but I tuned it out.

Yang and Wei reappeared soon after. Wei eyed Yue with utter contempt.

"I don't like her either," I reassured Wei, "but you can't deny how powerful she is." Besides, I was her creator. I could fix her.

Time left: 0 seconds
Percent killed: 57%

With a blue flash, the timer for the first chapter finished, marking the end of the first challenge.

Chapter #1—Prerequisite has concluded.
Stars received: 21,400
Congratulations! You have cleared the chapter.

CHAPTER FIVE

Name: Liu Peijin
Age: 24
Sponsor: None
Skills: Hindsight lvl 1, Editor's Pen lvl 1, Scathing
Reviewer (awaiting application)
Stats: Strength lvl 15, Physique lvl 15, Agility lvl 1, Health lvl 1
Evaluation: After living a miserable and wasted life,
Liu Peijin finds salvation in the apocalypse.

Who the hell wrote my evaluation?

Yang helped me move Yue into the pest control van while Wei stood to the side for a while, looking conflicted, before he helped too.

The three of us stood just outside the van in silence and read through our own stats windows.

I gently scratched my chin as I evaluated my skill set, tapping my foot on the ground as the blue window glowed in front of me.

I didn't recognize any of these skills, but they were clearly related to me being the author of *Surviving My First Run*. I'd already used Hindsight, and I was curious what Editor's Pen could do.

My mind flashed back to the attachment MolaMola had sent me. Was the skill Scathing Reviewer the gift he'd been referring to?

> **Editor's Pen activated!**

> **Please type the edit you'd like to make.**

A glowing blue keyboard appeared before me, and my face twisted into a slight grin. If this skill really worked the way I thought, surviving this apocalypse would be a breeze. I typed out my edit.

> **After Chapter #1—Prerequisite, the richest disciple
> in the area will receive a star bonus of 5,000 and
> gold-tier access to the Azure Dragon Store.**

I couldn't give myself a higher boost—if anything, this skill's existence already pushed karmic restraints. Despite being the writer, I had to give some care to the laws of the narrative within the confines of the readers' expectations. The karmic system meant every single action taken—positive or negative—would come back and impact the entity in the future.

A divinity outright murdering a disciple they didn't like? Karma would jump in and bring immense sorrow, death, or destruction to temples of worshippers.

A moderator, like the Azure Dragon, changing the course of a chapter or arc? Karma meant they'd face the brunt of a grotesque death or eternal financial failure.

The Goblin King abusing Yue to influence the events of the first chapter? *Poof.* He was probably reeling from the physical or mental injuries that karma had brought in the demon realm right now.

This rule was the same reason powerful divinities couldn't directly communicate with disciples right now. The only way around karma would be overriding it with an abundant amount of spiritual energy. This was easier for more powerful and well-known gods with massive followings, since they had more to waste.

Spiritual energy funded their magic, grandiosity, and influence by allowing them to skirt around karma. Still, the amount of spiritual energy needed to massively influence a challenge was incredibly high.

All individuals contained a small bit of spiritual energy. They could grow it in a similar way to the gods—by winning more challenges, their fame would increase, and the more supporters they had meant the more energy they could expend. Humans could even achieve the status of gods by succeeding in this world.

Editor's Pen already seemed to test karma, and I didn't want to find out what would happen if I abused it.

> **Edit granted.**

I awkwardly waited for the star payout while watching Yang and Wei chat about their skills and play around with the Azure Dragon Store, but nothing came.

> **[Observers Chat]**
> **Socrates:** . . . This is seriously painful to watch.

Was I using the skill wrong? It said my edit was granted. I waved down the Azure Dragon, who popped up in front of me.

"We're starting the next scenario soon, so could you keep this brief?" he asked, trying to look dignified.

I gave the dragon an annoyed stare. "What's your name?"

"Chang."

"Chang, who's the richest disciple right now for this specific area?"

The Azure Dragon puffed and grabbed one of his whiskers, twirling it in between his claws. "As an astute and hardworking moderator, I cannot give such classified information to a puny disciple such as yourself."

I looked at him expectantly. "Do they have more than me?"

"A bit less than double."

Less than double? Who was strong enough to kill that many people or goblins this early on? Even Feiyu got fewer stars than I did during this chapter, and he was the richest disciple of all divisions.

"Who the hell came up with this stupid system?" I grumbled, kicking the side of the van and putting my hands in my pockets.

Instead of retorting, Chang perked up and teleported to a more gruesome and interesting scene.

I let out an annoyed sigh before I saw Yang sitting beside Yue in the van, holding a miniature vial of kraken mucus.

Yang looked up, sensing my eyes on him, and said, "I bought it from the store. It said it was good for healing and soothing injuries." His hands were covered in the slimy substance as he gently rubbed it onto Yue's skinned joints and oozing cuts.

"It's not cheap. How much did that small vile cost? Three thousand stars?" I asked.

"It's fine. I have more than ten thousand stars left," Yang said. "I'll save the leftover mucus. I'll be stingy with it."

It was the end of the world, and Yang was still preoccupied with caring for others, even at his own expense.

"You should save your stars for more important purchases. Yue could have healed from those injuries on her own."

"Sorry, it was my idea," Wei cut in, awkwardly rubbing the back of his head and avoiding my gaze.

No, it definitely wasn't, but whatever. I was more worried about the next chapter, even though it was easy.

The blue screen appeared before me with its big white text.

CHAPTER #2—PARTY TIME!
Difficulty: F
Task: Team up with at least two other people by high-fiving them. Appoint a group leader and choose a name.
Time: 5 minutes
Reward: 100 stars
Failure: Death

This chapter was solely meant to sabotage people like Yue, rendering the savages incapable of finding teammates. Yue managed to make it through this chapter in *Surviving My First Run* by using her surprising power to knock out two other people and force them to join her party.

I turned to face the group, tying my shoulder-length black hair into a short ponytail. "We'll be a party, but keep it to just us four." I raised my hand into the air and slapped all their hands, lifting the unconscious Yue's arm and giving her an unnecessarily hard slap.

[Observers Chat]
Nipon23: why are you bitchy in real life, online, and in your own fictional world?

. . . Okay.

I was definitely not going to check MolaMola's attachment, and hopefully whatever the hell my skill Scathing Reviewer was, it would remain far, far away. However, I wondered why MolaMola wasn't sending any observer messages. I did block him, if that was a requirement for being an observer.

"Everyone, let's go!" I motioned for them to get into the car. Yang circled back to the passenger seat while Wei uncomfortably got into the back beside Yue.

I climbed into the driver's seat and tried to slam the door shut, but it slammed on someone's hand instead.

"Oh my god." I pushed the door open and faced a trembling woman outside. "Are you all right?"

Her voice trembled when she spoke, and her hand was bloodied and crushed. She held it tightly against her chest. "You need to let me join your party."

I gave her a dumbfounded look.

Hindsight activated!

A blue box hovered over her head to identify her, but I immediately recognized her frail limbs and tired expression as those belonging to Wang Ting.

In the fourth arc, Ting had developed a romantic relationship with her party's leader. Out of paranoia that her fellow party members were jealous and would soon sabotage her, she began hiding significant portions of the party's food, elixirs, and weapons. She would die in that arc, and the rest of her party would only survive thanks to Feiyu's charity.

Obviously, there was no reason to team up with Ting, nor was there a reason she should live as a character.

"I'm sorry, but my party is full." My voice was firm.

"Please, I'll even pay you. I saw you in the first chapter, and I can't team up with anyone else. I won't survive." Her voice was frantic, and she grabbed onto my collar now, practically pulling me out of my seat.

Yang reached over and gripped her wrist until she released me, but she only became more desperate.

"Okay, look," I said. "If you head farther back down this lane of the freeway, you're going to find a group of around seven people who you can team up with, okay? And they're all very qualified," I said, offering an alternative. I felt horribly guilty for crushing her hand, even if it was by mistake. The party I suggested was pretty good, too. I brought them up in *Surviving My First Run* quite often, though they were still far beneath Feiyu's party.

I tried to shut the door, but she stuck her entire arm through. I stopped myself and swung it back open.

"Are you insane? Don't shove your arm in when I'm about to shut the door!"

"I'm begging you! Please! You want money, right? I'll give you all my stars. All of them. I'll do anything—I mean it!" Ting reached into the car and fumbled for my arm, struggling due to her shattered hand. She grabbed onto me again and tugged me toward her, trying to force me to give her a high five.

I instantly pulled my wrist out of her grasp and shut the van door, making sure not to close it on any of her limbs. She began furiously banging on the door. Blood from her shattered hand smeared all over the window.

> **[Observers Chat]**
> **Socrates:** ?? Jia Li, what are you doing?? Have you seriously lost your mind??? That's Wang Ting, you need her!

I shook out my shoulders. My interaction with Ting ruffled me more than I'd expected. I could feel Yang's and Wei's stares burning into me, but I wasn't worried about that. An ominous blue screen had appeared before me.

> **Warning: This action will have unforeseen consequences.**

Wei gave Ting a sympathetic look as she cried out and slammed her body against the side of the van.

"How can you be all right with this, Peijin?" Wei asked me.

His words startled me, but I regained my composure. "We're only alive because more than fifty percent of the population had to die. If we must team up, I need a group without liabilities."

"You have an awfully transactional mindset for someone who complains about their exploitative job all the time," Yang added.

I glared at Yang, pursing my lips, but I knew part of what he said was true. Rather, none of this felt real to me. I was trapped in a job I'd hated for years with no hope or fulfillment in sight, but I was now in a world that I had crafted with my own two hands for a decade.

Still, this was only a story, with fabricated characters and fabricated opportunities.

The banging on the van stopped. I peeked out the window to see Ting vigorously waving others toward the pest control van. She caught my eye and glared at me. Chills spread down my spine.

A large group of people turned and raced toward the van with their arms raised in the air and their voices clamoring over one another. Some were gesturing high fives while others already had their hands clasped together, ready to beg to join my party.

Ha. At least now I didn't need to feel guilty about my decision.

I started the car and drove farther down the freeway, trying to throw the crowd off my tracks. Survival meant partnering with people who adapted the fastest and oftentimes abandoning people like Yue, so I wasn't surprised that they were flocking to me. After all, Wei, Yang, Yue, and I had already established ourselves.

I noticed a small girl on the side of the road. No one was near her, and she was weeping into the body of a puppy in her arms, her shoulders shuddering with every racking sob. The puppy was clearly deformed, with some of its limbs and features bulging out due to the previous chapter's monsterization.

I decisively shook my head. *No.* I couldn't let it get to me. I made it clear— the party was solidified. What kind of party leader would I be if I broke my own rules?

But I immediately pulled the van up beside the little girl and leapt out beside her. Her blond hair waved in front of her face, and she had stunning and crystal-like blue eyes that peered back at me with tears spilling out. The dew of youth seemed to have kissed her skin and gave it a lively appearance. I had a warm smile on my face, my hand outstretched toward her.

Her hair and eye colors told me she was a foreigner. I peered into the destroyed car behind her and winced at the sight of her two dead parents who had clearly been gored by goblins. She must have been forced to kill her puppy to survive the chapter.

"Do you have a party yet?"

Time left: 2 minutes, 3 seconds

I turned around and saw the crowd of people storming toward me again, and I turned back to the girl with an almost-impatient look that was disguised under my hopefully sympathetic expression.

She responded in a language I couldn't understand, tears streaming down her face. She held her puppy tighter and pressed her back into her family's car, fearful.

I gave a little sigh and shut my eyes, slightly frustrated. Would I really have to buy this skill? The Azure Dragon Store opened before me as I swiped, looking for the Translator skill.

Before I could purchase the skill, the little girl slapped my hand, and the puppy's corpse was now carefully laid down on the car seat.

"Amelia." She murmured the words under her breath with hesitation, her large blue eyes still full of tears that clung onto her blonde lashes.

This was the world I had created and thrown her into. Even if this was just a story, I felt an odd pang in my heart at the pathetic sight.

"Amelia," I awkwardly repeated, unfamiliar with the word. I grabbed her forearm and threw her over my back in one movement to get back into the van. As soon as I locked the doors, the crowd reached us.

"Stop banging on the door!" I shouted angrily at the people outside the locked truck while I gingerly passed Amelia over to Yang in the passenger seat beside me. "This isn't an orphanage! Just team up with the people next to you!"

I drove off while Yang held Amelia tightly in his lap, both swaying with my atrocious driving; Yang let out a surprised shout as Yue rolled onto the floor of the van and banged against his seat. Wei hesitantly lifted her back up.

For some reason, Yang seemed unnecessarily tense around Yue, even though he was in the front of the van. His brow sweated more when he saw her, and he would nervously bite his lower lip, but he hadn't made any complaints.

Yang spoke to Amelia in English, and she gave a little nod of her head, receptive. He guided her through the Azure Dragon Store and transferred enough stars to her for her to purchase the Translator skill.

This man spent money like water. Good thing I was the richest disciple so far.

Well—the richest disciple in this party. Stupid Editor's Pen skill.

Time left: 1 minute, 38 seconds

"We need to come up with a group name. It's temporary for the next few rounds, but does anyone have any ideas?"

"You should pick, Peijin!" Wei said enthusiastically, leaning into the gap between the driver and passenger seats. "You should be the party leader for sure. You're the one who saved all of us."

"Of course I'd be party leader," I replied with a satisfied expression on my face, my chin held high.

"I love your confidence, too!"

That sounded passive aggressive. Wei's childish character was predominately based on the type of character I'd idolized since I was a child—funny, brave, and handsome. He was cute like a puppy and as loyal as a dog. I garnered the inspiration for his character based on my weirdly idealized version of my first crush, and Wei was the complete opposite of Feiyu.

I was deep in thought for a moment before replying, "What about Peijin's Pest Control Corporation?"

Yang let out a boisterous laugh before going dead silent when I shot him a glare. He said, seeming perfectly serious, "Why not Yang's Pest Control Corporation? People might be driven away if they see your name in the title."

I stuck my tongue out at him, blowing a raspberry. "Not a single entity in this world would want to watch a group with that stupid of a name."

Party Leader: Liu Peijin
Party Name: Peijin's World Dominion

I winked in the rearview mirror and laughed before leaning over to cover Amelia's eyes as the scenario ended and anyone who failed to complete the scenario exploded, their heads swelling as their eyes popped and they turned into puddles of red sludge.

I could see Ting in the background. She stared straight into the van, even though she was too far to see inside, before she exploded.

Yue was beginning to wake up in the back of the car, groaning as she sat up before punching Wei straight in the face, startled. Amelia let out a horrified shriek, and Yue became even more panicked at the sight of an unknown child.

This was going to be a fun party. If things worked out how I planned, we'd be in the top three strongest parties in China by the second arc.

Chapter #2—Party Time has concluded.
Stars received: 100
Congratulations! You have cleared the chapter.

CHAPTER SIX

Although currency in *Surviving My First Run* was technically based on stars, there was one thing far more valuable: worshippers. Every worshipper you gained meant the chances that your story would be passed down increased, more temples were constructed, and more sacrifices were conducted. This popularity manifested into a god's spiritual energy.

Nothing in this world was immortal, not even the divinities, and once someone died, they could only live through the stories people passed down. Every experience or life event was a story, and the more well known you were, the more widespread your existence became.

Of course, stars and worshippers still went hand in hand—a positive feedback loop of sorts. The richer you were, the more famous you got. The more famous you got, the richer you were, and more entities would be willing to make sacrifices for you.

Gods—which included divinities, ghosts, and demons—all rose to their powerful status because their many believers heard their stories and worshipped them.

Which was why choosing a good sponsor was critical. Not only would they be able to support their disciples materially, but through skills as well. A disciple and their sponsor were bound for life—this was undeniably one of the most important decisions that could be made. A bad sponsor could ruin even the best disciples.

Although any disciple could sign a contract with a god the way Yue and the Goblin King had, you could only ever have one sponsor, and you would rely on them for every aspect of the system. A contract was a temporary transaction, lacking a bond that typically defined the relationship between disciple and sponsor.

Now that I'd become part of this system, I wanted to craft the perfect story for myself—one devoid of unnecessary sacrifice or loss. One of success and fame.

CHAPTER #3—SPONSOR SELECTION
Difficulty: F
Task: Select a sponsorship from any of the gods that have made offers. Once you have picked a sponsorship, declined gods may offer sponsorship to other members in your party.
Time: 15 minutes
Reward: Sponsor

Now that we were far enough from the chaos, I pulled to a stop on the side of the freeway. As expected, my list of sponsors was pretty impressive—though I was disappointed not to see any ghost offers. None of the gods used their true names, but I could determine who they were based on their titles.

POTENTIAL SPONSORS LIST
Great Sage Equaling Heaven
Great Sage Who Pacifies Heaven
The One Who Fights in Front
Abyssal Kraken of Black Seas
Eternal Wish

Great Sage Equaling Heaven . . . Sun Wukong was here? Sun Wukong as my sponsor—that was the dream.

I let out a nervous laugh, scratching the side of my head once I finished rereading the list. This might have been a bad list. I was doing pretty good in terms of the number of offers, considering Chang's channel was tiny and new, but this list was . . . contradictory, to say the least.

There was no failure scenario for this arc, which meant that if I didn't pick a sponsor, nothing would really happen; however, I'd miss out on a lot of buffs. Feiyu never picked a sponsor to rebel against the gods, but I didn't have the luck of the protagonist.

I opened the Azure Dragon Store before buying ten prayer candles with decadent designs carved into the wax and laid them out across the dashboard.

"Yue, light them."

Yue snickered in the back seat. "Ha, why would I do that?"

It was her first time talking since our earlier skirmish. Her bitterness was apparent, but she made no idiotic attempts to overpower me.

"It'll help you, too. Don't pick a fight when you've already lost one," I said.

Yue let out a loud huff before using Demonic Fire to ignite all the candles—although I supposed it was a bit offensive to use a demon's power to worship divinities, I didn't want to spend extra money on a lighter.

I whispered the names of all my divinities, and five of the candles turned crimson. Now my sponsors would be allowed to easily communicate; the candles served as a gift of worship and helped manifest their spiritual powers into early rounds without the drawbacks of karma.

Yang looked at me curiously. "Are you praying?"

"Say the epithet of your sponsors. This serves as a prayer gift and will let you have minimal communication."

The first of my sponsors was Sun Wukong from the iconic *Journey to the West*, and he was arguably the strongest Chinese god, who I was dead set on selecting at first. His epithet was Great Sage Equaling Heaven, despite him being arrogant and snobby. The only entity who'd ever been able to overpower him was Buddha.

The second was Sun Wukong's main enemy, the Bull Demon King. He virtually matched Sun Wukong's level. I never really considered him much of a villain in *Journey to the West*. Picking Sun Wukong as my sponsor would turn the Bull Demon King directly against me unless I found a way to keep them both.

The Bull Demon King's epithet was similar to Sun Wukong's, but he cockily made it Great Sage Who Pacifies Heaven to appear superior to Sun Wukong.

> **Demon Great Sage Who Pacifies Heaven sponsors 1,000 stars.**

> **Divinity Great Sage Equaling Heaven expresses contempt toward Great Sage Who Pacifies Heaven.**

> **Divinity Great Sage Equaling Heaven sponsors 1,001 stars.**

I placed my hands on my hips and faced the wide sky. "Don't bother bribing me with stars. I already know who I plan on picking!" I shouted.

> **Divinity Great Sage Equaling Heaven says not to make stupid considerations.**

"Your third sponsor is Athena, right?" Yang chimed in, peeking over at my screen. "That's one of her epithets. It's how the Greeks referred to her."

Since this chapter involved the entire party, we could see one another's choices.

I shifted away, awkwardly leaning over to try to block my screen.

"Stop being nosy."

Yang sarcastically placed a hand to his chest. "Sorry, CEO Liu, but this requires teamwork and talking. Yue also got a Greek goddess sponsor."

"Who the hell would sponsor Yue?" I grumbled, glancing over my shoulder. Yue was slumped in the back seat, her arms crossed and her lips forming a slight pouting shape. She looked far smaller and less . . . unhinged than earlier. The scrapes and cuts on her legs were already healing thanks to the kraken mucus.

I gawked when I read her screen. She had only gotten two offers, a far cry from the original novel, but I hadn't expected such a good divinity after her embarrassing loss.

POTENTIAL SPONSORS LIST
King of Resourceful Goblins
Far Shooting Queen of Beasts

I looked back and forth between the blue screen and Yue. "You got Artemis? You didn't even do anything in the Prerequisite chapter!" I exclaimed, slightly jealous and fully ignoring the Goblin King's offer.

"Beast class divinities usually don't make offerings un—" I awkwardly stopped, realizing I let too much slip. "Until they see something more impressive. At least, they don't in video games."

"Ha, 'impressive'? Wait until I gut you," she threatened, her eyes like black holes.
Gut me?

"I'd like to see you try. It's stupid for anyone to have made you an offer at all," I said.

Yue snorted at my response. "You jealous?"

"Me? Jealous?!" I grabbed the back of Yang's seat and leaned over to the back of the cab. "Hey, I didn't spend the last two rounds blacked out in—" Yang let out an awkward laugh and clasped his hand over my mouth.

My fingertips gripped my blue screen and shifted it into Yue's view, showing her my list of offers.

"Oh," she said.

[Observers Chat]
Socrates: It's almost like you're a cheap cosplay of Feiyu! Did you know observers might be able to sponsor stars after this arc? Better be nice to me :D

Socrates was really pissing me off. Besides, there was no way observers would get access to an abundance of stars when one needed to be a powerful god to have any impact . . .

I shot a judgmental glare at Yue, my brown eyes narrowing to form an exaggerated expression, before I looked at my own offers. The third was Athena, who was undeniably one of the most well-known mythological figures. If I had her, I'd receive the best war advice and immediate connections to the Greek divinities.

But . . .

My eyes wandered to the fourth offer. The kraken was by far the most powerful water beast in *Surviving My First Run*. And, of course, he was indirectly angry at Athena, since the sea serpent, a fellow water beast, was slain thanks to Athena lending Perseus Medusa's head and a shield.

No one else in my party had any beast offerings or any water skills, though, so lacking in those categories could put us at an early disadvantage—a disadvantage that Artemis could make up for. Especially in the fourth arc, which would take place in the middle of the sea with pirates and sirens, a beast or water disciple was crucial.

As for Eternal Wish, I had no idea who that was. I'd never even thought about a character with that name when writing *Surviving My First Run*. Given the rather weak and stupid epithet, I assumed he must have been a pathetic god.

"Wei, Yang, and Amelia, what offers did you get?"

Amelia looked nervous before speaking, brushing her hair behind her ear and looking down at the floor. Her voice was a whisper. "I didn't get any."

Her expression was incredibly shy, almost ashamed, like she was expecting better from herself. It reminded me of someone or something I couldn't remember.

"It's all right. That's why we're in a party." I gave her a bright grin before rubbing the top of her head, her blond hair immediately frizzing.

"Peijin is so understanding," Wei chimed in from the back seat, turning to Yue.

Yue rolled her eyes. "Yeah, right. All of you are delusional," she muttered, kicking her feet against the back of my seat to throw me forward into the steering wheel.

I looked at Yang, who was regarding Amelia with a mixture of fondness and protectiveness. "Yang, who do you have?"

"I have Chang'e. She must be good for healing, then, right? I can pick her if you think that'll help the rest of the group."

Chang'e was an incredibly popular and beloved goddess among Chinese culture, and she was frequently celebrated at the moon festival, but if Yang picked her, he'd be limited to being a healer. Even though that was a crucial role for every group, couldn't Yang do more?

I inspected his features. In the time that the world had turned into this devastating apocalypse, he adapted into a supporting role.

"Let me think about it. What about you, Wei?"

"Ah," he said, seemingly startled, "I got the Supreme Commander of the Heavenly Hosts."

My face spread into a stupid grin as I gave him an enthusiastic double thumbs-up. Some things remained the same as the web novel. "Pick him—that's perfect."

Without any hesitation, Wei selected his sponsor. Despite his almost-intimidating appearance, he was an incredibly trusting and kind man, and his nature never changed, not even down the line in *Surviving My First Run*.

"I'm sorry, Peijin, but I'm not as good at recognizing myths as you or Yang," Wei said. "Who exactly is my sponsor?"

> **Divinity Supreme Commander of the Heavenly
> Hosts lets out a booming laugh.**

> **Divinity Supreme Commander of the Heavenly Hosts sponsors
> 1,500 stars to all members of Peijin's World Dominion.**

I didn't get what was so funny, but I appreciated the fat paycheck.

"The Supreme Commander of the Heavenly Hosts is Archangel Michael. He's one of the strongest divinities from the Abrahamic religions. Don't worry about it, he's perfect for you," I reassured Wei. "He's a symbol of justice and strength against evil."

Wei's face lit up, and he brought both of his hands in front of his face. "Do you really think so highly of me, Peijin?"

I let out an awkward laugh, patting his broad shoulder. I could see why Feiyu liked him—he was like a golden retriever. "Yeah, yeah, but don't start crying, or you'll change my mind."

> **Time left: 6 minutes, 29 seconds**

"Amelia, Yang, and Yue. Don't pick a sponsor yet. The arc instructions show that there's no failure, so there must be another time for us to pick a god in the future. I'll pick first, and we'll see if any of my gods move to one of you."

Yue interjected. "Who are you picking?"

I tilted my chin up and narrowed my eyes arrogantly. "Sun Wukong."

Her nostrils flared. "You can't pick him!"

"And why not?"

"Do you really think a bitch like you should have a sponsor like him?" Yue snapped back, slight blue sparks at her hands.

Wei promptly covered Amelia's ears and eyes.

I pulled my lower eyelid down and flipped her off. "What happened to all that big talk about how good your sponsors were? Careful, you might piss off your only good one, and then you'll really be stuck at rock bottom," I taunted.

I moved to click on the glowing white *X* in the corner of the blue window, but an invisible force suddenly slammed my hand into selecting a different sponsor option.

Congratulations! You have selected Eternal Wish as your sponsor!

CHAPTER SEVEN

Divinity Great Sage Equaling Heaven is tearing out his hair in offense!
Divinity The One Who Fights in Front no longer thinks you're very wise.

H uh?!" I cried out in anger, staring at the blue screen in front of me. "I swear, something pushed my hand!"

[Observers Chat]
Socrates: What are you doing. You had Sun Wukong.
Hedgehog1938: LMFAO NO WAY SHE JUST FUMBLED THAT
Nipon23: . . .
CactusLiver: STOP HAHAHA
Nipon23: I actually can't even process what I just watched
Socrates: ☹

You have received a new review!
HEDGEHOG1938 REVIEW: ★ ☆ ☆ ☆ ☆
Liu Peijin is an absolute idiot when it comes to her decisions.
Not only is she hypocritical in who she saves, but she
can't even make rational decisions during chapters.

You have received a new review!
CACTUSLIVER REVIEW: ★ ★ ★ ★ ★

> **Liu Peijin is SO bad at this it's seriously the most
> entertaining thing I've ever seen LOL**

I could hear Yue burst out laughing in the back of the van, clearly finding my disastrous error to be funny. "What happened to being a fortune teller?"

All of a sudden, Chang, the Azure Dragon, appeared in the center of the car with a small blue flash.

"What's with all the commotion here? This is a no-risk scenario, and you still manage to blow up my system with messages."

> **309 observers are leaving to watch a different disciple.**

Fuck! If I wanted to grow in status, I needed as many cheerleaders as possible.

"Can you please let me reselect my sponsor?" I pleaded with Chang. "Somebody interfered with my selection. My hand was pushed, and I made an accidental selection."

"If something interfered, I would have been alerted. There's no godly interference to that extent this early in the scenario."

"Did you not just broadcast what happened with the Goblin King?"

"Yeah, but the karmic system handled that. It would've handled any interference here, too."

I buried my face in my hands and groaned in frustration. Where the hell was karma? Influencing a disciple's decision like that should've been immediate sentencing.

> **Editor's Pen activated!**

> **Allow disciples to make edits to their sponsors if
> there is still time left in the scenario.**

Whatever. If Chang couldn't fix this, then I would.

> **System error: Edit cannot be processed.**

"What the fuck?" I cried out angrily, waving my hands around. "How can you call this a system when sponsor selection and my skills don't even work! Can't you open an error ticket?"

"Why would I open an error ticket when you're blatantly lying? It's not my fault if you stupidly misclicked," Chang replied.

"I'm telling you that my hand was pushed!"

"All selections are final."

Without processing his words, I continued scolding the dragon. "How can you criticize humans for living monotonous, meaningless lives when you can't even do your job? You're the equivalent of a minimum wage customer service worker, but you have the audacity to scold us? What the fuck!"

Chang's blue skin flushed a deep purple as he nervously looked around the car, surprised at the angry outburst. We were now centered on a bridge above a deep bay.

"Ha ha, you see, I'd love to help, but I'm actually getting a really important call, so I need to go. Also, weren't you a pest control worker? I wish you luck, though!"

The dragon vanished with a poof.

I groaned, bashing my head repeatedly on the car horn. This sucked. I was just as unlucky in this new world as I'd been in my original pest control life.

Time left: 4 minutes, 39 seconds

The gods were now forced to pick other disciples from my party. I looked around the van looking at all the visible screens. Yang now had Chang'e and . . . Sun Wukong. My face flushed red.

Fucking Yang! If he wasn't so nice and virtuous and perfect, I would've murdered him already. Dammit, I really wanted Sun Wukong. I would have killed for Sun Wukong.

"Yang, you should pick Sun Wukong as your sponsor. We'll find a healer later," I ordered.

Yue now had the Goblin King and the Bull Demon King. Amelia now had Athena and the Abyssal Kraken of Black Seas as options. Artemis, however, was dissatisfied with the rest of the party and withdrew her sponsorship entirely.

"As for you, Yue, pick the Bull Demon King," I said. "It'll be advantageous to have both of them in one party. And . . . he's a very fitting sponsor for you."

Yue's face twisted. "Hey, what the hell does that mean?"

I ignored Yue and turned to Amelia with a pleasant smile.

This was a significant moment—Artemis could have provided a beast controller to the team, with the Abyssal Kraken of Black Seas providing a vastly superior water advantage, but Athena was one of the strongest Greek warriors.

"Amelia, don't pick a sponsor yet. Let's wait till you have another opportunity, all right? You might not get the same sponsors, but you'll be stronger then and have more options."

"Were none of my sponsors good?" Amelia frowned, tearing up again.

"Huh? No, that's not what I meant!" I turned to my side and squeezed her face, dramatically fake-sniffling. "You're perfect. Don't worry about a thing."

Yue pretended to gag in the back before letting out a surprised yelp as Wei punched the side of her leg.

I was going to get Artemis to sponsor Amelia no matter what. Not only did it anger me that Artemis so easily gave up on the rest of my party, but she was a god that provided my team the benefits of both Athena and the Abyssal Kraken of Black Seas.

It was advantageous to choose a sponsor earlier on for various reasons—a higher chance of survival, various buffs, and relationships to certain gods—but I was confident that I could cultivate Amelia into a formidable disciple without a sponsor.

> **Demon Abyssal Kraken of Black Seas feels slightly sad.**

> **Divinity The One Who Fights in Front seriously regrets trusting you.**

I really had to give it to public figures for keeping all their fans happy. It was only more of a misfortune that there was no block or report feature. I'd try Editor's Pen, but I'd had enough of my awful skills.

> **Chapter #3—Sponsor Selection has concluded!**
> **You have earned the achievement Beginner's Luck.**

> **Congratulations! You have cleared the chapter.**

This was definitely not beginner's luck. I hated my younger self a bit more with each passing hour.

> **HOP ON THE TRAIN!**
> **Please head over to Futian Station immediately.**
> **The next arc will commence in 23 hours and 59 minutes.**
> **The atmosphere will become more toxic with each passing**
> **hour until you reach Futian Station. If you do not make it**
> **to Futian Station in time, you will succumb to illness.**
> **You will now be marked by a specific color and symbol for**
> **your party. These will remain private until the third arc.**

"Futian Station?" Wei repeated, his head tilted a bit in confusion. "Isn't that pretty far?"

"It'll be fine since we have a full day. Right now, we should focus on our skills and get some more stars," I grumbled, trying to mask my indignation. "If it's an underground station, it's probably a dungeon arc."

A blue message flickered before me. Socrates had a habit of messaging me privately rather than in the public chat. He'd only call me Jia Li in private—I guess I was grateful for his consideration.

> **[Observers Chat]**
> **Socrates:** Jia Li, all the observers have spiritual energy. And there are a lot of us. You're going to have to be careful.

At that little message, my blood immediately ran cold. If they ever found out I was the infamous author, I'd be seriously screwed the moment they decided to work together. *Socrates, please keep my identity secret. I swear I'll be less of an ass!*

A firm kick to the back of my seat launched me forward. I whipped my head backward and glared at the snickering Yue.

She sat up in the back of the van, running her fingers through her silky ink hair. "You seem to know a lot about this world, Peijin. And you're definitely not a fortune teller."

Her left eye glowed purple as she stared at me. For a moment, I was reminded of Yang's eyes in the sunlight.

"What's Scathing Reviewer?" Yue said. "How do you have a skill that isn't equipped?"

Dammit, so Yue already got the skill Profiling, which allowed her to view everyone's skills and stats.

"H-hey!" I protested, waving my arms in front of myself. "Should you really be so invasive of your party leader?"

"My party leader? You kidnapped me!"

My face flushed. I was hoping to gain that skill soon, but Yue beat me to it.

I opened the party settings before me. As party leader, I could toggle certain features.

> **Make all system notifications of Peijin's World**
> **Dominion visible to party members.**
> **On / Off**
> **Toggle: On**

> **Disciple Yue activated Profiling!**

I glared at Yue. "Turn that off."

Yue's nostrils flared out of anger, but she obliged, turning off the skill and slumping back in her seat. "At least answer my question," Yue said.

I let out a dramatic sigh and ran my fingers through my short hair. "Whatever, fine. I lied about being a fortune teller."

Yue let out a satisfied huff and crossed her arms. "Then, how do you know so much?"

My phone buzzed in my pocket, and I removed it with sweaty hands. In *Surviving My First Run*, technology ceased to work unless it was powered by the system. Thus, most phones and alternate forms of communication were shut off. Only certain people had tech-related skills and maintained access to the web. So . . . why was my phone working?

MolaMola's message and the attachment titled 'Scathing Reviewer' appeared again, sounding off despite me having dismissed it before.

It was a miracle my phone was working at all. But I couldn't stop feeling dread at the convenient timing of the notification.

Who was MolaMola, and how could they have sent me a skill? Not to mention a skill that sounded detrimental to its user more than anything?

"Peijin, are you going to answer?" Yue cooed in a mocking tone.

Wei responded for me. "There's no need to interrogate Peijin. She's already saved us, so let's just trust in her."

Yang seemed more skeptical, eyeing me from the passenger's seat while still holding on to Amelia. "How do you know so much about what's happening, Peijin?"

"I read a lot of books," I said.

"Like Shakespeare?" Yang asked.

"What? Why the hell would I read Shakespeare?"

"Never mind," Yang responded, with a strange look of satisfaction. "But you're still lying."

"Am I on trial or something? Look, we can host a slumber party and play truth or dare when we get to the station."

Yang's confrontation caught me off guard. I figured he'd be more predictable and controllable given his laid-back nature that I'd gotten familiar with. I didn't trust him any less, but I was certainly more tense now.

I began driving on the freeway again. Other parties searched for any working vehicle they could, tossing out and running over dead bodies if they had to. The freeway was elevated above a river surrounded by a mountainous landscape full of trees and large rocks.

Thankfully, I had refilled the gas tank before our job this morning, so we would be fine for the rest of the trip.

"If the air outside is going to be toxic, we should all buy pigeon's lung from the store," I said while swiping through the store, my eyes flicking between the blue screen and the road.

A pink and lumpy ball appeared first in Yang's hands. It had a hardened texture with a place to bite down on and breathe through. Yang attached it to his mouth; it expanded and deflated with each breath he took. He then removed it and stuck out his tongue for a moment. "Are these actual pigeon lungs?"

"I really hope not." Wei gagged, covering his face with one hand, the pigeon's lung in the other.

Amelia squished the pigeon's lung in her hand and looked mortified when she realized it was far firmer than she'd expected. Yang helped her get used to breathing through it, but she looked ready to burst into tears.

Laughing, I continued to drive, breathing through my own pigeon's-lung attachment. "If the next arc is a dungeon, then we'll have a good chance to level up our skills and get some weapons."

"Peijin," a sharp voice called out from the back seat.

I groaned at the sound of Yue's voice. "What?"

She finally seemed to get used to the setup and was much less tense, even leaning in toward the front of the vehicle. "Do you think we'll be all right and that this apocalypse is just temporary?" She added, "I'm only asking because you know a lot." She bit down on the pigeon's-lung attachment and stared at me expectantly.

My face remained unfazed despite my surprise at her words. Even though these were characters I'd created, characters as psychotic and insane as Yue, they still wanted to return to their own normal lives. They still had desires beyond what I'd brought out in *Surviving My First Run*. They were their own people now.

Had they had lives before the apocalypse, though? After all, they were just characters. Had they just randomly appeared today, thinking they had existed before?

I was looking at Wei and Yue in the rearview mirror when an odd movement caught my attention.

I tilted my head at my reflection. It didn't tilt back.

My reflection moved independently from me, mouthing something.

Found you.

A wide grin spread across my reflection's face and it winked at me, giving a peace sign beside one eye. Childish laughter echoed in my ears, but no one in the van was laughing.

My chest tightened so much I forgot to breathe. Nothing like that ever happened in *Surviving My First Run*, and for a being to appear even in an alternative form meant they had an incredible amount of spiritual energy.

Before I could process what I'd seen, yellow sparks appeared all over the freeway before exploding with a deafening crash. Debris blasted the van forward.

I cried out, squinting to try to see through the sudden dust. I stomped on the gas and swerved the van toward the side of the road. Everyone shouted, their bodies slamming into the sides of the car. Yang hugged Amelia while Wei tightly held on to Yue in the back.

Yellow sparks? What the hell were karmic restraints here for?

The van rocked dangerously from side to side but then came to a halt. I let out a relieved sigh, pressing my forehead to the steering wheel.

Chang's voice boomed over the entire freeway. But I couldn't spot him.

"All right, meeting's over. None of you had a good enough performance to satisfy your benevolent gods, so let's make things more interesting, shall we? A big thanks to the demon realm for their massive donation of spiritual energy. A show like this wouldn't have been possible otherwise!"

Hindsight activated!

The sound of rushing water erupted in the distance. I whipped my head around and saw dark blue waves come crashing over the hills with an explosion of white bubbles. With terrifying speed, a tsunami raced toward us.

A few years ago, an aquarium had been built in a nearby town—all those creatures would have been impacted by the last arc.

A giant blue sea serpent with red scales and whiskers around its face crashed through the mountains and trees, its massive jaws snapping, tearing, and chomping through entire buildings in a violent frenzy. Its bright red eyes locked on our van. It lunged, following the rushing waves that were flooding the land beneath the freeway.

This was a perfect opportunity. I could practically feel my heart skip a beat from my excitement.

"Yang, you're the driver now! Get everyone to the station no matter what, and make sure our party is the ruling party. Don't let anyone else control the station!" I threw open the door and leapt out, scrambling toward the serpent.

Yang immediately obeyed, crawling into the driver's seat while calling after me. "Wait, Peijin, where are you going?"

I sprinted down the freeway, not wasting a second. "I'm going to kill this son of a bitch!"

"Peijin!" Amelia cried, trying to crawl out of the car and run to me. Yang held her back, a small feeble hand reaching out the car before Wei pulled her into the back seat. Yang shut the door and drove off.

I was analyzing the scene before me with Hindsight. The road trembled beneath me, and I clung to the safety bars that lined the side of the freeway to avoid the other disciples who were scrambling away.

I could see the snaking body of the serpent swim through the waves toward me. Water droplets splattered against my face, and I wiped them off.

Had this degree of godly influence ever happened so early in *Surviving my First Run?* The demon realm must've been infuriated by the Goblin King's embarrassing performance and collectively chipped in enough spiritual energy to permit this wicked situation.

If these demons wanted a show, I'd give them one.

My vision was blue with countless possibilities scribbled all over the serpent. It snapped forward, its teeth gnawing through the freeway as if it were nothing more than a soft, malleable plastic.

In *Surviving My First Run*, the sea serpent was a gluttonous beast that consumed everything in its path. It didn't care about other demons, didn't care about anything other than satisfying its insatiable bloodlust for destruction and chaos.

I gripped the metal bar even tighter while the street crumbled under my feet. I was dangling above the flooded canyon now, my sweaty hands holding the bar for dear life. I spared a glance behind me to see my party members racing away, becoming a speck in the distance.

The sea serpent locked its eyes on me and bolted forward, jaws wide open.

Dammit, dammit, dammit! I seriously did not want to die!

At the perfect moment, I let go of the bar, just missing the sea serpent's jaws. It ate meters of the bar in a single bite, tearing it apart with frightening ease.

I tumbled backward toward the rippling water, looking up at the open jaws of the sea serpent lined with horrific teeth. I reached up to the sky and braced for impact.

SIDE STORY—SEA SERPENT
Difficulty: C
Task: Survive the sea serpent.
Reward: 10,000 stars
Failure: Death

CHAPTER EIGHT

Physique level 15 → level 20

My body slammed against the raging water, sending a painful shock through my limbs. I gasped in surprise, and the pigeon's lung fell out of my mouth. Polluted water flooded my throat.

Massive chunks of debris crashed into the water and sank just beside me; I jerked to avoid them, but some still struck my shoulder and leg, forcing me deeper down. Streaks of blood flowed out of the resulting cuts before they vanished into the raging water.

My legs flailed beneath me, and my hands clawed through the water until I reached the surface. I coughed and sputtered, wheezing to catch my breath.

Waves continued to force my head down, but I struggled back to the surface. I rubbed my eyes to clear my vision. The pigeon's lung was being washed farther away; I reached for it and reattached it to my mouth, taking in a big breath of air.

Thankfully, upgrading my Physique level before the fall made up for most of the pain, but my body was still throbbing from the force of the impact. I would definitely have a nasty purple bruise in a few hours.

I pinpointed the sea serpent, Hindsight still guiding me through all of its movements. Having finished its destruction of the freeway, the sea serpent dove back down into the water, its body barely leaving a ripple. Despite being used underwater, Hindsight continued to track the most likely moves of the serpent.

I surveyed the underwater landscape and was amazed I could no longer see the bottom in some areas. It was so deep that it looked pitch-black.

From the depths, there was an occasional burst of color from the hundreds of other water beasts that flitted in and out of the darkness. I could see the glint of thousands of menacing eyes, but they all kept their distance, deterred by the sea serpent's overpowering presence.

I swam toward the shallower end, which was still too deep for me to feel comfortable. I was surrounded by the towering landscape and huddled toward the edge of a steep cliff, clinging to the rocks to save my energy.

The serpent's body was a dark shadow darting through the water until it suddenly vanished, diving deeper until neither my eyes nor Hindsight could track it.

My heart froze in my chest. Dammit! There was no way I could get through this. It hadn't been possible in my novel, and it wouldn't work in this world, either.

I steeled myself, closing my eyes and slowing my breathing. This was the perfect opportunity for me to elevate myself to observers and gods alike. If anybody could accomplish this, it would be me. Or Feiyu, but he wasn't here.

I looked around the water to make sure the pest control van wasn't caught in the collapsing freeway. Various cars floated atop before sinking, but I recognized none of them. The others must have made it. Yang could take care of all of them, and with Archangel Michael and Sun Wukong, they would be just fine.

A massive sense of foreboding shot through me. At the last second, Hindsight warned me of a rapidly approaching entity.

Then the sea serpent appeared beneath me, its jaw unhinged and ready to snap shut on my legs. I rushed to the side to avoid its attack, but its massive body whizzed past me and sent me soaring into the sky with an explosive rush of water.

I flailed in the air while I hovered in between its gaping jaws, looking down its fleshy burgundy throat.

I let out a surprised scream, and my eyes squeezed shut with terror. This was far scarier than what I had originally imagined, and this serpent was young and inexperienced—what would the rest of this world look like, with insatiable demons, wicked ghouls, and vile beasts?

Agility level 1 → level 10

I grabbed a fang of the serpent, trying to swing myself onto its scaly nostril.

A blue flash appeared before me, and a small dragon popped up. Seeing Chang and the sea serpent side by side, they looked incredibly similar with their same-colored scales and red eyes.

"Look at what we have here! It's very impressive you haven't died yet, but you're sure to meet your end soon."

This damn money-hungry moderator. To these gods and observers, I was nothing more than a character. It was like they were tuning in to their favorite show.

But just like how Archangel Michael sponsored coins when he enjoyed what was happening, gods could sponsor me now. I needed to put on a show of defeating the serpent—not only to save my life, but to win the approval and money of the gods.

I dug my nails into the serpent's palm-size scales, pulling myself up and grabbing its whiskers. It let out a horrific cry, its voice reverberating throughout the air.

The sea serpent was one of the most powerful demonic beasts. Unlike most dragons, where there were hundreds of tales involving their brutal deaths, tales of a serpent's death were much less common. Even in *Surviving My First Run*, the most powerful sea serpents were talked about like myths and hardly appeared.

---

108 new observers have joined to watch your struggle!

These observers were no different from gods.

[Observers Chat]
Socrates: This is so cool. It's like I'm watching you write a new chapter before my eyes, Jia Li. Unless you die, obviously.

You have received a new review!
<u>IHARU REVIEW:</u> ★ ★ ★ ★ ★
**Liu Peijin is really impressive and a bit crazy. Who
would ever run straight into a situation like this? I
don't know. Still, I applaud her determination.**

The serpent slammed back down into the water, dragging me along as I struggled to keep my grip. I inched up its whisker while my fingers and knuckles turned white from the pressure.

I held my breath and puffed my cheeks—although pigeon's lung helped me filter the toxic outdoor air, it didn't help me breathe underwater. Thankfully, the spiritual energy from the positive review gave me a slight boost, letting me hold my breath for longer than normal.

I grabbed both whiskers and entangled them around my forearms, tugging them back and bringing the serpent to a momentary halt before it thrashed uncontrollably, infuriated by my sudden control over its movements.

Using its whiskers as reins, I forced it to the surface of the water. I gasped for air before holding my breath again. The serpent took a wild dive to drown me, but I pulled it back up.

Looking through the water, the mountainous terrain led to giant caverns and towering underwater structures. I tugged on the whiskers, forcing the sea serpent into the jagged rock.

It let out a loud cry underwater, bubbles shooting out of its mouth. I could feel myself running out of oxygen—I tugged the serpent back to the surface to catch a breath.

> **You have received a new review!**
> **PINKPINEAPPLE REVIEW: ★ ★ ★ ★ ★**
> **An amusing mess! Liu Peijin's personality isn't very good, but there aren't many disciples who show so much promise.**

> **You have received a new review!**
> **SAPLING123 REVIEW: ★ ★ ★ ★ ★**
> **Leaving this review bc I don't want Peijin to drown**

> **You have received a new review!**
> **UGGSHOES REVIEW: ★ ★ ★ ★ ☆**
> **Liu Peijin is very interesting to watch. Maybe a bit less than Qiu Feiyu, who I've also been following . . . I just feel like I could do a better job than Peijin.**

I could feel a surge of spiritual energy through me from the positive reviews, but I did my best to limit its flow throughout my body. There was something I wanted to test, and I needed all the spiritual energy I could get. I also needed to show that drowning was one of my biggest obstacles.

The serpent dove back down underwater, and I forced it straight into another jagged rock. The terrain exploded from the force of the sea serpent's body. I could sense its growing panic.

Desperate, the serpent began to viciously thrash underwater, bucking its body to throw me off. The serpent violently flung me into the riverbed as I gagged, spitting water and saliva down my chin.

I scrambled for the pigeon's lung that started floating up toward the water's surface and reattached it to my mouth. I coughed, and I instantly felt the water enter my nose and mouth. My face burned and chest tightened while I struggled to get to the surface.

Was no god going to sponsor me some coins? Anything at all?

I finally broke the surface, sputtering and breathing as hard as I could through the pigeon's lung. Bright blue sparks erupted next to my face.

"You're still putting up a pretty good fight. I'm surprised you're not dead yet, Liu Peijin." Chang cackled, a devious glint in his eyes. "This is such fun. You really don't want to die!"

I wanted to reply with something snarky, but I thought I would choke and die the moment I tried to speak, so I stupidly continued gasping for breath.

Editor's Pen activated!

Having enough spiritual energy invested in my edit would allow me to make changes without worrying about Editor's Pen stopping me like it has been. My edit was a small one, but it was better to be safe.

**Pigeon's lung not only filters toxic air pollutants,
but also allows for underwater breathing.**

One concern had been burning in the back of my mind, and this was my opportunity to finally test it—were the edits I made detectable? If the function of pigeon's lung suddenly changed, would gods and observers question how I could now breathe underwater using the pigeon's lung even though I almost drowned moments earlier? Or would gods and observers simply think that my edit had always been reality?

Edit granted!

My entire body was aching by this point, and my arms were covered in various gashes and bruises. I stuck my head underwater, using Hindsight to analyze the current situation.

The sea serpent was still throwing a fit underwater. There were now dozens of other demonic sea beasts swimming around—though none posed as big of a threat. They were attracted to the sporadic movements of the sea serpent but kept a safe distance.

Some were oversize fish with mutated razor-sharp teeth; others were sharks with terrifyingly swollen flesh and fins, making them look ready to pop.

All beasts were demons, and all demons hated one another. Even though demons all belonged to the demon realm, none of them ever got along, and constant warfare was at play.

While the serpent was currently acting as a deterrent to other beasts, since it was only targeting me, if I could get the serpent to accidentally attack some and cause internal fighting, I could defeat the serpent through the number of lower-ranked beasts that would attack it.

It was like the goblins all over again.

I sucked in a breath through the pigeon's lung and dove back underwater, this time thrashing around to attract the sea serpent's attention. Its bright red eyes were narrowed and its rage evident. I could feel a shiver travel up my spine.

I swam deeper down, keeping my eye out for any messages about my new ability to breathe underwater, but none came even as I went deeper and deeper. I couldn't stop a small smile from creeping onto my face.

Even if Editor's Pen rarely worked, it became an increasingly formidable skill. I just needed more spiritual energy to wield it.

I swam just in between the sea serpent and a school of mutated fish, waving my arms frantically.

358 new observers have joined to watch your struggle!

The mutated fish snapped their jaws curiously in my direction but kept their distance, warded off by the overwhelming aura of the serpent. The serpent, however, paid no attention to any other beasts.

It whipped its head around and roared underwater, causing a flurry of bubbles and a current to shoot right into me. The disoriented demonic fish were spinning in the current, unsure of what hit them. The serpent darted forward, jaws wide.

Just before it could latch on, I exhaled all my air into the pigeon's lung while kicking up toward the surface. It inflated like a balloon, almost to the point of popping, but it lifted me just high enough to avoid the jaws of the serpent.

The sea serpent latched onto one of the fish and tore into it, shaking its head and causing strings of flesh to dissipate into the water. The rest of the fish immediately swarmed the serpent like piranhas, biting down and tearing through its thick flesh.

[Observers Chat]
Socrates: This is so stressful to watch.
ZebraMM: You got this Peijin! I'm rooting for you!!
CommerceADK: Thank god I'm not a disciple . . .

The serpent only seemed more enraged, completely ignoring the fish that tore through its body. It let out another vicious roar and headed straight toward me.

My eyes widened in fear. I was relying on the air I'd exhaled into the pigeon's lung to bring me to the surface, but the serpent would reach me before then. Instantly, I set Hindsight to focus on finding a place for immediate shelter and spotted a nearby cave.

However, with my attention turned away from the serpent, it caught up to me. I dove for the cave's small opening the moment the serpent's front teeth snagged onto my leg. I winced, slowing down as the serpent moved to finish me off. I pulled my leg from its jaws, mangling it but holding in my cry.

I gripped the edge of the cave with my fingertips and pulled myself into it. The sea serpent raged outside, slamming its wide-open jaws into the rock to try to grab me. I could feel myself becoming more and more lightheaded. My vision was fading in and out of darkness, and I swam farther into the cave before reaching a small air pocket.

623 new observers have joined to watch your struggle!
10 major gods are watching you!

My head broke from the water, and I spat out the pigeon's lung into my hand. I brushed my slick hair off my face. My surroundings were pitch-black, and I could sense nothing but the pain in my leg and the sound of sloshing water on the cave walls. I was so exhausted I could faint, but the panic was welling inside me.

Blood was oozing out of my calf from where it had bitten me. The pain shot up my body. The cave was already crumbling from the serpent's relentless attacks—my time in this pocket was limited, and my chances to defeat the serpent were dwindling fast.

It was true that there were hardly any ways that the sea serpent had been previously defeated in mythology. However, there was one well known one—and it involved Medusa's head.

In fact, it was the exact reason why I didn't want Amelia to side with Athena or the Abyssal Kraken of Black Seas as her sponsor. I didn't want to make enemies of either of them.

Perseus was able to slay the sea serpent when Athena gave him a shield and Medusa's head to turn the serpent into stone. Similarly, by recreating that myth, I could do the same.

But due to my low spiritual energy and star count, I would have to sign a contract with Athena to get Medusa's head. It would be like what Yue had done with the Goblin King—I would sacrifice something worthy of Athena's contribution, and I would be contractually obligated to execute my half.

If I failed to do so, I'd face horrific consequences the same way the Goblin King did when he took advantage of Yue's body.

I opened the system, checking how many stars I had.

Stars left: 18,800

"Socrates!" I shouted. "Give me some of your spiritual energy so I can talk to Athena!"

[Observers Chat]
Socrates: What? No way.

"Even if you hate me as a person, you can still like me as a character," I gasped, barely able to steady my breath while treading water with my injured leg. "You said you were excited by this, right? I'll show you something even better. Watch me defeat this monster."

"You're the only one aware of . . . me other than Nipon and one other. You've been sending me private messages instead of public ones, so I know you're only interested in watching me through these arcs."

"Can you not do this whole secret-messaging thing right now?" Chang interjected. "You're upsetting the viewers by being cryptic right now."

Suddenly, my breathing calmed completely as if a restorative wave rolled right through me. Ha, so Socrates really did give me a bit of spiritual energy. This would be enough just to spark a conversation and permit Athena to send me messages.

"Chang! I want to sign a contract with Athena!" I cried out at the creature, wet hair clinging to my skin in the dark.

"A contract? With Athena?"

Chang burst out laughing, holding his stomach before his eyes turned menacing. Chang's fangs seemed to grow before me as he took on a horrific look reflecting that of the sea serpent outside.

"You think you can open a contract with her? You're weak. Here you are about to die after making it past just the introduction to this world."

"Athena!" I shouted, completely ignoring Chang. "I know you're watching me! Let me sign a contract with you. I know of a god far stronger than you, and you, the almighty Athena, have never even heard of him. Don't you want to hear all the nasty things they had to say about you and your inferiority?"

With Hindsight activated, I could see the faint silhouette of her figure staring at me, an owl perched on her shoulder. She bristled at the mention of the "unknown god."

I knew of Athena's immense pride, given the myth of how she turned Arachne into a spider for claiming she was better than Athena at weaving. I wanted to grab Athena's attention no matter what.

I scowled under my breath; the constant attacks of the sea serpent caused small rocks to crumble and smack down into the water beside me. I groped along the dark walls, trying and failing to find a tunnel I could squeeze through.

Had I known it would play out like this, I would've done more to gain Athena's favor.

I opened the Azure Dragon Store, swiping through the long list of items until I found the one I wanted.

Shield of Truth: 30,000 stars

It was that expensive? It wasn't that strong of an item outside of any arcs involving Medusa, but I needed to replicate the original story to have a chance at escaping.

Editor's Pen activated!

Shield of Truth costs only 2,000 stars.

Error! Impossible within karmic restraints.

Potential edit: Broken Shield of truth costs only 15,000 stars.

Was my skill seriously bargaining with me? *Well, there go all my stars.*

I made the purchase and a burst of blue sparks appeared before me. They dissipated and revealed half of a large stone shield, which fell into the water and began to sink. I panicked and reached down, pulling it back up.

Despite being split in half, the shield had some good weight to it and elaborate engraving across the surface depicting various Greek myths and achievements. Thankfully, it still covered most of my body.

I lifted the shield above my head to protect me from the crumbling cave while kicking to keep myself afloat in the pitch dark.

Divinity The One Who Fights in Front realizes your plan.

Divinity The One Who Fights in Front sponsors 5,000 stars.

If this was going to be the only star sponsorship I got throughout this entire ordeal, I would never live it down. I glared at the notification before looking up at Chang.

You have returned 5,000 stars to divinity The One Who Fights in Front.

Divinity The One Who Fights in Front is angered by your hubris.

"Athena, I'm not asking for your money right now," I declared loudly while I continued to search the Azure Dragon Store for what I needed. "I need you to sign a contract with me. Send me your stars after."

Sending back star sponsorships wasn't something the disciples dared to do in *Surviving my First Run*, but I needed to show Athena that I was serious about the contract. I also didn't want to show my reliance on the system or gods. I was only willing to abuse the system.

Admittedly, I needed the money, but my pride and the contract mattered more.

"Chang, open up a contract."

Chang puffed out his chest and crossed his arms in a stubborn gesture. "You're making a lot of enemies, Peijin."

"You're about to be one of them. Open a contract," I said.

"If you keep this up, I'm going to have to report you to my supervisor. A disciple like you abusing and ordering around gods? Ha!"

Like everyone else in the system, Chang was incredibly money-driven.

"Chang," I said, "I'll let you have a say in the contract terms."

I could virtually see Chang's eyes fill up with dollar signs. "Deal."

He floated up into the air, batting his long gold lashes again and holding clasped hands cutely against his cheek. "I'm so sorry to all my beloved viewers, but unfortunately the next segment will be ads. Feel free to buy the platinum subscription to my channel to skip them in the future!"

1,129 observers and gods are crying out in anger!

[Observers Chat]
Aslan: ARE YOU KIDDING???
ZebraMM: This is corrupt. You're a shitty moderator!
CommerceADK: This is such a bad story. Contemplating leaving a 1 star review. I can't believe you're making us pay for this.
Evian: How are we supposed to know what's being negotiated then??

Chang looked at Evian's message and gave a dismissive wave. "Don't worry about something like that. Karmic restraints check everything. Besides, it's just an ad break. Don't go around spreading conspiracies on my broadcast."

---

104 observers are rooting for Liu Peijin's death!

. . . Okay.

Chang winked, bringing two of his claws beside his eye to form a peace sign before flicking off the broadcast. Now only Athena, Chang, and I remained.

"I'm sure they don't really want you to die. It's just so exciting," Chang said.

A bright blue screen opened before me, and this time it was iridescent, gleaming with an almost-gold sheen. It lit up the cave enough for me to inspect its current state.

Half of my small cave had collapsed, and I could see the sea serpent's bright red eye staring at me through a gap, its thin line of a pupil flickering back and forth. Gold and brown veins gave it a horrific look as it continued to peer at me.

> **Divinity The One Who Fights in Front warns that you're setting dangerous precedents.**

If other gods discovered that Athena was making this deal, she could face severe backlash—same for Chang, but I didn't care about what happened to him.

I hardened my expression and proposed my plan.

"My sponsor Eternal Wish isn't a god anyone would recognize. For you, that might not be so strange, given that there are thousands of gods far weaker than you. Of course you can't be expected to know all of them," I began.

> **Divinity The One Who Fights in Front claims you know far too much given your current status.**

I needed to come up with a convincing enough lie that would work for the gods and disciples. Telling them I created this world would just be a death sentence. I let the gears turn in my head, stalling. "I'll get to that later. Let me finish with the Eternal Wish. One of my skills allows me to manipulate what happens in an arc. I'm allowed to use this skill once at the start of a chapter, side story, or arc. No one is aware of the edits I make."

Of course, that was a lie. Now that I knew my edits went undetected, I wanted to sow seeds of fear into Athena. Still, I didn't want to give away the full parameters of my skills—thus, I claimed I could only use it once at the start of the arc.

> **Divinity The One Who Fights in Front says that no such skill would be permissible in the system!**

> **Divinity The One Who Fights in Front claims that you are nothing more than a fraud.**

I lifted my broken Shield of Truth up. "See this? My edit for this side story was that I would obtain this item despite the fact that I'm too weak of a disciple for something like that. Of course, that fact must have slipped your mind because you would've otherwise questioned how I got this item.

"My edit for the last chapter was for Sun Wukong to be my sponsor. Despite my ability to make edits, I couldn't influence anything involving Eternal Wish," I said. "Do you know why?"

Chang blinked absentmindedly at me, clearly confused—but the flashing blue notifications appearing before me gave me enough of a sign.

**Divinity The One Who Fights in Front says that
what you're suggesting is impossible!**

I smirked at the screen, looking up at Chang with a cocky grin. "Eternal Wish is a completely unknown god, but he has enough power to heavily influence the early arcs. Even you, Athena, can't do that. It's impossible for any god given karmic limitations. That's what Editor's Pen told me when my Sun Wukong edit fell through."

Editor's Pen hadn't explicitly stated that; however, the fact my edits were impossible in the earlier sponsorship selection implied that Eternal Wish had unspeakable power. Editor's Pen wasn't even able to provide an alternate edit like it just had for the shield.

"Eh?! How could you have put all of this together? Are you really a fortune teller?" Chang replied, completely stunned as he tugged on his whiskers, stressed. "Ahh, I could make so much money off this! A disciple this powerful in my broadcast? But I thought Yue said you weren't a fortune teller."

I replied firmly, staring at him, "Yue is right. I'm not a fortune teller."

His small blue head cocked to the side as he stared at me, confused.

"Then, how do you know so much?"

With the blue glow of Hindsight in my eyes, I appeared menacing in the cave while glaring at Chang. My voice remained steady despite the water splashing against my parted lips.

"I'm a god."

Chang burst out laughing, throwing a complete fit while rocking back and forth in the air. His clawed hands grabbed his tail, tugging and pulling it with each cackle he let out. "You should go into comedy! There's always an opening with a pretty good star salary."

"Qiu Feiyu is a disciple in this area who has not chosen a sponsor and has sworn to tear all gods down from the heavens or drag them through hell. The next arc is a personalized dungeon room that'll test every single person in the parties we made. After that, the top parties will battle, and the winning group will pick the following arc out of three proposed options. And in the fifty-third arc, Athena will fall at the hands of Feiyu."

At my words, the entire cave fell silent except for the sloshing of water against the cave walls. Chang froze, staring at me with widened and shaking red eyes. Even Athena seemed to vanish.

". . . What are you the god of?" Chang asked hesitantly.

"Fate and fortune."

"Why are you here as a disciple? You should be in one of the realms if you're that powerful."

"That's where I'm trying to get back to. So, help me, and I'll make you unparalleled in your power and wealth."

> **Divinity The One Who Fights in Front is stunned.**

> **Divinity The One Who Fights in Front says you're**
> **relying on too many assumptions.**

"No assumptions if I'm a god," I said. "Besides, what other disciple could have a skill as powerful as mine? Athena, grant me Medusa's head so I can survive this. If you do, I'll show you the best story of any other disciple here. I'll uncover Eternal Wish."

CHAPTER NINE

SIDE STORY—SEA SERPENT
Difficulty: B+
Task: Defeat the sea serpent.
Time: 30 minutes
Reward: 50,000 stars
Failure: Death

"Are these the side story edits you wanted?" Chang asked.

I stared at the blue screen in front of me, the broadcast still hidden from everyone but Athena.

"What about seventy-five thousand stars for the reward?"

"Are you trying to get me fired? Stop being greedy."

"Do you even know what that means?"

Divinity The One Who Fights in Front wants
to discuss details of the contract.

"Whatever, that's fine for the side story. As soon as you restart the broadcast, assign it to only me. As for the contract . . ." I typed my terms into the iridescent blue box.

The entire system was, in a way, a manifestation of an uber-capitalistic society.

One that had people turn into disciples and work as slaves for the gods—and apparently observers as well.

Simultaneously, it was the most pure and elite form of entertainment. That meant if I could do something interesting, more gods and observers would watch me. Oh well, more spiritual energy and stars for me, then.

Although Socrates did go radio silent, it wasn't a big concern. I still had enough spiritual energy to get through this.

LIU PEIJIN CONTRACT

A) **Liu Peijin will receive 100% of profits from all messages sent within the broadcast.**

B) **Liu Peijin will receive Medusa's head from Divinity The One Who Fights in Front.**

C) **Liu Peijin must uncover Eternal Wish.**

D) **Liu Peijin may only be streamed directly from Azure Dragon Chang's broadcast.**

E) **Liu Peijin will ally with Greek divinities.**

F) **All parties involved in the signing of this contract will not disclose any details to any external parties.**

G) **Contract will only be terminated in the case of Liu Peijin's death.**

H) **Under the circumstance that Liu Peijin fails to meet any of these obligations, Liu Peijin's death will occur.**

"Are you insane?! One hundred percent of profits earned? How do you ever expect me to agree to that?" Chang erupted.

Divinity The One Who Fights in Front says the contract is fair.

A god needed to pay fifty stars and expend spiritual energy to send a message to a disciple through the system. This was easy for most prominent gods like Athena or Archangel Michael, but smaller gods struggled without enough believers or worshippers—disciples were a chance to bring more fame.

At this point, I didn't know how much observer messages were costing, if anything at all.

Chang gawked at Athena's messages before protesting, "Are you delusional, too? In what world does one hundred percent of profits ever exist in a contract? You may be a god, but you are by no means a businesswoman. Peijin is completely screwing us both ov—"

Divinity The One Who Fights in Front is warning the Azure Dragon to watch his tongue.

Chang was a young Azure Dragon, and he was thus in charge of a relatively unimportant broadcast. He was lucky to have both Feiyu and me. Even though one hundred percent sounded like a lot, it would only help me during the earlier stages. Once karmic limitations permitted gods' descent, there would be no incentive to continue sending messages through the broadcast system.

"Athena is right. The profits will only help me in the short-term, and you gain most of your finances from channel subscribers anyway," I said. "Term D ensures that I'll only be streamed from your broadcast, and I can promise you that I'll give you the best stories out of any other disciple. Besides, I'm now bound to Greek divinities. How limiting do you think that is, Chang?"

> **Divinity The One Who Fights in Front says**
> **you're overestimating your abilities.**

> **Divinity The One Who Fights in Front laughs and says**
> **you're not the most promising disciple in the area.**

I glared at the words, biting my lower lip—Socrates also mentioned that I wasn't the strongest when he threatened to watch other allegedly interesting disciples.

I figured that I wasn't the richest disciple from my earlier fail with Editor's Pen, but this confirmed it. How could there be anyone else stronger than the writer of the story? I should've been beating Feiyu.

"Well, there must have been a reason for you to want to sponsor me instead of them, right? No reason for you to have forced me to ally myself with you otherwise." I grabbed the rock above my head and pulled myself up to avoid the rising water.

"Eternal Wish is my current sponsor," I continued. "So, I'm the only disciple with the best shot at uncovering them. If I fail to, then I'll die for breaking the contract unless it's terminated by my death."

> **Divinity The One Who Fights in Front adds a condition**
> **that you must read her fate and explain her death.**

"Ah, but what would that do? I'm sure you remember the story of poor Oedipus. I've already given you the name of your killer and the time," I said with a wide smile on my face.

Saying I was the god of fortune and fate was especially impactful on any Greek gods; with their heavy religious emphasis on oracles, they were terrified of playing around with something inevitable.

> **Divinity The One Who Fights in Front adds a condition
> that she must become Amelia's sponsor.**

"Can't do that, either. That's her decision. I won't stop her from picking you if it's what she wants, but this deal is already against my favor. You want me to bring down my own undefeatable sponsor, or I'll die."

"Why would I make this deal with you if you aren't even the best disciple here?" Chang interjected stubbornly.

"I will be once you sign the contract. I'll even lower my profit to eighty-six percent."

The Azure Dragon huffed before signing his name down on the contract.

Chang began growing in size, spikes tearing through his back and his jaw unhinging. "Do you have any idea what this means, fool?" Chang roared. "If you fail Athena or me, you will d—!"

"I'll die," I said, annoyed. "I'm aware." I typed my name into the screen and waited as Athena reasoned through her options. As soon as she agreed, the broadcast would open, and I'd need to defeat the sea serpent. If I failed? Well, there was nothing to blame but my own skill.

> **All signatories have signed! The contract is now
> in effect until Liu Peijin's death.**

Chang reopened the broadcast, and a flood of messages appeared from during the ad break.

> **You have received 43 stars!
> You have received 43 stars!
> You have received 43 stars!
> You have received 43 stars!**

Blue screens erupted all around me, blocking my vision. I toggled my personal settings so that the small star notifications would no longer be seen.

"Hello, everyone! So sorry about the ad break, but it's mandatory in terms of my managers. Special treatment could get me terminated. I take my job very, very seriously here. So does karma."

Any spiritual energy I had was fully expended now, and all messages from Athena were terminated. I was alone with not even Socrates to bother me.

There was nothing Athena feared more than defeat. She was overwhelmed by her reason, but even then, her rage was unparalleled when she lost against those she viewed as weak enemies. Thus . . .

Medusa's head appeared in my hand, and the snakes on her head wrapped tightly around my wrist. The Shield of Truth glowed in my hands; an orange light seemed to make up the missing half. It was incredibly heavy and glistened in the water, painting beautiful orange reflections in the blue waves. I reattached the pigeon's lung to my mouth.

By buying the Shield of Truth, I would fight with a symbol of Athena. To lose against an easy enemy in her eyes would bring shame to her name. If I wanted to survive, I needed to play to the god's desires for entertainment, money, and greed.

Before I could be crushed by the crumbling cave, I dove back into the tunnel and swam out. The sea serpent slammed against the cave, and it finally collapsed on itself.

1,583 observers and gods are crying out in anger!

[Observers Chat]
Nipon23: booo, the wicked witch of the west is back

The dark water surrounded me, and I swam back from the sea serpent as its fangs became embedded in the rock from the collapsing cave. I hid Medusa's head behind my shield; I had only one shot to kill the serpent, and I couldn't let it discover my plan so soon.

Just a few feet away, the sea serpent broke free and shot toward me like a jet. I raised the shield in front of me, grunting as the glowing orange light pushed back against the serpent. It roared underwater, sending a current that forced me back, but Hindsight calculated its next move.

Was Hindsight keeping me calm and levelheaded? The shrieking sea serpent snaked closer, and I lifted my shield. With my right arm, I revealed Medusa's head just before the serpent.

As soon as Medusa's writhing head locked eyes with the sea serpent, the vicious beast froze. Its eyes took on a hazy gray color before hardening and turning into stone. The back end of its long body thrashed and slammed into the side of the river.

Fate. Something I knew and could alter in this world. My survival was proof of that.

---

638 observers are screaming in excitement!

[Observers Chat]
Hedgehog1938: How is Peijin pulling this off? I thought she was stupid?
CommerceADK: It's clear she cheated! What do you think that ad break was for??

Socrates: Peijin isn't cheating. She's using the system. Isn't that the whole point?

With the last ounce of its strength, the sea serpent crashed into the sides of the river, violently spasming and trying to break free of its curse. The river collapsed in on itself, clouds of soil and rocks blurring my vision.

Dammit! I dodged the debris and swam toward the head of the sea serpent. If the sea serpent didn't kill me, the underwater landslide would.

Avoiding a crashing rock, I latched onto the now-stone whiskers of the sea serpent. I gripped my shield and slammed it into the eyelid of the serpent, watching the stone crumble away. I dug and pried into its eye socket to remove its eye.

The entire river floor was shaking violently, causing countless rocks and sediments to cascade down.

The eye shifted, half of it popping out. I was so close; it was almost loose. Just a bit more, and—

A rock smashed the front of my face, knocking the pigeon's lung out of my mouth.

> **Divinity Supreme Commander of the Heavenly Hosts is urging you to swim to the surface!**

Water flooded into my nose, sending a sharp stinging pain. A flurry of bubbles burst from my mouth, and I choked, losing oxygen. The serpent's eye finally fell loose, the eyelid crumbling away as fine gray dust. I desperately grabbed and held onto it.

Kicking, I hacked underwater, my body spasming as I tried to break through the surface. The sun's rays were beaming down into the deep river, casting bright ripples on my skin.

The influx of messages had brought in thousands of stars, but I was forced to spend all of them.

> **Agility level 10 → level 20**

I moved with unparalleled speed as my hand broke through the surface of the water. I sputtered, spitting up water while swimming over to floating debris from the freeway. Pulling myself onto a chunk of concrete, I vomited all over it.

I had made it. Broken Shield of Truth, Medusa's head, and Petrified Eye of the Sea Serpent. I had all of it.

> **Side Story #1—Sea Serpent has concluded!**
> **You have earned the exclusive achievement Butcher of Abyssal Horrors.**

> **Congratulations! You have completed the side story.**

This was the world I knew. This was the world I fabricated with my own hands and mind, and it was a world I knew better than anyone.

I wouldn't fall back into the way of my old life. This was my playing field; I was going to become a god and make it all the way to the last arc. Then I'd tear down this wicked system piece by piece with my party beside me. Karmic restraints, Eternal Wish, gods, and the observers—I wouldn't allow myself to lose to any of them.

Hindsight, the skill that had served me most so far, began to flicker before me. The screen crackled, glitching as the pixels shifted into a deep red.

> **THE MAJOR ARCANA HAVE SPOTTED YOU.**

. . . The Major Arcana?

My eyes grew wide in confusion and fear, my throat feeling thick with anxiety. Had I written about such a thing in *Surviving My First Run*? The system glitched at times, but it was promptly fixed by one of the thousands of gods like Chang that kept it running. Never did it display a red screen. The idea that the system was hackable was even more impossible than the existence of Eternal Wish.

> **THE MAJOR ARCANA HAVE SPOTTED YOU.**

The screen glowed, wavering as bright orange sparks flew from the red screen and burned my skin. This one notification sent the most dreadful rush of anxiety through me more than anything else had up till now.

> **THE MAJOR ARCANA HAVE SPOTTED YOU.**

CHAPTER TEN

I crawled back onto the shore, trudging up into the sweeping trees. I purchased another pigeon's lung to stop myself from breathing in the toxic air. Just the few breaths I took when fighting the serpent caused a burning sensation that lingered in my lungs.

Apart from me, the rest of Peijin's World Dominion, my party, was far gone. Yang was empathetic but also possessed a strong sense of responsibility. I trusted that he would safely get my party to the station.

Small scrapes and cuts littered my skin, and my leg was torn through. Still, I was lucky to have survived. Whoever Eternal Wish was, they didn't seem remotely concerned with the status of their disciple despite the big investment made. As of now, I theorized that Eternal Wish and MolaMola might've been one in the same.

Even if I didn't sign the contract with Athena, I still wanted to uncover the identity of Eternal Wish. I knew for a fact I didn't select Eternal Wish as my sponsor. Whatever or whoever smacked my hand had an ungodly amount of spiritual power to have influenced my decision—an amount of spiritual power I couldn't fathom, even in *Surviving My First Run.*

I would need to become a real god to contest it; the spiritual energy that observers could give suddenly seemed much more appealing. If I could earn enough achievements from the arcs to gather enough spiritual energy, I'd one day receive the option to become a god.

Honestly, it pissed me off a bit, too—the fact that I, the author, didn't know such a pivotal "character."

Though I felt the same frustration with the Major Arcana notification, there was nothing I could do until they made the first move. Unlike Eternal Wish, they hadn't changed the course of anything yet. I would work my way up to that mystery.

Looking up at the sky, I noticed the sun was already setting behind the mountainous horizon. Today officially marked day one since the apocalypse began, yet the sun still drew watercolor strokes of soft pinks, baby blues, and deep oranges that kissed the expansive sky. The world kept moving as if this situation was simply fate bestowed upon humans alone.

It would typically take one day to get to the metro station on foot, but it should only take me around two hours, given my enhanced Physique and Agility. But no matter how much was spent on status upgrades, I still needed rest.

I purchased a small tent and crawled inside. Once inside, I saw it was far larger than its appearance suggested; it shifted to accommodate my supplies. The weather was far cooler now, and given that all my clothes were drenched, the icy air was stabbing into my skin. I tucked my knees beneath my chin and tried to ignore the cold.

Instead, I focused on patching up my leg, wrapping it in some purchased gauze and applying some healing ointments. With my improved physique levels, I wasn't too worried about this being a fatal injury, but I didn't want it to hold me back.

I finally finished and lay down on the floor of the tent. Rolling onto my side, I felt an awkward lump on my thigh.

"My phone!" I gasped, sitting up and patting my pocket. It was definitely dead now after being drenched from the earlier encounter with the sea serpent. I guess it didn't really matter, since it was the apocalypse, and I hadn't brought my charger, but still . . .

My finger rapidly and impatiently clicked on the power button. To my surprise, the black phone screen flickered to life, reflecting my wide-eyed expression back at me.

The same notification from MolaMola as before was on my home screen, and with a trembling finger, I tapped it.

Spiritual power could be used not only for a god's power, skills, or weapons, but also to influence the trajectory of the story by influencing karma. Therefore, divinities like Archangel Michael, Athena, or Sun Wukong were especially powerful. If enough spiritual power was used, the story progression could be bent by their will.

Just like Eternal Wish's interference seemed impossible, the same applied for the Major Arcana notification. Hijacking the blue screens wasn't something I ever considered possible.

So, who was MolaMola? Were they the Eternal Wish?

> **MolaMola:** Thanks for writing *Surviving My First Run*. As promised, here's the surprise.

> **Open attachment**

I nervously tried to chew on my lower lip—a habit I most likely picked up from Yang—before I remembered the pigeon's lung in my mouth. Why was my heart beating so fast? Was this not my world?

> **Download Scathing Reviewer?**
> **Cancel / Download**

I saw my trembling iris reflecting in the blue pop up. Seriously, this skill had a name that seemed more detrimental to me than anything.

"Socrates? Are you still stalking me?"

Nothing but an eerie silence and the muffled chirps of crickets followed my words.

A thought suddenly popped into my head: What was my personal goal?

Sure, I wanted to uncover the Eternal Wish and do something supercool, but I didn't know what kind of life I wanted for myself.

Every character envisioned themselves at their desired end. Whether that was being a happy billionaire, finding the love of their life, or just cultivating a small garden, there was always something. Did I have something like that?

Just yesterday, my only focus was surviving. I wasn't really living in any sense of the word as much as I was scraping by. Writing was simply a means of survival—an escape. Then, when the apocalypse started, my focus was still surviving.

I just didn't want to die. That would be too pitiful, especially given my already-pathetic life. I wanted to make a name for myself, and I wanted to tear down the system. That was what I wanted to accomplish. Part of the reason for that was that I wanted to prove I was just as good as Feiyu; the other part was that I wanted to see my own story carried out to the end.

Lying in my cold tent, my leg throbbing despite the healing ointments, I felt a bit lonely. I had spent so much of my time alone that loneliness became normal. But now I was surrounded by people. It felt unfamiliar. My thoughts drifted to my party.

Wei and Yue were just characters, so did it really matter what happened to them? I wanted to protect Yang and Amelia first. I felt a pang in my heart at the thought, but they were the two who were truly innocent in this situation.

But wasn't it Wei's duty to protect the innocent? Could two characters with the exact same goal exist in one story?

I had fallen out of love with my story and its characters long ago, and if any of the millions of readers still loved this marred adventure, they could go ahead and frolic around in this world themselves. So, what did I want? After I defeated Eternal Wish and destroyed the system, what kind of life did I want to live?

My phone beeped, announcing the download.

> **Downloading Scathing Reviewer . . .**
> 1% . . . 5% . . . 29% . . . 48% . . . 79% . . . 89% . . . 91% . . . 95% . . . 99%

> **Scathing Reviewer has been successfully downloaded!**

> **Scathing Reviewer has been equipped.**

My breath hitched, and I anxiously waited for something, anything, to happen. My eyes skimmed across the inner seams of my tent but found only that familiar and eerie emptiness. The chirping outside of my tent continued aimlessly, and the wind brushed against the thin walls.

I let out a pitiful laugh, putting my hand down as my hand ran through my short hair. "I've gotta have the worst luck out of any other disciple here," I muttered. I collapsed onto my back and stared at the ceiling of the tent before shutting my eyes.

The next arc would be the dungeon series, and I should be able to get to the train station just before it started. There was only so much toxicity the pigeon's lung could filter, so I should make it to the station before needing to purchase more powerful items.

This arc would be when Wei would start to regain his memories, and I needed to be there. If I didn't make it in time . . . then hopefully Yue could kill Wei before he would kill everyone in that train station.

Wei managed to survive in *Surviving My First Run* because of Feiyu's skill and my favoritism as the author—but he only came to his senses after slaughtering more than half of Feiyu's party in cold blood.

Even though it was technically a dungeon, it was very loosely based on the term. It would start out similarly, with generic mobs, grinding, and rewards; however, it would contort and twist into individual rooms designed for each party member. At the end, the top three teams would compete against each other for an achievement.

The moment I'd arrive tomorrow, I would buy Wei a nice set of clean, white robes. The classic set was on sale in the Azure Dragon Store. By making him wear them, it would not only boost his stats, but it could jog his memories just a bit.

It wouldn't be enough for him to go berserk, but it would hopefully be enough to allow a trickle of some memories in so he wouldn't have to face all of them at once.

There was also a sword hidden beneath the flooring of the currency exchange booth at the station. Feiyu wouldn't discover it until after the third arc, and I would make sure I was the first to take hold of it.

I fell asleep eager to wake up and execute my plans at the station the next day.

CHAPTER ELEVEN

The rising sun's rays bled through the thin fabric of the tent and onto my face, waking me. I rose, my back aching and sore as I let out an exhausted groan. Opening the Azure Dragon Store, I bought the Boundless Bag, which was a sort of backpack that had endless capacity, although the weight of all items held would remain the same.

I packed the tent, serpent's eye, and Medusa's head into the bag before draping it over my shoulder and holding on to the arm strap. I wielded the Shield of Truth in my free hand and began the trek to the metro station.

Agility level 20 → level 25
Physique level 20 → level 25

The longer I spent outside, the more I could feel my lungs tingling. I could see the train station in the distance and approached it. Once I got close enough, the air instantly cleared up, and I spat out the pigeon's lung and took my first breath of clean air.

I squinted to better make out a white figure walking in front of the entrance.

"Wei?" I sped up my pace as I approached the man. "Wei!" I ran forward but stumbled over the heavy shield, falling forward.

Wei darted forward with surprising speed and stabilized me, grabbing me by my shoulders. "Peijin?" he whispered, surprised. "H-how did you . . . ?"

"It's a long story. I'll explain it when all the party members are here." I sighed, clinging to him for just a moment too long and finally letting myself relax.

I looked around the metro station, peeking down the escalator to notice how packed it was with people. "Are you patrolling? It looks like you got new clothes, too," I said, gesturing toward his long white robe. I did my best to mask my surprise.

He gave a curt nod before peeking over his shoulder. "When we got here, there was already another party in control, but don't worry. I'll call Yang over to show you around."

My eyes were glued to the white robes. Had someone told him to wear these exact clothes? After all, long white robes weren't the most convenient for an apocalypse. If an observer tried to tell him to wear them, I figured karmic restrictions would've stopped that conversation from happening. But if a disciple told him, then my theory on observers was incorrect again.

"Did you get that outfit yourself?" I asked. "I could get you a nicer one."

He shook his head. "No, they were given to me by the other party. Not sure why, but it's nicer than my old blood-soaked clothes."

"You don't think it's strange they asked you to wear something like that during an apocalypse? I can buy you a better outfit from the Azure Dragon Store."

Wei cocked his head, giving me a strange smile. "Don't worry about the other group. You can trust them." He emphasized the last part slightly, trying to convince me.

"Peijin!" I heard the familiar voice call out to me, and I whipped my head around to find Yang's arms. He gave me a tight hug, leaning to bury his head in my shoulder. "You're all right! You don't know how worried I was." Yang's words jumbled together in a quick mess, barely comprehensible.

I tried to power through his hug, but it was far too tight—I could feel my limbs compress together as the air was forced out of my lungs. I lightly tapped his back, trying to signal for him to let go. "Yang," I choked out, heaving for air. "Yang!"

What the hell was his Strength level for it to be suffocating my level-15 Physique?

Scathing Reviewer activated!

Bright blue sparks flew out from my skin, causing Yang to let out a small yelp before he let go of me and leapt back. My hands still had a small blue sheen on them, minuscule particles flying off as if my skin were burning. This flurry of sparks must have been from my Scathing Reviewer skill.

Yang looked at me, wide-eyed and embarrassed. "S-sorry! I'm still trying to get used to the levels. I just upgraded my Strength level a bit."

"A bit? How high is your Strength level for you to almost strangle me to death?!" I replied, exasperated, my hands on my hips like I was scolding him before I bent down to pick up my shield.

"It's only at level twenty-five."

My jaw dropped at his statement. Did I fight the sea serpent for nothing? There was no way Yang could nearly match my stats when I was the one who had to defeat a mythical beast. "Where'd you get the money for that? Did you commit fraud or something during the few hours I was gone?"

Yang scratched at his head and laughed. "Well, the reigning party here set up a whole monster-farming system in the train station. It's impressive. I was there all night getting stronger."

I gave him a blank stare. Feiyu certainly didn't put together such a complicated setup in *Surviving My First Run*. Did his IQ go up or something?

So, fighting monsters in the dungeon could single-handedly boost a disciple's early stat levels by a very significant amount . . . My victory over the sea serpent felt less impressive now, and my cheeks flushed from embarrassment.

Well, no matter what, I caught the eyes of observers and gods through my earlier performance, not to mention the achievement and reserve of stars I had. That fame couldn't be earned by farming monsters.

Wei patted my shoulder reassuringly. "Don't worry, Peijin. I'm sure you still have the highest level in our party if you survived the serpent."

My cheeks burned even more at Wei's callout. "Hey, who said I was worried about Yang's stats? I know I'm still first."

"But, Peijin, I didn't say anything about Yang."

"Go back to patrolling, Wei." I was flustered, and I could see the playful glint in Wei's eyes. He briefly lowered his head before leaving Yang and me alone.

"Don't mind Wei," Yang said. "He was nervous the entire time you were gone, but everyone at the station thinks you're a legend now with how much Wei raved about you. I'm sure the reigning party moved him to outdoor patrol just to get him to stop talking about you and fighting with Yue."

"You weren't nervous?" I asked.

Yang glanced to the side. "I couldn't console Amelia if I was also upset."

I gave him a smug grin. "Yeah? Well, since you were so calm, I was hoping you'd be able to bring the train station under my party's domain."

Yang's face lit up. "Oh, just wait until I introduce you to the other party. Qiu Feiyu is just great. You'll love him."

[Observers Chat]

Socrates: LOL Jia Li, aren't you excited to see Feiyu? Technically, you've known him since you were fourteen. All those pages you wrote describing him really paid off, even if they were boring at the time.

My eye twitched, and I awkwardly cleared my throat. "I'd rather see Amelia."

We approached the staircase at the entrance of the train station. It was a massive structure of concrete and glass with signs pointing in the direction of various train lines.

Yang led me down, and the sight before me was astounding. Thousands of people were sitting on benches or leaning against the wall—which was completely typical of a Chinese subway station—but the station's various service centers had been turned into a food-and-water-distribution system, a cooking station, a medical treatment room, and a strange rendering of a barracks where a constant flow of men and women were exchanging weapons.

Yang navigated through the crowd. We were at the top of a staircase leading down to platforms one and two. He pointed down the stairs. "Platforms one and two are where monster farming is set up. We're currently at the east gate, which is the main hub for the disciples because all the supplies were here."

"I can't help but feel like I missed a lot when I was gone," I muttered, feeling rather bitter that I wasn't excelling in my own world. Not only that, but I wasn't even a necessary member of my own party.

Yang let out a little laugh before walking to the barracks to pick up a glowing sword from a reserved section. It was an intermediate level, not high enough to have any special functions, but Yang had clearly established himself at the station.

"It's not as utopian as it seems. Give it another day for infighting to start. It'll be just like the pest control office."

I scrunched my nose. "Don't even bring up that place again. But, Yang, don't you think it's suspicious that they're this organized? We're in an apocalypse, and they seem too prepared."

I crossed my arms over my chest before my eyes locked on a figure leaning back on a pillar by the east gate, nonchalantly polishing a blade.

Based on the wide back profile, the person was a man who regularly worked on his physique. He wore a tight black button-up. The fabric stretched around his muscles when he twirled the gorgeous blade in his hands and carefully examined it.

It was the exact blade I wanted.

"Hmm?" Yang lowered his head to meet my eye level, a mischievous grin on his face.

"Stop it. I was looking at his sword." Was that a lie? Partially.

"Didn't you mention once that your type was men like that?"

"Men like what?"

"Brooding, wearing all black, and—"

"No."

Yang snickered and continued to walk forward. However, as we were passing by, Yang suddenly pushed me straight into the stranger.

I stumbled and fell straight onto him, pushing myself off and blinking rapidly in my shock. I stammered, completely embarrassed. "I'm so sorry!" I saw his face for the first time, and my jaw instantly dropped in horror and awe.

His sharp nose perfectly complemented his angular features and drew one's eyes to his mischievous, slightly upturned lips that parted just enough to show pearly white teeth. His thick eyebrows were raised in surprise and perfectly framed his pitch-black eyes. They squinted in a condescending and intrigued manner with his long lashes twinkling under the harsh station lights.

Who else could this man be but Qiu Feiyu?

[Observers Chat]
Socrates: Whoa.
Hedgehog1938: He looks even better than I thought he would . . . ToT
Sapling123: And his skills surpass his looks. He might be better here than in the original, too.

Feiyu aimed his sword right for my throat. I swung my Shield of Truth just in time to clash against it, causing a loud ring to sound through the station.

His smile grew, and his chin cocked upward as if he were observing all my movements. "Not bad. You must who Wei was talking about."

Yang awkwardly stood on the sidelines and brought both of his hands to cover his gaping mouth. The station quieted down at the sound of our clashing weapons before Feiyu pulled back.

"What a bummer. I was just finishing up polishing my sword," Feiyu pouted, his eyes still mocking.

"You're the one who swung at me first," I panted before pulling back, holding the shield in front of me. For once, I was glad the shield was so large and clunky; it hid my trembling arm.

Feiyu smiled, his eyes curving into pleasant crescents. "Forgive me. I recognized the look in your eyes, and I thought I'd make the first move."

Yang clasped his hands together and let out a very nervous laugh, walking between us and separating us with his long arms. "Peijin, meet Qiu Feiyu. Feiyu, meet Liu Peijin."

Feiyu took a step back and leaned on his sword casually, tilting his head. "Peijin. That's a loaded name. You must be very ambitious, then."

Cocky bastard.

"There's not enough room in this station for the both of us," I said, my voice cold.

I meant every word. Even the sword he was holding, a sharp black blade with dark purple iridescent highlights, was the one I had wanted to snag at the station for myself, but somehow he'd gotten it first.

"Really?" Feiyu asked. "I was going to say I found you intriguing."

"Don't play with me."

My palms became clammy, and I tried to mask my discomfort. Since I created Feiyu, I knew he was the biggest wildcard—no disciple ever came close to challenging him. The only true threat to Feiyu were the gods, and he killed them.

"Wei and Yue . . . Those two disciples are great, aren't they? You're really lucky, Peijin. I would've loved to have them in my party."

I bristled, instantly defensive. We were two wolves fighting for territory. "What are you getting at?"

"I'm just excited, is all," Feiyu said in a friendly tone. It only set me more on edge. "It's still just the beginning, so I'm sure a lot will change."

Yang was burning up out of embarrassment from how poorly the introduction was going. "Ha ha, you guys are both so . . . intense. Peijin and I will get out of your way now." Yang bowed his head in an apologetic manner before dragging me away.

We had only taken a few steps before Feiyu's deep, calculating voice rang out from behind us.

"Wait." The sound of his slow footsteps approached until he leaned down to whisper in my ear. "You can't replicate what my party has created, so don't ruin it. I want to work with you, not against you."

I looked over my shoulder to meet his gaze, my eyes cold. "I wouldn't need to replicate it when I could make something greater."

"You really are ambitious," Feiyu said.

If I heard that phrase one more time, I would truly go insane.

"I'm just a pest control worker."

Yang exchanged a few words with Feiyu, but I tuned them out, distracted by my racing thoughts.

Truthfully, there was nothing inherently wrong with Feiyu as a character. His prior occupation was as a relatively popular online streamer, and once the apocalypse started, he was incredibly cunning, cold, and calculating.

What sparked fear through me was that he was created as a reflection of myself. He was equally selfish and pathetic—looking at him caused rage to surge through me. It was as if I were staring at an alternate version of myself, but a far better one. Feiyu lacked all the qualities that I hated about myself.

If Wei and Yue's connection to my identity startled me, Feiyu's appearance was a punch straight to my liver.

"Peijin? Hello? Earth to Peijin . . ." Yang waved his hand in front of my face. Feiyu was long gone.

I snapped out of my thoughts. "Huh? Oh, sorry."

"You look a little pale. Do you want to get some rest before the next arc? It'll be starting soon."

I shook my head. "No, it's fine. I want to see Amelia and Yue first," I muttered, rubbing the back of my neck. I checked how long was left until the commencement of the second arc.

> **Please make your way to platform 1 in the next 12 minutes.**

"Then, let's go straight to platform one. Amelia, Yue, and Wei are supposed to meet me there in ten minutes," Yang said, grabbing a sword as we walked by the armory and tossing it toward me.

The sword was relatively heavy and I inspected it, fiddling with the handle. It was by no means a very good one, but it could work for now. Yang and I headed for platform 1, but before I could descend the stairs, a man blocked my path.

"Sorry, princess," he said, leaning on a run-down and unimpressive axe. "We're full here, and we wouldn't want you to get hurt, either."

I quirked a brow before peeking around him. The tracks were full of small monsters, but farther back, it was clear that more giant and treacherous beasts weren't being fought. The entire station seemed to tremble at their roars as they pounded against the walls.

Looking back up at the man, my cold eyes met his. "Doesn't look very packed. This is where the next arc is, and it starts in a couple minutes."

He gave a condescending frown before leaning down to match my eye level. "Do I need to repeat myself?"

"She's with me. Let her in," Yang retorted from behind me, taking a few steps forward.

"Yang, are you this girl's babysitter or something? Did boss tell you to watch over her?"

> **Divinity Supreme Commander of the Heavenly
> Hosts cries out at the man's injustice!**

Another message from Archangel Michael. He was strangely devoted to my party.

> **[Observers Chat]**
> **Socrates:** Take this abuse and I'm never giving you spiritual energy again.

I let out a humored exhale before turning around, ignoring the man's comment. There was no point in arguing with trash like him. As I began tying my cropped hair into a short ponytail, two hands grabbed my shirt before throwing me as hard as possible at the staircase. I only stumbled.

A normal person would have gone flying, but now it was clear to me that my level was far higher than whatever this guy's was.

I whipped my head around to face the man, but Yang was a step faster, already shoving him against the wall.

My sword let out a loud ring, piercing the space between the man's wrinkly neck and the wall behind him. The man's pupils shrunk into tiny dots as he stared at me in horror.

Divinity Great Sage Equaling Heaven sponsors 3,500 stars.
Observer Socrates sponsors 5 stars.

My eyes lit up with total excitement, and the dreadful feeling that I was a failure finally lifted just a bit. It was my first real star sponsorship!

A shocked Yang turned around to see me standing with an outstretched arm. The sword he handed me just moments before was now mere millimeters away from having pierced the other man's neck. I walked up and pulled the sword out from the wall before turning my back on him.

"I'm so sorry about that, Peijin," Yang apologized, running up behind me moments later. "I didn't think they'd act like that toward you. He scrambled away as soon as you turned around."

At my silence, Yang grew increasingly apologetic. "Peijin? Is everything okay?" He hurried his steps to see my facial expression but paused once he saw me.

I burst out laughing, clutching my stomach as I leaned forward; my hand gripped Yang's shoulder for stability. "Did you see that look on his face? He won't last another arc! God, that was hilarious."

Yang paused in surprise at my reaction before letting out a little laugh himself, shaking his head. "I shouldn't be surprised by your reaction."

"Peijin!" A shrill voice called for me, and I turned my head to see Amelia darting over, her arms outstretched. I hoisted her up and spun her in the air while Wei and Yue approached.

Amelia's hair was tied up into a beautiful braided bun. Yue's hair was also braided—if you could call it that. It looked like a total disaster, but I just smiled. Amelia and Yue must have done one another's hair.

Disciple Yue activated Profiling!

Yue let out a slow whistle as she read my new stats.

"Busy without us? Hey, you've even activated—"

Before I could make a snarky retort, Yue let out a surprised gasp. Sparks erupted from her eye, and she painfully clasped a hand over it, wincing.

"The fuck?!" she cried, vigorously rubbing her eyes and glaring up at me. "Since when could you disable skills like that?"

Shrugging nonchalantly, I turned away. "Scathing Reviewer doesn't seem to like you very much."

Make your way to platform 1 immediately for the second arc.

My party made its way down the stairs. The select few who were brave enough to farm leapt up from the tracks and waited patiently while thousands of disciples flooded the platform. Trains would serve as transport during some of the arcs, operating with the system's magic.

Thankfully, it was big enough to accommodate all of us, though it became increasingly cramped. Amelia clung to my leg while we edged closer to the platform, where the first car's doors would open. Wei stood behind my party, extending his arms to protect us from the crowd.

A roaring erupted from the tunnel, causing the station to rumble. A set of blaring lights emerged from the darkness to reveal a train hurtling down the tracks, crushing all the creatures and beasts in its path.

"Ready for the next arc?" I said, a cocky grin on my face.

Yue cackled from behind me, cracking her knuckles. "Bring it on."

CHAPTER TWELVE

Hundreds of people shoved one another and clamored like rolling waves to reach the train, but thousands stood back, hesitant of what could potentially emerge. Feiyu was casually inspecting the clean cut in the wall from my sword, tapping the ground with his long blade.

As the number of adults increased, Amelia grew more intimidated and clung to me harder. I lifted her into my arms, and she buried her head in my shoulder.

I thrust my sword into the train car's door, trying to pry it open. Wei held the shoving parties back, his body a barrier.

Only one party was allowed per train car. Although there would be enough cars to satisfy every party, thanks to the magic of the system, entering the first car of the train gave a perceived aura of power. There was no material benefit to it, but gods who were joining broadcasts late gravitated to the ones in the earlier cars. More liked to select Broadcast Car #1 over Broadcast Car #47.

The train skidded to a halt when I finally managed to crack the door open. With a nod of my head, I gestured for my party to follow, but when I tried to step inside, an invisible barrier shoved me back. My shoulder pressed into the barrier, and I strained to enter, but it shoved me back again.

"Sorry, Peijin," Feiyu called out, easily maneuvering around the crowd that shrunk in his presence, "but my party has already claimed the first car."

"But this car just opened . . . ?" I gawked as he led his party into the train. There were four people in total from his party walking in, but I only recognized two of them as characters. The one I didn't recognize was a young girl who looked oddly familiar.

When I peered inside, forcefully pressing my cheek against the invisible barrier, I saw the door connecting the first and second car had already been opened. Their party must have claimed the first car using that.

I scowled and was about to pull back before a small black figure at the very front of the first car turned to meet my gaze. A fifth party member. Shrouded in darkness, I was unable to make out any discernible features, but a shiver traveled up my spine. They must've been the one who used the connecting door. I pulled back.

"Nice one," Yue called out, rolling her eyes. "You can't even enter the arc properly."

Yang promptly elbowed her in the side, which caused her to reel for a moment before cursing.

The front of the claimed train cars changed to display the party's name. My eyes widened when I read what formed in black ink before me.

Twenty-Two. Feiyu's party.

Hindsight activated!

I stared at the name of Feiyu's party for a moment, stunned. "Twenty-Two" wasn't the name of his party in *Surviving My First Run*. So far, the apocalypse played out the exact same as it had in my novel, unless it was directly influenced by a disciple's actions . . . What could have possibly made Feiyu change the name of his party?

"Yang," I said, "do you know why the name of the party is Twenty-Two?"

Yang shrugged. "Apparently the party leader is really into tarot cards. Twenty-Two is the number of cards in the Major Arcana deck."

Feiyu was certainly not into tarot cards.

I shook my head, getting rid of the thought. Was I a hired detective or something? Why the hell would I care if Feiyu now liked astrology or palmistry? Quite frankly, if I was rich and alive, life was good. My top priority right now was the arc.

The cabin door shut as the train shifted, the next one opening with the sound of scraping metal. I instantly jumped in along with my party members and entered our party name to claim the car.

Peijin's World Dominion.

"More like World Tyranny . . ." Yue muttered before sitting on one of the cushioned chairs.

Earlier, I had told Athena and Chang that I knew these dungeons would devolve into personalized horror rooms for each party member; however, if they asked for any specific details, they would discover me to be a fraud.

Apart from Wei and Yue, I had no clue what these rooms were going to look like. This arc was full of uncertainty, even for me, the author.

But one thing was for certain—my party needed to survive so I could make the most out of this room. It was easy to lie to Athena and Chang by telling them I was a god—our contract discussion would remain private, and they wouldn't be able to tell any other parties.

But I needed to convince the other disciples that I was a god, even if I was a fake. Words and promises were more convincing to the gods—man, however, would only consider a display of power as truth. I needed to become a stronger disciple by leveling up as much as possible before declaring I was a god.

The biggest threat and key to my goal was . . .

My gaze shifted over to Wei; it was clear to any onlookers that he was . . . beyond strange. He resembled a historical cosplayer, if anything.

For most of his life and the present time, Wei had been like a foolish dog, blindly loyal to whoever he latched onto. But on the tragedy of his eighteenth birthday, Wei's entire world crumbled, and he found himself truly alone for the first time.

People cursed him ever since, calling him a dog. Men cursed him as a son of a bitch, women called him a rotten mutt, and worst of all, his friends damned him as a good-for-nothing mongrel.

Luckily, Wei had no recollection of this. But Wei's dungeon room would rekindle these lost memories—and he'd become a ticking time bomb with too much power for his own good.

If things went awry, I wouldn't hesitate to kill him.

For now, the best thing I could do was show my trust in him. Then, when the time came, he might remember me through his madness.

I handed Amelia to Wei, and he sat down with her on his lap, holding her still in case the train started moving.

"Yue, do you have to argue with everything Peijin does?" Yang said, letting out a sigh. He was peering at the posters on the wall, tilting his head, curious.

"Don't worry about it, Yang," I replied in a cheery tone. "Everything she says is either wrong or stupid. When she disagrees with me, it reassures me that my decision is the right one."

"The hell? Are you sure you're older than me? You act like a child!" Yue spat back.

I shrugged. "I'm not the one throwing a tantrum."

To my side, Wei covered Amelia's ears and made a hand puppet that blabbered incessantly, making fun of Yue.

"Wait, Yue, how old are you?" Yang asked, seeming to be entranced as he stared at the posters lining the windows of the train. They were large and elaborate, detailing countless scenes with small plaques below them.

Yue huffed as she crossed her arms, turning her head to the side. "What a rude question to ask a woman."

Yang then turned to me, jerking his chin up to signal for me to answer the question if Yue wouldn't.

Noticing his gesture, Yue chimed in before I could respond. "I'm twenty-two."

Yang's gaze then shifted to the next poster, his hand tracing the strange, embossed plaque below. "And Peijin is twenty-four . . . Amelia, how old are you?"

"If you already knew how old Peijin was, why were you acting like you were going to ask her?" Yue quizzed, her brows furrowed.

"Because that's the only way to get you to do something," Yang replied nonchalantly.

"I really hate you guys."

Wei uncovered Amelia's ears and quietly repeated the question for her.

"I'm nine," she replied, her voice still quiet and reserved.

"That's strange," Yang whispered, staring at the posters. "All of these posters have our corresponding year of birth under them . . . Wei, how old are you?"

"I'm eighteen. Why?"

"Your poster . . . It's not here."

Yue scooted closer to stare at her own poster. Her face immediately drained of color, turning a ghostly pale as she looked at what was depicted on it. "What the hell . . ."

The poster displayed a girl who shared a shocking resemblance to Yue. She was sitting on a remote island, completely alone. She was shrouded by darkness, with nobody and nothing in sight but herself.

Amelia let out a choked gasp at the sight of her own poster. To my surprise, instead of the poster showing a scene of her losing her parents, it was the large sea serpent from the first arc roaring as it hovered over a bridge. Wei tightened his grip around her and shifted his weight to block her view.

I hesitantly looked at mine. It was . . . A terrible wave of fear hit me all at once, and I froze in place, my thoughts a jumbled mess. My hands became clammy, and my throat parched. I looked at Yang, trying to ground myself in the familiarity of his existence.

I already knew my room was going to be one of the worst. It was a psychological one, so my entire mind would be toyed with. Ha, I really hated fourteen-year-old me for coming up with this cruel idea for an arc.

"What do you mean my poster isn't here?" Wei said. "I'm eighteen. Just look for my year."

"There's only one other poster," Yang said, pointing all the way at the end of the car. "And it's dated back more than two thousand years ago."

Wei stood up, gently passing Amelia to me before rushing to the end of the car. He stared at the poster there; it depicted a stunning ancient Chinese temple, with curved red-tiled ceilings and a golden bell in the center. Countless floral trees surrounded it, disguising the cliff's edge. Out of all the posters, it was the only one not outwardly horrific in its appearance.

"I . . ." Wei trailed off, his eyes repeatedly darting between the written year and the poster.

I watched Wei, glancing up his sleeve and noticing the band around his arm beginning to slither away.

"Are you hiding something from us?" Yue questioned Wei, her voice pressing. "The posters match for the rest of us. Why would yours be any different?"

Wei shot me a pleading look and put both his hands in the air as if surrendering. "I swear I'm not! Believe me! I really am eighteen. Do you want my ID?"

Disciple Yue activated Lie Detector!

Yue was constantly surprising me despite me being her creator. She was gaining key skills left and right, and although they weren't anything major to her character, her growth was unparalleled. The system truly rewarded people who shifted right into what it wanted.

Disciple Wei is telling the truth.

Both Yue's and Yang's faces contorted into confusion, speculation, and hesitancy. My hand gripped suspended strap from the ceiling as I readjusted my hold on Amelia.

Yue's eyes tracked my movement. "What are you holding on for? We're not even mov—"

The train lurched forward, causing Yue to slam into Yang with a loud cry. Yang steadied her, grabbing her shoulders and holding her still. The lights flickered out, and everyone was sent into pitch blackness.

[Observers Chat]
Socrates: Jia Li, you already know what's happening. Why aren't you explaining it to them? You're making Wei anxious.

I felt my way along the wall until I brushed against loose, flowy robes. "Wei," I whispered into his ear. "Calm down. I believe you, but the last thing you should do is get overwhelmed right now. That's how you become nothing more than fodder to the gods."

Divinity Supreme Commander of the Heavenly Hosts is filled with a deep sense of dread.

Archangel Michael had way too many stars and too much spiritual energy if he was wasting it on messages like these.

The slithering on Wei's arm calmed for a moment, and I could hear his breathing slow down. The lights soon flickered back on, and the clinical interior of the train greeted us, but the doors were open now. The sight of a run-down and cracked dungeon appeared before us, stretching out from the train platform.

As my eyes adjusted to the dim lighting, I pointed at Yue and burst out laughing, doubling over. She was fearfully hanging on to an awkward Yang, his eyes wide and pleading, lips pressed into a thin line.

"Shut up!" Yue cried, shoving herself off Yang.

[Observers Chat]

Nipon23: Good luck, Jia Li. You'll need it this time. Even if you pretend it doesn't exist, you saw your poster, and you know exactly what it means.

ARC #2—DUNGEONS OF GREAT TURMOIL

Difficulty: D

Task: Kill all the beasts in as many dungeon rooms as possible. Each room will get progressively more difficult. Rewards will be given out at the end of each room. The more kills correlates to more stars for that party member. You will not proceed to the next room until all rewards are collected.

Time: 20 minutes

Reward: All items collected from dungeons and 10,000 stars per party member.

Failure: Death

CHAPTER THIRTEEN

We stepped off the train and onto the dungeon floor. The train wasn't operating on tracks anymore but rather magic, flying us to our destination before it shot off, vanishing into a black hole that appeared and promptly disappeared.

The dungeon was a small, run-down room of cobblestone full of mossy cracks. It was completely barren with not a creature in sight. My party members remained close to one another, not daring to take a step too far.

Despite being shaken from his poster and Yue's accusation, Wei confidently held his sword in front of him, scanning the dungeon for any entities that might appear.

I walked up to Wei, putting my hand on his shoulder. "Don't get worked up over things you can't control. We'll deal with your dungeon room when you get there, but we need to survive first."

Wei gave me a firm nod. "I trust you, Peijin, so I hope you trust me, too."

"I just told you not to worry about this nonsense."

A familiar blue flash appeared, and Wei swung his sword with terrifying force toward it. I could barely process the speed of his swing. This man really was impressive.

From the portal, a familiar creature popped out.

"Agh!" Chang cried, curling his body like an armadillo to avoid Wei's assault.

Wei stopped midswing and looked at me, a question in his eyes. I shook my head, and he lowered his sword.

A small jar of candy was held in Chang's arms, and he moved to protect it.

Chang let out a fiery huff before unfurling, his body seeming longer and larger than when we had last met.

I groaned at his appearance. This nuisance was back. "What do you want, Chang? Why would you even appear during the middle of a dungeon arc when everyone is on edge?"

"I didn't come to get scolded! But, Peijin—" Chang cut himself off as he surveyed the room. "And Peijin's friends . . . I need a big show this arc. Something that'll stun the gods and observers. It would be much appreciated by your favorite moderator." He put his clawed hands up in front of him like a prayer and bowed his head.

"When do I not give my best? I can beat all the monsters in this room in a few seconds after they spawn, so keep the camera and all the divinities here," I said with a wide smile, my eyes closed into happy crescents.

"By the way, what are you holding?" I gestured toward the candy jar in his hands.

Chang had a proud smile on his face. He lifted the candy jar up before him like it were his most prized possession. "The other party tipped me. Have you ever heard of something like that?"

"Mm-hmm, that's really sweet, Chang," I replied, nodding. "Can I have one?"

"What?" Chang asked.

"I'm your moneymaker, aren't I? Do you want a show or not?"

I opened my eyes to meet his distraught gaze, one of my eyebrows raised. Chang let out a sigh before popping open the jar and pushing it toward me. He squeezed his eyes shut and turned his head away.

My hand shuffled through all the wrapped candies before taking out an orange lollipop. I unwrapped it and popped it into my mouth.

"Thanks, Chang! You're the best," I said, handing him the empty candy wrapper to discard.

He shot me a bitter glare before he vanished.

Countless blue flashes appeared all over the dungeon, and dozens of the same goblins spawned, wandering aimlessly. I stole an awkward glance toward Yue, but small blue particles were already sparking all around her.

Disciple Yue activated Speaker of Goblins!

The goblins froze before bowing to the ground by Yue, their pointy green noses awkwardly forcing their heads to turn to the side when they tried to press their foreheads down.

Yang's stance became loose, and his shoulders fell at the goblins' passivity. "Can we clear the dungeon level just by taming them?"

"That would make this too easy for teams with beast tamers. We should all kill an equal number and get the stars before moving on," I declared, bashing a goblin into a mushy pile of guts beneath my shield. Despite the gross impact and subsequent squelch, my shield was left spotless. The goblin soon dissolved into ash.

Yue crossed her arms and glared at me. "Shouldn't I kill the goblins and get the most stars? I'm the one who tamed them."

"Are you trying to make this a competition?"

"I'd win if it was."

My eyes narrowed. *Sure. See if you can.*

Yue was visibly seething beside me, her fists clenched, but she thankfully kept her mouth shut and speedily killed all the goblins in her vicinity. Under her command, they didn't even spare a hurt glance at her when she pierced her sword through their small, fleshy brains.

When it came to killing demons, ghosts, or divinities, the process could be complicated. At a lower level, these entities could be killed the same way a disciple would—a head injury, a vicious stab wound, or a strong enough kick.

But stronger demons, ghosts, and divinities could manifest a spiritual energy core; they could condense all their spiritual energy into a single form, usually an orb, that they would secure in their body. If this orb was destroyed, they would die. Some gods could give their spiritual core to others, but there was only one instance this occurred with the God of Death in *Surviving My First Run*. It took incredible skill and was the biggest gamble a god could take.

> **Disciple Yue has deeply betrayed Demon King of Resourceful Goblins!**

> **Hindsight activated!**

Now, when I looked at Yue through my skill, the only god behind her was the Bull Demon King; however, there was now a blue box floating above her head.

> **Warning: This act will have unforeseen consequences.**

"Wait, Yue," I called out, stopping her with my sword.

> **Scathing Reviewer activated!**

"Let me do it. I'll let you get the next room, all right?" I continued. My expression was serious as I looked down at Yue's hard face—although I usually tried to make her life more difficult, I couldn't let her face a potential punishment under my orders.

> **Disciple Yue activated Lie Detector!**
> **Disciple Peijin is telling the truth.**

Yue let out an annoyed sigh before grumbling, "Fine, whatever. These are worth nothing anyway." It finally seemed like there was a bit more trust between us.

Although my Scathing Reviewer skill activated, I couldn't tell if it did anything. Nothing was out of the ordinary, and I felt completely fine while slaying the rest of the goblins.

Once all the goblins were dead, each providing about ten stars, their bodies dissipated into dust and a deep brown chest appeared in the center of the dungeon. Wei popped it open with a single flick of his blade and peered into the glowing interior.

Amelia ran over and got on her tiptoes to peer inside, but I placed a hand to keep her at a safe distance.

Since this was an incredibly easy dungeon level, the rewards weren't that good. There were a few random scraps of metal, but most importantly, there were a handful of healing elixirs, a vial of kraken mucus, and multiple enhanced bandages.

"Really? That's it?" Yue asked.

"We need these supplies, since we don't have a healer," Yang said, sifting through them with his sword. He stood as far as possible from Yue.

I bent down and began shoveling all of it into my Boundless Bag. All the metal and elixirs piled up, making it much heavier. However, thanks to my high stats, it practically weighed nothing.

Still, I exaggerated my movements like I could hardly lift the bag. Immediately, Wei grabbed the strap of the bag and swung it over his shoulder like it weighed nothing, even though I was still holding on to it.

"Peijin, let me carry it," Wei said.

I shook my head. "I got it. Our most valuable fighter shouldn't have his hands full."

Wei looked embarrassed, and he became even more resolute in his decision. "That's not true. But if you believe in what you said, then let me hold the bag, so you can focus on getting us out."

I pretended to give in, letting go of the bag. Until it was time for Wei's room, my goal was to make him trust me, and I wanted him to think that trust was mutual. Admittedly, I felt bad about manipulating him like this. But when he regains his memories and subsequently his loss of faith in humanity, I needed to represent a promise of a future.

It was funny that I, the infamous JiaLi1825, was trying to become a symbol of humanitarian ideals to a man as righteous as Wei. I guess my name "Peijin" finally held more merit.

Once the chest was cleared, it vanished as a new portal opened to spawn in the next creatures. This time, six large ogres appeared; their crackled and dry skin was littered with deep, oozing scars. The largest, bearing two horns jutting out from its grotesque forehead, immediately roared and spat all over Wei's face.

The ogre lunged and gripped Wei's throat and hoisted him into the air, but Wei slashed through its arm in one clean movement. Blood splattered out from the ogre's small shoulder stump as it cried out, causing the rest to lunge toward Wei.

Despite the ogres being much more formidable opponents than the goblins, everyone had leveled up enough to handle them with relative ease. In *Surviving My First Run*, most parties never passed the second level. Many survived the first arc thanks to luck and running—this arc forced ordinary citizens to pick up a weapon and fight, and that was not something everyone could do.

Each dungeon level, however, would get five times harder than the previous, which meant the round after this would be exponentially more difficult and match the party's skill level.

Disciple Yue activated Demonic Fire!

Yue's fists erupted in black flames, but before she could pummel the ogres with her bare fists, I darted in front of her and stabbed through them, killing them.

"You're going to steal my kills?" Yue said furiously, slamming her shoulder into mine and sending me stumbling forward. I shot her an infuriated glare.

She turned around and targeted the next ogre. Whenever they got too close, she would leap back, and Yang would charge forward. He sliced the ogres into small pieces before Yue delivered the final kill. They worked in perfect harmony despite their disdain for one another.

"At least I don't need someone to help me," I retorted.

The glow of gathered stars filled the air like shimmer, and Yue immediately reinvested them into her levels.

If only I had Yue's plethora of skills, I would have done the same. I stood beside Amelia, helping her make rather feeble attempts at killing the ogres Wei already injured. A chest appeared on the bloodied floor.

[Observers Chat]
Socrates: This is so much more disgusting to watch than read about.

This time, the chest contained better items. There was a hoodie, a suit, and a beautiful silver cuff. I gasped and grabbed the blue hoodie with a cartoonish graphic on the back and threw it on; the fabric immediately readjusted to fit perfectly around my figure.

> **Agility level 25 → level 29**
> **Physique level 25 → level 29**

It was becoming more expensive now to upgrade levels, and the clothing was an easy way to increase personal stats while also adding a layer of very fashionable armor. Not liking the odd number for my levels, I invested a few thousand stars.

> **Physique level 29 → level 30**
> **Agility level 29 → level 30**

"It suits you," Yang said with a polite smile.

"I agree," Yue said, giving a thumbs-up. "It makes you look immature and foolish."

I scrunched my nose at Yue, making direct eye contact with her while picking up the silver cuff. Shallow but highly ornate engravings of dragons, a phoenix, tigers, and serpents covered it, and it reflected a slight sheen of glowing white light. I popped it open before locking it around Amelia's wrist.

My tone was much more hushed when I spoke to her and got down on my knee to speak to her eye to eye. "The engravings here imply that it's either a defensive cuff or will help you with taming, just like Auntie Yue did with the goblins."

Amelia inspected the cuff, gripping it with her other hand and fidgeting the fitting. "Then, shouldn't you give it to Auntie Yue?"

"No."

Yue huffed behind me. "Am I even a party member?"

"Are you so weak that you need a protection amulet? Should I not give it to Amelia?"

Yue shut up.

I continued to look through the chest, pulling up the last clothing item—a black tuxedo suit and red tie.

The suit was definitely one of the better outfit finds in all the dungeon chests, since it offered the biggest boost in personal stats. I was biased in wanting to give it to Yang, for two reasons, but Yue needed it significantly more than he did.

I groaned but relented, leaving it in the chest. "Yue and Yang, you two can fight over this."

Yang looked awkward, balancing on his sword and rocking his weight back and forth. "You can take it, Yue."

For once, Yue seemed a bit hesitant. "It's fine. You'll need it more."

I was surprised by Yue's sudden generosity. I figured she must have had a change of heart when fighting so harmoniously alongside Yang just moments ago.

Yang flushed and grabbed the suit while letting out hesitant laughs, looking apprehensively at Yue. No matter how hard he tried to mask it, he was visibly uneasy around her.

Once the suit was removed from the chest, the next round immediately began. This time, twelve giant portals appeared all over the dungeon, and the dungeon walls shot back dozens of feet. The room was far larger now, enough for more serious fights to occur.

Time left: 5 minutes, 42 seconds

Massive dire wolves spawned to form an entire pack over the dungeon. They were around fifteen feet long each, their hackles raised as they bore their teeth. The largest was around twenty feet long, and it led the pack to circle around my party members.

The room filled with an ominous air; these wolves were clearly a formidable opponent, and the number made them incredibly dangerous.

The largest wasted no time. It lunged for me, but I jumped to the side, bringing my shield up to force it back. Yang launched forward at incredible speed toward the flank of the pack, but the wolf predicted his move and snapped at his leg.

Before its teeth could latch on, Wei's sword made a loud clash with the wolf's jaw, and he twisted his sword out of its mouth and thrust his sword into the wolf's flank. It let out a desperate howl and wrangled its body off Wei's sword, jumping back and snarling.

A smaller wolf snapped at Amelia's ankles. She cried out in fear, falling to the ground and scrambling back. Jolting at the sound of her scream, Yue grabbed her and pulled her back on her feet, forcing Amelia into the middle of a protective circle formed by all the party members—except for me.

"Wait!" I cried out, blocking an incoming attack. "Let Amelia try to tame one of them!"

She was tightly gripping the silver cuff now, staring up at me with trembling blue eyes. Before I could say any more, the alpha wolf saw an opening and its jaws flew wide open, wrapping around my entire abdomen.

CHAPTER FOURTEEN

P eijin!" Yang screamed, darting toward me and flinging his sword forward, but the wolf had already reached me.

Just before the wolf could clamp down, the blue sweatshirt thrust upward into the air, dragging me with it. I slammed into the ceiling of the dungeon, cracking the bricks with my body before the sweatshirt dragged me across the ceiling like a mop.

My hands wrangled with the sweatshirt. Rocks and debris filled my mouth. "S-stop! I'm already out of the way!" I shouted, twisting the fabric of the sweatshirt while I was being flung like a rag doll; my body was being smashed and dragged along the eroded walls of the dungeon. Dirt, moss, and jagged rocks came tumbling down.

[Observers Chat]
Socrates: . . . this is giving me really bad secondhand embarrassment
Hedgehog1938: STOP I'M LITERALLY GOING TO GET AN ANEURYSM HAHAHAH
Nipon23: I'm about to join you

Dammit! This was completely humiliating! I bit down on the fabric of the hoodie, but it seemed to retaliate by repeatedly flinging me side to side and smacking me against the ceiling, then floor, then ceiling again. I was a flattened pancake with all my screams cut short every time I caught a mouthful of moldy brick.

**Divinity Supreme Commander of the Heavenly Hosts
turns away from the broadcast and mutes it.**

Even Archangel Michael??

Scathing Reviewer activated!

Blue sparks flew off the hoodie, and it fell limp. I crashed into the ground one last time and formed a human-shaped crater. I groaned as I got onto my feet, my legs trembling and my messy, untied hair prickling at the back of my neck.

The shield was heavy in my hand, but I lifted it before me and prepared to face the wolves; however, when I looked around, the wolves were latched onto one another's throats, sending blood flying in long red streaks. With wild snarls, they launched at one another and gored each other. One dug its hind legs straight through another's stomach, striking with rapid and deep strokes, spilling its organs all over the dungeon. Another tore off its packmate's nose.

My eyes flicked to Amelia.

Amelia stood before the mad wolves, the hand with the silver cuff outstretched before her. With blue sparks flying from her, Amelia wielded the power and drove the beasts toward one another. Yue was kneeled beside her and whispered into her ear, presumably guiding her.

Hindsight activated!

Hovering above Amelia's small frame, the towering silhouette of a woman holding on to the antler of a deer in one hand and a bow in the other peered down: Artemis.

The alpha wolf snarled in front of Amelia, its massive, scarred nose a few inches from Amelia's own face, but it wouldn't move any closer. Wide and ferociously animalistic eyes peered into Amelia's. She didn't back up. Her hands trembled with the effort, and the light from the cuff flickered.

I opened the Azure Dragon Store and searched for a powerful mana potion, throwing it at the ground before Amelia. It erupted into a deep blue gas that whirled around her in a blinding shimmer. Blood dribbled from the corner of my mouth, but I wiped it away and darted up to Amelia, a mixture of amazement and awe in my expression.

With one last violent snap in the air, the alpha wolf was subdued. It pointed its ears back and bowed before Amelia, pressing its head against the dungeon ground. Amelia let out an exhausted sigh and fell to her knees before the wolf.

I gently guided the cuff to the wolf's nose, and the wolf exploded into white shimmer. Looking down at the amulet, a new engraving of a beastly dire wolf was etched into the metal.

Time left: 19 seconds

The moment the chest appeared, I flipped it over and dumped out everything, immediately starting the next dungeon level.

"Peijin, we don't have enough time to beat the next round!" Yang cried.

"She'll have a plan. Fall back!" Wei replied, grabbing Amelia and shielding her from whatever might appear.

A giant portal was forming behind me. I latched onto the Boundless Bag and tore it from Wei, immediately shoveling through it. The dungeon expanded, this time to accommodate a creature of horrific size. "Trust me! Shut your eyes now!"

A massive foot the size of a car exited from the portal, causing the entire dungeon to violently shake and tremble. Then a pointed snout appeared from the portal, covered in azure scales. Rows and rows of snaggled white teeth covered its face, and menacing red eyes peered down at me.

It was an Azure Dragon, the same kind as Chang.

Appearing before me at two stories tall, I gawked at it in amazement while it opened its jaws, letting out a deafening roar that threw all of us into the back wall of the dungeon. I scrambled back onto my feet and darted forward, a thin smile growing on my face as I took a step back, admiring the creation before me with wonder and horror.

Yang shouted for me again, both loud and hoarse. "Peij—!"

"Keep your eyes shut!"

Time left: 4 seconds

At the sound of my roaring voice, the dragon lunged for me before I could even process the movement. I ducked down and buried my face into my shoulder while thrusting my arm forward.

Medusa's head squirmed in my hand, and all at once, the dragon's roar was cut off. I opened my eyes to find myself peering straight down the throat of the dragon with its jaw unhinged. Its lower body thrashed, and its hind legs kicked against the walls in a futile attempt to escape before its entire body became no more than a stone statue.

Peijin's World Dominion has completed four dungeon levels.
Your party now has 5 minutes to collect rewards
before the next set of dungeon rooms.

I collapsed in exhaustion before the new, glowing chest. The rest of my party members uncovered their eyes, surveying the empty room.

"What happened?" Wei asked, walking up behind me.

Amelia replied, her voice louder than it was prior to the arc. "Teenage Azure Dragon. A lot scarier than Chang."

Yue's hands were placed on her hips while she berated me. "What the hell happened to splitting the stars and teamwork? How much did you get from that alone?"

"Fifteen thousand stars," I whispered, slightly embarrassed.

"I want to appeal for a shared party bank account. And a union," Yue angrily retorted as Yang and Wei sifted through the chest.

This time, the chest held various exclusive or rare items and four weapons: a dao, spear, staff, and jian. My party would now have the four Chinese martial weapons.

The jian was a double-edged sword, and this specific one was the Dragon Gulf sword, part of the legendary and precious swords of ancient China. The initial owner stabbed himself in the thigh with the sword to atone for killing an innocent person.

An intricate gold dragon was detailed on the hilt and appeared to be swallowing the blade of the sword. This sword was excellent, even in later arcs, for disciples determined to be "judges." Judges were individuals who had a strong sense of justice or morality and would execute judgment on those who violated core principles. They were especially effective against demons.

My gaze shifted over to Wei, who glanced at the sword with a conflicted expression. It was possible he recognized it from a past memory, but it wouldn't have been recognizable to him yet.

"You should take the Dragon Gulf sword, Wei." To my surprise, it was Yang who had spoken.

I gave Yang a surprised look, and he let out a repressed laugh before elaborating. "I was a history major and mythology minor in university. This is a sword of justice, and if Wei's sponsor is an Archangel, it fits him the most."

I nodded in agreement, and Wei took the sword. A part of me felt awkward now knowing that I had missed such a key part of Yang's personal life despite knowing him for years. No wonder he picked up faster on the mythological references than the rest of the party had.

The spear had a glistening silver leaf-shaped blade and a red horse-hair tassel below. A sword was attached to the long shaft to make it all the more deadly and written on the blade was the name Hua Mulan.

"*The* Mulan?" Yue posed the question with immense interest, immediately bending down to stare at the spear.

I nodded and handed it to her. "Do you want it? It's pretty powerful, since Mulan is a popular legend."

For once, Yue was grateful as she took the spear, testing the weight of it in her hand. I sighed before looking into the chest. Clearly the only thing I had to do to get on her good side was to play into her fangirl tendencies.

"Yang, you should take the staff. It'll work best with you, since Sun Wukong wields the Ruyi Jingu Bang," I said. My hand gripped the wide band before I handed it to him. Yang spun it around for a moment, inspecting the ends before tracing the inscription with his fingers.

"The Golden-Bound Staff of Cruelty," he whispered, reading out the engraved words. "What a mouthful."

"Think of it as just a weird rip-off version, but it suits you more than the rest of us."

The last weapon left in the chest was a dao, also known as a saber. It was a long, thin, single-sided sword. Despite recognizing which weapon family it belonged to, I didn't recognize the actual sword.

It was a somewhat-dull silver and seemed to have a dark gray stain within the detailed engravings. The end of the hilt was carved to resemble a flame, the rain guard twisted into opposite directions to look like snaggle teeth. Most notable, however, was the shut eye just below the rain guard. It was a simple thin black line, almost unnoticeable.

"Yang, do you recognize this? I've never read about a dao looking like this."

He shook his head, confirming my suspicion. "It's not in any myth I've studied."

It reeked of an ominous spiritual energy—was it potentially a ghost or demon's sword? Gods typically had spiritual weapons associated with them that were incredibly powerful, but they were subsequently deeply cherished. It should never be found in a dungeon chest of all places.

"Yue, can you grab it?"

"Why? So I die first if it's evil?"

I mean, she wasn't wrong, but she didn't have to put it like that.

I grabbed all the miscellaneous items around it, including a dragon's broken heart, countless powerful potions, and small sheets of glowing blue paper before dumping it into my expandable bag.

"Are you going to grab it or not, Yue?"

"Am I seriously going to die?"

I shook my head and continued to stare at the sword. "No, but your sponsor is a demon, so he probably clashes with other demons," I explained, trying to sound like I was crafting an elaborate theory. "If you reach for it and can grab it, then it's a ghost's weapon. If you can't, then it's a demon's."

Yue sighed but reached down to grab it. Just before she could, an invisible boundary pushed her back and small blue sparks appeared.

"Must be demonic, then. Thanks, Yue." I gave her a friendly, but rather powerful, slap on the shoulder before bending down to grab the dao.

It was heavy, not because of the material but rather how overwhelmingly powerful the evil spiritual energy was. I spun it around a bit before inspecting the stunning hilt. Although Hindsight was helpful, it didn't seem to recognize the weapon at all—this dao must not have originally existed in *Surviving My First Run*. But was I going to turn down a demon's spiritual weapon?

Absolutely not.

"I'll take this one, then. No clue what it is, though."

Suddenly, when I grabbed the blade, my arm locked, and my hand felt welded to the silver hilt. I let out a sharp cry as the dao began to violently tremble, sending giant yellow sparks flying off my arm. It carried waves through my body as I gripped my shoulder to regain control of my arm.

The eye on the hilt opened instantaneously, revealing a bloodred iris with a snake's pupil glaring straight at me.

CHAPTER FIFTEEN

wrestled with the sword, gritting my teeth from the amount of energy that was being forced through my arm. Stumbling backwards, I could feel my grip on the hilt beginning to slip, and the red eye darted all around the room as if taking in the sights for the very first time.

"Peijin!" Wei immediately reached out to try to help steady the hilt, but it suddenly zapped him with a violent spark of yellow electricity. He reeled back in pain, clutching his completely seared hand.

My eyes matched the panic of the red one embedded into the dao. "Don't come near me!" I shouted, taking a few stumbling steps back in a futile attempt to distance myself.

> **[Observers Chat]**
> **Socrates:** Jia Li! Let go!

> **Divinity Supreme Commander of the Heavenly Hosts is warning you to let go!**

A sudden burst of electricity shot out from my arm, sending beams of yellow sparks and streams of lightning out and across the room. I let out a surprised shout, curling up to try to avoid the sporadic bursts. Lightning? Was this . . . karma?

Amelia let out a horrified scream and barely dodged a massive bolt before Wei picked her up with his uninjured arm and shielded her.

An ominous burgundy began to creep up my arm before shooting up to my shoulder with alarming speed, a deep black following suit. In fact, it was such a deep shade it looked as if my arm had simply vanished entirely. The blue screens around me flashed with that familiar bright red, but the sparks suddenly froze.

Scathing Reviewer activated!

At once, the flying sparks immediately calmed down, and all the screens returned to their familiar blue color. The growing red and black patches on my arm were suddenly stamped out; my regular skin returned in large patches as if it were being slapped on. My arm was glitching back to its original appearance chunk by chunk.

I blinked in surprise. Scathing Reviewer appeared to be a multifaceted skill without a clear pattern. It got me out of danger, which I appreciated, and kept my privacy from other disciples.

I let out a loud sigh of relief as I felt the energy sizzle out, but my eyes widened at the image remaining on my arm. Just above my wrist and stretching partway up my forearm was a black-ink tattoo.

It depicted a crashing and inflamed building as a female goddess and demon were tearing it down. Lightning and fire erupted, the two parties raining heaven and hell down upon the structure. Just below the piece, Chinese characters marked my skin in blurry writing: *The Tower.*

With a blinding flash, Chang appeared while the background of the dungeon shifted back into the moving train. The walls of the dungeon contorted and waved until they became the metal ones of the metro, and the posters were plastered onto the wall.

"My system reported that there was an unusual amount of spiritual energy here." Chang spoke nervously, a massive array of blue screens in front of him. He was anxiously swiping them away, but more continued to pop up like he had a system virus. The eye in the dao continued to stare at me before blinking once.

Immediately, the entire train came to a crashing halt. Amelia let out a scream, but Yue calmed her while Chang panicked more.

"Peijin! You're emitting too much spiritual energy—you're going to destroy the arc!"

"I'm not emitting any spiritual energy!"

The lights in the train burned out with a frightening *pop!* that shot the train into complete darkness except for the blue screens lighting up before Chang. My skin was glowing white with an unbelievable amount of energy, and my hair was whipping all around my face.

Chang turned to me, gripping my ears with his pointy claws and violently shaking my head.

"I mean it, Peijin, so stop fooling around! If you take advantage of this much spiritual energy so early on, you're going to summon a calamity."

Demon Supreme Commander of Heavenly Hosts is deeply disturbed by the spiritual energy you're emitting.

The metro began to tremble violently, the entire train rumbling before lurching into the air, bouncing on the metal tracks. It creaked and groaned, seeming to cry out in pain as loud bangs were heard around the metal.

This wasn't right—really, this wasn't right at all. It was impossible for a disciple to emit spiritual energy like this unless they themselves were a god, and even so, the amount present around me would throw the arc into complete chaos. If I potentially received this spiritual energy from another force, they had to be indescribably powerful to have bypassed all of the system controls and karma.

I grasped my head, panicking as my breaths became shallow and rapid. If a calamity spawned here, at this very moment . . . all of us would die. Absolutely nothing could save us. God or not, I wouldn't be able to save them.

With my unmarked hand, I immediately dug my nails into the tattoo, trying to tear it off. "Dammit . . ." I grumbled, my voice a desperate whisper bordering on a plea. "Dammit!"

Divinity Supreme Commander of the Heavenly Hosts is pleading with you to stop!

Yang stumbled toward me, grabbing my tattooed arm. His eyes peered into mine, and his expression seemed to demand that I calm down.

I let out a shaky breath as my arms fell to my side, taking in each breath. The presence of the other party members grew around me, and I could feel their reassuring presence.

Wei's voice was a deep hum in the sound of screeching metal. "Peijin, please, calm down. If there's a calamity, we'll deal with it as always."

What stupid, childish naivety.

I would have thought the same, too, except that this was all wrong. None of this could exist in the world I created.

Yue said nothing, but I could feel her hair gently brush my shoulder, signaling to me that she was nearby as well. Amelia clung to the loose fabric of my pants tightly, and I could feel her straining the cotton material.

A deep breath and subsequent sigh helped me loosen my tense shoulders, and the spiritual energy calmed immediately. Before my identity as a pest control worker, before my identity as Liu Peijin, before my identity as a god, I was a writer. I wasn't limited by the confines of my own work.

"It's probably my sponsor that's providing the spiritual power," I declared resolutely, any hint of panic vanishing from my voice. "I'm still convinced they influenced the sponsorship selection, which means they'd be powerful enough to allow me to wield this weapon."

I continued to inspect the sword before me. It was undoubtedly a spiritual weapon—therefore, similar to my blue hoodie, it had a consciousness of its own, yet it was forever bound to its creator.

Some were deeply sentimental items that had ascended with the god; others were forged by the most talented and skilled blacksmiths. However, a very select few required the sacrifice of a loved or sacred life.

My eyes flitted over to Wei.

I looked down at the sword and smiled, petting the hilt. "Aren't you cute!" I cooed, running my hand over the blade. "What should I name you? You don't have an engraving."

Yue's face twisted into one of complete distaste and embarrassment. "Peijin, have you seriously lost it? Yang and Wei, you need to stop enabling her."

The sword's eye pressed into a small crescent as if it were smiling before it vibrated and grew larger.

The train immediately calmed down, the banging stopped, and the lights flickered back on, revealing my disgruntled party and a very stressed Chang.

"Wha—?"

My hands clapped together, and I was truly overjoyed in such a seemingly odd moment. Spiritual weapons were only attuned to a few people—people they had an immediate bond or soul connection with.

"Peijin, the next set of dungeon rooms are going to start soon," Yang said.

"Then go inspect the posters," I retorted. "Let me play around with this sword."

The red eye blinked at me joyously now, and I decided to run my fingers directly down the sharpened edge; however, it immediately dulled itself upon sensing my intentions before sharpening after I removed my hand.

"What was your past name?" I whisper quietly to the sword.

It jumped out of my hands, floating in the air before carving it into the metal walls of the metro.

"Appalling Horror of Bloody Fangs. My owner called me Haimo. 'Hai' for evil, and 'mo' for devil."

"That's not a very pretty name."

My brows furrowed, my expression deep in thought, before I came up with a response. "What about Zhige? Zhi, for infantile, and ge, for dove."

Zhige moved to etch a response on the wall, but yellow sparks appeared before Zhige clanged to the ground, having fallen. Well, it wasn't fully immune to karma, then.

I leaned down, picking up the blade and staring at the wide snake eye. "Zhige it is, unless you'd rather go back to being Haimo."

Yang, who was inspecting the posters like I told him to, snapped me out of my thoughts. "Peijin, is your poster depicting a—"

"Yang, don't try to change the subject!" Yue shouted. "What the hell is your poster? Are you some pervert?!"

"W-what?" Yang exclaimed, flinching back from her, his hands hovering in front of him as if he was trying to back away from a predator.

Yue took more steps forward, her hands on her hips. "I'm going to be so pissed off if I ended up in a party with a dirty pervert! I'll kill you myself!"

[Observers Chat]
Hedgehog1938: Bye if I got that poster, you'd never hear from me again. I'm embarrassed just watching him.

**Demon Supreme Commander of the Heavenly
Hosts stares awkwardly at the poster.**

Wei was attempting to distract Amelia with his own poster, pointing out the beautiful details. Out of all of the ones displayed, Wei's was the most gorgeous. Stunning pastel colors, lavish red temples with cyan-tiled ceilings, and a man dressed in all white in the center with ribbons of gold and red swirling around him.

"I swear! I'm not a pervert! Why the hell would I be into plants?"

"Then explain your poster, you creep!"

Yang covered his flushed cheeks with his hands, clearly deeply embarrassed and flustered. Taking another step forward, Yue was about to hoist him up by his collar, but the train doors suddenly opened to a vast bridge.

My party exited to find themselves beside a white pest control van. Looking down, beautiful ripples of water were formed from the razor-sharp spikes of a sea serpent slicing through the black waves.

Amelia let out a violent shriek as she noticed the dead, deformed puppy that had appeared in her arms, and with a deafening explosion, the serpent leapt out of the water and toward the freeway.

**Custom rooms now commencing!
Tailored for: Disciple Amelia Silva**

CHAPTER SIXTEEN

The custom dungeons were tailored to each party member's greatest fear. Beginning with the youngest party member and progressing to the oldest, the rooms would get increasingly more difficult. I wasn't enough of a monster to forcefully torment children and give them no chance of surviving.

However . . .

Amelia's face was deathly pale as she stared up at the sea serpent, her entire body trembling like a leaf. She was the weakest and least reliable member of the party despite being the only potential beast tamer.

Now that I had defeated the sea serpent before and earned the achievement Butcher of Abyssal Horrors, I could easily use Medusa's head to defeat this level in seconds without causing Amelia any unnecessary fear.

Yang pieced together the same solution after seeing how I defeated the Azure Dragon. He looked at me expectantly, but his face fell at my expression.

The sea serpent crashed down on the road, splintering it. The force flung Amelia across the freeway dozens of meters from us, and she let out a loud cry when her small body slammed against it. She skidded across the pavement until finally coming to a stop. The freeway was quickly crumbling away behind her, but she desperately crawled forward to a more stable portion.

"Amelia!" Wei shouted. He sprinted to her, his arms outstretched and ready to pick her up.

I intercepted and pushed Wei back. Tears sprang in Amelia's eyes while she looked up and reached out for me, crying out feebly.

"The wrist cuff! Use it!" Zhige trembled in my hand with an eager anticipation.

Amelia blinked at me, unable to process my words. The serpent roared, spraying water before it darted forward, chomping through the remaining freeway and approaching us. The water swirled below, rising higher and higher.

I felt a sudden blunt pain on my wrist, and I turned back to see Yang tightly twisting my hand, his eyes glaring at me.

"Peijin, what is the meaning of this?" he hissed.

I returned his glare coldly, my voice a low threat. "Don't pretend your moral compass matters, Yang. It means nothing here. Amelia will survive."

I turned to face Amelia, my voice loud and clear for the rest of my party to hear me. "Amelia, these dungeons are custom rooms because they're meant to help you evolve your skills. You're in this room because you're supposed to tame it!"

That was partially true. It was an opportunity for Amelia to level up, but I knew this serpent was far beyond what she could handle. It would be impossible for her to tame—instead, I was banking on the fact that the gods who wanted her as their disciple would find it within themselves to intervene.

Finally, the sea serpent caught up to us. It chomped down on the bridge, barely missing Amelia's leg. She stumbled forward, trying to run, but her movements were disoriented. Turning around, she thrust out the cuff, and a white light exploded with immense power.

[Observers Chat]
Socrates: Jia Li, stop! Amelia will fail without a sponsor!

The dire wolf appeared, immediately latching onto the sea serpent's nostrils. It violently tore into the monster's flesh, sending red chunks flying all over.

The sea serpent shrieked and swung its head in a futile attempt to throw off the wolf. The wolf only sank its claws and teeth further into the serpent and shredded its face.

With the freeway collapsing rapidly, Amelia sprinted in hopes of making it to the mainland. We were across from her, and my party continued to attempt desperate strides toward her even when I held them back.

The wolf flew across the freeway and crashed into the ground before Amelia with a heavy thud. Amelia flinched, perhaps feeling some of the wolf's pain as her own, and the sea serpent continued its pursuit with renewed vigor.

I stalled my party, blocking their movements when they tried to reach Amelia. It was cruel of me, but Amelia needed to adapt on her own, so I needed to push her beyond her limits. She couldn't keep relying on the party.

"Peijin, what are you doing?" Wei asked. He readjusted the Dragon Gulf sword in his hands and darted past me. I let him go.

When the serpent neared for its next attack, Wei saw his opening and leapt into the air. He braced his sword against himself before bringing down a heavy slice between the eyes of the sea serpent, resulting in a long slit with blood spraying out like a hose with a thumb pressed over the nozzle.

Amelia's eyes were squeezed shut, her forehead pressed against that of the wolf. She cupped its gray cheeks, and she was whispering to it. I could barely make out the shape of her moving lips, but she was murmuring something with frantic speed.

Soon after, the wolf unsteadily got onto its feet and charged at the serpent, this time darting up the snakelike body. Its claws dug through the scales and into its flesh, causing crimson streaks to appear and bleed down all over the serpent.

"Amelia!" I screamed. "You need to tame the serpent!"

Tears of fear and exhaustion streamed down her battered face. Her hands were outstretched and trembling.

Disciple Amelia activated Beast Taming!

Her hoarse voice shook violently as she shouted to me, "It's too strong! I can't tame it!"

I intentionally spoke louder to ensure the rest of the party could hear me. "Yes you can! We're weakening it by attacking it!" I screamed over the chaos, sprinting to Amelia and standing behind her.

I pulled my blue sweatshirt off and threw it over her head. It shrunk to fit her, though it wouldn't do much to protect her in this situation other than give the illusion of greater security.

"Amelia, I wouldn't tell you to tame it unless I believed it was within your skill set. You're strong enough," I whispered into her ear.

Yang, Yue, and Wei had attacked the sea serpent with vigor, motivated by their desire to protect Amelia.

"I—I can't do it," she stammered, her hand flailing behind her to try to hold on to mine.

"You can," I insisted, my voice forceful. "Artemis sent me a message. She says that you must tame the serpent if you want her to consider sponsoring you."

Divinity Far Shooting Queen of Beasts is stunned by your lie.

Divinity Far Shooting Queen of Beasts is enraged by your cruelty!

Yellow sparks immediately erupted from the blue message boxes, forcing them to disappear before Amelia could fully read them. Clearly, karma was still overpowering godly messages—except for those who used enough spiritual energy, like Archangel Michael.

I held Amelia's shoulders as I knelt to match her eye level. "Amelia," I whispered. "Turn off your system notifications. Focus only on my voice and the serpent."

Divinity Supreme Commander of the Heavenly Hosts is mortified by your sudden actions.

1,893 observers are watching you with immense interest!

[Observers Chat]
VegasDuck: Holy shit Peijin is not playing around
Nipon23: Poor Amelia. Who knew Peijin cared more about the gods than her own party members?
CactusLiver: Peijin wouldn't just let Amelia die. It's obvious she cares about her party members. I'm sure Peijin has a plan.
Nipon23: when have you seen Peijin genuinely care for someone else? she always has other motives.
CactusLiver: And that's exactly how the system works?? You can't blame her for doing that

Using Hindsight, I could see a string from the sky attached to Amelia's wrist. Artemis was on the other end. Her heavenly silhouette practically floated right above Amelia, far closer than before. Reaching out a hand, Artemis pressed through the shadows for the young girl.

Blue sparks flew around me from the sudden surge in spiritual energy, causing the massive bursts of karma's yellow lightning. Artemis was trying to interfere with the course of the scenario, but she was forced out.

I covered Amelia's ears and defiantly shouted at the sky. "Artemis, if you wish to protect this girl so badly, then do something about it and sponsor her!"

Warning! You have outraged a divinity!

[Observers Chat]
Socrates: Jia Li, stop this! You're going to get Amelia killed!

Of course, Athena wanted to be Amelia's sponsor, but it was clear now that Artemis was the superior fit. Artemis was ready to risk her own skin for Amelia—Athena wasn't.

"Amelia, raise your arm to the serpent, and ensure the cuff is well within your line of vision," I instructed. "Focus all of your attention on it, just as you did with the dire wolf."

Sweat dripped down her brow in thick streaks, and Amelia's breathing was rapid and shallow. I could see the concentration swirling in her wide blue eyes.

With unbelievable horror, the sea serpent let out a pained roar. It flung its tail, crashing into the freeway and causing Amelia and me to fly into the air.

Amelia's concentration broke and she screamed, but I dug Zhige into the flesh of the dragon and flung her up, the blue hoodie pulling her onto the head of the serpent.

"Peijin!" Amelia shrieked. Her small hands reached out for me.

I gave a curt nod before flashing her a bright smile. "It's up to you, Amelia."

I fell back toward the water, and I dragged Zhige down the entire length of the serpent. My feet landed on something solid, and I looked down to see myself standing on Yue's spear.

"Peijin, you fucking bitch!" Yue roared, hoisting herself up onto the other half of the spear and squatting to maintain her balance as the serpent continued to thrash. "You have Medusa's head! End this!"

"I can't!" I screamed back. "Amelia is on the serpent's head, so it's too big of a risk if she locks eyes with Medusa! The rest of you are still attacking it, so I can't use it without hurting one of you."

I leapt off her spear and sprinted up the beast's body. I climbed up toward its head.

Suddenly, her spear whizzed just past me before impaling the beast's flesh. I froze. I looked around for Yue angrily before realizing that she was gripping my ankle, dangling above the water. "What the hell are you attacking your own party leader for?" I shouted.

"I'm not attacking you!" Yue retorted in frustration, trying to grab hold of her spear. "Look up!"

With a loud crash, the serpent's tail smacked where I would have been had Yue not stopped me, and the violent thrashing almost threw me off the serpent. I grabbed her spear. Yue still dangled below me, clinging onto my foot for her life.

Yang, Wei, and the wolf had restrained the serpent to some degree, digging their weapons or teeth into the flesh of its vulnerable snout, head, and neck. The serpent let out a violent scream, but Amelia clung to its head using its whiskers, just like I had when I first battled the serpent.

Her skin was deathly pale, and she was sweating profusely while murmuring under her breath. This was by far too big of a skill jump for her, and blue sparks were flying out of her skin as if she were a firework.

"Come on, come on . . ." I whispered beneath my breath, looking up into the sky. This would be a complete waste of time if *she* didn't interfere with the arc to help Amelia.

An abnormal number of blue sparks continued to explode all around the bay.

Yue was climbing up my leg, and her long fingers dug into my calf and knee. Her black hair whipped her face, and she spat out a mouthful of salt water.

"Stop scaling me like a damn monkey!" I shouted.

"Do you want me to drop down and die instead?!"

I remained silent while using her spear and dao to scale up the serpent's body, alternately stabbing one weapon into the serpent's flesh, then another before pulling myself up. Each slice sent a deep gush of blood flowing, and the serpent was becoming more and more frantic.

It jolted, and Yue's grip on my ankle slipped. Her eyes lit up with fear. I reached down and grabbed her wrist, hoisting her up until she could reach her spear. She was surprised at my gesture and confusion clouded her expression.

"What the hell are you plotting, Peijin?" Her shout was barely audible over the sound of crashing waves.

I ignored her, my focus on Amelia. A thick line of blood trickled down her nose and into her mouth. She clasped a hand over her mouth, then swayed as if she were about to fall.

"Nothing," I replied coldly. Then, with Yue gripping her spear, I grabbed her and threw her as far up the serpent's body as I could. "Stop Amelia when you reach her! She's going to faint!"

But before either of us could begin our mad dash, the serpent slammed its head into the freeway and threw Amelia off.

CHAPTER SEVENTEEN

Amelia let out a bloodcurdling scream. Her small body flew and was hurtling straight for the water. Wei made a desperate attempt to reach her, but a massive explosion of blue sparks prevented him. The explosion was so violent and bright that for a moment, everything seemed to freeze before chaos ensued.

The figure of a small child with flowing auburn locks materialized from the yellow sparks, and the sight of her could be described as none other than blinding. Her skin glowed white, and every detail of her elaborate robes glimmered like gold.

Artemis.

How much spiritual power did she exhaust just to appear in the weak form of a child?

My eyes widened at the sight of the glowing, luminous girl easily catching Amelia in her small arms. The girl floated upward and gently set Amelia upon the serpent's head before pressing her forehead against the serpent's. At once, the serpent slumped.

The string between Amelia and Artemis tightened, and Hindsight confirmed my suspicion—Artemis was ready to sponsor Amelia the next time the opportunity arose.

With a deafening scream, the auburn-haired girl was assaulted by a flurry of yellow sparks that dug into her white skin like daggers until she vanished. A single star in the sky flickered out.

The punishment for interfering so heavily in an early scenario would be absolutely detrimental, especially given Artemis's status. She had clearly grown incredibly attached to Amelia during the short time they'd noticed each other.

[Observers Chat]
Socrates: So, this was Jia Li's plan . . . You've sent the divinities into a flurry in the heavenly realm. They're astonished.

You have received a new review!
<u>MAGICTAPE REVIEW:</u> ★ ★ ★ ★ ★
Liu Peijin is wickedly cruel, and it is thrilling to watch her actions. However, I pity her party members. Even though she cares for Amelia the most, she was willing to sacrifice Amelia's security just for a sponsor.

Amelia weakly pressed the iron cuff to the sea serpent's head, and it vanished, becoming no more than a silver engraving.

Suddenly, my entire party was free-falling straight toward the water.

Amelia made no sound.

Her body was limp, and the blue hoodie was trying to jerk her higher into the air.

"Zhige! Get her!" I commanded, throwing the sword in her direction.

Zhige pierced through the hoodie, which flailed angrily and threatened to tear. Though Zhige and the hoodie slowed her fall, Amelia was still headed toward the waves at a dangerous speed.

Lengthening his staff, Yang managed to hang on to one half as the other dug into the riverbed below. Wei grabbed his arm and swung before they both descended toward the water, trying to meet Amelia.

I wrestled for my bag, my limbs flailing in the air. Before I could pull my shield out, I felt a strong hand pull me in.

"Peijin," Yue whispered, frightened. She held me tightly.

"Don't worry," I reassured her, shutting my eyes from the wind blowing debris into them. "I can break your fall. My Physique level is high enough."

Riding his staff, Yang reached out to grab Amelia and hooked her small, limp body over his arm. Wei, Amelia, and Yang soon crashed into the water with an explosive splash. They resurfaced, alive.

I shifted Yue on top of me while lying within the inner curve of my shield. When we hit the water, the shield and I would break her fall, and if any of us were hurt, I'd use the potions collected from the last dungeon room.

I tightened my grip on Yue, making sure to protect her head. My muscles tensed up as I prepared for impact, but instead of landing in water, I slammed against metal. It felt as if every bone in my body shattered on the impact.

[Observers Chat]
Nipon23: karma.

I had slammed against the top of a train. Since we had completed the round, it flew back in, only to leave me splayed out like a starfish on the dented metal roof.

Yue got off me and dusted off, snickering and pointing at me. She jumped off the roof and swung inside the train while I stared at the sky, contemplating my life.

I followed a few moments later, spotting the beast-themed chest beside me. We were back in the same train we were in earlier, the posters still lined up.

"Amelia," I groaned, heading toward her. She was clinging to Yang, who was rubbing the leftover kraken mucus into her wounds. I wheezed while searching through my bag for a restorative potion to help her recover her physical health and mana. There were only two left, and I pulled one out and crawled over to her, dribbling the liquid into her mouth.

"Amelia?" I repeated.

I tried to take her from Yang, but he held her tightly. Amelia swallowed the liquid, and I wiped the blood off her face. She opened her eyes.

"Peijin," she sobbed, reaching her arms out to hook them around my neck. Yang relented and begrudgingly handed her over. I gently threw her over my shoulder while rocking her to soothe her.

When I stood up, pain seared through my body, but I ignored it and paced around the inside of the train. "You did well, Amelia. I'm proud of you. You were the reason we beat that level," I whispered into her ear while patting her back. I discreetly looked over my shoulder and gestured for the rest of the party to raid the rewards chest.

With Amelia now possessing two beasts under her command despite being an initially very weak disciple, there was no doubt that she could survive alone in this world.

Admittedly, a part of me felt remorse over forcing her through such an experience, but she was insignificant to this story and nothing more than an anomaly in a fictional world.

Scathing Reviewer activated!

A wave of guilt rushed through me. Amelia tightly gripped the back of my shirt.

"Amelia, you did what no other disciple could in all of China. You even got a Greek goddess looking out for you," I reassured her until she seemed to calm down. "You should check out the chest. There will probably be some awards for you."

Tears still fell down Amelia's face. "Peijin, I was so scared."

"You handled it perfectly. I'm proud of you," I said.

I inspected the silver cuff on her arm. The sea serpent was now a part of the intricate ornamentation. The cuff already contained other beasts, including a phoenix and a white tiger, but those would be far too strong for her—in fact, they were far too strong for almost all disciples, even later into *Surviving My First Run*, since they were members of the Four Auspicious Beasts like Chang.

To get an item like this from a simple dungeon room . . . It felt impossible. It felt like something karmic restraints should have prevented. The same applied for the various other items my party received, including Zhige. I pushed the thought from my head, focusing on the moment before me.

Yang called, "Amelia! There are three skills for you to pick from."

Three blue screens were glowing from above the chest. The rest of the rewards were miscellaneous items that the rest of the party had already bagged.

POTENTIAL SKILLS LIST
Universal Communication
Stone's Aura
Mark of the Beast

Universal Communication would allow Amelia the ability to easily communicate with all creatures: wolves, dragons, serpents, and insects. More powerful beasts were incredibly hard to connect with or speak to, and this skill would bridge the gap.

Still, Amelia had already proven herself very capable of talking to various beasts. There were better options for her.

Stone's Aura was a rather interesting skill; when equipped, the user's aura or energy would become like that of a stone. In later rounds where demons or ghosts could detect people and divinities, it would completely protect her. It was a primarily defensive move, but it was perfect for an ambush.

Mark of the Beast was by far the most complicated one. It had demonic connotations that threatened the Abrahamic divinities. It would make other divinities, like Artemis, nervous. But it wasn't a demonic skill.

The user would be able to merge and turn into a beast hybrid for a period of time if they so desired. It got its name from the fact that humans who merged themselves permanently with a creature—typically serpents, bulls, and dragons—became demons.

**Demon Great Sage who Pacifies Heaven encourages
Disciple Amelia to select Mark of the Beast.**

That was the first time the Bull Demon King expended a significant amount of spiritual energy, and it was over a weak disciple's skill.

"Wouldn't Mark of the Beast align Amelia with demons?" Yang asked, looking skeptical. I could tell that he had much more to say to me, but he bit his tongue while we were in front of Amelia.

"The description makes it sound like a temporary shift. It's probably just named after the fact that demons are typically merged with some kind of animal, and the skill permits that."

[Observers Chat]
Hedgehog1938: That's sick asf pick it

I wasn't sure how far I should stretch my lie about being a god. Should I presume omniscience or take a middle ground?

**Divinity Supreme Commander of the Heavenly
Hosts says Stone's Aura is difficult to attain.**

**Demon Great Sage Who Pacifies Heaven says Supreme
Commander of the Heavenly Hosts disagrees just to disagree.**

**Divinity Supreme Commander of the Heavenly
Hosts takes offense to such a claim.**

**Divinity Supreme Commander of the Heavenly Hosts is
threatening to torture Great Sage Who Pacifies Heaven for fun.**

Yue was now glaring at Wei, her arms crossed over her chest while the spear was held in a threatening manner. "Your sponsor better mind his place, Wei."

"I'm just a disciple. There's nothing I can do."

**Divinity Supreme Commander of the Heavenly Hosts
finds Disciple Yue to be very entertaining.**

**Divinity Supreme Commander of the Heavenly Hosts
has sponsored Disciple Yue 2,000 stars.**

Two thousand stars?!

Yue's body immediately tensed at the mocking sponsorship, but after noticing the amount, she kept her mouth shut.

In monotone, Wei replied, "Is money the only way to shut you up?"

"It's one of the ways."

If the Bull Demon King and Archangel Michael theoretically fought, it would be a rather difficult battle for both sides; however, Archangel Michael had the advantage of killing many demons in the past. He was by far one of the cruelest Abrahamic gods, and he frequently tortured and mutilated Demon Kings when bored. The only reason he wasn't doing so now was because he was more entertained by the splendid show I was putting on.

Amelia, still wearing the blue hoodie, tugged on the bottom of my dark brown pants. "Peijin, does Stone's Aura apply to the animals I tame?"

"Uhh . . ."

Editor's Pen activated!

**When equipped, the skill Stone's Aura applies
to all of the disciple's tamed entities.**

Edit granted!

My face softened, and I smiled at her. "I believe so."

"Then I should pick that one, right?" she stammered, unsure. "I—I don't know. What would you pick, Peijin?"

"Stone's Aura is a daoist and defensive technique, and Mark of the Beast is more offensive and has indirect correlations with the Demon Kings," I replied. "Both are good options. It just depends on what you want, although you can theoretically work your way to both."

I wasn't lying this time. Whichever she picked, either would work out well. Personally, I doubted her ability to get Mark of the Beast—she was still rather weak and not a very formidable opponent—but Stone's Aura would take the average disciple hundreds of years to attain.

Amelia's small hand reached up and selected a skill just before the timer ran out. Once she selected Stone's Aura, the train sped to the next room. Yang looked like he was dying to say something, but he held himself back.

"What is it?" I asked him.

He gave me a complicated expression and glanced at Amelia. I covered her ears despite her protests.

"You let Amelia suffer like that just for Artemis to interfere? For what? Her sponsorship?" Yang finally said. His arms were crossed.

"It'll be better in the long-term. It's better for Amelia this way, too. She'll know how to take care of herself," I said.

"You knew it was her biggest fear, and you left her in that moment."

Yang and I weren't very close before the apocalypse, so we'd never argued.

Part of me was taken aback, but another part also knew he was doing this out of genuine concern for Amelia and not anger.

"If there was any moment of danger for Amelia, I would've stepped in instantly."

Yang's brow furrowed, but before he could say anything, Wei chimed in. "Peijin hasn't done anything that hasn't been in our best interest."

"I know you don't agree with what she did, Wei," Yang said.

"I don't, but I believe in Peijin."

"You don't need to justify what I did for me, Wei," I said. "Yang, I hope you trust me enough to know that I care about Amelia, and I wouldn't let her get hurt."

Yang looked down at the ground for a moment before nodding. "Peijin, I want to put all my trust in you, and I will until you prove otherwise."

"That's very ominous," I said.

Yang quirked a brow suggestively, and I laughed. The tension lifted until Yue spoke.

"If it was in the party's best interest for her to go through that whole room alone, would you have let it happen?" Yue asked. A flurry of emotions swirled in her gaze. It caught me off guard.

But I just smirked at her. "Why? Are you worried I'm going to leave you behind?"

Yue scowled. "You bitch. You wouldn't dare."

I shrugged and turned away.

The train slowed to a stop.

I confidently turned to Yue, spinning my blade in my hand. "Yue, do you have any idea about what your room—"

"No."

I grew disdainful. "Are you seriously going to act like this right now?"

"These rooms are based on our biggest fears, right?" she asked, ignoring my question.

I paused for a moment before giving a slight nod. I looked back at her poster, expecting to see the isolated island, since that was what I had written in *Surviving My First Run*. But here, the poster showed a girl who bore a shocking resemblance to Yue. She was bent over in agony, screaming in an empty white room as dozens of black swords, spears, and staffs pierced through her abdomen, black blood pooling beneath her. Behind her, silhouettes of people loomed, watching the scene take place but not doing anything.

Her deepest fear had changed after we'd gone through Amelia's room.

Yang gently placed his hand on Yue's shoulder, looking at her with those reassuring brown eyes. "What do you want us to do in the next room?" His question still felt like a direct attack on my reaction to Amelia's room.

Yue spared a short glance at Yang, and the hand that clutched her spear trembled. "Don't leave," she said.

The doors opened to a vast theater. Lights beamed on and illuminated the room.

Custom room now commencing!
Tailored for: Disciple He Yue.

My eyes took a moment to adjust to the light as I blinked rapidly. I could hear the train vanish into the distance once every party member had exited. When my vision finally cleared, I turned to face them.

The spot beside Yang was now empty. His hand was still hovering as if it were on someone's shoulder. Yang's eyes widened.

"Yue?"

CHAPTER EIGHTEEN

Zhige swung through the air where Yue had been standing moments before, unleashing a sharp ringing sound.

"Huh. She really isn't here," I said.

If she was, Zhige would have sliced her apart, regardless of whatever arc spells she might've been under.

Countless rows of red theater chairs surrounded us, and on the other side of the seats was a glass wall. I headed over to it and tapped it with Zhige, causing blue sparks to fly off and prevent Zhige from passing. We were on the theater balcony, and below was a dark stage.

Hindsight activated!

This room was vastly different than what I'd originally written, but as the author, I tried to piece together the new dungeon room in my head.

"Peijin, what do you think is going on?" Yang asked, stepping forward to look over the edge with me.

"Right now I'm thinking about your annoying voice."

In the train, the second iteration of Yue's poster was the most disturbing of all, even though Yang's had been the most peculiar. In it, she was being brutally stabbed by hundreds of weapons, and her face was covered by a half smiling, half crying mask. Four figures hovered behind her.

My blood ran cold, and my gaze surveyed each party member.

"What is it? Peijin?" Wei asked, growing more nervous. He placed a comforting hand on my shoulder.

Yang's face fell, and I knew he had come to the same conclusion I had.

The stage lights flickered on, blaring down on a small female figure standing proudly on the stage before a twisting maze. It was Yue. Behind her were four other figures—their features were completely indistinguishable, and they shifted and floated like a black fog.

Ghosts.

"But I wouldn't do that!" Yang's voice shook, and he grabbed my arm, shaking it.

In the poster, there were multiple weapons piercing through the masked Yue: a dao, staff, and jian. At the time, I hadn't considered such details. But now that we had passed through those dungeons, it was clear they were the three weapons the rest of us were carrying.

But the fourth weapon . . . It was a spear. In the poster, there was only one— and it was piercing straight through Yue's heart.

The four figures onstage behind Yue transformed, their bodies warping and shifting to reflect my party's features perfectly. They now took the form of two men, one woman, and a young girl. The illusion was masterfully crafted—they looked identical to us.

My counterpart turned to face me, lifting a finger to her lips in a "silence" gesture.

"Backstabbing," I murmured. "That's her biggest fear."

Divinity Supreme Commander of the Heavenly Hosts feels pity for Disciple Yue.

[Observers Chat]
Socrates: Jia Li, you should be nicer to your party members. You're probably the cause of her fear after she saw what you did to Amelia.

Wei reacted first, stabbing the glass barrier. Sparks flew and landed on his skin. With an echoing boom, he was sent flying back.

Not a single scratch on the glass.

This was a psychological room, by far the most ruinous for its victims. By forcing them to confront the horrors of their own being, the chance a disciple could become traumatized and never recover was high. In fact, most would end up killing themselves before escaping.

Yue's memory of the poster and her senses would be severely diminished, and she'd inherently be reliant on the puppet versions of my party. For someone as headstrong and stubborn as Yue, such a dungeon room would be absolutely crippling.

Yang rushed forward and elongated his staff, stabilizing it between the back of the theater wall and the glass. He tried to pierce through the glass, but his staff instead shot straight through the wall.

"Yue!"

There were two ways to beat this room: one was for Yue to recognize the mental manipulation and finish the room, and the other was for Feiyu to break her out.

In *Surviving My First Run*, Yue's dungeon wasn't centered around abandonment, although it still was a psychological room. With a mighty roar, Feiyu had raised his sword to the sky, called down a god, and torn apart the entire dungeon.

Was I Feiyu now?

No.

Was Yue strong enough to withstand the room alone?

Maybe, but probably not, considering that her fear was being backstabbed.

Scathing Reviewer activated!

Guilt tore me up. I almost keeled over before I grabbed Zhige, stabilizing myself and slowing my ragged breathing. I felt Yue's fear as if it were my own, and the prospect of my party one day not needing me filled me with dread.

Anytime Scathing Reviewer activated, I became racked with regret and pity. What kind of skill would do that? I scowled at the thought of my skills making me weaker.

I was a part of Yue's biggest fear, even though I had written a predetermined fear for her. Was it that fundamental of a shift in her character, or were my words not as set in stone as I'd thought?

I stabbed Zhige into the glass. Its red eye blinked wildly at me. Under the immense pressure, the glass warped around Zhige like hot plastic, trying to mold together. Zhige shrunk into my hand, then elongated once it managed to escape the shifting glass.

The theater balcony was the perfect height to watch Yue, who was solving puzzles with the puppet party, running around the maze. She had found something similar to a Rubik's Cube in the maze, and with every twist of the cube, certain maze corridors would shift. Her pseudo party members followed closely behind, acting as if they were diligently trying to find their way out.

Inconspicuously, the puppet version of Amelia lagged behind, then wandered into a hall out of Yue's vision.

The real challenge was starting.

Wei cried out, his knuckles bleeding from his desperate attempts to break through the glass. His chest heaved with every breath, and his shoulders were slumping in defeat. "Peijin, what do we do? Do you have a plan this time?"

Yang's expression was cold and hard, and he continued to violently bash at the glass; blue waves erupted like raging waves out of each hit. Amelia had summoned the dire wolf, but even its vicious fangs and claws couldn't damage the glass.

"I'm thinking!" I shouted, my hands trembling. "We need to stop the impostor versions of ourselves from killing Yue, and then we need to get her out of the maze!"

Dammit. What the hell—there was no way I could be as lucky as a protagonist. In Feiyu's dungeon, he received a rare item that would allow him to call down a god for an arc.

Wei grew more desperate, his strikes sharp and frenetic. "Can you call down a god like you did with Artemis?" His voice was high-pitched, and I could barely hear him over the sounds of Yang's banging.

> **Warning! Dozens of gods are glaring at you**
> **with overwhelming animosity.**

Artemis's descent was an attempt at the same premise, but without the item, she had faced the immediate consequences of karma despite manifesting in the weak form of a child. She would undoubtedly have faced harsh scrutiny from the other Greek gods, but it was a risk she took in hopes of securing Amelia as a disciple.

Yue held the cube in her hand, examining it with Puppet Yang. Puppet Yang twisted and interlocked the different pieces with one another to shift the doors of the maze.

Yue seemed confused by Puppet Yang's demeanor.

Please, let her realize. She knew it just as well as I did—Yang was deeply frightened of her and trembled every time she was near. Yet here, Puppet Yang moved confidently and intelligently.

Such a sight seemed to send the real Yang into an even greater frenzy as he continued to violently swing at the glass. Amelia's eyes welled, her brows knit together.

"Amelia, can you use Stone's Aura to get through the glass?" My voice raised an octave from the mounting pressure I felt as Puppet Wei slipped away into one of the corridors.

> **Disciple Amelia activated Stone's Aura!**

Her hand slipped right through the glass, and she looked up at me with large, hopeful eyes.

I grabbed her arm. "Don't go in there. Yue will think that you're the impostor and kill you."

"We're running out of time, Peijin," Wei protested. "At any moment, your puppet or Yang's puppet is going to kill her!"

"I'm not blind, Wei. I can literally see that happening!"

Even though Yue seemed to be growing suspicious, she hadn't yet realized that the puppets weren't us. If I were writing this scene now, how would I have it play out? The people who Yue would least expect to betray her would lead her to the very end before backstabbing her, leaving her trapped. It would've been the ultimate heartache.

With Hindsight activated, I could see the looming silhouette of the Bull Demon King hovering over his disciple. I looked up, shouting at the ceiling of the theater.

"Bull Demon King! Sign a contract with me!"

His silhouette immediately vanished.

> **Demon Great Sage who Pacifies Heaven adamantly declines!**

"What the hell do you mean no?" I shouted. "Do you want your disciple to die? You'd be a complete laughingstock, given how powerful you are!"

> **[Observers Chat]**
> **Socrates**: Because you're poor, I'll lend you enough spiritual energy to talk to him. But if you let Yue die, I'll make every god turn on you.

That didn't seem quite fair.

> **Demon Great Sage who Pacifies Heaven asks what you want.**

"Grant me the ability to use Stone's Aura for the next five minutes."

> **Demon Great Sage who Pacifies Heaven says that is an even greater violation of the karmic restraints than Artemis helping Amelia.**

> **Demon Great Sage who Pacifies Heaven calls you idiotic.**

"Are you saying you're weaker than Amelia? You can recover from karmic restraints." Behind me, my party continued their fight against the glass.

> **Demon Great Sage who Pacifies Heaven says he'll agree to a contract if you pay the price for the violation of karmic restraints.**

"What do you want in exchange?"

> **Demon Great Sage who Pacifies Heaven says he'll agree to a contract if you feed him an immediate family member.**

I forgot he was a gross murderer in *Journey to the West.*

Regardless, his words reminded me of a third method.

I sat down on one of the theater chairs. Zhige was sheathed on my hip. I shut my eyes and focused.

Gods like Hermes were famous for gambling, but in *Surviving My First Run,* such sins were much more prosperous in the ghost realm. Red-light districts, gambling, alcoholism—all of it ran rampant in ghost cities.

Deals with ghosts were risky, but they were fast and direct, with no compromise needed. With Wei, Yang, and Amelia distracted, I whispered, "Chance Sought Gold Serendipity, I would like to wager a bet with you."

A few moments passed. Nothing happened.

"Ahem," I loudly cleared my throat. "Chance Sought Gold Serendipity. I would like to wager a bet with you."

More silence.

"What the hell? Are you too entitled to answer or something? I said I'd like to wager a bet!"

Suddenly, a pair of small red dice rolled out from beneath the chair at my feet. They stilled, and their bright white dots taunted me, an ominous air to them.

Chance Sought Gold Serendipity was a powerful Ghost King, and he spent most of his time gambling. Although he never lost, he was always fair whenever it came to bets that did not involve him personally.

Many disciples would travel to the ghost realm and make countless bets: on the death of an enemy, for infinite stars, to pass a scenario. To grant such wishes, Chance Sought Gold Serendipity had to be powerful enough to snap his fingers and confidently declare, "There—your reward has been granted."

However, each bet carried a great risk.

I stared down at the dice. "Allow Amelia to temporarily transfer her skill Stone's Aura to members in the same party."

A small blue flame appeared beside the dice before it vanished, leaving a piece of rustic-looking paper with writing in black ink.

Big reward. You want me to save a life, mess up the scenario, and transfer skills. What are you betting?

"I'll bet Medusa's head and the broken Shield of Truth."

The note burned to ash and a new one appeared.

Not enough.

Editor's Pen activated!
Lower the betting amount when gambling with ghosts.
Edit granted.

"I'll add on serpent's eye."

Not even close. You really underestimate how much Artemis sacrificed for you.

Time was ticking. Even though I hated Yue with what sometimes felt like every fiber of my being, she was necessary for my team. I needed a powerful magic user, and a future Demon Queen couldn't be topped by much.

Not only that, but I was her creator. More than anyone, I knew she just wanted to be cared for. Who was I to deny her that?

Zhige was a strong enough blade to take me through the entire apocalypse, so I couldn't give him up. I didn't have any other material possessions, either.

I sighed, rubbing my head. "Fine. Instead, I'll wager a year of my life."

The note remained, signaling that my offer still wasn't enough.

Really?

[Observers Chat]

Hedgehog1938: Why would you ever risk your own life for someone you obviously vehemently hate? You've done nothing of the sort this entire time.

CactusLiver: Why are you still here if all you'll do is complain? If anything, I'm glad she's not being stuck-up like before . . .

Nipon23: he's prob here for the same reason I am. a good time

---

"Five years."

The note didn't budge.

"Seven."

The note burst into flames, and the dice rolled closer to me. A new note appeared.

Roll higher than or equal to seven to win.

I reopened the Editor's Pen skill. Even though I had bet seven years of my life, I didn't plan on losing. It was a game of complete chance, and I knew Chance Sought Gold Serendipity wouldn't interfere.

A disciple's first bet will be a win for them.

Error! Impossible within karmic restraints.

As expected. My original input was too far of a stretch, but the system would automatically adjust my edit to the maximum capacity. I wasn't sure what that was, so allowing the system to decide was the most risk-free.

Potential edit: On a disciple's first roll, their luck will be tenfold.

Accept / Deny

My trembling finger tapped "accept," and the blue screen vanished with a blip. My breath caught in my throat when I took the dice, shutting my eyes and shaking them in my enclosed hands. A tenfold increase was enough to practically guarantee me a number over seven.

With a deep inhale, I gave one last shake and threw the dice on the ground.

CHAPTER NINETEEN

The first die had rolled a one.

It was a terrible start, but it must have meant all my luck went into the second—the other could still be a six.

I leaned over in my chair and checked the second die.

One.

A terrible pain ripped through my entire body. It felt like every bit of flesh was erupting into flames at once, and I fell off the chair, shrieking. At once, Wei and Yang appeared at my side, both of them trying to hoist me off the floor.

I gritted my teeth to hold back my cries. The pain traveled like seismic waves through my body, volcanic and explosive.

"Peijin! Are you all right?" Wei shouted. He lifted me up and gently placed me down on the chair. I could tell he was trying to say something to calm me down, but his face was a blurry mess behind my tears. Yang was searching through the Azure Dragon Store for something that could ease my pain.

Amelia was horrified, the dire wolf nudging her cheek in a feeble attempt to comfort.

"I'm fine," I groaned, reaching for the dice. Sweat dripped down my face in thick beads, and I could taste the saltiness as they ran down the cusp of my upper lip and into my mouth. Parts of my body were flaking off in golden sentences. Those were all my future years, in the form of stories, slipping away.

I was watching my future disappear before my very eyes.

If that roll was the result of my luck tenfold, and the chance of rolling a sum of two was already incredibly low, how bad was my luck?

Even with the tenfold increase, I wasn't guaranteed to roll a sum over seven. Perhaps I'd just gotten unlucky—though I knew this was flawed logic. In part because I failed the probability assessment at school, and because if my luck was that bad with the Editor's Pen, there would be no hope for me during a second bet.

Yue struggled to reach the end. Beside her, Puppet Yang used his staff to break through pieces of the maze to find the correct path, while Puppet Peijin now scrambled the cube. Yue wielded her spear, fighting off the creatures that were approaching from behind.

Puppet Yang snuck up behind an unsuspecting Yue and lifted his glistening golden staff just behind her head, tensing his arm as he got ready to strike.

"No!" I screamed. "Yue!"

The staff sped right past Yue and pierced a humanoid creature in front of her, instantly killing it. Yue turned around, grateful and trying to hide her trembling. With a warm smile and quick pat on the shoulder, Puppet Yang continued to fight the beasts.

My heart was racing now, and not from the pain. My hands trembled violently at the sight of Yue being so blatantly manipulated because of the trust she had in her party. For once, I couldn't take her for granted.

Wei's hands were clamped firmly on my shoulder, but I gently pushed them off. If he was saying something, I wasn't processing it.

I glanced back down at the two red dice in my pale hands.

This was the only way.

Squeezing my eyes shut, I shook the dice, not bothering to read the ghost letter before rolling again. "Same bet, all right? I'm going to get it this time, you fucking ghost asshole."

**Divinity Supreme Commander of the Heavenly
Hosts is begging you to stop!**

Yang looked at me, lines forming on his forehead. "Peijin? Are you gambling?"

The dice bounced on the carpeted floor before rolling to a stop. I scrambled to check. My lips were tightly pressed together in a line.

One and one.

This time, I was prepared for the pain. It ripped through me again, like a sword had stabbed my stomach before stirring and tearing into all my organs. I gripped the soft floor and cried out in pain as more gold phrases flew from my body.

"Peijin! Peijin!" Wei's face twisted with worry, and he foolishly tried to grab the gold phrases to contain them. He saw Amelia's tear-streaked face, and he hesitated, torn between sheltering Amelia from the sight and caring for me. He shared a brief glance with Yang and moved to Amelia.

"Peijin, stop!" Yang shouted, gripping my shoulder and kneeling before me. His eyes peered straight into mine, and his expression was firm and unrelenting. I could hear Amelia wailing.

I groaned and wrestled to stay conscious. My hair was strewn across my face, stuck to the beaded sweat on my skin. I didn't have the energy to brush it off.

"Peijin," Yang said. "You need to tell us what you're doing. You can't keep doing everything on your own! I don't care if you're a fortune teller or anything else!"

Ignoring him, I reached my hand out for the dice, but he slapped it. I shoved him away and crawled to the dice, cupping them in my hand.

"Come on, Chance Sought Gold Serendipity. Do you offer discounts when I'm rolling this many times for one outcome?" I let out a strained laugh, spit thick in my throat. "Fourteen years is really cruel, you asshole."

You have received a new review!
<u>POCKETRECORDS505 REVIEW:</u> ★ ★ ★ ★ ★
Peijin is like a tsundere. She pretends she doesn't care about her party members, but here she is convulsing on the ground and giving up her life span. Good stuff, good stuff!

Yang tackled me to the floor. One of his hands pressed right against the Tower tattoo as he lifted me and slammed me back down with a loud thud.

"Let go of me! You're wasting our time!" I struggled against him before I kneed him between the ribs; he violently hacked, and his grip slackened. I got up in an attempt to run.

Yang coughed, struggling to catch his breath before grabbing my ankle. I fell, my forehead bouncing off the floor as I tried to crawl away. I kicked him repeatedly in the head during the struggle, but he flipped me over and his long arms reached up, trying to pry open my hands, which still held the dice.

"Do you not trust us enough to tell us what you're doing?" Yang shouted over the chaos. "What the hell are you thinking, Peijin?!"

I pursed my lips and avoided his gaze—my focus was on breaking free so I could roll the dice again. If I told Yang or any of them my plan, they would try to stop me, and Yue's death would be certain.

A small flame burst beside my head, and another note appeared. Yang's eyes flicked to it. He let go of my hands and pounced for the note.

My shoulder pushed into the floor to propel myself upward, and I planted my knee into his lower back. Looking over his shoulder, Yang shoved my head back and caught the note.

Zhige unsheathed itself and jumped out of my holster, darting over to Yang's head to knock him out.

"Zhige, down!" I shouted, and the blade halted in midair before returning to me like a scolded puppy. Practically crawling up Yang, I grabbed for the paper, but he had already read it.

He flipped over to face me. I was frustrated and nervous.

Yang's voice was considerably softer than before, and his brows furrowed. "Are you gambling years of your life away?"

I couldn't meet his gaze and tell a lie at the same time.

"I'm not. Give me the paper back, or I'll roll the dice right now." Kneeling above him, I raised my hand up in the air and showed him the dice, reminding him that he couldn't stop me if I decided to roll now.

"If I give you the paper, are you going to roll the dice?"

"I'm rolling either way."

His expression was complicated; his lips were pressed into a line and the corners were curved downward, as if he was trying to hide his offense or disappointment. "Let me roll. Please."

"No. Hand me the paper."

"It says the penalty will decrease by one year for each of your rolls. Tell me, how many years have you already lost? Were those the gold words coming off you?" Yang demanded.

"Hand me the paper," I repeated firmly. What Yang had told me was most likely the truth, since he was able to deduce the penalty, but I had to be sure. I shook the dice in my hand as a threat.

Yang gripped the fabric of my shirt. "Peijin," he whispered, "I can't watch you kill yourself for any of us. You matter too much."

I froze. My heart thumped in my chest.

Scathing Reviewer activated!

Admittedly, I was rather nervous to go through the pain again—having pieces of my life forcefully extracted wasn't the best thing. But if losing my years could save Yue, I'd do it over and over again until I died, and even then, I'd come back as a ghost to haunt this shitty world.

"I'm sorry, Yang." I brought up my hands and shook them one last time, closing my eyes and praying the outcome would be better.

A blue notification appeared before me.

Divinity Supreme Commander of the Heavenly
Hosts is willing to gamble with you.

CHAPTER TWENTY

My brows rose in surprise at the notification. I got off Yang and looked at the ceiling of the theater again. Even though there was a roof above me, I could see the small twinkle as if the star symbolizing Archangel Michael shone through.

"Chance Sought Gold Serendipity has the best deal," I replied nervously, my hands trembling.

> **Divinity Supreme Commander of the Heavenly Hosts is willing to take the consequences personally.**

My spit thickened in my tightening throat. If I accepted, then we would most likely make a deal that wouldn't have such a severe payment, and he'd have to boost my luck. To do such a thing would require an unbelievable amount of spiritual energy.

> **[Observers Chat]**
> **Socrates:** Take it, Jia Li. You'll die otherwise D:

I blinked solemnly at that notification. The knowledge that I blocked Socrates before he could see the full extent of what I'd created in *Surviving My First Run* now weighed on me.

Archangel Michael undoubtedly had enough spiritual power to execute the deal, but did he have enough to fully push back karma? He'd fall victim like Artemis, and I just couldn't do that to him.

This was different. Socrates's notification blinked, but I refused to look at it.

> **Divinity Great Sage Equaling Heaven is warning**
> **Supreme Commander of the Heavenly Hosts.**

Gambling was a vice, and for an Abrahamic god to engage in such a deal with me, it would wreak absolute havoc on his status.

"I'm sorry, Archangel Michael. But I can't." I prepared to roll again.

Although I was endlessly grateful that Archangel Michael would have made such a bold offer this early on, the rest of my party would have to deal with gods hesitant to help or pay back my debt. I'd be screwing over everyone but myself because no matter what, Yue would make it out.

> **Divinity Supreme Commander of the Heavenly Hosts**
> **is willing to create a contract with you.**

> **Divinity Supreme Commander of the Heavenly Hosts says he**
> **will help you when necessary during Yue's dungeon room.**

"I want you to descend into the dungeon room and protect my party from karmic restraints. I'm asking more of you than I did of Chance Sought Gold Serendipity."

> **Divinity Supreme Commander of the Heavenly**
> **Hosts says it's no challenge.**

> **Divinity Supreme Commander of the Heavenly Hosts says**
> **he'd never embarrass himself when demons are watching.**

> **Divinity Supreme Commander of the Heavenly Hosts proposes**
> **that you ally your party with Paradise for the contract terms.**

I hesitated, my hands frozen in the air. Taking this deal would mean my party would forever be bound to Paradise—a collection of every Abrahamic divinity. My party would forever be bound to their will and their goals, along with their fight against the demon realm.

Not only that, but I'd already promised to align myself with Athena and the Greek divinities. Well, I guessed Archangel Michael didn't know that, though . . .

There was no direct conflict as of now. The rest of my party would be allied with Paradise, while I was individually tied to Olympus. It would be a mess, but I'd deal with that fallout later—and find my way out of the deal.

"Archangel Michael, I'll sign a contract with you. I'll need you to trust me, though."

An iridescent blue screen appeared before me, and I typed in the terms. As ironic as it sounded, I had faith in him.

> **All signatories have signed! The contract is now
> in effect until Liu Peijin's death.**

Smiling solemnly, I whispered a quick thanks under my breath.

> **[Observers Chat]**
> **SageDrunkKitty:** Sending you my spiritual energy, Peijin! Just remember to return it to me later.

My body was thrust forward, and I was pinned to the glass wall. I whipped around to see who my assailant was, only for it to be Yang, who pressed his staff firmly against my back to detain me. He pried the dice from my hand and shook them.

"I don't know who you are, but let me place the same bet," Yang whispered into his hands.

"Yang, you don't need to anymore!" I screamed. "Zhige!" I strained to break free as my entire body squished and contorted against the glass.

Zhige flew forward, and its hilt smashed into Yang's back, making him stumble and lose the dice beneath random seats.

He had rolled them.

Blue sparks burst throughout the theater—there was a considerable amount of spiritual energy flowing through the room now. My eyes darted around expectantly for Archangel Michael, but he was yet to appear.

> **Divinity Great Sage Equaling Heaven is fascinated
> by the story taking place before him.**

> **Demon Great Sage Who Pacifies Heaven reminds Great Sage Equaling
> Heaven that he should be concerned about his disciple's life instead.**

> **Divinity Great Sage Equaling Heaven sponsors Disciple Yang 500 stars.**

Yang's staff shrunk, releasing me. I fell to the floor but climbed back to my feet to chase after him. Staff flying back into his hand, Yang began to destroy the seats in search of the dice.

Wei's panicked voice could be heard over the chaos. "Yue is almost at the end of the maze!"

As he spoke, Wei's hand was on Amelia's back. Beads of sweat fell down her head as she whispered to the dire wolf, their foreheads gently pressed together.

If Yang never found the dice and knew their sum, then he would forever be in a stalemate. There would be no risk of him losing seven years of his life.

Chance Sought Gold Serendipity would force Yang to look at the results of the dice, but I could prevent that from happening if I increased my power.

Yang froze, having suddenly spotted something.

My gaze followed Yang's to a small, glistening shape on the ground. "Zhige!"

Zhige darted forward to stop Yang, but Yang leapt and covered the die. He looked at it cupped between trembling hands, and his blood ran cold.

I had caught up to him now, and I peeked over to check the value.

Two.

"You stupid, stupid idiot," I muttered, my chest heaving from how out of breath I was.

Goddammit, goddammit, goddammit. If Yang lost years of his life, I'd never forgive myself.

What if he didn't have seven years left? What if the pain would be too much for him to handle? What if I still couldn't save Yue with Archangel Michael, and I lost Yang in the process?

A thick bead of sweat rolled down my cheek.

[Observers Chat]
Nipon23: jia li, stop it. you know this world better than anyone else
Nipon23: this is YOUR element

"The second dice might be a five or a six," Yang replied, but I could hear that he was far less than confident.

I looked over at him, my voice soft. "Don't take that risk, Yang. Don't search for the second die."

Amelia activated Stone's Aura for the dire wolf, and it quietly slunk through the glass after both Amelia and Wei's encouragement. The dungeon didn't sense the beast, and he slunk down into the maze to reach a still-unaware Yue.

If Wei hadn't pulled Amelia together, I think I would've broken down in that very moment. The anxiety of needing to save Yue and stop Yang was only piling up.

"All right," Yang relented, getting up onto his knees.

I tried to keep my breathing slow and steady, disguising my trembling frame.

A small shape was wedged between my shoe and the ground. Amid the chaos, I had managed to spot the red glint of the second cube and stepped on it.

The dire wolf let out a loud snarl before pouncing, snapping its jaws at Puppet Yang and Puppet Peijin. Yue looked at the wolf in surprise, gripping her spear and attempting to pierce it, but not before turning behind her and realizing that Puppet Amelia and Puppet Wei were already gone.

She froze, stealing a nervous glance at the situation in front of her.

Scathing Reviewer activated!

In *Surviving My First Run*, Yue grew up in the foster care system and was only adopted when she was a teenager. Yue's fear of abandonment was instilled due to my writing. She deeply feared being left again, deeply feared the unknowing emptiness that followed the word "home"; however, this still hadn't been her original fear in *Surviving My First Run*.

This was the result of me and my actions here, in this world. Even if Yue was nothing more than a character, she lived beyond the pages I'd written.

"Yang, help Amelia and Wei," I ordered.

He looked at me. "You first."

I hated people smarter than me.

Yue glanced around in the maze, panicked. Puppet Yang, though gone, shouted reassurance and comfort, and she persisted.

Mere words were all Yue needed to hear. I supposed I knew that very well, more than anyone in the world.

"Why? Do you not trust me?" I replied nonchalantly. My foot was still pressed on the second die, and I refused to budge.

"I trust you very much, which is why I think you'd lie to me." Yang gave me that smile of his, and I watched his eyes wrinkle into those thin crescents.

I let out a weak laugh. "When'd you find out?"

"I know you very well, Peijin. You're a bad liar."

With my eyes shut, I thought, *Thank you, Archangel Michael for that goddamn contract.*

I lowered my head and let my shoulders droop. Blue sparks erupted all around me like a firework, creating a bright and radiant aura.

Slowly lifting my foot, I revealed the glaring red die.

CHAPTER TWENTY-ONE

Six.

Yang let out a massive sigh of relief, his forehead falling to meet the carpeted floor.

> **Divinity Supreme Commander of the Heavenly Hosts is jumping with joy.**

> **Divinity Supreme Commander of the Heavenly Hosts sponsors everyone in Peijin's World Dominion 5,000 stars.**

I smiled at Yang before sprinting to Amelia.

I shook her by the shoulders, and her head swayed side to side.

"Amelia, call back the dire wolf and let me use Stone's Aura!" I urged, not waiting for a response. "Keep the hoodie for now in case something goes wrong."

Amelia's large blue eyes widened in confusion, but she followed my command. After a few moments, the dire wolf appeared beside her, his face bloodied. I promptly pressed my forehead against hers and blue sparks flew between us.

> **You have temporarily acquired the skill Stone's Aura.**

With Stone's Aura equipped, I could easily bypass my way into the dungeon with Yue, as the karmic parameters would not sense me.

I flew through the glass with Zhige in tow. Thankfully, Zhige's aura was also masked since he was my sword. I quietly slunk through the maze before finding puppet Wei. He held his sword tightly, and his steps were barely detectable as he stalked a distracted Yue.

The white ribbon on his arm, however, was not present.

I drew in a deep breath before launching myself at Puppet Wei, slashing through his abdomen with Zhige. Zhige's power was unbelievable, and I looked down in pure amazement at the clean cut. Although Zhige managed to cut straight through his entire body, no blood or organs came out.

Puppet Wei let out a ghastly howl, turning and trying to stab me while his upper body slid off his lower body. He began to disintegrate—black ashes falling from his skin and leaving nothing behind but a foul stench.

I knelt on the ground, bringing my hands to my chest in a prayer.

"May you find peace beyond this world," I whispered earnestly, my eyes closed in a solemn manner. After pausing for a moment, I gathered the ashes and placed them in my bag.

> **[Observers Chat]**
> **Socrates**: Who knew you'd treat ghosts with such kindness and respect?
> **CactusLiver**: Damn ☹ Anyway, isn't Zhige kinda OP? Sick

> **Divinity Supreme Commander of the Heavenly Hosts**
> **is moved to tears by your generous display.**

> **Divinity Supreme Commander of the Heavenly**
> **Hosts sponsors 5,000 stars.**

I smiled internally at the sponsorship but kept my expression solemn. Zhige looked at me, blinking expectantly.

"Good job, Zhige! Aren't you just the cutest?" I gently rubbed Zhige and the red eye squinted into a pleased crescent.

Typically, the puppets used in arcs were lowly ghosts. In the ghost realm, ghosts still had to make a living and survive, and there were different categories— the ghosts impersonating my party members often forgot their past lives but struggled with poverty, illness, and abuse in the ghost realm.

Thus, they were easy for the broadcasters and gods to get a hold of for the arcs. Regardless, they were ghosts, not demons, and Archangel Michael inherently had a soft spot for wronged humans, even if they were alcoholics, gambling addicts, and scummy people.

They rejected becoming demons, and that was enough of a justification for salvation.

Suddenly, the black floor shifted beneath my feet, sending me crashing into the wall. The maze walls shifted around me.

> **Hindsight activated!**

Yue must have been playing with the cube again. I was running out of time—soon one more puppet would slink away and prepare to kill her.

I darted through the maze, now unsure of where I was. The walls shifted, and I crashed face-first into a black wall.

"Urgh! Hindsight, is this literally not your job?" The bridge of my nose ached from the impact, causing me to sniffle.

My body stiffened as Hindsight analyzed the situation, and an ominous shadow loomed over me.

I leapt to the side of the wall, pinning myself against a corner as a vicious tarantula burst through where I'd been standing.

Shaking itself off, the creature crawled up the wall with its large furry legs striped red and black; its beady black eyes and sharp fangs glistened under the theater lights.

The tarantula raised its two front legs in the air in a threatening manner before pouncing for me—I ducked and slid under it, whipping my head around to see my attackers.

Of course I was transported right in front of Puppet Amelia.

"Zhige, go!"

Zhige flew out from my hand and immediately stabbed through Puppet Amelia's stomach, twisting its blade before shooting up vertically and splitting her upper body in half. She dissipated into ash.

It was a rather gruesome sight to see the body of a child get viciously torn apart.

No longer under her control, the tarantula froze awkwardly on the wall. Zhige flew back into my hand, and I slashed the head off the spider.

"May you both find peace beyond this world," I prayed, bowing my head. I gently scooped up their ashes, mixed them together, and put them in another compartment of my bag. Before they became ghost and beast companions, they had probably been owner and pet in the real world.

> **Divinity Supreme Commander of the Heavenly**
> **Hosts is searching for more tissues.**

> **Divinity Supreme Commander of the Heavenly**
> **Hosts sponsors 7,000 stars.**

> **Demon Abyssal Kraken of Black Seas is happy you cared about the beast.**

> **Demon Abyssal Kraken of Black Seas sponsors 2,000 stars.**

A warm smile grew on my face from the Abyssal Kraken of Black Seas' messages—they were few and far between, but they were earnest, unlike those from other gods.

Demon King of Resourceful Goblins wishes for your death!

Was that guy seriously back already? I hoped karma would keep him out of commission for a bit longer.

The amount of spiritual energy here must have been permitting more of the gods' involvement—he was certainly too poor and lacking in spiritual energy to ever send a message right now otherwise.

Since the maze was shifting again, Yue must have been close to the end—and to her death.

I navigated toward the end using the age-old hack of only turning right. I looked up and spotted the entire crew watching me from the glass, and they were pointing their fingers at me, their mouths saying something I couldn't make out.

I grinned and gave a thumbs-up, continuing to sprint through the maze. Yue's annoying and ear-piercing voice could be heard now; following the sound, I finally spotted them near the edge of the stage.

Peeking past the black wall, Puppet Yang and Yue were bickering. Yue stubbornly held the cube above her head, glaring at Puppet Yang as he tried to explain his idea on the proper path. Puppet Yang did a perfect job of mimicking the real version—his voice was firm but still soft enough that Yue didn't feel suspicious.

My blood ran cold at the sight.

Where was I?

Puppet Peijin was nowhere to be seen . . . and if the person who Yue trusted most would leave last like I theorized, then I was the wrong person to send down.

I shook my head, brushing off the idea. Even if Yue drove me up a wall, she knew I held the party's best interest at heart. I wanted to believe she valued me that much, at least.

"Zhige, can you sense Puppet Peijin?" I whispered at the blade, twisting it in my hands.

Zhige spun around before pointing at a corner, directing me toward it. My arms trembled slightly as my grip tightened on the handle, and the giant black tattoo on my forearm wasn't helping ease my nerves.

Above me, the rest of the party was still gesturing toward me. They must have realized first that Puppet Peijin had gotten in position.

"Good, Zhige," I praised the blade, stealthily approaching the corner. After a deep inhale, I burst out from the corner and surged toward Puppet Peijin.

To my surprise, she was already facing my direction, and as I approached, she easily dodged my attack. Her face was cold as she faced me, and in her hand, she held a replica of Zhige without the blazing red eye.

Zhige seemed to shake at the sight of the phony blade and grew larger in my hands, spiritual power raging through it. I prayed that Stone's Aura would continue hiding its energy.

Puppet Peijin brought the blade parallel to her cheek before soaring at me, striking.

Sparks flew as our blades made contact, but she was pushing me to the wall.

"Dammit, I'm not going to lose to a stupid puppet like you!" I hissed, jumping back and lifting my sword into the air.

At my words, Puppet Peijin's face flared with incomprehensible rage, and I was reminded that she, too, was human, even if she was not me.

"Zhige, go!"

Zhige flew forward and pinned her against the wall before pulling back, fighting her alone. I ran to Yue, my feet thumping on the hollow wooden stage.

"Yue!" I finally managed to catch up to her, and I was now staring at both her and Puppet Yang. My chest heaved with every breath, and I was a far cry from the composed Puppet Peijin fighting with Zhige back in the corridor.

Yue's face immediately fell at the sight of me. "Weren't you going to look for any traps? Why are you suddenly incompetent again?"

"Y-yeah," I stammered, sparing an awkward glance at Puppet Yang. "I think I found one. You two should come check it out."

Even if Yue didn't trust me as much as Yang, I needed to pull this off. There wasn't enough time for me to head back up and exchange places with Yang because Yue had already reached the end of the maze. The moment she'd try to leave, she'd be brutally betrayed by the puppet party. I needed to kill them and have her break free of the illusion before leaving.

Yue must have noticed all the red flags by now, especially when one of them was blaring alarm signals right next to her.

Puppet Yang grabbed Yue's sleeve before she could step forward and quietly murmured into her ear. "Why is Peijin suddenly so breathless? She was perfectly fine moments before."

My muscles tensed, and my throat was dry. Yue turned toward Yang receptively before glancing at me once again.

"Seriously?" I gestured toward myself. "Yue, remember that conversation we had fighting the sea serpent? The one where you called me a bitch?"

I let out a big sigh of relief as soon as I saw her face drop in exasperation at my comment. Yue might have been insufferable, but so was I.

"Yang, she probably just ran back here to tell us about the trap. Besides, we already found the end. Let's just check."

Yes! I loved Yue!

> **[Observers Chat]**
> **Socrates:** Come on, Yue!! Get out of this!

> **Divinity Supreme Commander of the Heavenly
> Hosts is leaning on the table in anticipation.**

Puppet Yang shook his head insistently. "Do you seriously think the real Peijin would have told us that? When has she ever told you anything, Yue? And now she suddenly wants us to head back into the maze."

Fuck!

On cue, all the maze walls dropped immediately, revealing Puppet Peijin fighting with Zhige. Zhige froze as if suddenly gaining stage fright and flew across the stage into my hand. Putting on a perfect performance, Puppet Peijin called out to Yue.

"Yue, run! It's a trap!" Puppet Peijin cried before collapsing onto a knee, clutching an "injury."

I now stood on a completely empty stage with the white lights searing into my skin, making me feel hot as sweat dripped down my brow. Holding Zhige's menacing blade in my hand, I realized how much of a monster I looked like.

Yue's eyes surveyed the now-empty stage and she realized that Puppet Amelia and Puppet Wei had vanished. In a panic, Yue grabbed Puppet Yang's arm and made a dash for the exit.

I looked back at the window, watching my party scramble and pound against the glass frantically. Even if this was my world, I wasn't the protagonist of it. I couldn't force my characters to be saved by me.

Regretful and bitter about my weak bond with Yue, I lifted a hand. My unwavering finger pointed straight at Yang.

"You," I mouthed, jumping back to avoid Puppet Peijin's flurry of attacks.

His eyes widened in realization, but I nodded my head in affirmation.

Yang would use Stone's Aura and descend; since I wouldn't have time to rush back behind the glass, I'd have to deal with karma myself.

"Archangel Michael, are you ready?" I called out, balling my hands into fists.

> **Divinity Supreme Commander of the Heavenly Hosts
> is ready to fulfill his side of the contract.**

With a loud crackle, all the spiritual energy in the room seemed to suddenly condense into a glowing blue sphere at the center of the room before erupting in a blaze of light.

CHAPTER TWENTY-TWO

A small doll appeared on stage before the sparks vanished, and it fell limp.

I darted forward, picking it up. It was a traditional rag doll with large black button eyes—it had pieces of yellow yarn for hair and white wings attached to its back with flowing blue robes.

In my hands, it looked like a normal angel doll—completely lifeless and still.

To make a descent like this, it would have cost Archangel Michael an unspeakable amount of spiritual energy given how immeasurably powerful he was.

You have received a new review!
CIDER988 REVIEW: ★ ★ ★ ★ ★
**I want to see Peijin do cool things, and if bad reviews are
what kills her, I might as well leave this good one.**

[Observers Chat]
Socrates: Hurry, Jia Li! You can only hold off karma for so long.

I felt a small burst of spiritual energy within me, though I knew it wouldn't do much to the amount of karmic restraint. Gently placing the doll on my shoulder, I offered it a large smile. "This form is quite cute for you. I wouldn't mind signing more contracts if I could keep you perched here."

The doll was still hunched over on my shoulder, the big button eyes unblinking. I held back a snort.

"Zhige, here," I called out, slapping the side of my leg as if the blade were a dog. "Can you feel pain?"

Amelia was now pressing her forehead against Yang's, and soon I would be thrust into the arc's punishment for invading the dungeon room.

Zhige shook back and forth to reassure me before nuzzling against me.

"Lucky you."

I leapt off the stage and tried to run as far up the auditorium as I could toward the glass, but Yang descended before I made it.

At once, massive sparks flew around me and, like a swarm of infuriated hornets, surrounded and seared into my skin.

"Urgh!" I exclaimed, falling to one knee.

My limbs kicked and convulsed from the burning pain. More and more sparks emerged around me and bit into my skin, vanishing and leaving burn wounds behind. Zhige trembled violently against me and tried to ward off some of the sparks.

Even if my Physique level was at 50 or 100, the arc's punishment would've overwhelmed me. I was breaking the room's rules by passing the glass without a skill—allowing me to survive would be a massive flaw of the system.

I groaned, trying to stand up as the flurry around me began to completely block out my vision with nothing more but bright, angry sparks.

"Zhige, can't you try a bit harder?"

Rather offended by my remark, Zhige flew above my head and grew in size—with the blade pointed at the floor, it spun rapidly in circles to deflect the sparks around me.

Surprisingly, most likely due to Zhige's incredible spiritual power, it deflected most of the sparks. Soon the system would come for Zhige, but I could finally fight for a few desperate inhales.

"Archangel Michael . . . !" I wheezed, unable to finish my plea for his help.

To outsiders, I would look like a burning tower, sparks of fire and pure energy exuding out of me.

Before me, there was a sudden blue flash that I could hardly make out. It creeped closer until a small blue snout poked through the whirlpool of sparks.

"Chang?"

Oddly enough, he seemed strangely concerned, with his scaly brows furrowed and his lips dipping into a frown.

"You need to get back behind the glass, Peijin."

"I can't."

"You can never outdo karma. God of fortune and fate or not."

I laughed pitifully, standing up and readjusting the doll. "You wanted a good show, right?"

Before me, Yang made it onto the stage and was fighting Puppet Yang. Yang swung his staff at Puppet Yang, but Puppet Yang matched his pace and swung back with equal force and superior skill. He wielded the staff seamlessly, creating distance between the two as he continued pulling Yue toward the end of the stage.

"Yue! Stop!" Yang cried, trying to reach her, but the staff beat him back ceaselessly.

<hr>

Scathing Reviewer activated!

<hr>

I looked up at Chang with a small smile on my face. "I can't leave until this dungeon ends. I trust Zhige and Archangel Michael."

<hr>

Divinity The One Who Fights in Front nods at your display of bravery.

<hr>

**Divinity The One Who Fights in Front also
criticizes your behavior as unwise.**

<hr>

Chang's expression fell immediately at my words.

"The doll . . . Is that . . . ?"

"Yes, it is."

"Do you understand what you're doing, Peijin? How did he even agree to let you do that?" Chang's voice grew louder and louder.

"Since when did you start doubting the gods?"

"If you're a god, I can see why you got banished."

Sparks continued flying around me as Zhige attempted to swing them off, but he was being forced closer and closer against me. Sparks broke through his defense and ripped through my skin.

"Zhige, you need to leave me and help Yang kill Puppet Yang," I whispered to the spinning blade above me.

Faltering for a moment, Zhige hesitated with the command—as soon as Zhige left, the sparks would reattach themselves to me.

I let out a little laugh, brushing my hair back. "I know. I'm pissed off that Yang hasn't ended this yet." Gripping the doll tightly, I took in a breath.

"Zhige, go."

The blade darted forward, and I was immediately engulfed by the yellow sparks.

Yue

Liu Peijin has my best interest at heart.

That was a phrase Yue truly believed.

In fact, if she were asked to, she'd swear her life on this belief; however, she'd never confess to that. Peijin's ego would get far too big.

Yue didn't know where this belief came from, but it felt like it was an ingrained part of her.

The two deeply resented each other, but there was an unspoken tension of respect between them. Yue deeply admired Peijin's cunningness, and Peijin acknowledged Yue's unparalleled growth.

But there was another truth that Yue believed.

If it's in my best interest, Liu Peijin will abandon me.

These two truths managed to coexist within Yue and, in only a few days, cultivated a garden of fear in her heart. For one, Yue did not yet know if Peijin would abandon her for Yang or Amelia or Wei, as Peijin always managed to achieve everything; she never had to make such decisions.

Peijin, however, was still deeply cruel. Yue saw, felt, and accepted this when watching Amelia tremble with fear in the past room, and Peijin permitted it. In fact, Peijin fostered it.

"Y-Yang!" Yue screamed, wielding her spear nervously in front of her as the two identical figures viciously battled one another.

How could anyone tell them apart?

"Get out of here!" Yang screamed, looking over his shoulder while slashing through the air with the golden staff. "You're at the end. Make it through! Peijin and I will hold off these impostors."

The other Yang shouted, but his breaths were labored and weaker. "Don't listen to him, Yue! He's not real!"

The Peijin that had burst through the maze now vanished, erupting into no more than a golden flame, but the one that had been with Yue this entire time continued to fight relentlessly before a gray blade with a red eye suddenly appeared.

It swung at Peijin with unspeakable force, throwing her back with a loud cry.

A blade that can move on its own?

Yue couldn't quite recall through her foggy memory.

The gray sword was coated in thick layers of the yellow sparks, crackling and popping like a firework—shaking them off, it lunged at Peijin again.

Yang drew his staff into the air, swinging it down and causing the entire stage to splinter in half, sending everyone flying back. With a deeply fearful look, he turned around to make sure Yue was okay.

That's right, he was the real Yang. The one who had gone through the maze with her, because Yang hadn't left.

Yang was different than Peijin. It was clear he harbored a deeply odd fear for Yue, his entire body trembling like a weak autumn leaf around her, but Yang was a person who stayed. He stayed with her at the station, he stayed with Amelia during her level, and now he stayed with her through the maze.

With a loud cry, Yue darted forward, pinning the impostor Yang against the floor with a flurry of attacks.

"Yue? What's gotten into you? You can't recognize me?" the impostor shouted. He raised his staff to prevent himself from getting battered by her spear, but the impostor never struck back.

He craned his neck and saw the glowing yellow figure in the audience, and his face fell, his eyes growing wide in horror. For a moment, his grip on his staff slackened.

"Peijin . . . ?"

That wasn't the real Peijin. It deserved to die.

Yue's spear breached through the impostor's defense and slashed his face, causing a deep cut to bleed down his cheek. With a quick movement, the impostor tucked his legs in before kicking out, sending Yue flying.

Suddenly, Peijin darted in, throwing the impostor to the ground. The blade chased after her tail, stabbing deeply into her back.

Peijin let out a deep guttural cry but continued to fight the impostor.

"No! Peijin!" Yue screamed, reaching out for her.

"Yue!" the impostor shouted. "Don't you remember when I patched your wounds with the kraken mucus? Or when we saved Amelia from the serpent? I promised I wouldn't leave you, and I didn't!"

Yue paused, struggling to piece the events together. She could vaguely recall a promise being made.

Before she could reflect further, Yang's hand firmly grabbed her wrist. "There's no time, Yue. We need to get out of here. Peijin will catch up with us, believe in her!"

Yang tugged her firmly, sprinting toward the end of the stage and flinging her forward. With one last jump, Yue leapt for the end of the stage.

But she suddenly stopped.

Two arms were hooked underneath her armpits, pinning her tightly against a body.

Yue blinked, confused, as she looked over her shoulder and met Yang's eyes.

"Yang?" Her voice faltered now as the betrayal set in. She had chosen wrong. "Yang?"

A blade thrust straight through Yue's abdomen, causing a line of blood to shoot out and splatter onto the ground. The blade let out a metal ring as Peijin removed the sword in a quick movement before piercing Yue more, over and over and over while Yang held Yue in place.

With a violent, guttural sound, Yue cried out as blood spurted from her mouth.

CHAPTER TWENTY-THREE

I fought to see Yue through the yellow sparks that surrounded me. They swarmed in thick layers, but I pushed through them with my hands until I could finally catch a glimpse of Yue on stage, her eyes darting between Yang and the puppet party.

"Yue! Yu—!"

The flurry of karmic sparks stung my skin, leaving red burns in the shape of scars. I pushed through the pain and waved them away. They chewed through my hand, and my eyes burned like they were being sliced open. Still, I stumbled toward the stage, the doll perched on my shoulder.

> **[Observers Chat]**
> **Socrates:** Turn back, Jia Li! You'll die if you continue this for much longer!

"Fuck, Archangel Michael, are you going to do something or not?!"

Finally, the sparks flew back, leaving an empty halo around me like I was in a protective bubble. The sparks clashed against the invisible barrier, struggling to get through.

I hissed air in through my teeth, trembling from the pain on my whole body. Now that I could catch a breath, it felt even worse than when I was being assaulted.

"You couldn't do that sooner, Archangel Michael?"

The little doll still hung limply on my shoulder before falling over and leaning against my neck. I knew it was the best that Archangel Michael could do given the amount of karma surging around me, but I was still pissed that it took so long.

"Thanks anyway. Save your energy until we get closer, then I need you to fling everything off. It'll only take a few seconds, and I'll try to save your energy."

> **115 gods are shocked by the actions of Supreme Commander of the Heavenly Hosts!**

> **1,039 demons are enraged at the interference of the divinity!**

> **Demon King of Resourceful Goblins attempts to rally demons against Disciple Peijin and Supreme Commander of the Heavenly Hosts!**

> **Demon Abyssal Kraken of Black Seas glares at King of Resourceful Goblins.**

> **Demon King of Resourceful Goblins accuses Abyssal Kraken of Black Seas of turning against the demon realm.**

> **Demon Great Sage Who Pacifies Heaven says only weak demons would be bothered by contracts.**

> **Divinity Great Sage Equaling Heaven says stupid demons should keep their mouth shut.**

I lifted leg after leg, lurching forward with each heavy step. It felt like I was dragging my body through quicksand. Whipping my Shield of Truth out from the bag, I began pressing my way forward.

The entire theater was rumbling; loud crashing and bangs threw me back. I gripped onto the side of the chairs, shoving myself forward until I could finally see the elevated stage before me. Yang was struggling on the stage, having suffered a grave wound to his leg that he was struggling to heal. His whole body shook with the effort to stand.

Suddenly, I heard an earsplitting shriek cut through even the crashing stage, and my blood ran cold.

Yue.

Yang and I cried out for her at the same time, our voices cracking and violent alongside the sounds of Yue's pained, animalistic screeches.

"Archangel Michael, now!"

The sparks all erupted away from me, glimmering and vanishing into the arc as I darted forward, leaping up onto the stage. Zhige, finally battered down by the sparks, raced toward me and flew back into my hand, gaining the protection of Archangel Michael.

Yue was being gored, Puppet Peijin rapidly stabbing straight through her abdomen repeatedly. Puppet Yang held her in place without a flicker of emotion crossing his face.

"No! No!" My words came out as a scream. Goddammit, even if Yue was the biggest asshole in the party, she didn't deserve this.

Disciple Yue activated Demonic Fire!

Yue's fists lit up with the black flames, but they weakened with each stab she faced. Tears streamed down her pale face. She kicked her feet, screaming and crying and thrashing.

I let out a loud scream as I lunged at Puppet Peijin.

Zhige pierced straight through puppet Peijin's back before I dragged the sword up, splitting her in half. With a brutal cry, she attempted to reach behind me and grip the sword, but Zhige's red eye furiously blinked, and the blade swiveled to cut off her arms.

Zhige diced straight through Puppet Peijin with such ferocity, it was like Zhige had a personal vendetta against the ghost. The blade made quick work since puppet Peijin had been distracted by Yue, cutting her into small ghost cubes that began to disintegrate.

Yang, who had finally gotten to his feet, tore Puppet Yang off Yue, who collapsed. Yang struggled against his demented self; his moves were frenzied, frantic, and panicked—only growing in intensity when Puppet Yang suddenly lifted the staff and aimed it for Yue's heart.

Some spare sparks cut into my skin like little paper cuts, but I swung my arms before me and pushed them back, stumbling forward to control and speak with Zhige.

The last thing I would die from was some stupid sparks from hell, but I couldn't be the reason Yue died, either.

"Zhige! Help Yang!" My voice was strained now from the repeated onslaught. I'd need to use some of the elixirs and potions gathered from earlier rooms to heal my wounds, but I needed to make sure Yue survived.

Zhige froze, looking back and forth between the two versions.

"Are you serious right now? The real one!" I was swarmed, my voice and strength were fading.

I clutched the doll closely against me like it was a protective amulet, but its stitches quickly began unraveling. I could tell Archangel Michael was rapidly running out of spiritual energy in this feeble form.

"Archangel Michael, redirect most of your energy to protecting Zhige." I cried out in obvious pain from my past injuries and the new ones being inflicted by karmic restraints.

I looked up at the balcony seats—Wei was covering Amelia's eyes as she hugged his leg, clearly deeply frightened by the sight.

I had to last until the end of this dungeon.

Please, let that be soon.

Or I'd come back as a ghost to haunt Yue forever and give her a new fear.

Puppet Yang flung his staff and smashed Yang against the stage wall, a loud crash erupting. The fall was hard, causing him to cough and spit a mixture of saliva and blood all over himself, but Yang still got up and ran over to Yue.

Zhige was beside him, both moving as one to catch up to Yue.

I sprinted toward Yue, trying to reach for her and tend to her injuries.

"I'm sorry. I'm really sorry, Yue. Let's get out of here, okay?" I pleaded, still holding the shield above me to hold back the sparks. But at the sight of me, she tried to crawl away.

Ah, right. In her confused and disoriented state, Yue needed Yang, not me.

My face twisted into a pained smile.

I didn't think it would feel this bad to be rejected by my own character. I guess not all of them needed me the way I wanted them to.

Karmic sparks forced me down again, and I collapsed onto my knees beside Yue, who only further distanced herself from me.

Puppet Yang lifted his staff up into the air with incredible strength, the muscles of his arm shifting under the theater light, before sending it straight through Yue's arm.

"It hurts! It hurts, it hurts, it hurts!" Yue screamed, trying to maneuver away before falling on the ground, a puddle of deep red blood pooling out beneath her. Thankfully, her high Physique level kept her alive despite the attempts of Puppet Peijin to kill her, but if she was not tended to immediately, she would die.

She looked up with a horrified expression, not seeming to believe the situation playing out in front of her. Her cloudy gaze flickered to the spear still clutched in her hand.

Zhige finally reached puppet Yang, and with one clean cut, pierced straight through his hard skull. Puppet Yang froze for a moment before gripping the hilt of the sword and trying to pull it out, but Zhige shook violently and gored Puppet Yang repeatedly.

Puppet Yang let out a violent cry before dissipating into ashes. Knowing my tradition of collecting ashes, Zhige gathered and piled the ashes of both Puppet Yang and Puppet Peijin together while Yang scrambled back onto his feet, darting toward Yue.

Suddenly, Yue tightened her grip on her spear and aimed at her own chest, but Yang ripped the weapon out of her hands, glaring at her furiously before shouting.

"I didn't leave. None of us did!" he shouted at her. "So don't ever do something so stupid!"

Yang's arms were wrapped around her neck tightly, and his face was twisted into a painful expression. He met her eyes dead on. "Yue, let's go. We're all waiting for you."

Despite his words, Yue could only manage to blink at him before her expression softened. Her shoulders slumped and blood spurted out of her mouth.

Yang tore off his jacket, tying it around her wounded abdomen. Zhige flew back into my hand, and I paid my respects. Finally, with Zhige back in my grasp, Archangel Michael could center the last bits of his spiritual energy on me enough for me to help Yang carry Yue out.

Although Yang's entire body was trembling, he didn't leave Yue's side.

Yang and I dragged Yue's limp body past the edge of the stage, finally bringing the dungeon to an end as the train appeared. The Shield of Truth covered most of my figure, and I collapsed into the train, letting it fall atop the rest of me. The train picked up Wei and Amelia just after.

I hit the cold ground of the train. The sparks vanished. The small rag doll was reduced to nothing more than yarn, but it, too, vanished before I could even process the sight.

"Thanks," I choked out. "I hope the contract helps you avoid any big punishment from Paradise."

Each breath I took let out a small whistle sound, and my eyes were still squeezed shut from the overwhelming pain. The golden flakes continued to leak out of my body, but their rate had slowed. My tattoo, however, was glowing white, emanating sparks of its own.

"Peijin!" Amelia's voice rang out and I could see the shadows from her footsteps as she approached me. She bent down and lifted the shield off.

The shield clattered to the ground beside me, and Amelia covered her mouth in shock.

[Observers Chat]
Hedgehog1938: Oh my god . . .
Cjst123: Holy shit. Even with all that spiritual energy it turned out like this?

You have received a new review!
BEIGETOWEL REVIEW: ★ ★ ★ ★ ★
Peijin has changed a lot. For someone who acts so cold and brutish, she is far more heroic than I'd have ever expected.

> **Divinity The One Who Fights in Front is stunned by your pain tolerance.**

The luminosity of the metro lights bored into me, and even with my eyes closed, I was blinded—my eyelids were worn so thin now that they couldn't even block the light.

> **Demon Great Sage Who Pacifies Heaven is amazed**
> **at how far you went for Disciple Yue.**

> **Demon Great Sage Who Pacifies Heaven sponsors 10,000 stars.**

Zhige nudged me, trying to get me to stand up. My skin was marred by deep red marks, entire chunks of my skin missing. Some were actively oozing thick streams of blood; I took in a shuddering breath that stung my throat.

If it weren't for the doll, I would have been torn apart. This? This was nothing. No one could escape karma.

"P-Peijin . . ." Wei said. He crouched beside me, his puppy-like eyes large. "I'm sorry I was too weak to do anything for you or Archangel Michael."

At Wei's words, Amelia teared up and sniffled loudly, on the verge of wailing. "Is Peijin going to die?"

My eye twitched. "No. Peijin is too angry to die," I said.

I sat up, moving at a snail's pace. I opened my bag to pull out a pink elixir. Blood dripped into my eyes and blurred my vision, but I stumbled over to Yue on the ground, kneeling beside her. Yang was holding her tightly, and he tried to reach out to grab onto my arm, but he hesitated when he saw the condition of my skin.

"Peijin . . ." Chang muttered.

I hadn't realized Chang had followed me. I couldn't process any of his words right now through my pain.

The pink elixir sloshed in the clear glass, and I tried to pry open the container's cork lid with my thumb; however, as soon as I put pressure on the lid, the skin on my thumb peeled off and revealed a raw flesh.

Yue's eyes followed my movements—her expression was that of a stranger. Every few seconds, she'd wince, and sweat that collected on her forehead would bead down her face and blood would gush out.

"I got it," Yang whispered softly, gently taking the bottle from my hands and tilting it above my mouth. "Here."

I shook my head and gestured at Yue, trying to take back the elixir. "Give it to her first."

Yang gave me a rather surprised expression, and I was glad that I hadn't looked in the reflective windows of the metro. Was my condition so bad that he thought I'd need the elixir before Yue?

I let out a small laugh.

Yue was still bleeding out on the ground before me, visibly in pain. She needed it far more than I did. If anyone was going to beat her to the brink of death, it would be me, not some stupid scenario.

Yang gently dripped the glittering pink elixir into her mouth before closing her chin, and she swallowed it with a wince. Her breath began to slow, and the blood began to clot.

"Give her some more," I commanded with a scratchy voice, leaning over to tip the elixir until it was virtually empty. "She needs to heal so she can pick her skill like Amelia did."

Once Yue finished drinking, she lay on the ground, unmoving, but her injuries were clearly beginning to heal.

Her eyes fluttered open, her eyelashes twinkling in the light, and she looked at Yang before staring at me, her face promptly twisting into one of horror at my condition.

"Peijin, drink the rest and then open up a new elixir for yourself," Yang said.

"I'm fine."

Yang glared at me, and I sighed. "Her lips touched it," I argued stubbornly. Every ounce of that elixir had to be preserved, and I was annoyed to have spent an entire one on such a trivial scenario. "Do you have any leftover kraken mucus?" I asked. "That'll fix this right up."

Yang didn't know whether to laugh or cry. "Just grab a new elixir, then."

"That was the only healing elixir we got." The lie slipped out easily, though it wasn't really my intention. It was the only healing elixir we should use—they were hard to come by, and we could always use more of a stockpile.

It wasn't really a lie if it was for everyone's sake.

To my fortune, Yang hadn't been paying enough attention to the collected elixirs, and since I was the one gathering all of them in my bag, he was unable to question me. My vision continued to blur as my hearing began to cut out, overwhelmed by a stuffy buzzing sound, but I still reached out and grabbed the kraken mucus from Yang's hand.

"Peijin? You're looking a bit . . ." Yang's words trailed off as I felt my entire body wobbling, blood still trailing into my eyes.

My body collapsed with a loud *thump*.

CHAPTER TWENTY-FOUR

My eyes fluttered open, but the first thing I sensed wasn't the blinding lights—it was that I was coated in a thick layer of slime.

> **Divinity Spirit of the Jade Moon is diligently instructing Disciple Amelia.**

I reflexively shot up: "Zhige!"

A little shriek followed, and I recognized it as Amelia and calmed down. She was holding a large vial of kraken's mucus in her hand. My reaction caused her to jump back and get the mucus stuck in her curly hair.

I scooted forward and was surprised to find myself slipping on the moving train's floor like it was an ice-skating rink.

"Sorry," I said, reaching over to her. "Some got stuck in your hair, Amelia."

I lifted my arm and wiped it off her, noticing that most of my wounds were healing . . . but my attire was different.

I could spot the others through the window connecting the different train cars, and I realized they had moved. Yang and Wei were speaking to each other, seeming rather tense, while Yue was moving her arms around her to test her strength.

I was now only in my tank top, and my pants had been rolled up past my knees. No wonder it was just me and Amelia in this car, but I still felt incredibly awkward in front of her, my cheeks flushing from embarrassment.

"Did they seriously leave you to play medic?" I ignored the way my clothes got dirty and oiled when I rolled them back down.

Amelia gave a nervous nod and looked at the ground. Even if we were in the same party, it was still humiliating for me to have been passed out and dependent on a child I just met.

[Observers Chat]
Socrates: Amelia wants your praise, Jia Li
Socrates: Archangel Michael better be ok :(I hope you thought this all through

---

The first notification caught me off guard. In paying closer attention to Amelia, I saw she was expectant.

I wiped down my hand before placing it on the top of her head, ruffling her blond hair. "Thank you, Amelia. I'm feeling much better thanks to your help," I said in a cheery tone, giving her a bright smile.

Hopefully I still didn't look like a knock-off Freddy Krueger or the effect would've been quite traumatizing. I didn't want to be the feature on her next "biggest fear" poster, either.

Amelia's face immediately lit up as she looked at me with sparkling eyes. "Thank you, Peijin!"

[Observers Chat]
Socrates: AWWWWWW OMG
Socrates: Archangel Michael gave me stars to sponsor you if you're nice, since he's on trial right now at the heavenly court for colluding despite his obligations as an Archangel

---

Observer Socrates sponsored 5,000 stars.

I didn't know how a child could be this pleased by a few words. It was rather cute to see how happy Amelia was from such a simple gesture. I never received words of praise when I was a child, and I wondered if I would've reacted similarly if I had. Maybe I wouldn't have become so twisted.

But how many stars did Archangel Michael give to Socrates? Did they talk with each other? Did Socrates talk to other people than me?

I shook my head back and forth. Of course they'd talk. Why the hell was I getting hung up on that?

"Let's head back to the other metro car, Amelia." I ushered her and threw on the blue hoodie she handed me.

As I was pulling the hoodie over my tender arms, she tugged on the jacket's fabric. "Wait, Peijin. Your tattoo."

"Ugh, I know. It's such an eyesore. I need to get rid of it," I grumbled, scrubbing at the top of my skin as if it were a washable ink.

Amelia interjected and brought her hands into fists in front of her. "No, it's not! I think it's very nice!"

I didn't need a skill to know that she was lying.

"But I meant that when you passed out . . . it wouldn't stop sparking. Even Chang showed up, since it was giving him an issue with the system."

"That's just because Chang is bad at his job. Let's head back."

> **[Observers Chat]**
> **Nipon23:** jia li forgets about her past occupation as a shitty pest control worker . . .

If it was up to me, I would've blocked him by now.

There were three big differences from *Surviving My First Run* that I still couldn't explain: Eternal Wish, the Major Arcana, and Scathing Reviewer. The observers, thankfully, were just like pleasing the gods, and as long as they didn't find out I was the author, I wasn't worried about review bombs and damaging my spiritual energy and potential of becoming a god.

The Eternal Wish was a deadbeat sponsor that had an unspeakable amount of power and used it only to tie me down to him. I needed to eradicate him to fulfill Athena's contract and for my own sanity. So far, I figured Eternal Wish and another mystery, MolaMola, were one and the same.

The Major Arcana rivaled karmic restraints to a terrifying degree. Hacking the system, branding me with this tattoo, and who knew what else they would do? The fact they could overstep karma gravely frightened me, and if they ever decided to come after me, there was nothing I could do.

I lowered the sleeve of my top, making sure it covered the entire tattoo.

Scathing Reviewer . . . It was a strange skill. It seemed to do a variety of things. It stopped any other disciples from analyzing me or my skills, but it also randomly activated. And when it did, I felt myself longing for my party. It made me soft.

Who could have corrupted my perfect novel so much that it almost felt foreign to me? Once I became a god, I'd destroy the system and take them all down with me.

"Hellooo, my lovely subordinates!" I swung open the car door and stepped into it, letting Amelia walk in before me.

Yue looked up at me with an already exasperated expression, like she wanted to pass out and die.

"The Wicked Witch of the West is back," she said in a slow, annoyed tone, sitting on the metro chair. A glowing chest was before her with three blue skills floating above it.

My eye twitched at her coarse remark, since I was pretty sure an observer had called me that before, and I moved to stand in front of her.

I had never been so inclined to hit a woman.

"Liu Yue!" I roared, grabbing her shoulders and violently shaking. "Do you know what I just went through for you? I can't believe you seriously trust Yang more than me! I went through hell to get you out of that dungeon, but you would easily run off with Yang?!"

We were back to stage one, but the emotion carried in our glances now held something different.

Her head wobbled back and forth before she grabbed my arm and stopped me.

"You're surprised by that? You fucking kidnapped me after knocking me out to make me join your party! And you hate me, too—of course I thought you'd leave me!"

"I'd never leave you, you idiot! I'm so pissed that you'd even say that!"

We both froze at my words, Yue blinking at me with an expression of utter disbelief. I let go of her and turned away.

> **Disciple Yue activated Lie Detector!**
> **Lie Detector has confirmed Disciple Peijin's words as truth.**

I turned to face Yue, this time gawking. "Are you fucking kidding me?! Stop using your skills on me! How the hell did you even get these skills, you damn farmer!?" I continued shouting at her, shaking her violently. "Did you make a deal behind my back with the devil or something? You're picking up skills like a scavenger. You're like a hyena!"

"A hyena?" she exclaimed angrily, but to my surprise, she suddenly burst out laughing. "Look how red your face is, Peijin!" She laughed so hard she held her stomach and wiped tears from her eyes.

I could feel the heat rise in my face before I scoffed and turned away from her.

Profiling and Lie Detector were rather passive skills, but obtaining them provided a significant advantage in this world. And with skills as unreliable as mine, I needed ones like those for me to count on.

"I'm seriously about to kill you, Yue," I grumbled and turned back toward the rewards chest. Technically, there wasn't any criminal justice system or death penalty anymore to punish me.

> **Disciple Yue activated Lie Detector!**
> **Lie Detector confirmed Disciple Peijin's words as false.**

I scoffed, and Yue snickered in response. Both of us were too shallow and cocky to ever address head-on how we felt after her dungeon room. But there was an air of respect between us that wasn't present before.

Above the chest, three blue skills were glowing.

POTENTIAL SKILLS LIST
Magician's Hand
Mark of the Beast
Possession

I began, clearing my throat. "Yue, you sho—"

Yue cut me off, shoving me aside. "I'm going to pick Possession."

I sighed and gripped my temples, already regretting the fact I'd survived the last dungeon.

Hindsight activated!

"Yue," I began, "you should pick Magician's Hand. It's an illusion skill, and that'll pay off a lot in the later rounds. If there's a skill like possession for demon disciples, there's a divine skill like exorcism that'll harm you."

Her nose scrunched as she looked down at me, crossing her arms. "Is there a reason you keep advocating for all of us to pick passive or defensive skills?"

Well, at least we both agreed that Mark of the Beast was out of the picture.

"Defensive skills take time and patience to develop, so it's good to get them early in the game. You can get more offensive skills like Possession or Mark of the Beast with strength later. Have you never played a video game?"

"Who made you the boss?"

"I did. It's tyranny."

Yang chuckled behind me before he decided to sit down on one of the train seats. Wei threw Amelia into the air and she landed on Yang's lap, who then threw her back, causing her to squeal in jittery excitement.

"Yue," I continued, "Magician's Hand allows you to warp the mind and space around people. It's the same thing as the dungeon you just went through. Possession requires you to actively control someone—you leave yourself vulnerable when using it."

Pursing her lips, Yue glared at me for a moment longer before letting out a long sigh and turning toward Magician's Hand.

I smirked as she did so. At the rate she was gaining skills, she'd pick up Possession soon in the future. My luck was so bad, it'd probably happen today just because I didn't want her to have it.

Before she selected it, Yue clarified her intention.

"I'm only picking this because you saved me. I'm paying back my debt," she said with a grumble.

"That's a bad mindset to have. Don't do something for anyone else, ever."

"Yeah, yeah, whatever." Yue waved her hand dismissively at me, throwing her long black hair over her shoulder and clicking the skill.

I smiled warmly and gave her a hard smack on the back. "See, you're not that stupid!"

Disciple Yue activated Magician's Hand!

Yue's eyes were glowing an ominous purple as she stared deep into my soul. The train around me crumbled into darkness until I was floating in nothingness.

"Stop."

The word immediately snapped me out of the illusion, and the train returned. Yue reverted to her original appearance, giving me a warm, innocent smile. She put her hand on her hip and swiveled around to face Yang while I dumped the rest of the rewards into my bag, rolling my eyes at her childishness.

The train had begun to slow before finally coming to a halt, jolting us forward. The doors were about to open.

"Pervert Yang," Yue said. "Any last words before we're teleported into your torture chamber?"

CHAPTER TWENTY-FIVE

on't call me that!" Yang protested, his face turning red.

Yue shrugged, grabbing her spear and spinning it around casually. "It's what you are, is it not?"

Wei tapped my shoulder, whispering into my ear above the chaos of their bickering. "Peijin, should we cover Amelia's eyes until we know what the dungeon actually is?"

That question took me rather off guard. I mean, sure, Yang's poster was pretty funny, but I hated writing any sexual arcs in *Surviving My First Run*.

Mostly for my own sake. Sure, a few readers complained about the lack of romance between Feiyu and his partners, but I just blocked them.

I probably shouldn't have blocked MolaMola, though.

"Yeah, let's just see what we're getting into," I said.

Yang seemed to hear my whispers. "I swear, it's really not like that! The dungeon took creative liberty with my poster. If it's my greatest fear, then doesn't that make me the opposite of a pervert?"

Yue tapped her foot before pointing at him. "Then, are you impotent or something?"

"Are you serious?"

Ignoring their conversations, I tensed up and stared straight at Wei's arm.

"Can we use the ribbon on your arm as a blindfold?"

"Huh?" Wei looked down at his arm, seemingly surprised by the mention of it. "Oh, sure."

Unraveling it from his arm, he handed it to me. It was rather long, as it was able to be wound around his forearm multiple times, but it would work.

"Amelia, come here." I knelt on the ground before her. I wrapped it around her eyes and tucked it beneath her hair. "Is that too tight?"

She shook her head, awkwardly turning around to try to face me, but she miscalculated and was staring at the metro wall. "No, it's good. Thank you."

I smiled, grabbing her small hand to gently guide her back to the train door. "Isn't it so convenient that Uncle Wei wears this ribbon?"

She nodded, gripping my hand tightly for comfort, since she was no longer able to see. "Uncle Wei, why do you wear this ribbon?"

Wei furrowed his brows at that question and met my expectant gaze. "It's just an aesthetic thing." His intonation hiked at the end of the phrase, almost as if his statement was more of a question.

"Where'd you get it from?" I asked.

"My younger brother gave it to me a few years ago on my birthday."

"He gave you a ribbon?" My tone was lighthearted. I tried to hide my laughter.

Wei avoided my gaze, looking rather embarrassed and fidgeting with the hilt of his sword. The outdoor environment was turning into a swampy forest, but the change was slow. Yue and Yang continued their fast-paced bickering behind me.

Amelia tried to turn toward Wei, her voice soft and sympathetic. "Where's your brother?"

This innocent question seemed to throw Wei further off his train of thought, almost like he was struggling to piece together every piece. "We haven't seen each other since I moved out for university. I'm sure he's doing well. He's far smarter and braver than I am. I'll look for him soon."

[Observers Chat]
Socrates: Jia Li, when are you going to tell him the truth? You know he'll never see his brother again.
Socrates: I pity him

Observer Socrates sponsored Disciple Wei 1,000 stars.

Wei looked at the notification, puzzled, before turning to me.

"Since when did observers have that many stars? Do you know Socrates, Peijin?"

"No. Don't associate with him."

[Observers Chat]
Socrates: Jia Li, you suck. You better make sure Wei is all right, or I'll get the observers to review bomb you.

Socrates had been talking excessively recently. I couldn't complain considering each message still sent me stars, but more important people, like Athena, hadn't messaged in a while. She was most likely dealing with the intense backlash on Artemis like Archangel Michael.

I shivered at the thought, remembering how bad it was just to be sensed by the arc and karma. Influencing it must have been torturous pain, even for a goddess as powerful as Artemis.

"Peijin, I'm sorry I didn't do much during the last room. I promise to make it up to you this time," Wei said, looking motivated.

I blankly stared at him for a moment before laughing at his eagerness. "Don't worry about something so trivial. Besides, it means I make more stars."

"But if I don't prove myself useful . . ." Wei trailed off.

Wei always wore his heart on his sleeve, and he had a similar conversation in *Surviving My First Run* with Feiyu.

"Are you worried that I'll kick you from my party or something?" I asked, already knowing the answer.

"You are very observant, Peijin."

"I won't do something like that. You're stuck with me till the end of the apocalypse alongside everyone in my party, so get used to it."

Wei finally let his shoulders relax. I could tell he was nervous ever since seeing his poster. It must be such a strange experience, to see your greatest fear display right before you and have no clue what it was.

The train finally came to a stop, and the doors opened. My party entered the swampy forest, the train charging off into the distance behind us.

Custom room now commencing!
Tailored for: Disciple Cai Yang

Dark oak trees loomed over us while we stood on a slightly paved path; flickers of light managed to fight past a few leaves, creating a beautiful effect of small rays and sunbeams. Nothing seemed that out of the ordinary. Luminous flowers and fauna splattered the dark forest with beautiful bubbles of color, like large brushstrokes of soft pinks and deep oranges.

"This is the mind of a pervert," Yue muttered, taking in the beautiful sight.

Any life left in Yang after her prior verbal assault died at that very moment.

Wei hoisted Amelia onto his back, and her arms wrapped around his neck. She blew and swiped at her face to try to get long strands of his hair off her face.

Hindsight activated!

I searched through my brain in hopes of remembering an arc or plot point like this: an unsettling but breathtaking forest full of flora and fauna that preyed on all who dared enter.

This was a demon's lair—that much was certain from the beings displayed on Yang's poster. Zhige trembled in my hand with nervousness and fury, confirming my suspicion as I cautiously wielded him.

"Everyone, stay behind me," I ordered, turning toward Yue. "Is this an illusion?"

Her eyes flashed purple, and she scanned the area. Magician's Hand should have been able to confirm if we were under any demon's spell. This environment was more difficult for demonic disciples like Yue, but it also made them more powerful and attuned to other demonic energies.

She shook her head. "We're in an actual forest, but it's been layered with many others."

I gave a curt nod. That meant even if we saw an exit within this swamp, it might have been a red herring and led us further into the forest.

"Yue, stay in the back. Sandwich Wei and Yang between us. Wei, make sure you're protecting Amelia at all times."

Even though we would usually bicker over every step, this was a dungeon that the two of us had a distinct advantage in. After all, we were both women.

The deep orange and pink flowers around us seemed to shift in the ground, as if their roots were moving and trying to dig out. Some of the leaves seemed to brush against Yang's ankles, and he shivered, swatting at his legs. Oddly enough, all the flowers seemed to gravitate toward him.

My eyes involuntarily squinted with the pressure of trying to remember what I'd written.

Back in the metro, Yang's poster depicted a rather odd situation. An exhausted and panting Yang was pressed into the back of the cave out of fear, gripping the rocky stone walls to hide. At the front of the cave, countless . . . voluptuous female figures peered in, their strangely textured hands reaching out for him.

Their delicate faces were framed by luscious green leaves, and though their upper bodies looked human, the rest of their bodies were made of the twisted roots of a plant. Flowers sprouted from their skin, bright red and orange.

It finally clicked. I knew where we were. "Everybody! Shut your eyes and don't open them!"

CHAPTER TWENTY-SIX

Yang was trembling in horror now, but he shut his eyes and extended his staff, using it as a walking stick to navigate the ground.

"I-I'm really sorry, Peijin!" Yang stammered, his face green.

He must have realized it, too—these plants were alive. This wasn't a normal forest, but it wasn't an illusion either. Rather, every single living thing here was a demon, and from our presence and attention, they began to awaken.

I looked down and noticed Zhige's bright red eye still staring up at me. "That includes you, Zhige. Shut your eye."

The red eye blinked shut.

These flower demons would lurk for their victims, often young men, before emitting a pollen that would first cause cloudy judgment and weakening muscles before driving them into a state of mania, where only satisfying their deepest desire could end the suffering.

Upon seducing and murdering them, the demons would thrive off their energy. Women had a distinct advantage, since they were better at resisting the demons' temptations, but that only meant the demons would react harshly at the sight of Yue and me.

The flowers all around me began to wiggle in the ground more fervently, their petals fluttering in an awkward manner.

"Don't apologize, Yang," I said, keeping my words calm. "Let's just get out of here. What do we need to do?"

In *Surviving My First Run*, I had only mentioned such a forest offhandedly in one of my many lengthy infodumps.

"We need to make it out of the forest or kill all of the demons here," Yang responded shakily.

Just like Yue had a sense of what to do in her personal dungeon by getting to the end of the stage, Yang would have that same intuition here.

"Kill all the demons? By what? Starting a wildfire in a wetland?" I grumbled, continuing to follow the path until a small fork in the path appeared. "Besides, lighting them on fire emits a poisonous gas and an aphrodisiac. We'd all die."

The more I kept my eyes open, the more I alerted the demons to my presence, but I had to guide the rest of the party. However, once I crossed the fork in this path, I'd shut my eyes and use Zhige to guide me.

You have purchased kau chim!

A small box filled with sticks landed in my hands. These were fortune sticks by the Oracle of Kuan Yin, and they were often used for guidance. This set contained many sticks with some denoting good, neutral, and bad fortune. These didn't require any actual gambling. It worked more closely to a magic eight ball.

I shook the box and inhaled. "Should I take the right fork in this path?"

A stick jumped out, landing on the poorly paved road. I got a weird sense of déjà vu as I bent down to the ground and picked it up.

It read the worst of luck.

Blinking awkwardly at the stick, I reread it multiple times as if to confirm the result.

I put it back into the box, shaking. So what if it read "worst of luck"? That meant the other path would be better.

"Should I take the left fork in this path?"

This time, when the stick jumped out, I already knew what it was. It was, once again, indicating that this path would bring me the most miserable fortune.

I squatted, looking down in annoyance, but Wei's voice rang out over my despair.

"Peijin, are you gambling again?"

"No. I'm not an addict, Wei."

"Let me roll instead. Your luck is very bad."

I turned around and handed Wei the box, ensuring his eyes were closed. He rolled for both paths, and I eagerly looked over to see what both sticks read.

This time, they showed the best fortune for both paths.

"Are they good?" Wei asked, obediently keeping his eyes closed.

"Eh, they're all right," I replied begrudgingly. "Let's go right."

Confident in the path, I closed my eyes and led the group forward, using Zhige to feel the path. If I could guide the group out, this would be a rather simple dungeon.

While gently skidding Zhige across the ground, the blade would bump into small rocks, pebbles, and a few pieces of tangled natural debris. Occasionally, it sunk into the mushy swampland, but I pulled the blade out.

But to my surprise, on my next swipe, Zhige slid over a springy, long texture.

I froze, extending my arm out behind me to stop Wei from moving forward. The right path was straight, and I didn't think I made any unnecessary or accidental turns. I continued to swipe Zhige across the ground, but instead of a scraping sound signaling the path, I only felt the same texture.

My eyes peeled open, barely more than a sliver, then shot wide open.

Before me were beautiful rolling plains. Long green grass tinted with burnt sienna blew in the wind, and countless wildflowers sprung up from the ground, dancing in the air. Bright red poppies the color of blood, weeping lilacs, massive sunflowers—we were no longer stuck in that earlier swamp.

A beautifully eerie voice rang out from the field. It was feminine, full of vitality like it had just been touched by the dew of life.

"Someone is watching us," it called out, alluring and smooth.

"Yes, yes, yes," countless other voices echoed back.

"Oh my, how long has it been?"

"Too long, too long!"

"Oh, we are starving!"

I squeezed my eyes shut, turning around. I could hear Yang let out another scream as a long strand of grass brushed up against his leg.

"We've taken the wrong path!" I said, circling the group around and using Zhige to direct me once more.

Apparently, my luck was so bad that I still managed to choose the wrong path when both sides were supposed to work out.

You have received a new review!
<u>FUJIFIJI REVIEW:</u> ★ ★ ★ ★ ☆
Liu Peijin's luck is so bad that I'm hoping this review
boosts her karma. I have no idea what she did for her luck
to be this bad, but I wouldn't want her to be
anywhere near me. Maybe my enemy.

Thanks, I guess.

Sweat began to fall down my brow now from the beating sun, but suddenly, a cold darkness blew over me.

"Shit," I murmured, opening my eyes to find myself on a cobblestone path with vines dangling overhead.

The path only changed when everyone shut their eyes. So, I had to keep mine open.

"Peijin!" Yue exclaimed. "What the hell is going on? How the hell do you mess up walking down a straight path?"

"The forest changes anytime we close our eyes." I was borderline breathless while leading the group away. "The demons have sensed us."

Beautiful red flowers were draping from the overhead vines, and they almost looked like bells the way they swished in the wind.

We were on a brand-new path now, another fork before us. I grabbed the kau chim sticks and put them in Wei's hands.

"We're at another fork. Could you see which way would be better?"

"P-Peijin," Yang's voice sounded. "Can I please open my eyes? Yue is doing something."

Yue angrily clicked her tongue, responding in an exasperated tone. "I told you, I'm not whispering anything in your ear! Stop being paranoid."

With his flushed face buried in his hands, Yang let out a loud sigh. "But you are, I can hear it!"

Yang yelped, and I could hear loud slaps from the back of the line as Yue yelled at him.

"You just touched my face!" Yang accused.

"What the fuck are you yapping about?!" Yue retorted.

"Stop it, both of you," I barked. "I feel like I'm a babysitter sometimes . . ."

Wei rolled the box and two sticks popped out, bouncing on the ground before they came to a rest.

They both read the worst fortune.

"Oh, we're so fucked," I muttered, staring at the two sticks.

Wei suddenly stiffened beside me and placed a hand on my shoulder. "Wait, Peijin, I hear it too."

"See, I told you I wasn't doing it," Yue exclaimed.

Yang's hands were covering his ears, and he looked like he was about to curl up into a ball. "It's so loud . . . It's like my whole head is ringing."

Since I didn't flesh this forest out in *Surviving my First Run*, this apocalypse must have been taking more liberty with the idea.

My grip tightened around Zhige, and I stared up at the black sky.

"Archangel Michael or Athena, are either of you there?"

The only thing that greeted me was an eerie silence.

"Sun Wukong? Bull Demon King? Mr. Kraken?"

. . .

I hesitated for a moment before the next god.

"Eternal Wish?"

It was as if the entire forest had stopped—there was nothing here. Nothing but that deafening silence and the shifting of the plants.

"Socrates, did Archangel Michael give you any spiritual energy?"

[Observers Chat]:
Socrates: *illegible*

My eyes widened at the message, causing me to freeze in shock.

I felt hot breath on the back of my neck, causing my hair to stand as a smooth voice spoke right in my ear.

"My, my, we have ourselves a new visitor," a seductively slow voice called out.

I whipped my head around, and a red bell flower fell right before my face. With one quick movement, it blew a golden dust straight into my face, causing me to violently hack immediately.

"G-get back!" I shouted at the party members while shoving Wei back as hard as I could, immediately keeling over. An intense burning sensation took over my face, and I wiped at it.

Countless cackling voices rang out from all around me. The flowers grew from the ground, their roots exploding from the soil as they began to walk around.

Their roots and petals formed and tangled into limbs before the forest was filled with the beautifully demonic female figures.

That's right, this was Yang's biggest fear: women.

CHAPTER TWENTY-SEVEN

> Editor's Pen activated!

> Demonic plants' pollen does not affect children.

> Edit granted!

> Editor's Pen activated!

> Delay the effects of demonic plants' pollen by 6 hours.

> Edit granted!

Since I hadn't written about this world extensively, Editor's Pen had far more influence over this situation.

It seemed like any contact with observers or gods was cut or diminished, but at least skills still worked. I'd worry about the communication errors if I didn't die.

> Editor's Pen activated!

> Increase the mental capabilities for victims of demonic plants' pollen.

Edit granted!

Zhige violently shook on the ground, having encountered the demon's pollen. While Zhige wouldn't face the same urges, there was no doubt the blade would be violently enraged.

I hacked up my lungs, gripping the cobblestone with my dirtied fingers and trying to regain my breath. It felt like my entire body had been lit on fire, and the demonic figures were approaching.

Wei shifted his feet forward until he bumped into the back of my leg, and he swung his blade around to defend me.

Suddenly, I looked up, and through my fading vision, I saw the correct path to the end of the forest illuminated by a fuzzy gold halo.

"You've got to be kidding me . . ."

Only those infected by the demon plants could see how to exit the forest.

"Ha ha ha! Look at her writhing on the ground like a fish!" one of the now-humanoid flowers said. Her hair grew past her waist in long black curls.

All the figures were undeniably beautiful—with jade skin and long vines that wrapped around their curvy bodies like makeshift clothes. Lavish wreaths adorned the tops of their heads, and bright red flowers blossomed off them. With long green lashes and endlessly deep eyes, the demons were stunning. It was easy to see why this was a dream for many and a demon's lair.

For Yang, however, this was the worst day of his life.

"Ooh, who is the man next to her? Let's get him!"

Another figure joined, cackling while she circled the blind Wei, like a predator encircling prey. "I want this one."

Licking her lips, she took another step forward and extended a hand to try to touch him. "What do you think he's hiding under his robes?"

"What a conservative man! Oh, someone like him is *so* easy to break."

"One look at us, and it's over!"

Another one of the figures let out a laugh equivalent to the beauty and resonance of ringing bells, and flowers erupted all around her.

"Ah, doesn't he remind you of someone? Perhaps he's paid us a visit before."

"Now that you mention it, I do recognize him. He's most certainly someone famous! I could never forget such a handsome face."

"Ha ha! Maybe he's visited us before and led them all down here for us! Oh, how lovely!"

Wei's calm facade finally broke, and his face twisted into one of rage as he suddenly thrust his sword out and cleanly stabbed the flower demon through the throat.

"Wei didn't do that," I said. Spit dripped from my mouth, and I wiped it away. "Don't believe them."

"This pretty boy's name is Wei? Now that you've mentioned it, I certainly know him!"

"The darling of the heavens!"

"That bastard! Wasn't he the one who tried to kill Daji?"

"Ha, you're right! Has his banishment sentence already ended? Let's remind him what happens when he messes with demons."

I could feel Wei tense up beside me, and his grip on his sword weakened from his trembling hand.

"Don't listen to them, Wei! Think of nothing but how to get out of this room," I said. My voice was hoarse now, and I couldn't stop myself from gagging.

Yue and Yang circled around me, helping Wei push back the figures.

"Yue," I began to plead at her weakly while still crawling on the ground, "give Amelia headphones or earplugs. Buy the best ones from the shop. I'll reimburse you."

"Peijin," Amelia cried out for me, the blindfold still over her face.

"Shh, don't speak. Can you hand me the ribbon? Keep your eyes closed, all right?" I hushed her, gently grabbing the ribbon from her hands. Amelia kept her eyes squeezed shut.

I was glad Yue couldn't open her eyes because she would have given me one of the most judgmental expressions ever at my state. A pair of sleek black headphones appeared in Yue's hands, and she brushed back Amelia's hair and put them on.

"E-everyone, follow me. I see the path out," I said.

I pulled the ribbon taut between my hands before weaving it along the wrists of everyone else in the group, effectively creating a rope to connect all of them. My breath hitched in my throat, my face burning. I stumbled forward and tugging the rope down the path.

Zhige violently shook in my hand like it was tossed into a flaming pit, jerking.

"Stop it," I hissed, banging the hilt with my hand before wincing again, nearly falling onto the ground. All my senses had been heightened to an extreme degree.

Lugging the rope forward, I heard Wei's frustrated voice behind me.

"Peijin! What's going on? Who are all these voices from?" Wei was still swinging wildly around, and the demons were now quietly lurking beside him, dodging his blind slashes.

Yang filled in for me, most likely having connected my state with the demons. "They're flower demons, like a succubus," Yang answered, his voice shaking. "I'm guessing they've infected Peijin, but don't do anything crass. It'll only rile them up."

"How the hell did your twisted brain even come up with this?" Yue shouted angrily, still swinging her spear wildly at the demons.

The path out of the forest was a straight stretch of black soil that occasionally dipped or weaved with the forest's layout. It was a mockingly simple path, but no one could see it but me.

"Fuck, this shit really sucks," I gasped.

Spewing profanities, I felt an unspeakable rage building up in me, and my grip only tightened on the rope. Instead of responding to Wei, I could only let out a loud, angry groan and continued moving down the path.

"Ha ha, do you see the girl in the front! I think we're really getting to her," cooed one of the figures as it began to morph, changing into the figure of a young man. "Huh, beautiful?"

"Fuck!" I screamed, throwing Zhige straight at the figure while blindly wiping at my face, sweat beginning to cloud my vision. My skin was practically dripping with sweat now, and when Zhige flew forward, it was with an indomitable speed and fury.

Zhige's strikes were sloppy. The figure let out a brutish scream as it tried to grapple with the blade.

Hindsight is flickering!

Suddenly, Yang's staff elongated and stabbed straight through the demon's head, pinning her against the trunk of the tree. A splitting sound crackled before erupting, sending the demon flying straight through the shattered tree.

Wei jerked his head over to me, grabbing my shoulder firmly. "Talk to us, Peijin. What's going on?"

The demons began to turn their attention toward Yang due to his sudden attack.

For a moment, the pain fully stopped, but it struck fivefold after. At Wei's touch, I let out a surprised gasp and immediately crumbled onto the ground, writhing in agony.

"D-don't touch me," I gasped, calling Zhige back over, my mind just as foggy as my vision.

My ears rang and my entire body swayed from the pain. How was this a diminished version of the initial effects?

With Zhige now firmly in my hands, I took in a deep breath while kneeling on the ground, trying to clear my mind. Yue and Yang began to shout in the background, but I couldn't hear them over the sound of the violent ringing in my ears.

The blade shook in my grip, but I readjusted it and prepared myself, trying to calm my shakiness.

When I initially came up with this forest, I figured it would prey on men's deepest desires. Typically, it ended up being lust, and with so many demons ready to prey on such a thing, it was convenient.

But there was something that snaked around that very same desire—violence. Brutality.

Murder.

After one more inhale, I stabbed Zhige straight through my forearm.

CHAPTER TWENTY-EIGHT

Gah!" My voice cracked as I let out a bloodcurdling scream. I pulled Zhige out of my arm, and a wave of relief flooded through me. I finally managed to catch my breath as blood trickled down my arm.

There was a deep-rooted desire to inflict pain, even death upon other people, for it was simply a repressed human desire.

Sure, perhaps I was just cynical, but was there not that inherent satisfaction in revenge, relief in anger, or humor in compilations of people accidentally injuring themselves?

"Peijin!" Yang shouted, his face contorted into extreme worry despite not being able to see me. He ran forward, trying to reach me, but Wei extended out an arm to stop him.

"Don't mutilate yourself, beautiful! We can make you feel so much better!"

"Won't you bring your friends over too?"

"Aren't we just beautiful?"

Some of the figures shifted to take on the form of men, their bodies twisting and contorting horrifically; I fought down the bile rising in my throat.

"Mm, do you like this more?"

"Oh wait, maybe this is your type!"

"Or maybe you're into a woman like this."

Blood was gushing from the wound on my arm, but I tightened my grip on the ribbon and began to sprint forward, dragging everyone along with me. This moment of clarity . . . I wasn't sure how long it would last, but I had to get everyone as far out of the forest as I could.

"Don't run away from us, beautiful!"

"You bitch, get back here!"

I couldn't hear anything but my shaky breathing in my ears as I whipped my head around and faced the howling demons.

"Get the fuck away from them!" I screamed, throwing Zhige forward.

The blade seemed to have a life of its own, undoubtedly affected by the pollen—it swung itself forward and stabbed straight through a row of demons, pinning them onto a tree before slicing them apart. Golden pollen seeped out of them, yet I had distanced the group enough to avoid the effect.

The demons let out a loud, garbled shriek as they tried to escape, their bodies returning to roots and vines, but Zhige cut them apart.

One managed to bypass him, shooting forward at me, but Wei extended his sword and cleanly cut it in half with surprising accuracy despite his eyes being shut.

Scathing Reviewer activated!

A small smile spread on my face before I winced, and it contorted. I could feel the pollen's effects returning. The pain returned in volcanic waves, sending me to the ground. With a loud swallow, I got back onto my feet and dragged the group forward.

Finally, like it was depicted in Yang's poster, a cave in the distance was approaching, its entrance dark and ominous yet eerily welcoming in this hellish forest.

"Y-Yue, when this dungeon ends, you can kill Yang," I tried to joke before covering my mouth to hold back my burning vomit.

To my surprise, I heard no response but a strange, muffled sound. I whipped around to check on my party, but only their weapons remained scattered on the black road. The ribbon I was holding now reached up into the trees. Barely able to catch my breath, I looked up to see Yang's mortified expression just before me.

One of the floral demons had reached him, and its long arms wrapped around Yang's body like luscious vines on a tree trunk. It whispered into his ear, one of her hands covering his mouth and nose.

Even Zhige was now restrained.

She peeled her face away from Yang to look down at me, a large smile creeping up her face. Her mouth opened to mouth a single word.

"Boo."

Countless of the same bell-shaped flowers dropped from the canopy of trees above us; red, writhing, and plentiful, they puffed out their petals in preparation to blow more pollen over the entire party.

"No!" I cried out.

If they were hit, that was it. None of us would be able to leave this forest—best-case scenario, we would murder one another until only one remained. Even then, that lone survivor would undoubtedly fall victim to the forest's hunger.

40,000 stars used.
Strength level 15 → level 35

I clung to Wei's white ribbon. "I know it's too early, but help out, please," I begged the ribbon until it finally whirled alive and meshed into my arms. At once, I whipped the ribbon forward, tearing my party out of the demons' grasp.

With a loud roar, I swung the ribbon straight into the cave, forcing everyone out of the grip of the demons and slamming them into the cave wall. Amelia's shrill scream rang out as she held on to Yue, both of them flying in.

Wei's white ribbon lengthened significantly in my hands before it vanished into the cave as well.

Like a roaring fire, the indignant flush rushed through me like a tornado, this time even less bearable than the past. I looked down at the blood trickling down my arm in thick streaks to find it had a strange gold shimmer now as it emitted a sweet smell. The aphrodisiac had spread to every part of my body.

Whoosh.

The plants spewed out the golden pollen from their mouths, causing it to rain down all over the forest. It was as if a golden powder had been dusted all over the forest, and I hacked and tried to spit out fat wads of the aphrodisiac.

35,000 stars used.
You have purchased Book of Seals.

"Zhige," my hoarse voice squeezed out, "get the hell out of that and watch my back."

I ran, crawled, and stumbled my way to the cave's entrance. My head was violently spinning, the entire forest blurring into a mess of brightly colored splotches. My hands became the only source of my navigation by brushing against the sharp shrubs and gripping onto patches of spongy moss.

I was so close to the forest's exit. So close. If pollen wasn't littering the forest and I could drag the party out now, I could make it to the end with everyone in tow—but I didn't have that energy. I couldn't put them all in harm's way, and my blood was already overtaken by that same golden sheen.

"Yue?" I croaked. "Is Amelia all right? Yue?"

My eyes could no longer adjust to the constant fluctuations in light, and I swayed at the cave's entrance like a wickedly intoxicated woman; however, I made sure not to step in any closer.

"Yue?"

"Medusa's head. Use it."

"I can't. This forest was made by Asmodeus, and these demons don't have eyes the way we do. It'll only make them pause."

A heavy silence followed.

"Why won't you come into the cave?" Yue's voice was firm and commanding.

I let out a weak laugh. "I'm glad you're all right, but close your eyes. You're making my job harder."

"Why won't you come into the cave?"

Just to sustain this brief conversation, I had already peeled off all the skin on the back of my hand. Kraken's mucus might have a hard time fixing this one.

I squatted down to the ground, flipping open the Book of Seals. Its old pages loudly fluttered in my bloody hands.

Even if they wouldn't forgive me, this was the only way I could ensure that they would all survive. If I stayed in the cave with them, it would be equivalent to locking them up with a ravaging bear. If I left the cave, they would come out and meet my very same fate.

My fingers dipped into the gushing blood from my arm, coating them in the sweet red liquid before I dragged them across the cave floor. My entire arm was completely gored at this point, but it was the only way I'd be able to transcribe the images from the Book of Seals.

I stood up, looking at the two bloody seals in front of the entrance. Because my blood was infected by the pollen, it contained a greater amount of spiritual energy, and it would be strong enough for a seal.

Yue appeared just in front of my face, but her eyes were still shut. She must have felt her way to the cave's entrance by dragging her hands along the cave walls.

"Peijin. You promised you wouldn't leave."

I wondered if she wanted to add "me" to the end of her sentence.

"I'm not leaving," I replied nonchalantly.

> **Disciple Yue activated Lie Detector!**
> **Lie Detector confirmed Disciple Peijin's words as false.**

Yue's lips pressed into a thin line.

"I'm sorry."

"What are you trying to atone for?"

I ignored Yue's question and turned away from the cave, looking back at the forest. Zhige was zooming around beside me, protecting me from the ever-approaching demons.

"Don't ignore me, Peijin!" Yue shouted, finally opening her eyes and trying to storm past the cave's entrance before an invisible barrier threw her back.

Jumping back onto her feet, she pounded on the invisible barrier with the look of a desperate, crazed woman.

"Peijin? Peijin, what the fuck is this?!"

Zhige flew back into my hand, and I tightly held on to the hilt. In my other hand, the Book of Seals continued to flutter in the wind. I stole one last glance at one of the seals I'd copied.

The Seal of Imprisonment.

CHAPTER TWENTY-NINE

I gave a warm smile while staring at the forest before me, the countless demons already swarming around me.

"Feel free to open your eyes now, Yue. Lead the party straight to the right no matter what you see. That's where the real exit is." Just to get out those words, I had to dig my nails straight into the soft flesh on my shoulder and tear off chunks.

Two seals were protecting the cave: the Seal of Imprisonment and the Seal of Isolation. Although typically used in grueling punishments, here they would prevent anyone from entering or leaving the cave, ensuring my party's safety.

Seals were complicated—they could be broken by an overwhelming amount of spiritual power, or if they were weak enough, just by repeatedly trying to bypass them. The stronger the user and the more power invested, the more powerful the seal.

It wouldn't be long before my party broke past the sloppy seals, but the pollen coating the forest would dissipate by then, and I'd hopefully have resolved the rest of the situation.

"Ready, Zhige?" I croaked softly while watching the blade's bright red eye swiveling in frantic circular motions.

With a deep inhale, my breath steadied for just a moment before I lunged forward, screaming at the figures.

"Doesn't this one have so much personality?" one succubus teased before he sidestepped me and extended his arms. They shot out in twisting roots, dodging and adapting to all my movements.

My sword pierced straight through where its heart would be before I twisted the blade in its body and swung it up toward the sky, splitting him in half.

Letting out a brutal shriek, the demonic man seemed to shift forms, taking on the appearance of Yang.

My entire body was trembling with the excitement of finally being able to attack and kill something, but at the sudden morphing in appearance, I froze, my eyes widening.

"I-it hurts," Yang pleaded, reaching out a trembling and gentle hand. "P-please, it hurts. It hurts."

His delicate hand reached up, brushing my hair off my forehead and away from my eyes.

I pulled back slightly, my back straightening, and the demon immediately took advantage of my weakness. It let out a shrill cackle, completely exuberated, before roots burst out from the ground and grabbed my legs, pulling me down.

"Gah!"

The contact was enough for me to collapse on the ground, wheezing.

"Z-Zhige!" I gasped, and my eyes squeezed shut in the struggle to hold myself back.

Flying from my grasp, Zhige easily cut me out before stabbing through the demon's head, pinning him against a tree. It tried to retake the form of Yang, but Zhige slashed the demon into small pieces before it dissolved into ash.

"So, her taste is the young man from her group, huh?"

"The poor girl has a crush! How cute."

"Ah, he's kind of frail, isn't he?"

"If you don't want him, I'll take him."

"Stop jumping to conclusions, you tramp!"

"Who the fuck are you calling a tramp?!"

Freed from the demon's roots, I jumped back to my feet and reached for Zhige, turning back to the dozens of demons in front of me.

I was seething now, my head throbbing and vision turning red. I could feel heat course through my entire body, causing me to tremble with excitement. I lunged forward again, swinging Zhige wildly at anything near me.

The bell flowers fell from the canopy and attempted to bite me, but with a quick swoop, I managed to slice their stems. They fell to the ground with a loud thud.

They continued to writhe, however, and their small rows of teeth gnashed together while they inched toward me. Their movement resembled an awkward snake's—they slid and bounced on the ground like water droplets in a hot pan.

Raising my foot in the air, I stomped down repeatedly on the flowers, smearing them into the ground.

Bam! Bam! Bam!

With a delighted giggle, I maniacally squished them under my foot before dragging them across the soil floor, no longer paying any mind to the pollen that still floated all over the forest ground.

My arm was completely gored at this point, and it hung limply at my side. Still, I forced my way forward and continued to attack the demons.

"Please don't hurt us!" A slithering root wrapped around my ankle.

"Come on, beautiful, why are you being so difficult?" Another gripped my wrist.

"We promise that whatever pain you're feeling right now, we can make all of that stop."

"Don't you want to feel good?" One trailed up the small of my back and nuzzled against it.

I grit my teeth, letting out another shout before another fiery wave ripped through me, causing me to collapse on the ground.

"Fuck all of you, goddammit! I'll tear every single one of you out of the ground, one by one!" By now, I was virtually blind, my vision clouded by a blurry red sheen.

My hand felt the ground in a futile attempt to grab onto Zhige, but the blade had already returned to the fight and continued to slash, gore, and mutilate the demons around me.

I was writhing in pain on the ground, curled up into a ball. I hissed through my teeth, gripping tightly onto my abdomen. This was by far the worst pain I had ever experienced in my life, and I was going to completely break apart soon.

I wouldn't need to be seduced to be convinced into giving up—the mere thought of any potential relief was enough for me to contemplate the option.

10,000 stars used.
Hellfire Lighter purchased.

Since this was a demonic swamp, an ordinary flame wouldn't be able to wipe out the demons—even if one were to possess a powerful, undying flame, hardly anything would combust in such a marshy, wet landscape.

However, with the abundance of pollen littering the ground and air in a gold sheen, the forest would practically burn down in a beautiful flurry of red flames. That being said, what I had told Yang earlier was true.

The plant's combustion would release wildly toxic gas into the air, and not even a pigeon's lung could defend against it. I tucked the lighter beneath my body while I continued to fight against the riveting pain.

"Aww, look how flushed she is!"

"Oh, but can you imagine how the rest of her friends would look?"

"You're so right! This girl is kind of ugly, but it's all right."

"Ha ha ha!"

"Careful, you're making her even more angry!"

Zhige was wildly fighting against all the demons now, barely in control of its own movements. The pollen clearly affected the demonic weapon's sensibility, and it was beginning to get bogged down behind a web of thick, ever-growing vines.

One of the female demonic figures slunk over toward me before squatting on the ground before me, pouting. "You're having a hard day, huh?"

She reached out a blossoming hand and brushed it against my ear, still pouting and cocking her head like a curious puppy.

"Give up yet?"

Turning away from her, I clicked on the edge of the lighter and kept it close to my side, sending a small blue flame bursting up, the edges tinted a soft orange and red.

By now, my entire arm was a dripping mess of tainted, iridescent blood and pulled flesh. The moment I dropped this lighter, it was practically a death sentence for me.

The cave was in the clear, though, and I supposed that's all that mattered. The pollen hadn't spread that far, and if they did escape, they could make it out of the forest. I was sure of it.

"Zhige, stop," I called the blade back, shakily peeking over my shoulder and staring at the creature before me. The demon was now sporting Yang's appearance, and more red flowers bloomed from his lean and bare chest.

Zhige was coated in the vile remains of demonic spiritual energy, but it still trembled with lust for more. The weapon was truly horrific—no wonder the karmic powers had such a strong initial reaction.

The demon's eyes widened in shock, halting after raising a pointed arm to attack me. Its figure was still one identical to Yang's, but my vision was failing, so I couldn't make out any of its figure other than those orange eyes.

"Is that . . . hellfire?"

I smirked, sitting up and letting the lighter fall onto the cushioned pollen surrounding me.

"Go fuck yourself."

At once, a horrific flame burst into life before my eyes, scorching me and the demons as they let out vile, desperate shrieks.

CHAPTER THIRTY

The flames grew higher and higher, licking the forest's canopy and immediately charring the moss and vines all around it. I felt the searing heat on my skin and instinctively flinched, but my mind was still too clouded for me to process what was happening. The flames seared straight into my skin.

Physique level 30 → level 33

Upgrading my Physique level would only delay the inevitable, but instead of feeling immense pain, each burn and scar left me with relief.

Demon shrieks and cries were heard all around me, the demons growing their arms and aiming for me in one last, futile attempt to kill me, grab me, and take me down with them. I took in a staggered breath and black smoke filled my lungs; I could only convulse on the ground.

Hellfire was unspeakably potent, but in my state, I could hardly move. My body hit the ground before I could even process the movement—the flames were unwavering as they grew even higher, burning the pollen and exploding in bright yellow sparks with every combustion.

The tattoo on my arm began glowing so brightly it could even be seen beyond the flames of hellfire. I would have tried to tear it out of my skin, and not just for the relief it would bring, but my other arm was far too gored for me to do so.

Instead, I planted my teeth in my arm, firmly clamping down on my skin and tearing at the tattoo before squeezing my eyes shut—the heat was so unbearable it almost felt like my eyes would start boiling.

Well, in the apocalypse, my death could've been much worse. At least the poison meant I would have a bit of peace in between the waves of pain.

Scathing Reviewer activated!

My eyes widened, shaking unsteadily.

"Yang," I gasped before wheezing heavily, resuming my feeble attempts to crawl away.

If I died, his stupid fear would undoubtedly be worse. I had no idea what would have caused women to be his biggest fear, but whatever it was, I didn't want to inflict a gaping wound upon him.

I spat out an entire strip of my skin, watching it be consumed by the fire, but the tattoo seemed embedded through my entire arm. It even appeared on my muscle. It burst with white light, and I looked away out of shock.

For a moment, out of the eruption of karmic yellow sparks and in my delusional state, I thought I saw a figure—a potentially frustrated expression was drawn on its face before it turned its back on me.

Squinting my eyes, I tried to make out the details in the twisted expression, but my vision was far too blurred. It was wearing long flowing pink robes, and its hair was partially tied up.

Did it come from my tattoo? Whatever. I was too high for this.

All I could manage was a pained groan. I writhed on the ground in a failed attempt to get away from the flames. The black smoke was blinding me now, and my lungs were filled with smoke and ash.

Suddenly, I felt a thick cloth being patted all over me, trying to put out the flames. Two arms lifted me up, initially slipping when trying to maneuver around my limp body, but they eventually succeeded in throwing me over their back.

Letting out a pathetic sound, I felt another wave of instant relief before pain tore through me. I cried out, my entire body feeling as if my skin were being peeled off from the burning sensation.

"I'm sorry."

Yang. He was here, doing his best to cover his face and hold his breath, but his face was twisted in excruciating pain. His skin was practically purple with how hard he was trying to hold his breath and avoid breathing in the toxic fumes.

"D-don't touch me," I pleaded, my eyes squeezed shut from pain.

Yang shook his head and turned around, struggling to find out where to go. He held Zhige tightly at his side. The forest changed its appearance again, switching between mountains, flower fields, and the dark forest. I feebly extended a hand toward the right path. With a sudden burst, Yang massively upgraded his agility level and brought me to the edge of the forest.

He finally breathed out, and Yang fought for his breath, hyperventilating. His skin was bright red, and his eyes bloodshot.

A vicious scream rang out as the entire forest lurched forward, thousands of roots and vines darting forward toward Yang. The trees grew rapidly, towering even higher, and began to form one collective figure.

"How dare you? How dare you!"

The voice was shrill and crackled—with each word, it strained and croaked like an ancient tongue. A giant hand reached out, smashing into the ground just before Yang. Sharp wooden and stone spikes burst out of it into fractal-like branches, one of them hooking the fabric of his pants but missing his skin.

If he was stabbed, he would be infected by the pollen.

"Z-Zhige," I stammered, reaching for my blade to help.

To my surprise, Yang firmly slapped my hand down before he threw his staff high up into the air; it grew to the height of a small building and he leapt up, grabbing onto it before swinging it firmly into the forest ground.

The entire world shook from the impact, and the train behind us jumped into the air before falling against the ground in a crash. The wind from the impact blew back the entire forest, raising the flames higher and higher on the demonic figure.

Letting out a deafening screech, the demon pried at its wooden figure, stripping off piece after piece and causing a gooey sap to seep out like blood. It shimmered in the light, clearly full of the pollen.

"I'll kill you! I'll kill you all! How dare you!"

I could barely hang on to Yang's neck as we landed on the ground, the entire floor splitting below us. He kept one of his hands to stabilize me while the other spun the staff high above him, cutting back the countless splintering branches.

His nervousness was apparent by the way he chewed on his lower lip, but he did not fall back against the demon. With a strong leap back, we made it to the metro and jumped into it before I was placed on the ground.

Hissing through my teeth, I let out a pained groan as soon as his contact ceased. My entire body writhed on the floor, blood seeping from my mutilated arm.

I tried blinking rapidly to clear my vision, wanting to check if Amelia was here. Yue had her held tightly on the opposite side of the car, blocking her view. Thankfully, she was still wearing the headphones.

My breathing came in a shaky pattern of shallow wheezes, each one forcing my chest to rise before falling deeply. The hot rush raged through my body, and I let out a loud scream, curling into a fetal position on the ground.

"Peijin! Peijin!" Yang shouted, rushing over and hovering his hands above me. He was clearly deeply frightened by my condition, and he reached down to grab my gored arm.

My unquenchable thirst for blood returned when I looked up at Yang, seeking any solace from the pain that I could get. I was disoriented, unable to piece together a single logical thought outside of what I needed in the moment.

It would be so easy to kill Yang right now. In one movement, I could swing Zhige up and slice Yang in half.

Then everything, this pain, this sickness, would cease, even if it were just for a moment. If I killed everyone on this train, I was certain I could find relief.

Gripping Zhige, I lifted the blade into the air and stabbed it straight through my shoulder, pinning myself onto the floor of the train.

I let out a blood-curdling screech, tears springing from my eyes as my entire body reeled once more. My mind cleared from the violent act for just a moment, and I could finally make out Yang's and Wei's faces.

"Oh my god, Peijin!" Wei screamed, darting toward me. "Stop it! Stop!"

What ignorant words from an outsider who did not know this story.

"Wei! Help me pin her down! She'll kill herself!"

In my moment of clarity, I leaned up, sliding up Zhige's sharp blade. "Don't touch me! You'll make it worse!"

I was losing blood at an alarming rate, but at least the searing pain paused. I gasped for breath, appreciating every single one because in a few moments, I'd suffocate.

Yang trembled above me, his hands hovering over me. He didn't look much better than me—his skin had taken on a sickly hue from both the stress and the few breathes of toxic air he inhaled.

"P-Peijin, I don't know what to do," Yang whispered, swiping through the Azure Dragon Store in a panic.

Hindsight activated!

If I died now, the party would move on. My dungeon room would be skipped, and they'd continue without me. They'd make it just fine with all of their current sponsors and weapons. And, when they made it out, it was clear that the rest of my party was on good terms with Feiyu. They'd be better off if anything.

But that was only if they made it through Wei's room. In fact, I even doubted my own capabilities to survive that room.

"Don't even think about something stupid right now, Peijin," Wei ordered sharply, his voice a higher pitch as he wrapped bandages around my arm. He was already halfway complete, working almost expertly, but I didn't even realize he'd begun.

My eyes widened at his words before I gave a small smile. I could feel the effects of the pollen growing once more, and I winced, my entire body trembling. Above this scene, I could see the silhouettes of the gods watching.

Fuckers. If they could watch, then they should do something about this mess. And goddammit, where was Socrates?

[Observers Chat]
Nipon23: don't be a failure in both your lives.

I seriously hated that guy. He only showed up at my worst.

"Yang, wait for me," I suddenly ordered, heaving.

"What?"

"Knock me out," I wheezed out. "Wake me up in six hours. The effects of the pollen will have worn off by then, and if you keep me up any longer, I'll end up killing someone."

I let my head fall against the train floor, and Yang raised his fist, smashing it against the side of my head.

I blacked out.

CHAPTER THIRTY-ONE

P eijin."

I became aware of my existence. My entire body was throbbing, and my senses were recovering. My spit was thick in my throat, and every time I inhaled, my nose let out a small whistling sound.

"Peijin, are you up?"

Was someone speaking to me? I tried to open my eyes, yet they remained frozen, along with the rest of my body.

"She's been drifting in and out. I wouldn't be surprised if she passes out again."

"Come on, wake up, Peijin."

"Are you stupid? She's not Sleeping Beauty. You can't just will her awake."

"..."

"Hey, couldn't Demonic Fire wake her up?"

"Are you trying to kill her?"

"No, but since demons all hate each other, then wouldn't Demonic Fire burn the pollen out of her body or something?"

"You sound like a European doctor from the 1800s."

"Could you not speak nerd for a second?"

"Both of you need to stop arguing with one another. The train is moving. We need to figure out what's going on. Yang, you should carry Peijin if we need to run."

"The doors won't open until I select my skill, so we should be fine. Has your sponsor said anything?"

"Archangel Michael? He'll be in trial for a while since he colluded in Yue's dungeon and got caught." The voice paused for a moment, and I could make out the slight banging of a weapon on the metro ground. "Apparently, Peijin's luck is bad. She's popular with the observers, though, so at least that helps her get some spiritual energy."

"Why the hell would they like Peijin? All she does is get mutilated every room."

"She's done it for you, too, so be more grateful Yue."

"Hey, I am grateful!"

"There's no point in bickering with everyone, Yue. Hey, are her eyes opening?"

"Ugh, I told you, I'm not—"

Before me, a fuzzy figure with long black hair suddenly hovered over my field of vision, peering closer before gasping and jumping back.

"She's awake!" Yue looked back down at me. "Peijin, can you speak?"

My eyes twitched, not having adjusted to the harsh train lights. I attempted to lift my index finger, yet it remained glued to the metro floor. My eyes darted around the car, and I found Zhige lying beside me. The blade's red eye was peering straight into my own eyes.

"Mmph," I groaned, squeezing my eyes shut and letting out a heavy sigh. The moment I moved, I knew I'd be met by searing pain.

Two large heads popped into frame, both looking expectant. Finally, the tiny blond head of Amelia joined.

"Peijin!" she cried, immediately jumping onto me and sobbing violently. Her fists crumpled up the fabric of my top, and I let out an involuntary, pained wheeze.

[Observers Chat]

Nipon23: welcome back jia li. your room starts soon ;) nervous?

Socrates: Do you know how hard it was to get observers to give you spiritual energy?? You're lucky you're popular because it's the reason you didn't die! Your whole party was scrambling, spending thousands of stars on medicine while I was stressed out of my mind trying to get you spiritual energy

Socrates: You drive me absolutely nuts, Jia Li. Don't go out and almost die like that again.

I shut my eyes again. Socrates was acting like a mother scolding their teenage son for staying out too late.

Yue lifted Amelia up by the back of the blue hoodie, holding her in the air like a small dog. "Hey, don't just jump on Peijin like that! She's delicate!"

"S-sorry Yue-ayi!" Amelia apologized through her flurry of tears. Wiping her face, she looked at me with furrowed brows.

I opened my mouth, trying to force the words out of my throat, but my voice failed me, and I looked as idiotic as a floundering fish.

Scathing Reviewer activated!

"Amelia," I croaked, reaching up to pull her out of Yue's grasp.

Suddenly, with a loud and violent creak, the entire subway lurched forward, causing everyone to stumble. I slid down the floor of the metro while Yue fell straight on top of me with a loud "hmph."

My entire body jolted forward as I let out a loud cough, immediately shoving off Yue. Finally, I caught sight of my arm.

The one with the black tattoo was still perfectly intact, but my other was bandaged from my hand up to my shoulder in a thick, white bandage. For a moment, it reminded me of a similar one wrapped around Wei's forearm.

I sat up and struggled to pick Zhige off the ground, the hilt feeling too heavy in my weakened state. When I finally got a firm grip on it, I sliced a small cut through my wrapped shoulder.

"Peijin!" Yang shouted, immediately slapping the blade out of my hand.

The blood that streamed came in red streaks—there was no more of that golden sheen. Letting out a loud sigh of relief, I chuckled for a moment.

With a closer look, I could now see that Yang's lower lip was peeling, dried blood in the cracks. He must have been nervously chewing on it again. My eyes lingered there for a moment before I gave a weak smile and looked away.

"I'm fine," I reassured him. "I was just checking something. How long was I out? I told you to wake me up in six hours."

Yang turned away from me, and Wei responded instead.

"Let's just focus on beating the next room," Wei said.

I glared at him, finally sitting up and taking Amelia's hand. "I need to know."

An awkward silence ensued, and my eyes drifted up to Yang's face. The cut was already gone.

"Four days," Wei murmured.

My body automatically got up before I could even process the words. Four days? Did I lose a lot of my observer and god viewers? Wei's room was already going to be a challenge to push through without their support.

"Peijin," Yang exclaimed, gripping my shoulders tightly. "Don't overexert yourself. Your room is next."

"What skills did you get? Have you picked yet?" My voice was rushed, but my words were still slightly slurred from my exhaustion. Even if my physique levels were constantly increasing, it didn't prevent mental burnout.

"Peijin."

"How many stars did you spend on treating my arm? You should've saved it. I'm fine."

Four entire days because I was knocked unconscious. I was the party leader, yet I couldn't even push through a single arc. I was holding my entire party back now.

How could I have let it get here?

"Peijin!"

Two firm hands gripped me, jolting me back to reality.

Yang's orange eyes glared into my black ones, and I finally noticed the deep purple eyebags that seared into his tender undereyes.

"Peijin, stop it. Calm down."

With a heavy inhale and exhale, he signaled for me to control my breathing.

Even now I was reliant on him. I was reliant on him in the first chapter, the second dungeon, and the third dungeon. If I was being honest with myself, who was saving who?

"I'm sorry," I blurted out.

[Observers Chat]
Socrates: Now I feel bad for yelling at Jia Li. You'll be fine, okay?

Observer Socrates sponsored 20,384 stars.

[Observers Chat]
Socrates: There. That's how much your party spent on your medical treatment. Archangel Michael probably would've paid for it.

There was a strange burning sensation in my nose, but I couldn't pinpoint the foreign sensation until my vision blurred.

I was tearing up. Did I really become this weak?

Scathing Reviewer is flickering!

My chest tightened. The anxiety of my room and what awaited me only made things worse. I hadn't cried since I was a child, back in that house. I couldn't cry. If I did, he'd be back, with that horrifying grin stretching from eye to eye, and then it'd begin again. I'd be back to fourteen years old and weak and helpless and still that same goddamn insufferable bitch, and—

Warning! Scathing Reviewer is flickering!

Yang's voice cut through.

"Peijin, are you okay? Is this about your poster? Your room?"

Scathing Reviewer deactivated.

My face fell immediately before I covered up my blank expression with a smile. A strange numbness took over my body, and suddenly, nothing was felt.

I stood up, my shoulder sloping downward. My hand was reassuringly placed on Yang's shoulder. "I'm fine now. Let's pick your skills and move on," I said. "We're more than halfway done with this arc."

Yang flinched in surprise, blinking at me and picking up on the strange shift in my demeanor. "Sorry?"

I approached the chest, looking at the three glowing skills before me.

POTENTIAL SKILLS LIST
Cloud Somersault
Alternates
Yaogui's Mask

"Which one do you want?" I asked firmly, looking blankly at the options before me.

"You're being weird again, Peijin," Yang replied softly. "Do you want to rest a bit before your room?"

"No, I don't. I don't want us to fall even further behind."

He bit down firmly on his lower lip before sighing, grabbing his temple with his hand. "I was thinking of Alternates. Yaogui's Mask sounds advantageous since it'd give me a similar power to the . . ." He trailed off awkwardly.

Yaogui's Mask would allow Yang to inherit similar traits to that of the flower demons, such as shape-shifting, seduction, and mind control—however, there was no doubt Sun Wukong would vehemently protest this.

After all, he used the term to berate the Bull Demon King.

"Did you talk to Sun Wukong?"

Yang gave a curt nod. "He didn't like the skill."

"Mm. Unfortunate."

Amelia looked up from below me, gesturing that she wanted to be lifted into the air. I picked her up stiffly, my body still aching and sore, before I gently threw her over my good shoulder.

Yang stared awkwardly, his brow furrowed, before he looked away again. It was obvious that he had much to say, but there were no words to communicate what he felt.

For an avid reader like him, that said enough.

I continued speaking: "You should pick Alternates, unless you plan on running away from everyone with Cloud Somersault."

Both skills were also inspired by Sun Wukong—by pulling out pieces of his hair, Sun Wukong was able to duplicate himself countless times, hence the name Alternates. Sun Wukong was also known for his incredible speed and distance, often flying on a cloud to efficiently fight and travel.

"Don't joke about something like that," Yang snapped, his expression only growing more tense. "You're acting strange." His cheeks were slightly sunken in, as if a deep hunger had been affecting him.

"I'm not joking." I shrugged. "You don't understand what the rest of this world holds. You're just as naive as when we were talking in the pest control van after I forgot the steamer."

"You're being cruel."

"Are either of us surprised?" I smiled. "You know me better than anyone else."

"And I'm telling you that this is psychotic," Yang said firmly, his expression hardening.

Amelia shifted in my arm, holding me tighter. "Peijin, please don't be upset at Yang-shushu."

"You're too old to be acting like this, Amelia." My hand brushed through her hair before I placed her back down on the ground.

I was promptly shoved forward before a hand spun me around. I was lifted up into the air by my collar.

"The fuck is wrong with you, Peijin?" Yue barked, glaring at me while thrusting me forward by my collar again. "Do you know how hard it was to keep you alive? You wake up, and this is how you start acting? This isn't a fucking hospital!"

I smirked up at her, tilting my head to the side as I gripped onto her arm. "Yeah? And who are you? Tell me that."

"He Yue. What bullshit are you spewing now?"

"Yeah, that's your name, but what was your childhood? How'd you grow up?"

"I grew up in a tumultuous household, got into university, and now I'm stuck here with the likes of you."

I let out a cold laugh, looking down at the metal ground. "Tell me one thing you were doing a week ago. Before all this."

"I was coming back from school the day the apocalypse started."

"That's not what I asked you. What did you do a week ago?"

Since the apocalypse began, I debated whether or not any of the characters I met were real. Did they have lives outside of what I'd written?

Yue froze for a moment, as if unable to recall anything she had been doing. She paused before glaring at me, pulling me up and slamming me against the wall of the car, her eyes dark.

It was just as I thought. None of my characters had lived through their backstories. All they had were prescribed memories that I spoon-fed them.

Her chest heaved up and down unsteadily now, and she trembled as she held on to me. "What did you do to me?"

"I didn't do anything," I said, finding my nose burning again. "I'm just a pest control worker, right?"

Wei shoved the two of us apart, separating us with his sword. "Yue, stop. Her room is next, and you know that anxiety."

Wei continued, "But, Peijin, this is stressful on all of us. Even if you are the one doing everything, don't pretend that it doesn't impact all of us the same. Sacrifice yourself, jump into the front lines all you want, but don't sit back here and pretend we don't exist every time you do."

But you aren't real. I know that now for certain was what I wanted to say. It was foolish of me to have thought I found something here. Yue didn't need me in her room, and in Yang's room, I became nothing other than helpless and humiliated.

I really was a loser.

The sound of a faint grumbling threw me out of my thoughts. I looked over to see Amelia avoiding my gaze while clutching her stomach. Immediately, my tone softened.

"Are you hungry?" Of course she was. It had been days that they waited for me to wake up.

She shook her head, her blonde hair swishing. "I'm not."

I walked over and gently took her hand. "There's food in the next room. Let's eat there, all right?"

Scathing Reviewer activated!

Yang selected Alternates, and the chest disappeared once I collected the rest of the rewards and placed them in my bag. The train shot forward once again.

". . ."

The metro car was filled with a heavy silence for a moment while I avoided the sight of my poster, instead staring down at the top of Amelia's head. I gently patted the top of it, ruffling it.

Nothing but the racing sound of metro tracks surrounded us until Yang finally broke the silence.

"Peijin, are you going to be all right in this room? It looks like it's a—"

"I know," I replied softly. "Thank you."

The metro finally came to a screeching halt, the doors sliding open.

Custom room now commencing!
Tailored for: Disciple Liu Peijin

CHAPTER THIRTY-TWO

My party stepped out of the train and were greeted by the inside of an eerie, ominous home. The lights were off, the house tinted in a cool shade of blue. The looming front door was behind us.

I looked around, inspecting the home. The childhood paintings stuck to the fridge and the decorations on the fireplace—it was just as I remembered.

"Peijin, where are we?" Yang asked, standing just beside Yue with his staff drawn.

Instead of replying, I confidently turned toward the front door and flicked on a switch, and the house now flooded with a cool, flickering light.

"A home," I replied nonchalantly, doing my best to keep my heart at a steady beat.

Amelia stood just beside me, and I comfortingly rubbed her back. "I'm going to take the hoodie for this room, okay?" I reached down to remove the blue hoodie before sliding it over myself.

"Ha, think you need the extra protection?" Yue asked, her eyes mocking and her grin wide. After my earlier explosion in the car, I could tell things were tense again between my party.

I had no idea why I acted so cruelly to them earlier. I would blame Scathing Reviewer except for the fact I only acted cruelly after it deactivated. Was that just my normal personality then when Scathing Reviewer wasn't influencing me?

I was the most unworthy being in the entire world.

Yang elbowed Yue sharply, causing her to whip her head around and glare at him. Wei let out a loud sigh and pressed the back of his hand against his temple before standing between the two.

I could only channel my emotions to the one thing I knew best. I gripped Zhige tighter and wielded it confidently before me.

"We need to get through the end of this house. I know where the exit is."

Bending down, I lifted the petrified Amelia up and threw her over my shoulders, holding her legs.

"Peijin, I'm sorry if I made you upset," Amelia murmured, wrapping her arms around my neck.

"Don't apologize when you didn't do anything wrong. I should apologize to you for snapping. It's okay to be scared."

Amelia's grip tightened, and she buried her face in the crook of my neck.

"Peijin, you still haven't told us what this room is," Wei chimed in, uneasily looking around. We had progressed through the first room and walked down a hallway, now approaching a large granite kitchen island.

Without a moment of hesitation, I easily turned around and flicked on the light switch, not even having to look to see where it was.

"Mm, I guess I haven't."

My shoulders tensed a bit more in this room, and I swallowed loudly. My anxiety only grew with each room. It had been so long since I last stepped foot here, and I did my best to keep my bitter memories at bay. The kitchen where my mother used to cook me breakfast, the couch where my dad watched football— my hands were trembling.

Wei was eyeing me nervously, picking up on my cues. "Aren't you going to tell us?"

"No need to."

Yue scoffed, rolling her eyes. "Can you stop acting like some emo teenager? You knew the rest of our rooms, but you won't tell us yours? The hell is so scary about a house?"

With a loud swoosh, a gust of wind flung open a window and blew past the group, causing the dusty curtains to blow around them.

Letting out a surprised yelp, Yue clung onto me before awkwardly pushing herself off and running over to the window, shutting it. Her expression was flustered, and she turned around, waiting for me to make fun of her and say something crass.

But my vision was longingly locked on the sofa in front of the television. I wondered how my dad was. Was he also going through the dungeon rooms right now? A part of me hoped I would run into him—a part of me hoped I'd never have to see him again.

The sound of Amelia's stomach grumbling jolted me from my thoughts. I made my way over to the fridge.

"You're not seriously thinking about eating out of there, are you?!" Yue exclaimed, her mouth wide open in a mixture of disgust and shock.

I rolled my eyes. Of course, I had no plan to eat whatever rotting demonic food was in the fridge. I subtly opened the Azure Dragon Store and purchased all the meals I thought Amelia would like.

1,935 stars used.

I opened the fridge anyway, blue sparks flying out before revealing a massive fridge filled to the brim with delectable frozen foods and ingredients.

Standing there frozen in shock, Yue watched as I let Amelia pick ingredients out, all of them looking fresh or recently purchased.

Even the freezer was filled with food, like pints of ice cream and congyoubing.

I looked over her shoulder, signaling for everyone to join.

"Grab whatever you want. Let's spend some time eating so we have enough strength for the next rounds," she said, giving a small smile to everyone before stepping to the side.

"Are you sure it's safe?" Yue asked, suspicious.

"I made sure it was."

Disciple Yue activated Lie Detector!
Lie Detection confirmed Disciple Peijin's words as truth.

Yue's face fell, giving me a doubtful stare. "And how did you 'make sure' of it?" she asked with air quotes.

My eye twitched before I reached into the fridge, grabbed a pear, and threw it straight at Yue's head before turning back to Amelia, gently speaking to her.

"What do you want? I'm not a good cook, but maybe Yang is."

"What's that?" Amelia asked, pointing at the frozen package of congyoubing.

My brow furrowed, and I looked at Yang and Wei for help, but they only shrugged back. I wasn't sure how to explain the dish to her, given she must have never tried something like them before.

"They're scallion pancakes. They're very savory," I said. "My mom used to cook them for me all the time, but it's been a while since then."

"What are scallions?" Amelia asked.

"Vegetables."

"No thanks."

"They're really good. I think you'd like them," I said.

"Peijin promises?"

"I pinky promise."

Amelia enthusiastically nodded.

I pulled the pack and tore it open, picking out one of the frozen pancakes. I opened a cupboard without hesitation and pulled out a pan—turning to the large pantry next, I grabbed a bottle of olive oil. It was instinctual.

"Yang, can you cook for her? I'd butcher it."

It wasn't difficult to see Yang's hesitant expression, but he hid it under a warm smile; the typical orange glow of his eyes was muted to a deep brown from the dim lighting.

"Sure. Could you grab me a set of chopsticks and a plate?" he asked.

I turned around and reached under the granite countertop, pulling out a barely visible drawer and taking out the plate and chopsticks before setting them on the table. I lifted Amelia onto a barstool and spun it, causing Amelia to let out a small laugh before swaying from her dizziness.

Yang walked over, turning the knob on the stovetop until a small red fire blossomed. He put the oil onto the pan before swirling it and dropping the frozen pancake in.

"You seem really familiar with everything here, Peijin," Yang said as if it were a casual conversation.

"Do I?"

"No, you must just have really good luck at finding things," Yang replied sarcastically.

I glared at him. "That wasn't funny."

Yang pouted before flipping the pancake, causing little bits of oil to spray out. "Your poster was a family photo taken in front of a house, was it not?"

My shoulders tensed, and a heavy silence followed. Yue was right—my posters showed my mother holding me as a baby while my father cheered beside us, delighted by the new home we had purchased in the background. Not one part of the image seemed terrifying. If anything, it was a beautiful family photo.

"I wouldn't know," I muttered coldly. "I don't have any family photos left."

"Aww." Yue pointed at Yang and me talking while Amelia spun in a chair just before us. "Don't these two look like a cute couple? Let's all go around and talk about our childhoods while in the middle of an apocalyptic dungeon."

Wei barked back at Yue. "Hey, every room has been different, and I'm sure Peijin knows what she's doing. She's gotten us this far."

Shrugging nonchalantly, Yue turned her focus back to the conversation between Yang and me.

"Really? How come, if you don't mind me asking?" Yang asked politely.

I braided Amelia's curly hair, trying to distance myself from confronting my childhood. "I moved out when I was fourteen."

"That sounds more like running away than moving out, no?"

I smiled bitterly. "Yeah, I guess I did run away."

"Bad parents?" Yang asked. He said it like it was the simplest thing in the world, and like there would be no judgment between us. It was my first time ever talking about myself since the incident.

"No. They were good to me," I replied honestly.

I couldn't say anything more because of how clouded the memory was. When I ran away a little over a decade ago, I buried those memories deep in my head, refusing to ever unearth them again. It was like blood on my hands that I finally washed off, but the feeling of blood lingered. My childhood haunted me, and I couldn't stop myself from trembling in fear at the thought of confronting my lost memories.

"I grew up in a haunted house," I finally said.

Yue paused for a moment before she burst out laughing, reeling over the granite table and smashing her close fist against it. "You mean ghosts and ghouls? Ha ha ha, you're kidding me!"

It wasn't that unbelievable of a statement considering that those very same ghosts and ghouls had manifested themselves into our lives, but my face flushed a deep pink.

"I mean it! This place is seriously haunted! The things here, they follow you around."

"Yeah, yeah, whatever. So, what, the boogeyman is your biggest fear? Did he grab your foot when you accidentally let it hang over the edge of your bed?"

I let out a loud sigh, running my fingers through Amelia's hair and undoing the braid. "It was a long time ago. I don't remember it anymore."

"Fourteen isn't that long ago."

Wei looked embarrassed now at the mention of my age and shushed Yue. The scallion pancakes were finally finished, and Yang placed it down before Amelia. She tore it into smaller pieces before biting down on it, her face lighting up at the savory and crunchy yet still-soft texture.

"You said your mom used to cook this for you, right?" Yang asked, tearing himself a piece. "Where is she now?"

"No clue." I shrugged. "Doesn't matter to me. I haven't spoken to her since I was eight."

"O-oh, I see." Yang flushed out of embarrassment.

I snickered at his response. "It's fine. It was forever ago. What's more important is what's going on right now. This is another bad room for Amelia. Wei, I want you to protect her."

"What?!" Yue exclaimed, offended. "What makes him so special?"

I rolled my eyes. "I'm not going to put a kid in the hands of a devil. Besides, your weapon is a spear. You're like a Neanderthal."

Yang slunk forward until he could whisper into my ear: "If this is a bad room for a little girl like Amelia, and this is the haunted house you grew up in, something bad happened to you, too. Right?"

My body immediately stiffened, but I continued to chew on my lower lip. Yang was so perceptive about my every move that it was scary.

"The only bad thing that's about to happen is me murdering you."

"Ah, with how bad your luck is, I'll end up becoming immortal," Yang teased, smiling and pulling back. "None of us will bring it up, but we're here for you," he reassured me.

"I know," I said. "That's why I'm not shitting myself right now."

I turned around and grabbed some instant noodles from the pantry, taking them out. "We should start moving soon. These have meat in them, so let's fill up then go." I slid the vegetable one over to Yue before heating up water.

"Did you seriously just give me the worst flavor?"

"If you eat your greens, you won't be so ugly."

"What the fuck?!" Yue exclaimed, furious.

I shot a teasing smile at Yue while I poured the hot water into her cup of noodles. In the swirling water, however, small vortexes formed to resemble a lopsided smiley face. My blood ran cold at the image, but I did my best to hide my expression, preparing the noodles for the rest of the party members before saying, "I'm going to use the restroom."

My heart was pounding in my chest, the blood pumping loudly in my ears. There it was—that fucking smiley face. There was no boogeyman or ghoul in the closet; this smiley face was my tormenter, the ghost that haunted me. I could feel my grip on my memory slipping, and I steeled myself.

Six steps down the hall and first door on the right. The second floorboard would creak, and I dutifully avoided it like second nature. I stepped onto the bathroom's tile floor and quietly locked the door, making sure not to bother anyone, before darting over to the toilet.

"G-gah!"

I hurled into the toilet, the vomit coming up like red slime with mysterious pink chunks. My stomach was too empty for any large chunks to be found in it. Wiping my mouth on my sleeve, I gasped before vomiting again, struggling to keep my hair out of the way.

"Goddammit . . ."

If I could change one thing about my life, it wouldn't be the pest control, the shitty writing contract I signed, or even my awful personality. If there was one thing I could change, I'd erase that smiley face from my memory forever. Maybe then, I wouldn't have turned out so twisted.

I stood up, flushing the toilet and wiping my face. I stood before the mirror now and stared at my appearance, inspecting my face even though my arm was still bandaged. My eyes lingered on something reflected behind me in the mirror.

A smiley face was carved behind me out of the black shadows, and it almost seemed to press out of the walls, reaching toward me.

"Ex . . . cuse me . . . Who are you?" a voice croaked from the wall, warped and vicious.

"You can't do anything. There are people at home," I replied.

Whenever Smiley entered my childhood, only that line would get it to leave.

At once, the smiley face shrunk back into the wall before dissipating. I turned on the faucet and splashed water on my face, letting out a shaky breath. I felt myself slipping further and further into the room, no longer certain of who I was.

"I am Liu Peijin," I said.

My reflection stared straight back at me, unwavering.

"I am Liu Peijin."

I repeated the words, but this time, they were more desperate.

Black eyes peered back.

Nothing was out of the ordinary.

I unlocked the door and walked back to the kitchen.

Yue's feet swayed back and forth as she kicked the base of the granite island. "Don't you think we should have Peijin sit back during this dungeon? She's been doing too much."

Wei slurped up the last of his noodles greedily while nodding. "For once, I agree with you, Yue. I want to take the burden off her shoulders, but she'd never let it happen."

"Ahh, do you really think she'd tell us the truth about this room?" Yue sighed. "There's no way this is just a haunted house. There haven't even been any ghosts."

Yang had cooked up slices of meat and was feeding them to Amelia, her face a wide grin.

Yue's eyes darted over to him. "Hey, you've known Peijin for a while, right? Was she always like this?"

He stopped to ponder the question for a moment, looking at the wall across from him. "I didn't speak to her much about our lives. We were just co-workers, after all. It was difficult getting close to her because she always had this big wall up around her. But that's what made it rewarding when she did reveal a bit about herself."

Yue looked at him suspiciously but let it slide, pouting as she rested her face on her hand. "I doubt she'd have any other friends. Do you think she'd worry about us so much otherwise?"

"How could she not have friends?" Wei blurted. "Do you not look up to her?"

"Eh?! Look up to her?" Yue's face warped as if she were about to profusely deny the statement, but she suddenly looked down at the ramen in embarrassment. "I might admire her intelligence, but so what? I admire a lot of people, okay?

"Besides," Yue went on, "she said something earlier that . . ." Yue's voice trailed off, but I could feel her hard gaze piercing into me.

I was standing in the hallway, but I was staring at an open bedroom door, my jaw slightly agape, my eyes wide, and my clammy hands trembling. A figure turned to me from inside the room, his voice hoarse and weak.

"Peijin, is that you? Oh, my sweet girl, you've finally come home."

CHAPTER THIRTY-THREE

Yue froze. Instead of seeing Peijin in the hallway, she saw a teenage girl blankly staring into a bedroom.

Her hair was that same, familiar bob with bangs, and those small black moles were dotted right beneath her pink lips and left eye.

It was Peijin, but she was significantly younger.

"Peijin, is that you? Oh, my sweet girl, you've finally come home," a chilling voice called out from inside the room.

The younger Peijin absentmindedly blinked before taking a step closer, her hand grabbing the door as she peeked in.

"Dad?" Her voice was feeble and shook unsteadily.

"Peijin!" Yue screamed. "Get away from there!"

Yue darted forward and thrust her spear forward, and the edge hooked onto the sleeve of Peijin's hoodie. Yue dragged Peijin back down the hallway, and Peijin seemed to age before her very eyes, growing taller and her face maturing.

Peijin's eyes widened in surprise, and she gripped onto Yue's shoulder and steadied herself, blinking rapidly.

"I . . ." Peijin trailed off, looking at the ground with an odd look of shame and embarrassment while Yue shook her shoulders violently.

"The hell were you thinking? You can't even take a piss without supervision!"

Peijin's face immediately hardened. "Nothing even happened! I wasn't going to go in there." Peijin shoved Yue's hands off.

The party stared at the open bedroom door for a moment, faint light flowing out of it and into the long hall, yet nothing else moved or made a sound.

Wei was wiping Amelia's mouth with a paper towel, since she had soup smeared all over it. Yang was the one to intervene between Peijin and Yue again.

"Peijin, what did you see in the room?" Yang asked softly, lowering his head to be eye level with her.

Biting her lower lip, Peijin averted her gaze again. "It was a ghost, so let's just get to the end of the house," Peijin replied again in her cold, firm tone. "Is Amelia done eating?"

The change in subject was obvious to the party—Peijin always did it anytime she felt uncomfortable with the progression of a conversation. In a way, it was her method of regaining control. And they let her.

It was difficult to press Peijin when she did such a thing. With her being so many steps ahead of the rest of the party, it was undeniable that the rest felt inferior standing beside her. As long as they believed Peijin knew what she was doing, they reluctantly accepted it.

Amelia gave a vigorous nod at Peijin's question, slurping up one last noodle before Wei wiped her face again.

"Peijin, do you want any food?" Wei asked.

"I'm not hungry."

Yang placed a hand tentatively on the small of her back. "You should eat something."

"I'm going to bite your hand off if you keep bothering me," she warned.

He rolled his eyes before he walked over to the pantry and grabbed a pack of mini chocolate sprinkle cupcakes.

"Still think so?"

Peijin stared hungrily at the cupcakes for a moment; at work events, he had often teased Peijin for having the diet of a fourth grader at a birthday party. A small glint in his eyes signaled their shared memory.

"I should probably get some sugar in my system," Peijin mumbled.

Yang gave a slight smile before waving her over. Peijin stuffed her face with some of the cupcakes. After she finished, she opened her bag and dumped the entire pantry of food in once making sure Amelia was full.

Amelia was now hoisted over Wei's shoulders as the group got ready to head down the hall. Wei's typically lighthearted voice seemed to fill with more and more anxiety as his room approached, but he kept his tone steady with Peijin.

"Do we need to worry about what's in the room?"

"Are you scared of old man ghosts like Yang is scared of women?"

Yang's jaw fell as Yue burst out laughing, reeling over.

"I'm seriously not scared of women anymore!" Yang exclaimed, the atmosphere in the house finally starting to lighten up. It even seemed as if the lighting became brighter, and Peijin's face lit with a cheeky smile.

Yue grinned, leaning in closer and speaking to Yang in a mocking tone. "Aww, is that so? If I lean in closer to you, are you going to start shaking again?" she teased. "You should've seen how scared you were when we first met."

Even Wei was chuckling now as he spoke over their bickering to answer Peijin's question. "I'm not scared of old men, but I am scared of ghosts."

"Then I'll protect you, even if this is my room." Peijin smiled.

"You really don't seem that scared or bothered. Do you have no fears?" Wei said, looking up at her with admiration.

Peijin let out a boisterous laugh. "Me? Scared? Never."

Wei paused for a moment, giving her a questioning look. "You looked like you were going to cry a bit ago, just before this room."

"..."

Peijin scoffed before pointing Zhige at the two arguing members and then at Amelia.

Since Yang's room, Peijin was off-balance—every word and jarring act was a misstep in everyone else's eyes.

However, she seemed to finally regain her brash but cunning impulsiveness. It was familiar. They found comfort in that.

"Let's get out of here."

Peijin led them out, still avoiding the creaky floorboard as they progressed down the long hallway. The rest trailed closely behind her or just to her side, ensuring that nothing could happen.

Since Yue was standing just beside Peijin, the small changes in her appearance grew all the more apparent.

"Peijin?"

Peijin had shrunk considerably, her cheeks widening and long lashes batting above big brown eyes. With every step, it was like watching her backward in a timeline, turning younger and younger until she looked only a few years older than Amelia.

"Peijin!"

She continued walking, not seeming to hear Yue until Yue firmly grabbed her shoulder, spinning her around.

Peijin looked just like Amelia had on the first day they met—her eyes were large and watery, her brows furrowed, and her lips quivering from immense fright.

"Oh, fuck me," Yue mumbled, gripping Peijin's hand and pulling her farther down the hall. Kneeling down, she looked at Peijin, staring at her.

"Who am I?" Yue quizzed, her hand raised at the rest of the party members behind her to silence them.

Peijin gulped, her eyes rapidly darting around. "Where's Feiyu?"

"The hell are you calling out to him for?"

"Where is he?" Peijin pleaded, virtually sobbing now as snot dripped down from her face, and she wiped it away while looking up at the ceiling, as if anticipating something to pop out. Despite her shaky voice and red eyes, tears never once spilled. "He's the only one that can help me escape!"

Peijin tried to scramble away from Yue, crying out and throwing her small fists at her, but Yue easily held Peijin's little body in place. Peijin's eyes darted around until they locked onto Wei.

"Wei! Wei!" Peijin cried. She was hyperventilating now as she clung onto Yue's pant legs. "Where is Feiyu? He's your party leader, so where is he?!"

Yue took a step back, looking down with a mixture of both disgust and pity. Yue was stunned to see her idol reduced to such a weak state, but she regathered her composure and lifted Peijin up.

"I'll bring you to Feiyu, all right? Come with me." Yue carried her back toward the kitchen. "Do you recognize this man with the orange eyes?"

Peijin's eyes glossed right over Yang and remained locked on Wei; Peijin was a few years older now but still young.

"Wei, your fate is black," she choked out, her face drawn into many worried lines.

It looked as if Wei had seen a ghost. Even though Peijin kept the source of her knowledge a secret, often dodging Yue's questions, Wei viewed Peijin's words as truth.

"You're lucky you always have that angel with you. I wouldn't have added him if—" Peijin was at the kitchen again, and she finally became aware of how she was wrapped in Yue's arms, bridal-style.

"Eh?"

Yue let go, causing Peijin to slam into the ground with a sharp yelp.

"The fuck was that for?! Why'd you carry me back here!" Peijin shouted, glaring at her. "Weren't we heading down the hall?"

Wei blankly stared at her before he finally gained the courage to speak. "Do you not . . . remember anything you just said?"

"What are you talking about?" Peijin said, looking around at everyone for some kind of explanation.

Yang let out a frustrated sound. He walked over to the granite kitchen island, burying his face in his hands. "We can't just walk out. When we do, you turn into a kid."

Peijin burst out laughing, wiping away tears from her eyes. "Are you playing some joke on me? We were talking the entire way."

"We weren't, Peijin. You rambled about Feiyu 'saving' you."

Peijin's expression had never dropped so fast, her cold expression immediately present. "I wasn't."

"You were. And you said Wei's fate was black, and he was lucky to have an angel."

"Consider it a prophecy. Maybe a moment of fortune telling came over me," Peijin replied, turning to head back down the hall again.

> **Disciple Yue activated Lie Detector!**
> **Lie Detector confirmed Disciple Peijin's words as false.**

Peijin's expression flared with rage. "How many times do I need to tell you not to use that on me?"

"Then explain this goddamn room to us, Peijin!" Yue retorted. "None of us know what to do when you start regressing in age!"

"I—I can't," Peijin stammered, wild. "I can't even explain this place to myself! This isn't real—I buried it long ago."

"Are you a fucking riddler now, too?"

The tension was growing between the two, which was nothing out of the ordinary, until they heard a small squeak from behind them.

Whipping their heads around, they noticed Amelia wide-eyed, staring at the ceiling of the kitchen.

A warped, smiling face was pressing through the ceiling, pushing farther and farther out until it was finally low enough to press its nose against Amelia. The gray ceiling warped around it like a thin skin getting ready to burst.

"No . . ." Peijin whispered, her shoulders slumping. "No, no, no! Amelia!"

At once, countless faces and arms shot out from all over the room, grabbing Amelia and tugging.

> **Scathing Reviewer activated!**

CHAPTER THIRTY-FOUR

Peijin

I reached for Amelia as she let out a bloodcurdling scream, her limbs being tugged in every direction.

"Stop it! Stop!" I flung Zhige forward, but Amelia summoned the dire wolf first. With a bright blue flash, it appeared and snapped at the ghost's hands.

The moment the grotesque hands were approached, they retreated back into the walls, meshing with the wallpaper and melting into it.

The house completely stilled for a moment, and Amelia fell onto the back of the dire wolf. The beast looked over its shoulder and licked Amelia's face, saliva coating her skin, and she wiped it away with a grossed-out expression.

Zhige flew back into my hand, and I rushed up toward Amelia and held on to her.

"Are you all right? Did it get you?" My hand brushed off the saliva from her face, flicking it onto the ground.

"I—I did good right? I summoned the wolf and fought it off myself." Amelia's voice quivered despite her brave words.

"Yes. Very good." I ushered the words out before pulling back, staring at her for a moment.

The entire house rumbled beneath our feet, and I grabbed Zhige in preparation.

Hindsight activated!

The entire house began to rotate, the floor becoming the wall then the ceiling. Furniture flew everywhere with each rotation. Amelia hung onto the dire wolf as it slid down the old wood floor and tried to claw its way up like it was running in a hamster wheel.

Yang extended his staff in the middle of the room, so it would connect with the floor and ceiling. One of his hands hung onto the staff, and his other arm held on to Yue.

"Peijin!" Wei's firm arms grabbed me, and he jumped around the walls of the house with me in his arms. It was like sprinting on a treadmill full of obstacles.

He was slightly panting, and his long hair was tied into a thick bun on the back of his head.

"Are you all right?" he asked.

I blinked at him for a moment, dodging the swinging lights as glass shattered across the wildly spinning room.

"Wei . . . I . . ." What could I even say to him? I was feeling something indescribable—a part of me wanted to reach out and embrace him, even if it were just for a moment.

But another part of me quivered from disgust at the thought of his very existence.

How could I, someone of no redeeming qualities, ever be worthy of his protection?

My entire body tensed up as I spotted the front door. A grotesque smile was plastered on it. Its lips were pulled up all the way to its ears, two dimples just beside its squinted and beady eyes. It grew larger, spreading through the wallpaper.

"No, no, no," I repeated, my voice getting stuck in my throat like a thick ball of spit. "He's here! He's here!" I screeched, pounding on Wei's wide back as my entire body heaved with every breath.

Yang reached down and grabbed onto Wei's arm, flinging him down the hall. I could already feel my body beginning to shrink, and I couldn't do anything but tightly grip his white robes.

"Feiyu . . ." I quietly croaked, holding on even tighter. My nails almost tore through the thick, enchanted fabric of his robes.

The house tilted again, this time tilting to an angle. Wei began sliding backward, but he dug his sword into the wall and still held on to me tightly. The ceiling was spinning around until it became the floor under Wei's feet.

I perked up instantly, Hindsight revealing the threat.

"Wei! Move! He only lives on the ceiling!"

The distorted, wicked smiley face appeared just below his feet, and everything froze. The house stopped spinning, and the sound of crashing furniture ceased. Wei's panicked face remained staring at me, Yue was clinging onto Yang, and Amelia was buried in the dire wolf's fur. But all of them were frozen. Even Zhige's red eye no longer twitched.

And the smiley face stared at me, its face twisting.

I tried moving my body, but it was like I was paralyzed.

"Please, please, please," I whined, my voice high-pitched.

Not a sound filled the house, nothing but an increasingly eerie buzzing that filled my mind.

"You're not real," I asserted firmly. "You're not. You can't do anything to me." I glared at its twisted eyes.

The smiley face opened its mouth, its dry, cracked lips morphing grotesquely.

"Be quiet." Its voice was hoarse and cracked like an old radio.

"You're not real," I repeated.

Its smile grew, its lips squeezing together to shush me. "Be quiet!" Its voice boomed louder now, a harsh whisper.

"No! Someone's home!"

I shook my head again, feeling my nose burn as tears came again. Bile burned my throat, and vomit threatened to burst from my mouth.

"Someone's home! You can't do anything! They're here right now, you motherfucker!"

"Be quiet! Be quiet!" Its voice grew louder and louder until the entire house shook around me, any remaining glass exploding all throughout the house.

"Be quiet, be quiet, be quiet, be quiet!"

"Stop it! Someone's home!" I screeched, wanting to cover my ears or shut my eyes, but my body refused to comply.

"Stop it! Stop it! Fuck you! Goddammit, I'll kill you!" I cried out.

"Peijin!"

A woman's voice pierced through the horrific cries of the beast, and my eyes searched for the source. Tears welled in them, but they were yet to fall down my face.

Yue appeared before me, and her hands had torn through an invisible layer like it was a film of thin plastic. Her upper body squeezed through, her eyes were glowing a deep purple, and her black hair was billowing all around her.

"Peijin, get out of here! It's an illusion!"

I blinked up at her, finally regaining minimal control over my body.

"Yue?"

So, this was what the power of the Magician's Hand looked like.

"Don't just blink at me, you idiot!" she shouted, her voice strained by her fury. "Get out!"

Gritting her teeth, she pushed her way through the illusion, tearing it apart with her bare hands before she extended out a pale palm before me.

"You're so pathetic sometimes, and it really pisses me off!" Yue said.

I laughed, looking down at the ground to find that the face had contorted into one of wild anger, its eyes wide and brown pupils quivering with rage.

My hand moved forward before I finally gained the strength to grab onto Yue, clasping onto her hand for dear life.

"You really are a bitch, Yue."

She tugged firmly on my arm and sent me flying out of the illusion until I crashed onto the ground of the haunted house.

"Humph!"

My body was a bit younger—I was maybe nineteen or twenty now. Looking up at the group, I apprehensively met their gazes.

I was shaking like a wet dog from my nervousness, but I attempted to quell it. To my surprise, despite the arguably horrifying event that just transpired, they didn't even look remotely fazed.

Were they even human?

Yue crossed her arms in front of her chest and glared at me. "You're awfully weak."

"At least I'm not stupid. I was the one who told you to pick Magician's Hand, wasn't I?"

Yue's jaw gawked as she looked stunned by my callout.

"I should've left you with Mr. Smiley," Yue said.

"Is that what you've named it?"

She raised her hand like a hand puppet and made it look like it was babbling nonsense.

Laughing lightly, I shook my head before I grabbed her sleeve and pulled myself up. "You really do get on my nerves. Thank you."

Suddenly, I heard a deep snarling from behind me, and I turned to face the dire wolf. Its massive lips were peeled back, revealing a terrifying array of menacing teeth. It snapped blindly down the hall, hackles raised.

"Peijin," Amelia's small voice called out. "There's something wrong here. I mean it."

Out of all of us, Amelia looked the most scared, her hands shaking violently in front of her.

"Do you have some kind of animalistic instinct now?" I teased her, ruffling her hair.

She furrowed her brow and her voice hardened, much to my surprise. "No, I'm serious. There's something wrong down the hall."

I pulled my hand back slightly, surprised by her reaction. "Let's get through it quickly."

"We can't," Yang interrupted. "You can't leave the dungeon room as a baby."

"Once we get out, I'll be normal."

"*If* we get out," Yang said, his orange eyes piercing my soul.

I pursed my lips, looking around the group. Since when did they start arguing with me?

"I'm telling you I'll be fine."

"It's not a risk I'm willing to take."

Finally, the crackling noise in the house came to a still, and the house no longer shook. I paused for a moment, hesitant to trust my senses given the past illusion, but when I met Yue's gaze, she gave me a reassuring nod.

"Let's go now. You guys can drag me back here if I turn into a whiny, gross baby, all right?"

Yang furrowed his brow but relented, standing beside me with his staff prepared. Wei flanked me as well, and Amelia rode in front atop the dire wolf. Yue walked behind, stepping on the back of my worn-down shoes to trip me.

We passed the bathroom door. Was I seventeen now?

I wondered if Feiyu would have gotten through a room like this by now.

Wait, what the hell was I doing thinking of a brute like him?

Bedroom door. Fourteen.

"Peijin, you can't walk past this." Amelia turned back, her wide blue eyes looking dark and foggy.

I was barely taller than her at this point, though part of it was because I had always been short.

"We're almost out. The exit is just after this hall."

I pushed her aside, standing by the slightly opened door.

"See? Don't worry, Amelia. I trust you guys to protect me, not that I'd need it," I replied cockily.

Amelia winced and moved to cover her ears for a moment, the dire wolf shifting uncomfortably.

"Peijin—"

A massive sound exploded from the front of the house, causing Amelia to shriek in fear. Debris erupted straight toward us. Yang whipped his staff forward and whirled it in the air, knocking back most of the chunks while Wei caught the rest.

"Peijin, are you all right?" Yang said, looking over his shoulder to where I was standing.

Or where I should have been standing.

Countless hands had erupted from the wall unnoticed, their long, pale blue fingers gripping onto my skin with overwhelming power. They were slick and sickening, forcing their way all over my face and even into my mouth, stopping me from crying out.

Before I could let out my muffled scream, they sucked me through the open bedroom door as it slammed shut behind me.

Bang!

CHAPTER THIRTY-FIVE

I wriggled in a feeble attempt to escape before the arms shifted behind me, merging together like clay until I felt only two, thin arms wrapped around my waist.

"Peijin, my sweet girl," a voice cried.

His voice was exactly as I remembered, even though I hadn't heard it in ten years. It was unmistakable.

"You're home."

My entire body trembled—was this fear? No, no it wasn't. I wasn't scared of anything in this world. I only felt deeper emotions. Anxiety, distrust, fury.

Relief, too.

"Hi, Dad." My voice quivered.

He finally pulled back, and I turned to face him. If I wasn't in my fourteen-year-old body, he'd be a bit shorter than me. But now, the top of my head barely reached his shoulder.

Small man that he was. Thin and tired eyes and a lean frame—but there was an odd serenity around him that made you feel all right.

"You never came to visit me."

I chewed on my lip. "I didn't see why I would."

He frowned, his shoulders falling. "You never even told me why you left."

What could I say? He was right. After I left home, I never reached out to him again.

"Can you blame me for that?"

Dad laughed a bit, a small chuckle as he gently rubbed his temple with his hand. "Your mother was the same way when she left. I admired her indifference for a while."

"Oh, fuck you," I spat.

"You were fourteen when you left. Do you know how petrified I was? I did everything for you. You know that. And how did you repay me?"

My nostrils flared, and I took a step back, pressing my palm against my chest. "You don't get the right to say that!"

"Would you have done everything I did?"

"Stop it."

"You can't keep pretending that it didn't happen."

"I'm not pretending!" I exclaimed, my back to him as I refused to meet him head on.

"Do you know how hard it was for me? Do you think I wanted to do it? For weeks, months at a time, I woke up and went to work until my skin turned black from the ash and metal, just to provide for you," he whispered, and the hairs on my neck stood up. "I did it because I love you, Peijin."

"Stop it."

"And then you left me with nothing. You really are just like your mother."

I whipped out Zhige and spun around, roaring. "Shut the fuck up!"

He gently stepped forward, pushing the side of Zhige aside with a frail hand. "Do you think I wanted to do that? All for a daughter who would grow to hate me?"

My entire figure trembled, my nose beginning to burn. "I don't hate you, Dad." The words involuntarily cracked as they came out.

I continued speaking, trying to even my tone. "But you should've never done it. I would've starved with you instead if it's what it took."

"And that's why you left? Without saying anything?"

"No," I choked out, "I left because of when you kept inviting your friends over for drinks until you'd black out. You were supposed to protect me. I was fourteen."

Tears welled up in my eyes, blurring my vision—but I fought them back. I blinked away my tears.

Dad's eyes widened with realization at my last words, and he rushed forward, pulling me into a tight hug. His frail arms suddenly felt wide and comforting around my small body.

And there we were—a thin, sad man hugging a small child in the middle of a cluttered room.

I remained frozen for a moment; I could feel each of his shaky breaths against my chest. How long had it been? A decade. I knew that, but now, I finally felt the weight of that time come crashing down on me.

My arms wrapped around his back as I buried my face into his chest, the top of my head barely reaching his chin.

"I've missed you so, so much, Dad." I choked out the words, melting into the hug.

The room remained silent apart from the sound of my beating heart and a strange radio static in the back.

". . . You're tarnished."

My blood ran cold at his words, and I stiffened in his grasp.

"What?" I whispered, trying to pull back, but his grip was too strong.

His fingers dug into my back. I felt the blue hoodie try to pull me away to no use.

"You're dirty and tarnished. How could you ever think someone like you was worthy of love?" The static grew louder and louder until the ceiling started to contort again, and a smiley face began to appear.

"Stop. Stop!" I shoved him back and held Zhige in front of me.

Zhige was far too big in my child-size hands, and the blade shrunk to be more manageable.

The smiley face on the ceiling dripped down like slime. It landed on Dad, absorbing him and taking his form.

I scrambled onto my feet, running toward the bedroom door and pounding on it.

"Help! Help me!"

Desperately shaking the doorknob, I peeked through the cracks in the door, watching shadows walk outside in the hall.

But none came to help me.

"Feiyu!" My voice grew louder.

"Feiyu!" A pleading whisper this time.

I lifted Zhige and tried to stab the blade through the door, but my blade bounced off, and Zhige went flying out of my hands.

I scrambled forward, trying to reach for the blade while Zhige also moved toward me, but I froze at the sight of the smiley face.

The smiley face had taken over Dad's body, turning into his friend. His face was just as I remembered—that terrifying, drooping smile that never went away, and the eyes that stared straight through me.

Even now, Dad couldn't protect me.

The blue hoodie jerked upward, trying to get me to stand on my feet. I complied, barely able to stand, before loud banging emerged all around the room.

The sound was so unbearably loud I thought the entire room would crumble in on itself at any moment. Each bang caused a seismic trembling of the room, throwing me back on the ground just before the smiling beast.

"Who are you?" I screeched, swinging Zhige wildly.

"Peijin, Peijin, Peijin, Peijin," my name echoed all around in short cries throughout the room in sync with the banging.

That's right—this room was my childhood bedroom with the trashy posters and books littering the ground. Here I was all over again, fourteen, begging, and with the smiling face in my room.

And Dad was gone again. Mom was never here.

"You're not my Dad! He'd never say such a thing!" Finally, my blade sliced open the chest of Smiley, causing a black goo to erupt from him in a thin line.

Suddenly, a chilling, high-pitched voice rang out from behind me.

"Of course not! But he sure thought it."

I whipped my head around and saw myself.

Myself?

No, that was impossible.

But she looked just like me. I recalled that time when the apocalypse had just begun, and my reflection in the rearview mirror of the pest control van moved on its own.

"Found you."

The figure's black, shoulder-length hair was styled, her bangs perfectly curled. Her skin was glowing white, and her red lips curved into a bright smile as she let out a childish laugh. Her laugh sparkled the way a young girl's would, not matching mine at all.

I looked over my shoulder, and the smiling man was gone. Instead, this freakish woman teleported into its place.

"Who are you?!" I looked at the woman with insane eyes. I crawled backward before I got back onto my feet. The room was silent, no more of the static exuberating out.

"Me? I'm Liu Peijin," she said.

"Don't spew such bullshit, you motherfucker!"

She knelt to match my eye level, speaking in that same, overly enthusiastic voice. "Ha ha, I can't believe I only now meet you here! Although, I do suppose it's a bit unfortunate in these circumstances."

My chest heaved with every breath I took. "What the hell are you bitching about?"

She entirely ignored me. "But oh well, I guess it doesn't matter. You reap what you sow, especially when it's about *you*."

She cupped her face in her hands, staring at me with her long eyelashes fluttering in the dim light.

I finally caught my breath, barely able to keep up with my thoughts as I stared at her.

"You're wrong. My father never thought that. He would've never said that, either."

Letting out another chirpy laugh, she reached into her pocket and pulled out two orange lollipops, handing me an unwrapped one and popping the other into her mouth.

I slapped it out of her hand and watched it roll across the ground.

"Oh, but he really did think that, Peijin. You won't believe how much he thought about it."

"Shut up! Who are you?! You're not real! You're not my fear, nothing of the sort. How did you get here?!"

"He thought about it so much, Peijin, that it drove him insane." She whistled toward the end, emphasizing it while she drew circles with her finger beside her head. "After you ran away and he found out what happened between you and his friend, he quit and searched everywhere for you.

"Don't you remember how happy he was the day you left? It was your birthday, and he managed to get the whole day off to spend with you. I guess you would've never known though, since you ran away that very day and left poor old Dad all alone."

My heart fell at those words. Every memory came rushing back, and there was nothing I could do other than grip my head in pain and stumble back, collapsing against the wall and hyperventilating.

However, she continued speaking in that childlike tone, and I listened to the words that flowed out of her mouth—my mouth.

"When you never came home, guess what he did!" She popped the lollipop out of her mouth with an exaggerated sound as her other hand pointed into the roof of her mouth.

"*Bang*. Don't worry, though, it didn't hurt him at all. Clean shot, straight out of the back of his head."

I lunged forward and gripped onto her throat, slamming her against the ground. My hands gripped tighter and tighter around her neck as I tried to crush her airway and strangle her.

She wasn't impacted in the slightest. Her face twisted into an innocent grin as she continued to speak to me. "I suppose it's only fair of me to tell you what happened with your mother, too. Congratulations, Peijin! You're an older sister! She's even in Feiyu's party. Isn't that so funny?"

Scathing Reviewer is flickering.

Incomprehensible emotions welled up inside of me as I tightened my grip, smashing her head against the floor repeatedly. My teeth were so tightly pressed together I was surprised my jaw hadn't broken. "Stop it! Who are you? You're not the real me!"

"Ha ha ha, of course not! I'm no monster. Who are you?"

I screeched, spit flying out with each word as my hair was plastered against my sweaty face. "It doesn't matter who I am! I'm the real me!"

"Oh, silly girl, of course it matters! But, it's alright. I already know everything about you, 'Jia Li.'"

She let out an innocent laugh again, and she easily sat up, removing my hands from her neck without looking at all impacted.

"As for me? I'm Karma."

CHAPTER THIRTY-SIX

My breath caught in my throat as my grip on Zhige's hilt loosened for just a moment.

"Karma . . . ?"

My voice was barely more than a whisper. This wasn't possible. Karma wasn't a being. Karma was a system, a control variable. Karma stopped godly beings from overstepping. It was purely reactionary force.

And I was an older sister. How could I describe the feelings storming through my heart at this moment?

Karma gave me an eerie smile before she sat up and put the orange lollipop back in her mouth, swirling it around as if nothing in the world could bother her.

"Cat got your tongue?" she jokingly called out. "I don't see why you're so surprised. After all, you created me."

"No . . ." I said softly, backing away from her. My feet tripped over themselves, but I steadied myself. I wielded Zhige before me apprehensively.

She—no, it—knew who I really was. This was impossible. I never told anyone, even my party. At most, Yang had an inkling. But for Karma to have called me Jia Li like that?

Was it Socrates, then? Or Nipon23 who leaked my identity?

My breathing came in rapid succession. I continued to shake my head, stepping back until my back pressed against the dark walls. I jolted forward, petrified by the thought of Smiley returning to grab me from behind.

"You're not real. I never created you!"

The haunting figure that looked just like me reached out to cup my cheek.

Zhige shot out from my hands as she approached—the blade pierced through her overwhelming aura and slashed a large *X* into her abdomen.

She remained still for a moment before blood sprayed out of her wound, and she stumbled backward, tripping over her feet before she stabilized herself on a sofa.

Even her movements mimicked mine.

"Ah, Haimo!" she exclaimed in a cheery tone. "It's good to see you're still alive! I'm sure he'll be thrilled to hear the news."

Zhige froze at the sound of its past name, or perhaps the mention of its past owner, before it darted forward again with enhanced speed.

Steadying herself, Karma easily reached out a hand just before the tip of the blade. Zhige stabbed straight through her palm, but she easily pulled out Zhige and spun the tip on her finger like it was a basketball.

"It's such a misfortune to see how weak you've become under Liu Peijin. You were very formidable before," Karma said in a soft tone, almost like the one I had just spoken in. "She even gave you such a silly name, and you let her."

"Weak?! The only thing stopping Zhige is your karmic restraints!"

Zhige thrashed, trying to break free of her grasp, but Karma held on tightly. "I'm not the one stopping Haimo. You are. Haimo has enough spiritual power to break through my aura even though it's only at a percent of its power."

She gave me a bright smile again and gently handed me the blade, holding the sharp edge herself and letting me grasp for the hilt. She was far more powerful than me, and we both knew that.

"I'm surprised Haimo liked you enough to let you become its new owner. You're extraordinarily lucky, Liu Peijin."

The irony of her words struck a chord as I shouted, rushing forward with Zhige held high above me. I tackled Karma to the ground—she restrained her aura, allowing me to get near her. I knew I would've been blown away if she used even an ounce of her power.

After all, karma controlled everything. Karma was god.

What a fool I'd been.

My hands wrapped around her throat. I strangled her thin neck in my teenage hands. I watched her white skin—my white skin—turn red under my fingertips.

"What the fuck have I done?! Nothing!" I shrieked, pressing down harder. My hand ran across the ground before I grabbed Zhige and plunged it straight into her chest, twisting the blade like the pin of a music box.

But no matter how much Zhige struck her, she remained completely unfazed. Even though blood gushed out of her, I knew no real wound was being left behind.

"Everything!" she cried out, ecstatic. "You've done everything, Liu Peijin! Even if you lived a billion years and only committed good deeds, you'd never be able to pay off your bad karma."

My eyes widened with her words before they narrowed in rage.

I knew her words were true. They weren't exaggerations. Karma didn't need to lie.

"Fuck you, you bitch! If anything, you should be on my side!" I grabbed Zhige and stabbed her again, but she still smiled at me. "You knew about my past, my family, and you still fucked me over. How is that karma?!"

She was pinned beneath my body as I relentlessly stabbed her, covering both of us in blood. With a laugh filled with the same joy of a young child's, she answered sweetly, "You know it's what you deserve just as well as I do. That's why you keep throwing yourself in the front lines. You know your debt to this world."

"That has nothing to do with karma!" I shrieked, tears threatening to break free from my eyes. "You don't know anything about me! Stop using my face!"

Scathing Reviewer is growing.

"Ha ha ha, but Liu Peijin, I *am* you. I am everything—the hairs on your head, the floorboards in this house, this entire universe. I am Karma."

She stuck her tongue out at me as blood dripped down her face in bold red streaks. It stained her precious skin, but she paid no mind to it. To her, the image of my body was nothing more than a vessel.

"You're not karma," I hissed before swallowing loudly. "This is torture! You're the one who has fucked with the whole system, and karma doesn't do that!"

Blinking up innocently at me, she furrowed her thin eyebrows. "And you, Jia Li, you're not an anomaly? My very existence occurred because yours did. When you didn't exist, did I?"

"Don't call me that!" I pressed the side of Zhige against her mouth and pushed down as hard as I could in a futile attempt to crush her jaw.

Being in my fourteen-year-old body meant that one thing was much harder: I could barely hold back my tears.

The moment I let one tear fall, I knew Smiley would be back. After all, anytime he was there when I was younger, I always cried. What else could a girl of only fourteen do?

But I knew one thing—fuck whatever karma thought I owed.

"I never asked for this. Do you think I wanted to be in this world? Even if I created it, I didn't want it to become a reality!" My blood pounded in my ears, and I could feel myself slipping from reality.

"But you love it all the same, Liu Peijin. You do. You want nothing more than to run back to your party right now and just live with them. You see bits of yourself in all of them, don't you? If they don't love you, how could you ever love yourself? You're nothing without them."

"Stop it. Please."

"You need to pay for making this world, Liu Peijin. Don't you get it? It's your fault this exists." Karma gingerly brushed a strand of hair from my face. "Even now, you wouldn't change a thing. You wish to live happily with all of them, but you don't wish for everyone's old life to come back, do you?"

I dragged Zhige straight through her throat to sever her head. Blood bubbled all beneath her body and my hands, but she continued speaking—none of Zhige's spiritual energy had a remote impact on her.

"You're the reason Amelia's parents died, but you picked her up right off the street and acted like her mother. How many other children have you orphaned? How many children have you murdered?

"And don't forget about how you killed Wang Ting by leaving her on the freeway! You created her to try to make sense of why your mother left you. You wanted a character that was loyal and reliable because every day you hoped your mother would come back. And when she never did, you grew to hate Wang Ting's character. Then, when you finally saw Wang Ting, your brain justified leaving her behind for dead."

My lower lip trembled as I thought back to the moment I saw Ting on the freeway. She crushed her hands in the van door in a futile attempt to join my party, and I still left her because I couldn't bear the thought of seeing someone like my mother. I lied earlier; I told myself that she killed her party, and that was why I couldn't take her. None of that was true. Ting was brilliant, powerful, and allied with Feiyu.

I wrote her because I believed my mother would come home, but she never did. I killed off Wang Ting later in *Surviving My First Run*. I also killed her here.

Each breath that squeezed out of my lungs was a mixture of a growl and a pained cry while I completely mutilated my spitting image. "You're wrong! I didn't cause anything! How could I have? If I was always this powerful, I would've never . . . never—!"

I couldn't finish the sentence through my sputtering lips. If I had been this powerful, nothing bad would have happened to me at fourteen. I would've wiped entire years of my life away, and Dad would be alive.

I would've apologized to him.

> **Warning! Scathing Reviewer is growing!**

Karma's gored flesh and mashed bones reformed into a perfect, vital version of my face appeared. "Silly little girl."

I finally pulled back. I dug my bloodied nails through the wooden floorboards, the sensation sending shivers down my spine. "If this is all my fault, then why am I still not the strongest disciple?"

"There are only two people above you," she sat up, too, as her body perfectly healed. She held up two fingers like a peace sign just in front of me. "Believe me, they will pay for their crimes all the same. You're not the only one being punished. You're merely the worst of them all, Liu Peijin."

"But I have been wronged! You call this justice? How can this be fair if I never knew I'd cause the apocalypse?!"

I wasn't going to deny it. Karma was right about one thing. I didn't find myself craving the mundane life of a pest control worker or the weight of my failure as a person when I sat before my laptop every day, writing *Surviving My First Run*.

I was addicted to watching my star count go up, watching more observer messages flood in every day, and watching the gods' fascination with me. In this moment, I wanted to murder the being before me and sprint back to the open arms of my party.

I didn't know whether to laugh or cry. Had I finally admitted that to myself? And it only took such a circumstance.

WARNING! SCATHING REVIEWER IS GROWING!

"You may be the author, but you can't change your fate, Liu Peijin. And I will adapt to whatever beast you become in this world." Karma stood before me in a short red dress that was the same color as her blood.

She continued to speak in that childish voice. "Hear that? *Bang, bang, bang,*" she mimicked. "Those are all your party members trying to rescue you. I wonder if you'll keep our encounter secret from them, too."

Scathing Reviewer has taken over.

CHAPTER THIRTY-SEVEN

Third Person

Karma's eyes immediately lit up at the shift in Peijin's demeanor. She darted forward and grabbed Peijin's small body, embracing her into a tight hug. She let out an excited squeal, jumping up and down.

"Ah, I think this is what you might call admiration? I can't believe I get to meet you."

Peijin's expression hardened, her eyes cold as she stared forward and spoke with a cold voice.

"I have done no wrong." The words were curt and held an indiscernible tone as Karma released her grasp on Peijin.

Karma pulled back and placed her glowing hands on Peijin's young face, squishing her soft cheeks. "It amazes me how the mind will split to preserve itself. We aren't so different, you know?"

"Was it so wrong for me to find comfort and live?"

"There is no such thing as wrong as long as you pay it off."

"There is nothing I need to pay off. Where was karma when Dad hopped from factory job to factory job? Where was karma when his friend assaulted me?" Peijin replied harshly, not skirting the story anymore. "You've never been just, and you're not now. Why make me remember everything?"

Karma laughed, bringing up a hand to cover her face. "You still don't understand karma after all this time. You've never lived a good life in any lifetime, and you've never made good decisions. Why else would you be standing before me right now? You aren't supposed to exist." Karma jabbed the question toward Scathing Reviewer before continuing.

"You pretend that all misfortune was bestowed upon you by the world. It wasn't. Whether or not this Peijin recalls it isn't of my concern."

Peijin's nostrils flared in rage, but she stood still, only clenching her fists. "Feiyu will kill you."

"He might," Karma replied sincerely, nodding her head. "But in the end, that doesn't matter. Peijin might change other's fates, but she'll never change her own."

Peijin lifted Zhige and pointed it straight at Karma's throat. "Then, before I die, I'll tear you down with this very blade. I swear it."

Karma gave a soft smile, her long eyelashes fluttering and dark eyes glimmering. A heavy moment of silence followed Peijin's statement before Karma finally posed a familiar question:

"Who are you?"

"I am me."

"But then, who am I? Am I not you, Liu Peijin?" Karma quizzed, placing a hand on her chest. "I know more about you than you yourself."

"Liu Peijin does not need to understand herself to live as long as she's in this world."

"And that is why she will be ruined," Karma replied sheepishly. "Liu Peijin is nothing without this world—she cannot survive without it. She only stands here, before us, instead of dead with her father because she wrote that story and damned the rest of us."

"Do not twist what happened," Peijin said. "This story is Peijin's salvation."

"And it shall be her damnation."

Eyes narrowing, Peijin glared straight at Karma, never once faltering. "Feiyu is Peijin's most beloved creation. You cannot win."

"Ha ha ha!" Karma laughed, her chest moving up and down with each breath. It sounded as if small hiccups broke up the laughter, like she was an over enthusiastic child. "Feiyu is merely Peijin. Everywhere you look, the only thing you'll find is Peijin. Yue is Peijin. Wei is Peijin. This world is Peijin. That is why you will pay. This world is the most beautifully selfish creation, and even if it saves you, karma gets everyone. I don't need to win. I am Karma."

Scathing Reviewer is flickering!

With a heavy sigh, Peijin responded, "Wait until Peijin meets Feiyu again, and you'll see the extent of her strength to protect him. Today, she has already acknowledged how she felt for the rest of her party without me influencing her.

With a wicked and twisted smile, Karma only said a few more words before Scathing Reviewer shattered.

"And even in this world, Peijin still cannot learn to love herself. You and I are more similar than you think. I believe we will become good friends."

"You forget that things are different now," Peijin's fading but firm voice declared. "Zhige has marked Peijin with the Tower tarot. Soon, she'll meet the other members. The Major Arcana already have their eyes locked on her. Once the Hermit and the Chariot tarot uncover Peijin's true identity, you'd be a fool to think they'd ever let her go."

Scathing Reviewer has deactivated!

Peijin

I coughed for a moment, placing my hands on my knees to steady myself. My head raced, and I felt it pulse as my vision blurred.

I spotted Karma's face peering at me curiously.

"Hello again."

Finally catching my breath, I wiped my dirtied face with the back of my hand and met her gaze. My mind was completely jumbled as if someone had shuffled and refiled my memories.

Why had Karma just said, "Hello?" We'd been talking this entire time, and our last interaction was about how I wasn't the strongest person here—that was Feiyu and whatever other monster of a disciple there was.

"I'm not the best in this world," I spat, steadying myself. "Kill the rest of them first, you motherfucker!"

I lunged forward and aimed Zhige straight at Karma's perfect figure, but she easily sidestepped, and I went flying into the wall with a flurry of curses.

"You misunderstand me, Liu Peijin. I don't intend to just kill you. Your fate is far worse."

I got back up, screaming as I ran forward again, this time making sure my blade slashed straight through her. I knew it was futile if I couldn't find her spiritual core, but I couldn't let myself get treated this way.

Zhige easily sliced through her body, but instead of being cut in half, she remained fully intact. For whatever reason, she was using more of her power now.

"Your curse is knowledge. Isn't it befitting? You'll try to save all of them by using your knowledge of the world, but all it will do is prove to you that you really can't save them." Her grin grew as she laughed, twirling away from my frenzied slashes before she calmly sat down on the armrest of a sofa.

"Shut up!" I slashed Zhige violently, but none of my slashes seemed to land on her. "Goddammit, Zhige!"

Zhige shrank at my harsh tone and words and a wave of sympathy immediately flowed through me. When did I get so attached to this world?

One thing was certain now. I couldn't lie to myself anymore—I really did care about my party. Whether or not Scathing Reviewer was activated, I started thinking about them more than I thought about myself at times. Yue's bickering, Amelia's smile, Yang's generosity, Wei's empathy . . .

And for that reason, I would kill Karma. No matter what it took of me.

Karma reached out an arm at surprising speed and grabbed my face, squeezing my cheeks. "I see why the gods and observers like you. You're so cute!"

I couldn't pull out of her harrowing grip no matter how much I tried—she didn't even budge despite my thrashing.

"I'll let you live, Liu Peijin. But you must know something." At once, Karma emitted gold karmic energy around her body, and I was violently flung into the bedroom wall with a sharp cry. I tried to lift a finger and move forward, but I was completely pinned down.

Even Zhige struggled to move from the overwhelming power.

Karma took step after step forward, almost floating across the room.

"You're the reason your group will suffer. Your karma is so terrible it impacts everyone else around you," Karma began.

"Weren't you curious why Yang's luck was so bad after his first dice roll? It was because of you, Liu Peijin. You're dooming everyone around you. Didn't it surprise you how well Yue did without you and with Yang, Wei, and Amelia instead?"

I wanted to scream in her face, reach out and cry and tear at her, but I couldn't even open my mouth. My eyes remained locked on her, a silent threat.

"No one needs you. They need Feiyu. He's always been the better version of you, and you made him that way. Every relationship you forge is your karma because you will always destroy the other person, Liu Peijin. You, you are destruction."

My blood ran cold. I remained still—not because of Karma's retracting aura but because of my horror.

Ha, this world really was cruel.

"Me?" I asked softly, meeting Karma's empty but glittering gaze. "Me?"

Karma walked forward and pulled my childlike body into a tight embrace before pulling back and looking down on me.

"That's your curse. But I won't go back on my word. I'll send you back, and your party will make it past this room safely as soon as you exit the house."

At once, countless hands burst all over the room and grabbed me, beginning to drag me into the walls. Their grip was cold, but their fingers moved frantically, pinching and tearing into my flesh.

"I'll kill you," I swore softly, my lips mouthing the words more than they were audible. "I'll tear down this entire universe and slaughter you to save them." My voice grew louder. "I'll hunt you down in any fucking timeline! In any world! You'll never get away with hurting them, you fucker!"

Karma smiled cruelly. "Then, if you're really worried about them getting hurt, you should be your first victim."

The hands continued to pull me into the wall, but I tried resisting, shoving my way forward until my face was just inches from her glowing one.

"You were right about what you said earlier," Karma said. "You're not the only anomaly. We're one and the same, Liu Peijin. And for this, this is why you'll survive."

Finally, the hands wrapped around my face and dragged me into the black abyss.

CHAPTER THIRTY-EIGHT

I burst out of the room and slammed into the wall of the hallway, but instead of landing flat on the ground, I fell onto a furry back.

"I got her! I caught Peijin!" a shrill voice cried out.

I was covered in a strange black goop that dripped onto the fur of the dire wolf, but it turned around and tenderly licked my face clean.

"Peijin!" Amelia crawled up the dire wolf and collapsed on top of me. "Did you see that? I can protect you now too!"

I remained silent for a moment, my head reeling at all of Karma's words, before I finally reached up and wrapped my arms tightly around Amelia, pulling her into a hug. The sides of our faces pressed together, but her curly blonde hair was suffocating. I gently brushed it aside and continued to hug her.

Karma was right. I had no right to care for or about Amelia after dooming her family and forcing her to kill her puppy. But at this moment, I couldn't let go of her again.

The last time. This would be the last time I'd indulge in the presence of others. If my bad karma rubbed off on them, I'd never forgive myself.

"Are you all right?" I spoke softly. "You don't need to worry about me."

She clung to me like a koala and wrapped herself around my abdomen. I smiled and tightened my hold on her. For some reason, I felt like she'd vanish at any moment, and I'd be all alone again.

The glint of a spear appeared just before my throat.

"You should be more worried about yourself right now," the voice barked angrily. "I'm so pissed off I could kill you."

I gave an exacerbated look, and the back of my hand pushed her spear away. "Good to see you again, Yue."

"You bitch, you—!"

Yang shoved her away, causing her to stumble in my peripheral vision.

I could see the sweat dripping down Yang's face, and when I looked into his dimmed orange eyes, I felt an empathetic pang in my chest—he was panicking to find me.

Ha, weird. I was never like this when Scathing Reviewer was deactivated. This story was changing me just as much as I was changing it.

"Sorry I'm late," I said before grabbing his extended hand and pulling myself up. Amelia was still clinging onto my abdomen, and my other arm supported her weight.

To my surprise, it looked like I had been fully healed. Bandages were no longer wrapped around my entire body, and my once shredded arm moved fluidly. Now the only sign left on my skin of any past arcs was the black Tower tattoo.

Yang continued to hold my hand after he pulled me up and sighed. "You really had me worried. Are you all right?"

I thought I'd cry just from seeing his familiar face.

Before I could respond, a man in white robes shoved Yang back and pulled me into a tight hug, making sure to avoid Amelia.

"Agh, Peijin!" he exclaimed, pulling back so I could make out his face. Wei's eyes were red and puffy like he was trying to hold back tears. "I feel horrible. I was supposed to protect you, and you just disappeared. I've failed again."

I was paralyzed by his dramatic response before I let my shoulders slump, a humored smile appearing on my face. "You're like a puppy." I laughed, putting my hand on his back after a moment's hesitation. "I'm really all right, everyone."

Yue finally came over and tore Wei off me but left Amelia hanging. "Get off her! You're acting like you just saw someone resurrect from their grave. Even Amelia is more mature than you."

Wei patted his swollen face and obediently nodded at Yue's words. I watched curiously; those two had hated each other at the very beginning, but here they were working together.

In fact, just watching everyone in my party interact with one another caused a fuzzy tingle and warmth in my chest. I watched them bicker with an odd sense of awe and wistfulness, and my most sincere smile appeared unbeknownst to me.

I shook the thought out of my head.

"Let's go," I said, grabbing Zhige and finally placing a calmed Amelia on the ground. "We can leave this house safely now, trust me. I won't randomly turn into a kid anymore."

"Wait, Peijin," Yang chimed in, standing beside me. "What happened in that room? Couldn't you hear us trying to get to you?"

I stiffened for a moment but relaxed. That must have been what all that banging and chanting of my name was—still, even knowing what it was now, it was still an unnerving memory.

"I couldn't hear you, but it's all right. I got out, didn't I?"

"Don't start distancing yourself again."

My nostrils flared in annoyance. "I'm not. Stop being annoying."

Yue shoved my head harshly. "Do you know how worried Wei was? He was *so* upset that you saw all our fears and saved us, but you were trapped alone."

I promptly punched her in the side before sparing a guilty glance at Wei and letting out a loud sigh.

"Fine. But Amelia can't hear."

"What?!" Amelia cried out in distress, looking up at me with pleading eyes.

"I'll tell you when you're a little older, okay? I'll take off your headphones for the parts that you can hear."

I signaled for Yue to put on the headphones, and Yue tightly held them against the squirming Amelia's head. She finally relented, pursing her lips and glaring at me.

"I'm gonna speed through my 'deepest fear' or whatever"—I added air quotes as I spoke—"But . . ."

Wait, should I tell them about Karma?

If I did, then there was no doubt they would act rashly in their weird fixation to repay me for helping them—and at their level and knowledge, I'd only be dooming them. Just by being with me, I was killing them.

That being said, Karma was after me, and I was actively hunting her, too. This was something that affected them as much as it did me.

Ah, Karma was right. My curse really was knowledge.

How cruel.

"But what?" Yang broke the silence and sent me back into reality.

"But I don't want to talk about it afterward."

Yang stared at me a bit before nodding. "All right."

"My mom left when I was around ten, I think? I don't know," I began in a nonchalant tone.

"My dad and I were dirt poor. Seriously. He became a factory worker just to make ends meet, but I'm sure all of you know what kind of job that is. I don't hate my dad or anything. He did what he had to. I just wish he didn't do it, you know?"

I felt an odd burning sensation spreading through my arm. I rubbed it in hopes of dissipating the sensation to no avail.

"But when I was about fourteen, he brought some friends over to drink. One of them came into my room and—"

Yue's eyes widened in understanding, and she clasped her hands over my mouth, silencing me. "You don't need to continue."

Pulling her hands back, I continued softly. "He had this big grin on his face, and at some point, I started to see it everywhere. That's why my biggest fear is a haunted house, since I never faced what happened. I ran away from home. I lived with someone for a bit, but I was mostly alone. I didn't have any other family."

Yue gave me a solemn look, her brow furrowed. "Then, when you got locked in the room just now, did something happen?"

"Nah." I shook my head, refusing to meet her gaze. "That's all. Let's go?"

When I finally lifted my gaze, I noticed all of them looking at me with a different expression now except for Amelia. But their faces didn't hold judgment or disgust, but rather it was a look of pity.

The burning sensation on my arm grew, and when I looked down, I realized my tattoo was glowing a faint white now.

"Don't pity me," I bluntly said. "I'm not a good person."

After all, I was the reason Dad was dead.

Two warm arms adorned in long white sleeves wrapped around my small frame. I could feel my breath catch in my throat, and I turned to Wei in surprise before Yang, Yue, and Amelia joined in, embracing me.

I blinked away tears and let my head briefly rest on their shoulders.

"Thank you for trusting us, Peijin," Yang whispered softly, and I was glad I couldn't see his expression right now.

Wei's response was silent and warm, and Yue's was a tight, almost painful squeeze. But all of it was comfort.

"Thank you," I choked out, finally wiggling my arms up and hooking the back of their necks, pulling them in tighter.

You have become the Tower.

The red notification appeared, and my tattoo erupted in a flurry of gold sparks—karma. I felt a surge of spiritual energy flood through my body, but I didn't let go of any of them. They held on too, until the flurry of sparks finally fell back.

I looked down at the tattoo. I still had no clue what it symbolized, but I knew it would cause me trouble.

I ushered the rest of the party out of the house first, practically dragging them down the hallway.

"I have something to do. I'll meet you all on the metro train."

Wei spared a nervous glance back, but I flashed a reassuring smile. Once they all safely made it in, I turned around and looked down the hallway.

I took two of the oranges I'd gathered and peeled them before using Zhige to slice them. They were my favorite treat to share with Dad. I placed one peeled orange on the table before me, and I ate the other.

"I guess this is as much of a meal as I'll ever be able to share with you, Dad."

I leaned against the wall for a moment, savoring the orange before I let out a heavy sigh. Things had gotten far more convoluted than I ever anticipated, but at least I was leaving with a clear head.

I stood up straight and grabbed Zhige.

"As for Karma, fuck you."

I lifted Zhige and slashed through the entire house, cleanly cutting it apart and causing the remaining décor and walls to crumble. The slices I had left for my dad remained perfectly untouched as I walked out of the tattered door and shut it behind me.

The silver train appeared just before me, and I could see all of my party members waiting for me inside. I stepped on, and the doors slid shut behind me with a satisfying click.

"The fuck were you doing in there?" Yue asked, raising an eyebrow.

"You'd laugh at me."

"Probably. You okay?"

I nodded, and my notifications exploded.

Communication resumed.

[Observers Chat]
Socrates: JIA LI OH MY GOD I CAN FINALLY COMMENT AGAIN WHAT HAPPENED????
Landescape: I don't care what all those "reviewers" say about Peijin, I'm rooting for her to live and succeed!

You have received a new review!
RZRHP REVIEW: ★ ★ ★ ★ ★
I didn't think I'd like Liu Peijin at all. She's been pretty
insufferable, but this room dragged her through hell and back,
and the first thing she does is care for her party members.

You have received a new review!
EIJIEKI369 REVIEW: ★ ★ ★ ☆ ☆
Good, but pretty unrealistic writing. Real people
wouldn't have cared this much.

[**Observers Chat**]
Socrates: Jia Li I'm sorry I was so mean to you please forgive me TvT You were really annoying before but still I'm sorry. I was so worried when the system shut down, and I couldn't see you.
Socrates: Also, I figured out what your tattoo is. It's the Tower from a tarot card deck. The tarot symbolizes destruction, painful loss, and tragedy, but the reverse meaning is resisting change and delaying the inevitable. It's pretty awful all the way around, actually.

"You're great at making me feel worse," I grumbled. My party turned to me in confusion, but I mouthed that it was an observer.

[**Observers Chat**]
Socrates: It's a sign for meeting a crisis head on and rebirth. I'm guessing you either got it because of this challenge or because something greater is coming, Jia Li.

"How many cards are in a Major Arcana tarot deck?" I asked Socrates.

[**Observers Chat**]
Socrates: 22

"Huh. Interesting," I said, recalling the name of Feiyu's party. Was it really a tarot reference after all, then?

I stepped forward, looking at the options of skills laid out before me.

POTENTIAL SKILLS LIST
Card Dealer
Divine Right
Grandmaster

I tilted my head curiously at Card Dealer. It was the only skill I hadn't heard of, so I opened the description and read it.

The key life moments, events, and emotions of those you interact with will be categorized into 56 different Minor Arcana tarot cards. Depending on how well you know the person or character, you will be able to take a card and alter it through various methods such as altering a card's contents, deleting a card's contents, or swapping people's cards. This will alter their current perception of an event, memory, or emotion. You will not have access to cards for events you

do not know. When using this skill, there is a chance of backlash, where one of your own cards is affected. You will not know which card it is or what happened to it. This skill relies on significant spiritual energy. Once you alter a card, you cannot undo this effect.

"What's Card Dealer?" Yue asked, peeking over my shoulder.

"It . . . allows me to edit memories of people." I contemplated falling back into my old habit of lying, missing the security it brought. But I knew I owed my party more than that.

Yue shot me a mortified look. "You should not pick that one."

"It could be useful though, especially in psychological rooms like the one we just went through," Wei said. "Besides, I trust that Peijin wouldn't use it unethically."

This skill was perfect for me, as I was the author of *Surviving My First Run*. I'd have access to a lot of people's "cards," since they would be characters that I created. Not only that, but if I was worried about Wei's resurfacing memories causing him to betray us, then this was the perfect fix. I could technically reconstruct his entire memory.

"There's no way to use that skill ethically," Yang said. "It's not like Magician's Hand, where only your surroundings change. You're changing a core part of the person."

"Peijin has a strong moral code. If she didn't, I wouldn't follow her. Besides, in the apocalypse, good people will need to do bad things. If anyone should have it as a skill, it should be Peijin," Wei said.

I felt bad to have Wei defending me like this, unaware of the fact that the first time I might use this skill could very much be on him.

"What about the other skills?" Yue asked.

"Grandmaster would allow me to control certain people as chess pieces after a murderous ritual, and Divine Right gives me greater influence over disciples if I become their ruler."

"How'd you get those as your options . . ." Yue murmured enviously.

Yang looked at me and gave a nervous laugh. "I'd hate to get on your bad side, ha ha."

I gave them both a slap on the back and a bright grin, feeling better in their presence. "Looks like we're all stuck with each other then. You're lucky you ended up with me and not a psycho."

I looked at the skills, contemplating my options before I eventually selected Card Dealer. Given its potential for backlash and its drain of my feeble spiritual energy, I wanted to use it only when it was needed.

I looked up to see Wei's still-anxious eyes. Despite my suddenly more cheerful tone, he couldn't mask his worry.

"Peijin . . ." he began, "do you know what my room might hold?"

A laugh escaped my lips. There was no time for breaks in this world—I was thrust back into my element as I felt the train speed up to our destination.

"Everyone, listen up," I ordered, my other hand holding Zhige. "Do exactly as I say, because if you don't, Wei will die at my hand."

CHAPTER THIRTY-NINE

Wei flushed bright red and gave me an astonished look before he took an anxious step back. "Ha ha, you're very funny, Peijin . . ."

I stared at him, my grip on Zhige's hilt tight. "No, I'm dead serious."

His pouting lips quivered as he stared at me, looking like a betrayed puppy. It already looked like he regretted defending me.

Yang grabbed my ear and tightly tugged on it, scolding me. "Stop bullying Wei and tell us what to do before the metro arrives at the destination."

"Agh—!" I exclaimed, wincing as I swatted at his hand. "Fine, fine!"

Wei nervously rested his chin on his sword's hilt. "Peijin, earlier you said my fate was black. What did you mean by that?"

"I did?"

"Yes, when you were in your younger form."

"Oh. Well, who said that was set in stone?" I shrugged simply.

"Earlier you said you were a fortune teller," Yue said. "But you're not. So what are you, actually? You know too much to be like the rest of us."

I smiled. "I'm the god of fate and fortune."

I wanted to fake being a god since the start, and now was finally the time. Not only was I directly shitting on Karma by proclaiming myself to be a god of fate, but it was best to do this before Wei's room.

It would give me greater authority over my party, since they would believe my word, and it would also draw the attention of the gods and observers to me. When they would watch me go through Wei's room with a surprising amount of ease, they would have no choice but to acknowledge my claim.

Disciple Yue activated Lie Detector!

Lie Detector confirms Disciple Peijin's words as truth.

My entire party gaped at the notification—so did I.

"See? I was telling the truth," I said, rolling with it.

[Observers Chat]

CannedWorms: Huh? She's really a god?

MoldyBlanket: I KNEW IT PEIJIN IS THE BEST DISCIPLE

CactusLiver: Now I won't have to regret defending you

Aslan: Ignore all my past messages very sorry Peijin </3

Sapling123: Don't forget us!! I've been here since the beginning!

You have received a new review!
MOLDYBLANKET REVIEW: ★ ★ ★ ★ ★
Before Peijin gets overrated, I want to say I was here
since Day 1. Never doubted her!! Don't forget me!!

2,947 observers are expressing shock at your statement.
56 gods are processing your claim.
104 new gods have begun to follow you.

The flurry of notifications surrounded me until I temporarily muted them, focusing on my party. I could feel a surge of spiritual energy flow through me from the incoming support and belief of thousands of observers.

Yue gave me a completely dumbfounded look. "So, this entire time . . . you've been a god."

"I'm exiled, so it's not like I have any special powers or anything."

"But that's how you've known everything?"

"Sure."

Yang turned to me, his brow furrowed. "Peijin, then when we worked together, were you a god then?"

"My identity wasn't significant until the apocalypse began." I brushed off his question. "I don't see why you're so surprised. After all, it's not like I'm the only god in this party." I pointed at Wei.

Wei couldn't even process what I was saying, only staring at me with a stupefied expression.

"There's a reason his poster is dated back to two thousand years ago," I said. "Wei's deepest fear is reliving his life from the time he was a god. He was banished then imprisoned, which is why he doesn't remember anything."

"Why?" Amelia blurted out. "Wei-shushu must have been unfairly treated. Why would someone not like him?"

I paused before replying to her question. "He was banished for the mass murder of his civilians when he was crown prince of an ancient Chinese city."

"Me? Murder? You must be mistaken. That's impossible. I don't remember any of that!" Wei insisted, clasping his white robes.

"Well, you won't remember anything when the room begins. You'll forget everything that happened since you were banished, including this conversation. You'll be sent back to your eighteenth birthday, which is the day you got banished. My party needs to stop you from committing the same crimes."

"What the fuck?!" Yue exclaimed. "Who created these torture chambers?"

I laughed awkwardly, running my hand against the back of my head while avoiding her eyes. "It's all right. I have a good idea of how to get Wei out, but I'll see how things play out."

"I'd rather not hear about any of this if it's so abysmal," Wei said.

"Don't worry. You have a strong enough character to beat this room," I declared confidently, staring straight into his eyes. "I know that for certain, and I won't let anything bad happen to this party."

He stared at me with glowing eyes before loudly sniffling, looking like he was about to cry.

"You better not start crying right now."

"I can't help it. Do you really think I have a strong character?"

I let out a loud sigh before I flicked his forehead and turned back to face the rest of the party. "Our first initiative is to meet up as soon as we end up in the other world. Some of us will arrive at earlier periods. All of us need to buy a skill called Continuous Convey." I pulled it up on the Azure Dragon Store and showed them all my screen. "This will let us communicate with each other. Amelia, I'll buy yours because it's expensive, and I like you."

Since our party would be split in two when we arrived, I hoped I would get stuck with Amelia, so I could look out for her, or Yang, since we worked the best in a team.

Continuous Convey was stupidly expensive at around twelve thousand stars—that's why I hadn't made them purchase it sooner. I was glaring at the purchase button as I clicked it before I spotted Amelia beaming with pride from my words, and it looked like she could burst at any moment. I snorted, placing my hand at the top of her head before ruffling her hair.

We all bought the skill and added each other, testing it out. Messages would be sent telepathically, and we could make individual chats as well.

[**Party Chat**]
Peijin: This is the main chat that has all party members. Don't chat here

> unless it's an emergency. You only get twenty messages a day.
> **Yue:** Twenty messages?? What kind of idiot came up with that?
> **Peijin:** Now it's nineteen.
> **Yue:** I'd curse you out right now if Amelia wasn't here. Can't we make an adults-only chat?
> **Amelia:** :(aww
> **Yang:** Wei is doomed

Yang playfully smacked Yue and me in the back of the head, and both of us cursed him out.

The train began slowing down, the path becoming increasingly bumpy.

I looked around one last time with a cocky grin, trying to ease their nerves. It was fun teasing them, but I would be lying if I said I wasn't nervous. The chance I'd end up killing Wei was high, after all. He already suffered amnesia to have lost all his past memories—now, he was about to lose all of his new ones. Once he regained both, who knew how he'd react?

"Don't panic. The first objective is to find one another and locate Wei, all right?" I said. "If not all of us appear, just wait. Everyone will show up eventually. Make sure to stay in contact using the convey."

"When will Archangel Michael be back?" Wei asked, looking up with a slightly more confident expression.

"Uhh . . . probably a while," I said awkwardly, rubbing the back of my neck.

> **[Observers Chat]**
> **Socrates:** He'll be out sooner because of the contract you signed with him. It lessened the karmic backlash.
> **Socrates:** Also, telling people you're the god of fate and fortune is cute lol I wasn't expecting that to be your excuse.

That damned contract. I was owing more and more gods with each arc.

Wait, did the observers or gods know about Karma? I doubted it, especially since the broadcast was cut—if they did, the entire system would have been heavily skewed considering that Karma knew I was Jia Li. I needed to confirm my suspicions.

I turned back to Wei, reassuring him, "Don't worry, he'll be out soon. There won't be much he can do in this dungeon room with you anyway since no one will be allowed to communicate with you."

The train finally came to a stop as the doors slid open. I gave Wei a hard slap on the back before we all walked forward.

All of them stood in a line before the open metro door, trying to squeeze in shoulder to shoulder. I held Amelia before me, apprehensive of letting her go.

"Take care of each other," I said softly, staring into the black abyss. Typically, the room would have appeared just before the doors, showing the scenery; however, there was nothing but a black void.

"Ah, I say we push Peijin in first," Yue sneered, giving me a mischievous look.

I glared at her. "Don't you dar—"

Before I could finish my words, the metro car erupted, the entire train bursting outward as metal panels flew all around the void before vanishing.

Custom room now commencing!
Tailored for: Disciple Jun Wei

"Amelia!" I shouted, looking down at my now-empty hands. I swiveled around the void for a moment, looking around to realize I was completely alone.

I let out an exasperated sigh as I floated around the emptiness. It was uncomfortable in how lukewarm it felt. Reaching for Zhige, I petted the blade in boredom as I waited.

Well, clearly, I was not in the first group to arrive.

"Sorry I yelled at you earlier, Zhige," I said softly. Since Zhige shrunk earlier, it refused to return to its original size.

The red eye blinked at me for a moment before rolling, clearly not convinced.

"Hey, I'm serious. I really am sorry."

Zhige's eye narrowed even more before the blade shrunk significantly as if protesting.

"You should be apologizing to me. Why does Karma know you, huh? She even called you Haimo. Do you guys go way back or something? Best friends, maybe?"

[Observers Chat]
Socrates: Wait, Jia Li, what are you talking about? Isn't karma just the power system?

Jackpot. The observers and gods did not know about karma.

The surrounding environment began to flood with colors and beautiful floral scenes that flew by—it was like I was watching an entire timeline float past me.

Zhige flew out before me and waved around frantically as if trying to justify itself.

"Uh-huh," I said with a raised eyebrow and my arms crossed, "I'm not convinced. I thought we had something special." I sniffed dramatically, wiping away fake tears.

Out of frustration, Zhige's red eye spun around wildly and shook back and forth again, insisting it had nothing to do with Karma.

I shrugged. "I don't believe you. It looks like we're even, so go back to your normal size, yeah?"

Zhige relented, finally reverting and flying back to my side.

This was the room where I was going to turn over a new leaf. No more impulsivity or half-thought-out plans—I knew this room like the back of my hand. That included the plot holes, I guess.

"Zhige, get ready. I'm going to absolutely wipe this room once I get there," I shouted, smashing my fist against my open palm.

Both of us suddenly froze at the appearance of a glitching red box—reminiscent of anything involving the Major Arcana—just before me.

UNKNOWN ENTITY DESCENDING INTO
WEI'S DUNGEON ROOM.

"No." I looked around, cupping my hands around my mouth and screaming into the flurry of images flying by. "Chang! Chang! Come and fix this bullshit!"

1% . . . 5% . . . 48% . . . 97% . . .

"Are you fucking kidding me right now?!" I cried out angrily, glaring at the screen.

Descent into a system implied it was being done by some kind of god—it was still too early in the arcs to have a being descend in their true form. That meant whatever spiritual energy they were backed by was enormous. It was big enough to deter karmic restraints.

"Fuck!" I screamed, smashing my fist against the red screen. "Is this from you bastards in the Major Arcana? You piss me off!"

Zhige's hilt bashed into my forehead, and I let out a grunt before wrestling with the blade. "Don't tell me you're on their side?!"

The sword shook back and forth at me, trying to convince me we were on the same team.

"What's your issue then? I'm going to lose my mind if I ever see this stupid Major Arcana bullshit again! This spiritual energy is literally—agh!"

Zhige smacked me firmly again, and I could feel a bruise already forming on my forehead.

DESCENT COMPLETE.

"Fucker!"

I reached for the screen with the intention of destroying it before the flashing images around me stopped, and I hurtled toward the ground. I crashed through countless trees before finally landing on the ground with a loud thump.

"Ugh . . ." Through my ringing ears, I could make out the sound of faint screaming gradually getting closer.

I stammered, "Y-Yang?"

The crushing body weight of someone fell through the trees and landed straight on top of me. The air was forced from my lungs.

"What the fuck?!" I exclaimed. I blinked repeatedly to try to make out the blurry figure on top of me.

The long black robes of a traditional Chinese hanfu dress were wrapped around her towering figure. She stood up and dusted herself off, her jewelry clinging. Her silky black hair was pulled up into a decorated half bun full of jewels, flowers, and pins; her lips were tinted a mauve color, and her eyelashes sparkled in the morning sun's light. I never realized it before, but she was very pretty.

She gave me a demeaning glare before opening her mouth. "Are you going to keep staring at me or what?"

CHAPTER FORTY

I can't believe I got trapped here with you, Yue."

"Excuse me?!"

I fell backward on the forest ground, clamping my hands over my face and kicking my feet. "Goddammit! At this point, God can strike me down!"

Yue let out a loud groan and reached over, trying to lift my limp body. "You're seriously annoying! Get up!" She tugged on me repeatedly, but I dug my body into the soft ground below me.

I was wearing a teal-colored hanfu with embroidered yellow flowers on the bottom and golden ornaments dangling from my high ponytail. My teal hanfu must've been the hoodie transformed to fit the dungeon room. My hairstyle was entirely different from the cropped one I've always had, but my bangs remained.

"Get up! The hell are you lying down for?" Yue exclaimed before pulling me upward and sending me stumbling forward.

I looked around to try to pinpoint our surroundings. Just a few feet away, the top of a temple was peeking through the trees.

"Let's go there," I said. "Then we can let Yang and Amelia know where we are."

As we headed toward the temple, our feet clicking on the cobblestone tiles, we were both taken aback by the landscape, staring at it like children. Unlike the towering skyscrapers of Shanghai and its neon lights, we were on a cliff's edge and surrounded by a wispy gray fog that seemed to move around the landscape with a mind of its own. The sun formed rainbows with the droplets of water and reflected beautifully off the colorful temples.

Reds, teals, and dark blues were sprinkled all over a massive temple hanging by the cliff. It was enormous—a massive gold bell hung in the middle of the outdoor gate with giant gods sculpted beside it.

Yue appeared beside me and let out a small gasp, the wind blowing her long black hair behind her. Her eyes were twinkling in amazement. "Whoa."

1,203 observers are amazed by the sight before them!

[Observers Chat]
Socrates: I'm sure you're glad you put more effort into describing the scenery than fixing your plot holes.

Socrates still read every single chapter before I blocked him, and now he stalked me. I must have done something right.

We walked through the entrance of the temple and entered the beautiful garden full of hydrangeas. I observed the signs and titles detailing who the temple was dedicated to.

"Donations to: The Blessed Martial God of Salvation."

"This temple is for Wei," I said, pointing at the sign. "Let's head in."

[Party Chat]
Peijin: Yue and I are here. We're at one of Wei's temples. It's by a cliff side. There's a large gold bell hung in the center.

I waited for a moment, but no response came. I sighed loudly and rolled my eyes in annoyance.

"Can they seriously not answer?"

"Maybe they're dead," Yue replied, shrugging. I promptly smacked the back of her head, and she let out a small yelp.

"Don't say stuff like that. You'll make my luck worse." I slipped off my shoes and walked into the temple to admire its beauty. I looked around in amazement and spun in circles, my feet almost tripping over each other.

Even on the inside, it was perfectly upkept. Before me, a beautiful and massive room covered with red and golden ornaments greeted me. In the middle was a luxurious marble statue of a beautiful woman sitting. Her eyes were closed and formed gentle crescents, and her marble hair was tied up to form elaborate buns. Flowers were spread all over her, and fake petals were spread out at her feet. Stunning robes wrapped around her delicate figure, and as the natural light poured in, it reflected off her sloping features.

This beautiful woman was Meihua—Wei's wife.

"I feel like I lived here in a past life," I whispered softly.

"Yeah, maybe as a servant," Yue replied in a snarky tone.

I glared at her. "Yue, remember those prayer candles I bought a while ago?"

She blinked in confusion before replying. "What?"

"We used them during the sponsorship to talk to the gods."

"Obviously I remember that."

"They're a bit too expensive for me, so I was hoping you'd buy them."

"Aren't you the richest in the party?"

I checked how many stars I had and smiled at the amount.

You have 203,495 cumulative stars.

"Are you conceding that you have less stars than me, Yue?" I asked.

Yue let out a loud sigh, and I gave her a beaming smile.

The candles appeared in her hand, and she handed me a dozen of them. I bowed before the statue before I offered the candles as worship.

"Peijin, I'm confused."

"Of course you are."

"Is this *our* Earth two thousand years ago?"

"The heavenly, demonic, and ghost realms existed prior to when the system was activated for us," I said, turning around and looking at Yue. "But Chang mentioned broadcasting for other planets before Earth."

"So, the heavenly realm is the same but this is a different mortal realm?"

I nodded.

[Party Chat]

Amelia: HI PEIJIN!!!

Yang: Wei, Meihua, Ailun, Amelia, and I are together. There are a lot of temples like that. Is it the one with the statue of the demons being imprisoned?

"Who are Meihua and Ailun?" Yue asked me.

"Wei's wife and younger brother."

"Wei has a wife?!"

"Yup. She's the one with the pretty statue."

Yue looked completely dumbfounded, staring at the glorious statue in shock. "But she's so much more—"

I elbowed her in the side.

[Party Chat]

Peijin: No . . . ? It's the one with Meihua at the front. There's a hydrangea garden in the front of the temple.

Yue and I continued leisurely walking through the temple until I spotted something on the ground.

Two drops of black blood splatter.

[Party Chat]
Yang: Get out of there. Now. We will be there soon.

"Someone else is here!" I shouted, wielding Zhige and stepping in front of Yue.

I waited to see if I could hear any sounds or if anything would appear, but it remained dead silent. Cautiously, I rounded the corner, ready to strike.

The entire room was littered with dying ghosts struggling to get up and stop their bodies from vanishing. Ash was scattered all over the floor from those that had already been slain.

Many of them were wielding weapons and sporting different military uniforms. Clearly, there had been some kind of skirmish here between enemy troops. Not only that, but some of the dying bodies were victims of disease. Buboes littered their features and oozed black pus and a putrid stench. The infections moved on their own, with some resembling limbs, but it was too early on to see the progression.

"Shit . . . what the fuck happened here?" Yue murmured, stepping back out of disgust. It was clear there wasn't a living threat, but the sight was grotesque.

I stepped over the bodies and inspected the walls. They were covered in gorgeous paintings depicting the rise of a god—Wei's reign. One showed him becoming the crown prince in a ceremony, wearing beautiful elaborate robes and a mask covering his face. The next showed him coming in victorious against countless demons and wicked humans as an embodiment of justice. Then came his marriage with Meihua, a beautiful flower divinity, and the final large painting showed Wei in all his glory.

Wei was standing among the clouds in white robes with streaks of red, blue, and gold. He was covered in golden jewelry, and his long sleeves were billowing out behind his outstretched arms. Beneath him, his temples littered the scenery—the tops of mountains, every village, and even the lakes had a place of worship for him. He was the darling of the heavens.

Except this painting had been desecrated. All these paintings had been. They were slashed through violently and splattered with the filthy remains of ghosts.

Below, in blood red characters, was the phrase *HIS HIGHNESS CANNOT SAVE US! TURN TO OUR RISEN SAVIOR DAJI!*

All of these paintings were clearly part of the temple's official artwork with the same brush strokes, paper, and canvas size. But, at the very end was a smaller painting. It was the newest addition, but it was also the most dirtied, on a pathetically small and tattered canvas.

In it, Wei was losing a vicious war on the outskirts of the city while everyone on the inside died of a plague denoted by the large purple welts on their skin. Their faces were haunted, torn apart, and pleading, but Wei couldn't do anything to save them. Only one figure was depicted well in this pseudo painting—it was a beautiful female fox spirit tending to the ill and helping them heal.

"Ha . . . what the fuck?" I murmured under my breath, staring out at the vile scene before me. Even though they were only ghosts and not real people, the scene was still painful. I put all of the ghosts out of their misery and dissipated their ashes properly.

"Peijin, mind catching me up a bit? What is this whole mess?" Yue pestered me.

In *Surviving My First Run*, Wei's room was the most challenging out of the ones that Feiyu's party had to face. It would also be the first time Feiyu would fail.

Unlike me, Feiyu had no clue Wei was a god or why they were suddenly in ancient China. But, as the story played out, Feiyu discovered that Wei, the totally beloved crown prince of the Shang dynasty, had come under attack by Emperor Di Xin and his most favored concubine Daji.

Daji was a demon with an unquenchable thirst for power. Disguised as a concubine, she manipulated Emperor Di Xin into letting his empire fall to the Zhou Dynasty and a mysterious demonic disease that she herself spread.

Then she would spread rumors about Wei and Meihua, claiming they had committed one of the worst heavenly offenses by switching the doomed fate of his younger brother with a would-be god. Subsequently, Emperor Di Xin and the Shang Dynasty would have a reason to turn their back on the crown prince.

In the end, Daji would pin the disease and war on Wei and Meihua's inability to save their people, and she'd steal all his worshippers and take his place.

The war with the Zhou was long-lasting and the disease crippling. Wei stuck to his values and labored strenuously every day to protect his citizens to no avail. But everything would collapse on the most miserable day of Wei's life—his eighteenth birthday. That would be the day his citizens turned their back on him and his wife Meihua. That would be the day Daji murdered his younger brother and wife.

Meihua would die at the border, defending her people until her last breath. She'd spread one of the largest protection seals of the time and maintained it for hours until she finally collapsed under Daji's repeated assault. Even then, she directed all the energy in her spiritual core to the seal, keeping it operative and protecting her people for days after her death.

This would be the first time Feiyu panicked. Feiyu didn't know the future the way I did, and he couldn't understand the events playing out before him. In the original tale, Wei went berserk and killed countless civilians before he was banished and sent to prison for two thousand years, only to become a disciple when the apocalypse began.

However, in *Surviving My First Run*, Wei's rampage had other victims. Specifically, Feiyu's party. Believing that all of humanity and the system wronged him, Wei successfully murdered half of Feiyu's party. At a loss for what to do, Feiyu gave in and signed a contract with a demon to possess Meihua's corpse and speak through it to convince Wei to stop his senseless massacre and return to the station.

Thankfully, the manipulation would succeed. Otherwise, Feiyu would be dead, and my web novel series a failure. But Archangel Michael witnessed it, and it would become a source of conflict later in the story, as the trust between Feiyu, Wei, and Archangel Michael had been shattered. Not only that, but Feiyu would be indebted to a horrific demon.

I made Feiyu fail because the point of the room was that it was Wei's fate to slaughter everyone—whether it be his party or civilians—after going berserk. Feiyu was only able to stop it by paying the high price of compromising his values and shattering his party's trust. At the time, I wanted to show off the karmic system.

But now that Wei was a member of my party, I wanted to break my own rules. I wouldn't let Wei massacre my party, and I wouldn't betray him or Archangel Michael. I fucking hated everything about Karma.

I was going to awaken Wei and calm him down to successfully clear the dungeon, and I'd do this with the least sacrifice possible. I was the writer, the sole creator of this world.

I didn't need to be the god of fate and fortune to rewrite my *own* story.

Of course, I couldn't say all of that to Yue. Her brain would've fried. Instead, I explained the paintings to her and Daji's plan.

"Why the hell would Wei's people betray him after he slayed all the demons in the city for them?" Yang said, growing frustrated.

"When people expect you to fix everything and suddenly you fail, they'll turn their backs on you. Wei wasn't as invincible as they once thought."

"That's just stupid! Wei should've gone berserk, especially if he had to watch his family get slaughtered."

"Don't forget that your sponsor is also a demon," I said. "Even if it's justified, if Wei goes berserk now, we'll be the ones who get slaughtered."

"You really think Wei would do that? He follows you around like a puppy."

"That's only because two thousand years of pent-up hatred haven't been released yet. Don't underestimate him."

"So, where are we in this timeline?"

Behind Yue, a group of people appeared from the dark. I instantly lifted Zhige in front of me but calmed down when I saw who they were.

His long black hair flowed behind him, and the outlines of his muscular figure could be seen through his white robes. The white bandage that was once on his arm was tying up his long, glistening hair. His large eyes glimmered and he had a cheeky grin on his face, but his good spirits couldn't mask his dully colored cheeks or his sunken-in eyes.

Beside him was the most stunning woman I'd ever seen in delicate pink robes and surrounded by flowers. The woman had long, flowing brown hair, and her gentle facial features sloped beautifully.

Just behind her were Yang and Amelia, and Amelia was holding the hand of a little boy.

Wei's soothing voice rang out in the desecrated temple, and he bowed before me. "You must be Peijin. I've heard a lot about you."

CHAPTER FORTY-ONE

I bowed deeply before Wei and Meihua, trying to show my utmost respect for them.

[Party Chat]

Yang: I told Wei and Meihua all about you and Yue since I got here about two weeks ago. I said you were going to help them. I'm assuming you know the jist of the situation?

Peijin: Yup. We saw the paintings in here, and I filled in the gaps for Yue.

Yang: We got into a skirmish there earlier today. Most of Wei and Meihua's temples have been overthrown, so they're low on spiritual energy.

Peijin: How did you manage to meet them and earn their trust?

Yang: Well, I don't know if they entirely trust me, but somehow Amelia met Ailun in a marketplace and convinced him to help her release dozens of pet birds from a shop . . .

I fought to hold back my laugh and instead cleared my throat.

"I'm honored to meet you, Your Highness," I said to Wei. "My subordinate and I are entirely at your service."

At the word "subordinate," Yue's expression turned into one of unadulterated rage. I was very glad she couldn't murder me in front of Wei at this moment.

Meihua flashed me a pearly smile, and I nearly died on the spot. "Your robes are too lovely for them to be dragging on such dirty floors. Let's head to the main room if you don't mind. It's a bit cleaner there," Meihua softly suggested.

Was this the perfect woman??

> **Many divinities now realize Disciple Wei's true identity.**

> **Divinity Spirit of the Jade Moon is stunned to see these divinities again.**

> **Divinity Spirit of the Jade Moon expresses great guilt over turning her back on them.**

Chang'e and Meihua were once incredibly close, bonding over their shared love for healing and medicinal studies. But the moment the persecution against Wei and Meihua began, Chang'e turned her back on them to protect her own skin. She harbored guilt ever since and struggled to atone for it.

> **Divinity One Who Fights in Front remembers this harrowing tale.**

> **Divinity One Who Fights in Front says it was popular among divinities to warn against the influence of demons.**

> **Demon Great Sage Who Pacifies Heaven says it shows the power of demons and their cunningness.**

We walked back to the main room of the temple while Wei led the way, and I couldn't stop myself from staring at Amelia. She typically darted to me the moment she saw me, but this time, she didn't. Rather, she was preoccupied by the little boy beside her.

"Did you know I tamed this massive sea serpent?" Amelia said. "I can't show you now because it's way too big. It's probably twenty times bigger than this temple, actually. But I'll show you next time. And . . ."

Ailun gave Amelia his whole attention, never once taking his wide brown eyes off her. He looked utterly fascinated by what this strange girl had to say. Ailun was a minor communication god and served as a midway point for various guards, gods, and even cultivators, but he himself was mute. It didn't seem that Amelia minded much.

Amelia pointed at me. "Sidang, this is the woman I've been telling you about this whole time! Isn't she so pretty and cool? She's my older sister."

"Sidang?" I cocked a brow. Had she named him "sworn friend"?

"Are you on nickname terms with him?" I asked.

She nodded ecstatically as she gestured for the small boy to wave at me.

I loved Amelia. She was adorable.

Yang was wearing long black robes with gold embroidery, and he easily shifted to Yue's side, talking to her with a pleasant smile on his face while she looked rather annoyed.

That left me with Meihua. I didn't write much about her *in Surviving My First Run*, since she was mostly just a plot device, but I felt intimidated now that I was beside her.

"Yang was telling me many good things about you," Meihua said with a brilliant smile. "He told me you were a god. Is that true?"

I looked down sheepishly. "Yes, but I'm not very well known," I murmured.

"Who cares about something silly like that? I think your skills are admirable. If I could see bits of the future, I probably wouldn't be in this situation. You know about the war, right? Yang said you would."

I nodded. "Yes, and about the conflict with Daji. It's so foolish that your subjects flock to her the moment you two don't fit their impossible expectations."

Meihua laughed, politely covering her mouth. "Ha ha, do you really think so? I suppose you're right. Though, I'm just a flower divinity. I'm lucky that I've had this much success in my life. I wouldn't be a percent of what I am now without my worshippers."

"You must really have faith in them to say something like that despite their abandonment."

"Ah, really?" Meihua's face flushed, and she scratched her cheek. "Maybe I am a bit naïve."

"No way!" I instantly replied, feeling defensive of her. "You're perfectly fine as you are. Lovely even! You're one of the most powerful Chinese divinities for a reason."

Meihua froze for a moment before she gave me the prettiest smile I'd ever seen. "I like you, Peijin. I hope this gets sorted out, so we can get to know each other more under better circumstances."

I clutched the hanfu fabric above my heart. Wei, you lucky bastard!

By this point, we'd all made it back to the main room, but everyone was still split up into their small groups, catching up with one another. Except for Wei, who pouted and waited expectantly for Meihua to finish her conversation with me.

"What's been harder to deal with?" I asked. "Daji, the enemy soldiers, or the disease?"

"It's difficult for me to choose. The enemy soldiers have been hardest on Wei, since he's out fighting all day, but I've struggled with finding a cure to the disease. It seems that no matter what I do, it just keeps spreading. Daji . . . I'm afraid she's far stronger than Wei and I are by this point."

"Nonsense," I said. "You and His Highness surpass her in terms of skill, regardless of the amount of spiritual energy you two have."

"I appreciate your optimism."

I would've never considered myself an optimistic person. If anything, I spent my whole life wallowing in my own sorrow. To be told that I was optimistic made me pause for a moment. It was like the apocalypse made me sappy and ambitious.

I reached into my Boundless Bag, which I grabbed onto before this dungeon began, and shuffled around it for a bit before pulling out a bright red sphere. It was the serpent's eye that I obtained in the first arc. "Tell me what you think, since a lot of this relies on your skill as a healer."

I tapped the serpent's eye. "The biggest thing you could do is either embed this into a weapon to make a spiritual weapon or you can absorb it. But since you and Wei are divinities, the demonic energy would clash with your existing spiritual energy and likely kill you.

"But if you take just a bit of the demonic extract from this, you could whip up a potion and feed it to those with the disease. That way, the demonic energy in this will clash with the demonic energy of the disease, since one is from a sea serpent, and one is from Daji. If you execute it properly, instead of killing the civilians as the two energies try to overpower each other, you could neutralize both demonic energies."

Meihua looked at me with interest, cocking her head. "The serpent's eye is certainly potent enough for a cure like that to be mass distributed . . . Is there a reason you want me to use the extract of the serpent's eye instead of the actual serpent's eye?"

I looked away and scratched the back of my head. "Well, I was hoping that most of it would still be intact, so I could use it in the future if I needed to."

This was just a dungeon room. I didn't want to waste such a valuable item on characters that didn't even exist.

"I understand. I'll certainly try it out. It could work, but the balance is incredibly tricky, and I'm not sure how the serpent's demonic energy and Daji's demonic energy will interact."

"I think it will work," I said confidently. "I have faith in your abilities."

Wei, finally bored of standing alone, walked up behind Meihua and rested his chin on her shoulder, analyzing the serpent's eye curiously. He turned away for a moment to quietly cough into his sleeve, trying to remain polite. "If anyone can do it, Meihua can. Isn't she perfect?" Wei said, looking at me for approval.

Meihua playfully slapped his cheek. "Shush. Don't worry about anything other than the troops, okay? I have the rest covered."

"But—"

"Your Highness, instead of stressing, you should get more rest. You didn't have those big eye bags when we got married."

"It's because I'm worried about you."

Yue gagged in the background, and Yang discreetly pinched her arm.

Wei stepped back and continued to cough; this time, it grew slightly louder as his eyes squeezed shut.

Meihua immediately turned to him with a concerned look in her eye. "Is everything okay, Your Highness?"

Wei nodded, covering his mouth. "Yes, yes, I'm okay. It's . . . the city of Anyang." Wei gasped for air between his coughs. "My temples and shrines . . . They're all being burned down."

Yue's eyes widened. "Does that physically hurt gods?"

Meihua nodded solemnly. "It can if they're weakened."

Wei began coughing again as he collapsed onto his knees, one of his hands still holding Meihua as she dropped down just beside him, her eyes wide with panic. Even Ailun, who stuck to Amelia like glue, darted forward in fear.

Scathing Reviewer activated!

Hindsight activated!

Editor's Pen activated!

Had Scathing Reviewer just activated all my skills?

The hairs on the back of my neck stood up, and I whipped around, looking for what might have set me off. My blue vision pulsed until I saw the outline of an eye hidden on the front of the bell. My breath hitched in my chest.

It was outlined in white with long eyelashes, and it blinked while staring straight at me.

I lifted Zhige and swung him forward. The blade pierced straight into the eye, and it shriveled up and oozed magic before vanishing.

"She's here," I declared, dashing forward and picking up the long strand of white hair that remained. "Daji is watching us."

With a massive explosion, hundreds of Daji officers erupted through the temple's floor.

CHAPTER FORTY-TWO

Z hige!"

The growing blade flew out from my side and skewered straight through half of the surrounding officers. With loud screams, their limbs flailed before Zhige cleanly cut them in half.

Their bodies dissipated into black ash; they were only ghosts from Wei's dungeon room, after all. In Wei's eyes, however, they must have been cut in half and bleeding on the ground.

To avoid the attacks of the other flanking officers, my blue robes lifted me up into the air before slamming me against the wall of the palace. I let out a pained cry but avoided the Daji officer's assault—all their weapons landed where I had just been standing.

"Gah! Can't you be gentler?!" I ridiculed the blue robes, and they angrily whipped around the air in protest.

Barely able to catch my breath, I opened a familiar blue keyboard.

**Decrease the impact of destroyed temples and shrines
by 50% of their respective divinities.**

[Observers Chat]
Socrates: Wait, Jia Li! Wei doesn't have actual temples or shrines. He's not a real divinity outside of this dungeon room.

Fuck! The room was messing with my head. All of it felt so realistic that it was hard to believe I wasn't transported into Wei's past.

**Prevent bodily harm to gods when their temples and
shrines are destroyed in arcs and dungeon rooms.**

That edit should work even when considering karmic constraints, and this edit was better than my previous since it wouldn't increase the difficulty of killing Daji. There weren't any other secret godly disciples except for Wei, so this would've only impacted our party.

Error! Impossible within karmic constraints.

This fucking system.

**Potential edit: Decrease bodily harm to gods when their respective
temples and shrines are destroyed in arcs and dungeon rooms.**

Decrease bodily harm by how much, though?

Accept / Deny

"Meihua!" I shouted, scrambling to her. "You need to get out of here and take Wei and Ailun."

A humored look crossed her face.

"Peijin, you worry about the wrong people." Meihua smiled politely, getting onto her feet and leaving Wei and Ailun with me. Meihua leapt into the air and unsheathed a pink blade, which looked more like a ribbon. Her spiritual weapon mixed the sharpness of a sword and the flexibility of soft fabric.

With a simple flick of her wrist, the ribbon snapped with a loud *bang* and whipped through countless officers at once.

She whirled her hand, and the ribbon wrapped itself around a group of soldiers and tied them together before tearing through them. When wielded properly, it was terrifyingly wicked despite its delicate appearance.

Rejected potential edit!

**Decrease bodily harm to gods by 50% when their respective
temples and shrines are destroyed in arcs and dungeon rooms.**

Edit granted!

Ha, so Editor's Pen could screw me over then if I wasn't careful enough.

"Your Highness, lean on me," I shouted over the chaos, trying to support Wei. I hoisted him up, my legs trembling from how heavy his presence was.

Wei's eyes trembled and his previously lavish hair style now left strands of hair in front of his face. Both dried and wet blood covered his mouth from his coughs, and a large red stain was left behind on his once pristine white robes.

A god having their temples or shrines burnt down was one of the worst things that could happen, regardless of if they were a ghost, divinity, or demon. The only way they gained relevance and therefore spiritual energy was through their worshippers.

Destroying their temples meant their inevitable death from becoming forgotten.

A pang stabbed my chest at the pitiful sight, so I turned away. Wei already had so many of his temples burnt down that the destruction of a few was leaving him in such a weakened state.

Amelia had run over to defend Ailun, bringing the dire wolf with her. It roared ferociously as it latched onto a Daji officer, shredding its body.

With his newfound trust, Wei gripped me tightly, stood straight up, and stared into my eyes.

"You can see the future, right?" he said firmly despite his trembling hands. "So, tell me how this ends."

My eyes widened at his demand, and I looked away. "It's . . ."

Really, what could I say? There was nothing I could say that wouldn't be blatantly cruel.

I continued stammering before a foreboding sense overwhelmed me; Wei looked behind me and pulled out his sword.

Disciple Yue activated Magician's Hand!

I whipped my head around to see a Daji officer wearing a white and bronze mask with a sword held high above their head, ready to smash into my back.

The scene dissipated with a strange film. The Daji officer missed, landing right beside me. He looked around in confusion like he could no longer see me.

I caught Yue's glare coming from my side. She gave me a curt nod, but her eyes still showed her pride.

Wei stared at the Daji officer, perplexed by the officer's sudden lack of aggression. He looked up at me, indirectly asking what was going on.

"Yue can create illusions," I replied. "They're pretty bad ones, but they work well enough."

I waited for Wei to finish off the officer, but instead of cutting him down with a quick move, he seemed to hesitate, looking at him conflicted.

My expression fell out of annoyance.

"You're not going to get out of this without killing people," I warned.

"Believe me. I've killed thousands," he said. Wei's face was drawn in a complicated expression, and I watched his throat bob from a heavy swallow.

With a wave of my hand, Zhige darted forward and stabbed the man through the heart before cleanly pulling out, returning to my side.

The man gagged for a moment and clutched at his body. While turning into ash, he tried to scoop together his disintegrating body and keep it together.

Wei's face lit up with alarm, but his expression hardened once he heard a loud commotion just beside him.

It wasn't that Wei was against killing people. Of course, he wanted to avoid it—hardly anything justified the murder of people regardless of their innocence—but when he did kill, he realized he was a little too good at it.

And that terrified him.

Yue's face was twisted into a pained expression. She held on to one of the divine statues and desperately tried to keep the illusion intact. More and more Daji officers were seeing themselves in an "empty" room, no longer able to see any of us.

"Fuck, hurry up and kill them!" Yue screamed from behind the illusion. It was wavering more and more, exposing Meihua as she relentlessly fought against nearly a hundred officers alone. Their relentless attacks were beginning to tear through the illusion, and Yue let out another pained scream. Her limbs were squishing together.

[Observers Chat]
Socrates: These officers are a lot stronger than I thought they'd be.
Sapling123: As long as Meihua is just as good as described though, they'll be able to stop the plague
MoldyBlanket: Hopefully Daji doesn't get to her before that

Yang expertly swung his staff around, whacking it into the sides of the officers and using it to elevate himself in the air whenever one got too close.

Until a man in a black fox mask darted toward Yang.

With a flick of Yang's hand, the staff spun before him in a protective circle, but the officer's sword seemed to twist and pass straight through, heading for Yang's face.

His eyes widened in complete shock—so far, spinning his staff had served as an all-purpose defensive move, but he was now face to face with the glistening sword.

Meihua leapt into the air, the fabric of her robes beautifully fluttering as she let out a burst of spiritual energy. Flowers rained down all around her. They were intoxicating; anyone in their vicinity would be overcome by a strange drunkenness.

As soon as she grabbed him, Yang let out a loud scream and covered his face, clearly flustered again and reminded of his dungeon room. Yue looked like she would have burst out laughing except that her face was instead twisted into immense pain as the illusion's borders shrank again.

As soon as Meihua and Yang began falling toward the palace floor, the masked officer lunged forward with horrifying speeds, another blade already in hand. The black mask signified the highest ranking Daji officers—although they themselves weren't martial gods, their power rivaled many. Despite that, this masked man carried a terrifying aura . . . as if he did have an abundant amount of spiritual energy.

Yang extended his staff and swung it at the officer's legs, but instead of sending the officer flying, the staff rippled and threatened to snap before Yang pulled it back.

Instantly, Meihua flung Yang back and gripped onto her sword, whipping it in the air as it wrapped itself around the officer.

The officer reached out, gripped the blade, and pulled Meihua in.

Meihua's face filled with shock as she was reeled in. Her feet skidded against the floor as she tried to push back—until the officer grabbed his blade and pierced straight into her abdomen.

CHAPTER FORTY-THREE

Meihua looked up with a threatening smile on her face. "A real opponent would know to target a god's spiritual core."

Before I could even process the scene playing out before me, Wei flew past, and his speed and force caused me to lose my balance as I swung my arms in the air to catch myself. My hair whipped into my face, and my eyes shut as the tile beneath his every step erupted.

"Ailun! Amelia!" I screamed, stepping back and reaching my arm out defensively before them. "Stay with me!"

Amelia summoned the dire wolf and used it to create a protective barrier around the three of us. It snarled and snapped at any nearby Daji officers, leaping around us in circles.

"Peijin!" Amelia cried out, her voice trembling. "You don't need to worry about me anymore!"

A puff of air left my nose at her confident remark.

Wei reached Meihua in an instant and grabbed onto the officer by his throat before flipping the man over his shoulder, body slamming him. Dust and debris flew up all around the two of them as a loud bang echoed through the palace.

The officer wrapped his legs around Wei's abdomen and flipped Wei over, now gaining the upper hand, but Wei gripped onto his wrist and twisted his arm around to lock his elbow.

Before Wei could snap the officer's arm in half, the officer rolled back and kicked Wei straight in the face, only causing Wei to skid back a few steps. Wei spat on the ground a mixture of saliva and blood. His gaze never left the skilled officer.

Wei's fighting style was typically more elegant and not so brutish. As a master of the sword, there was no need for him to resort to martial arts and his fists in a typical fight.

However, he was a complete master of hand-to-hand combat—and desperate times called for desperate measures. Bringing his opponent closer to him gave Wei an overwhelming advantage.

"Amelia, take care of Ailun!" I shouted, turning back one last time before sprinting for the countless shrines.

Another wave of pain seemed to shoot through Wei as he coughed up blood, faltering for a moment.

That opening was enough. The black-masked officer grabbed Wei's hair and slammed him into the ground, crushing his face into the tile. He grabbed the back of Wei's head and continued to bash him into the ground; for a moment, I caught sight of Wei's pained expression before it was buried into the floor.

Ailun's eyes were squeezed shut and his clammy hands were flying all over an invisible screen. Sweat dripped off his brow in focus. I tore the dozen prayer candles Yue gave me earlier today from my bag and lined them up before Wei's shrine.

Wei lifted his head up. His eyebrow was cut, causing blood to seep down his face. When he coughed again, blood flew out of his mouth. His fingers dug through the ground until he pushed himself up. His physical strength allowed him to match the man's skilled attacks.

"Grabbing my hair? Really?" Wei asked, one of his hands reaching up to try to retie his hair with the white ribbon.

He grabbed the hilt of his sword and pushed back at the officer, one of his eyes shut as more and more blood began falling down his face. The officer retaliated but was retreating, being forced deeper and deeper into Yue's illusion until he couldn't see Wei anymore.

"Yue! Light these candles!" I commanded, shouting over my shoulder so the sound would carry out to her. The only lighter my frugality let me purchase was during Yang's arc—and I dropped that on the ground when I decided to light the forest—and myself—on fire.

Yue's voice roared back, "No! Fuck off!" Her body trembled as she tried to regain control over the ever-fading illusion. She was beginning to slip out of it, more and more of her body flickering out of its barrier.

I ran out of the barrier, dodging a sword as I brought one of the candles up to her flaming arm and held it close until it lit.

"Thanks, Yue!"

"I'm going to fucking kill you!"

Rushing back to Wei's shrine, I skidded across the broken tile, slicing my robes and knees, and reached for the statue. I held the burning candle, now illuminated with a strong black and purple flame, to all the other candle wicks as they flickered to life one by one.

My breath caught in my chest as the scent of blood and fire began to fill the air. Explosive sounds erupted behind me, and I did my best to tune them out.

One of the candles refused to light, and I held the small flame even closer to it, my hands gently cupped around the flame.

"Come on, come on," I said, finally letting out a sigh of relief as the last candle lit up.

The candles were organized in a messy line just before a statue of Wei—he was wielding a sword elegantly by his side while small, hand-carved flower petals were sprinkled by his feet. His robes looked as if they were swaying in the wind, and the stone and marble were so elegantly carved that it looked like real fabric.

I could hear Wei let out another violent cough, and his relentless assault against the masked officer slowed. With a deep breath, I brought my hands together like a prayer before me and lowered my head.

"Give these blessings to Discip—uh, Divinity Blessed Martial Guard of Salvation." I rushed through the phrase and Wei's epithet before looking over my shoulder.

At once, Wei's shoulders relaxed as he seemed to finally take in a deep breath, his chest puffing out; Wei lunged forward and stabbed straight into the officer's side with brutal strength. The man pulled back in shock, retreating as far as he could.

"Daji! Pull me back!" the man cried out. Smoke enveloped his body.

Wei's face twisted out of frustration, but by the time he finally reached the smoky cloud, the man was gone.

Wei whipped his head around like a rabid dog before he shouted, "Meihua!"

He reached her, but she had already stood up, her blade extended beside her. She dismissed him with the swish of her hand.

"Your Highness, I'm fine," she replied breathily.

He sniffled loudly and wiped at his face, dragging her by the arm deeper into Yue's fleeting illusion. "We need to get you somewhere safe. Do you need treatment? Medicine? Stars? What about spiritual energy? I can give you some of mine, but I don't have much left."

Meihua grabbed his ear and tugged on it harshly as if she were scolding him. "Your Highness, I'm completely fine! You forget I'm a healer. And what do you mean, 'What about spiritual energy?' I have more than you!"

"Oh," he mouthed in a surprised tone, seeming to forget that she could handle injuries better than anyone else in their vicinity.

His head suddenly turned toward Ailun, and they exchanged a quick glance before Wei nodded. "Peijin," Wei said, "we're going back to our camp. I need to back the Shang troops, and Meihua has her medical supplies there. I'll reestablish control from there."

Finally, Yue let out a loud groan before she collapsed on the ground, her long black hair sticking to the sweat that coated her paper-white face. Daji officers immediately darted toward her, but Yang pushed them back with a sweep of his staff.

Yang lifted Yue into his arms and held her tightly as he desperately tried to push his attackers back. Blood shot out of Yue's mouth as her limp body struggled to cling onto Yang's. With feeble strength, her arms wrapped around his neck, and she pressed her face against his chest.

More and more Daji officers surrounded Amelia's dire wolf as their blades began to sink into its fur, large splotches of blood emerging in patches all over its body. A blade nicked Amelia's shoulder, causing a thin line of blood to dribble out.

Zhige's red eye flashed, and I swung the hilt, decapitating a line of officers just before Amelia. Leaving this many soldiers alive was a threat to Wei and Meihua later, but they seemed to be never-ending, more and more of them appearing every time we killed some.

"Amelia! Summon the serpent!" I commanded.

Meihua caught my eyes, but her expression hardened when she recognized my plan.

Amelia's eyes widened in fear; the moment she summoned the beast, although it was relatively small compared to the giant temple, it would completely destroy the room we were in.

I nodded at her with a faint smile, acknowledging her concern, before my voice hardened. "Wei, I'll pay you back later!"

Amelia held the metal cuff into the air; a bright beam of light shot out as the giant blue serpent appeared, roaring and immediately crushing dozens of Daji soldiers.

Meihua swirled her sword in the air, and it indiscriminately grabbed onto the remaining low-ranking officers before dicing them into pieces. Ash dissipated all around us before the palace let out a loud groan.

The palace roared and threatened to give way. I turned around and hooked my arm around Ailun and Amelia before sprinting toward Yang and Yue.

"Meihua!"

Her pink sword retreated as it wrapped around all of us, forcing us together as the palace completely collapsed with a massive roar. The entire room collapsed, and as I looked up, chunks of debris hurtled toward us.

Meihua scribbled a seal into the air before us, and then we descended—right to the front lines of the battle.

CHAPTER FORTY-FOUR

I screamed and wrapped my arms around Meihua's long neck while we fell through the abyss. Wind violently whipped all around us, causing everyone's robes to lash into their skin. Meihua gasped for air from my tight grip but didn't say a word.

The grip of the pink sword relaxed around us as it retracted, and I slammed against the dusty floor with a surprised cry. On the other hand, Wei, Meihua, and Yang landed elegantly just beside me, helping the other members of the group.

We were in what looked to be a makeshift camp. There were various medical tools and experimental spiritual objects lying around—clearly part of Meihua's journey to find the cure. Though this small room was peaceful, the howling of citizens in agony was easily heard from the outside.

To my side, Meihua was on the ground, treating a completely exhausted Yue. Well, it looked like Yue didn't really need one of the potions I'd gotten from the dungeon rooms. Better to save it.

Wei strolled to the side and tidied himself, exchanging his now dirtied and bloodied robes with a cleaner set. "Peijin, this is our camp. We're outside of the city walls of Anyang in the Shang dynasty. There was a huge outbreak of the disease throughout the dynasty, but this is the newest epicenter. Since the Zhou want a total takeover, they're targeting Anyang, since it is the capital city and what I reign over. Meihua and I are trying to hold back the enemy troops while preventing the spread of the disease by keeping civilians outside the wall."

"Understood, Your Highness," I said. "Have Daji's soldiers made any appearance here?"

"No, but after that fight earlier with the masked man . . . I believe he's one of her disciples. He poses a threat."

I nodded my head. In *Surviving My First Run*, Daji was set to attack today and successfully kill Meihua in her attempt to protect the citizens. I wasn't sure who this black-masked "disciple" was. That strayed from the original novel; it must have been the result of the butterfly effect from something that Yang, Amelia, Yue, or I did.

Meihua turned over and looked at me like she could read my mind. Even though she was far superior than me, she was also far more nervous.

I shook my head and slapped my cheek. This was just a ghost. A ghost that really should've pursued acting. I couldn't get hung up on this.

"Peijin, if I may ask," Meihua began, her large, light brown eyes blinking at me, "how much do you know about all this? Is the future set? Our futures?"

My chest swelled at the almost genuine sparkle in her eyes. This was indeed a very convincing ghost. It would've done very well in a C-drama.

"It's not set, but I don't know much," I tried to say convincingly. "I only know what I have to change."

"Then are we on the right track?" she asked politely, her hands folded on her knees.

"Yes. The serpent's eye is a good start. If we can handle the citizens and Daji as separate threats, we'll be fine. The Zhou soldiers don't pose a threat unless Wei's hold on the region slips."

Yang stared silently at the badly beaten Yue, chewing on his lower lip with worry before he rested his chin on his knees.

[Party Chat]

Yang: But, Peijin, how do we actually get out of this room?

Peijin: Wei needs to awaken. He needs to remember all of his past memories and choose to return on the train with us.

Yang: Then couldn't we just explain it to him?

Peijin: It's more . . . complicated than that. The biggest threat is that Wei explodes and shoots off his rockers. If he remembers all his memories, then he'll go insane and kill everyone, including us. And honestly, I don't know if we're strong enough to stop him. The best method would be for Meihua to find the cure → administer it → Wei's citizens believe in him and Meihua and their spiritual power returns → they can easily defeat Daji and the Zhou troops. When things deviate from his original memory, Wei will remember what actually happened, but he'll know there are people on his side who can change his fate.

Yue: Word vomit I am not reading all that

Amelia: What

Yang: So, what exactly were his old memories if it's so traumatic that he'll kill us? I can't imagine him doing that.

Peijin: Today, Meihua and Ailun will die trying to protect citizens from one of Daji's disguised attacks. Then, Wei will be defeated, go on a rampage and slaughter thousands of his people, and be banished for two millennia.

Yang: Then we only have one shot at this, right? It's today or nothing.

Peijin: Yes.

I could feel Yang's piercing gaze searing into my back. Ignoring it, I knelt beside Yue and prodded her face with my finger.

Suddenly, she whipped her head around and bit my finger.

Hard.

I yelped and jumped back as she glared at me with murderous intent.

"Can you not fucking poke me?! I'm an injured woman!"

"I'm trying to wake you up!" I lied.

Meihua gave both of us an intimidating smile, and we stopped our bickering.

"Peijin," Meihua said. "I'll know whether or not the serpent's eye is a valuable cure in the next hour or so. I'll do everything I can to make your efforts worthwhile, and I hope I don't disappoint you."

A fuzzy feeling spread through my chest at her selflessness. Despite being the writer, I was surprised by how much trouble Wei and Meihua had with some of the Daji officers. Although the soldiers missed the "spiritual core" of this ghost Meihua, they were certainly vicious. If ghost Meihua kept her fake core well hidden, things should be fine.

Wei suited up now, preparing to go out. "I'll return within an hour to see how things are progressing with the cure. I need to push back the Zhou soldiers again before they get too close and frighten the citizens."

"We'll accompany you, Your Highness," I said.

"Peijin, while I greatly appreciate your concern, it's best you stay here," Wei said.

"You two need to be safe first. That's my priority," I replied.

Meihua's face lit up with amusement. "You'll be helping us a lot just by staying here and advising with the cure. I think you're very capable, Peijin."

Wei's eyes stared at me, and his thick brown eyebrows were furrowed together, causing small wrinkles on his forehead. He rubbed his temple for a moment, wincing, before he gently placed a hand on Meihua's back.

She turned over, looking a bit surprised. "Did you sense something?"

Wei's luck had always been incredible, and Meihua trusted his intuition blindly. "I . . . Yes, I think so. I'm not sure what I'm feeling right now."

The dungeon was already beginning to resurface Wei's memories, since things were deviating from his past.

"Meihua, I just have a bad feeling. Peijin, your party will stay here, and they'll look over the citizens while Meihua focuses on the cure and I focus on the Zhou troops. Feel free to look around the base." Wei peeled back the curtain of the tent, and the sunshine was let in.

Yang and I stepped out, leaving Yue, Ailun, and Amelia with Meihua.

I was stunned by the disaster before us.

Far in the distance, there were hundreds of Shang soldiers pressing against Zhou troops, and yet they were clearly outnumbered. If there were at least one thousand Shang soldiers, then they were drowned out by five thousand Zhou ones.

All surrounding villages and homes were being set ablaze, vicious cries ringing out from dying families. Burning mothers pushed their children back as they fell on their knees, and the scent of charred flesh filled the smoky red air.

The sight of the civilians by the tent wasn't much better. Many of them were already infected and lay on the ground, gasping for air and shoving sand and sticks into their mouth—anything to push back their hunger.

Yue's face lit up in intrigue as she stared around at the destructive sight around her. I'd forgotten how, in the end, this was still her prime element—with a demon as her sponsor, there was an innate curiosity in the violence.

This was all part of Daji and the Emperor Di Xin's plan. They knew that, with how righteous Wei was, he could never leave his people to die. In the end, he would only draw more attention to himself and become an easier target for persecution.

To fail now meant to lose his worshippers. They expected Wei to protect them, and he could not disappoint.

A stumbling man slammed straight into Wei before falling back. His movements were crazed, and long black hair covered his face. He was clawing at his decaying body. The plague had clearly infected him to a severe stage.

The large purple buboes on his skin were turning into the limbs of a demon, and they moved independently. They tore at his body, trying to rip into his flesh. Hands, feet, eyes, ears—all of them sprouted from him. It was a vile sight.

"I-is that you, Your Highness? You've been gone all morning, where have you been?!" he asked in a wild tone, his wide eyes staring at Wei from behind the curtain of hair. "Blessed Martial Guard of Salvation, oh, please! Save me! I've been infected. Please, I'm begging you, give me some spiritual energy, okay?"

Wei didn't have any spiritual energy to spare. He needed all he could get right now. Still, he gently grasped the man's hand with utmost care and gave a small burst of his spiritual energy.

The man let out a relieved groan and crumbled to the ground, finally getting a moment of peace from his agony.

"Sir, I'll be back in just a moment, okay?" Wei said, soothing. "I can promise you Meihua is doing everything she can to find some kind of relief for you."

The man, however, didn't relent despite Wei's comfort and began to grip Wei's robes so tightly that dirty black handprints were left behind.

"Please! Please! Your Highness! Just a bit more!" he screamed, growing more and more panicked as his legs buckled and a spasm went through him. His emotions were overwhelming and his behavior became erratic.

Wei tried to pull his arm back, but the man threw himself onto Wei, screaming and clawing against him.

"Don't leave me, Your Highness! Please!" His tone became more and more shrill, cracking with every word, "Why are you keeping us out of Anyang? Please, let us in! We can't live like this!"

"S-sir!" Wei exclaimed, gently trying to take a step back and push off the man. "Please calm down. I'll help you, but I need you to trust me."

I reached down and pulled the man off Wei. "Back the fuck up! Who gave you the right to put your hands on His Highness? Do you not see the exhaustion dragging him into his grave?!"

He froze in shock and turned to me, his eyes begging the question of who I was to stop him when he was on the verge of death.

The commotion only drew more eyes to the scene, and Wei was becoming overwhelmed.

"Your Highness!"

"Save us, please!"

"You're our god, aren't you?! How could you ever let this happen!"

"Why won't you let us into Anyang?! Are you trying to keep us out?"

"Is your wife putting you up to this? You're a whore's whelp!"

"You fucking dog!"

"Son of a bitch!"

"A dead god is better than a failure!"

"What's wrong, Your Highness? Are you really going to run away from your own people?! Is it because we're not from Anyang?!" The ill man screamed in agony, grabbing his hair and ripping it out before his nails dug into his arms and legs, scratching violently.

Zhige's bright red eye was spinning in my sword frantically, its pupil a small slit. It was clearly deeply disturbed by the overwhelming demonic energy.

A good author had to kill their characters. And if they survived, a good author had to break them down into a shell of empty words before building them up off the backs of the characters around them—all of whom would, eventually, meet the same fate.

And yet, watching Wei at this moment, a blazing light of strength, passion, and naivety, I felt . . .

"Yang," I said. "You need to talk to the citizens and get His Highness out of this. You've done some PR stuff before when we had accidents at the pest control company, right?"

Yang looked nervous. "Well, it was nothing of this scale."

Considering my miserable track record in communicating with my web novel readers, it was either Yang or no one.

"You'll be able to do it, Yang. I believe in you. Tell them the cure will be developed by today. We only have one shot at this anyway. Your Highness, go push back the troops. I'll handle the situation here."

Yang purchased a tacky megaphone and got on an elevated stone, speaking to the crowd. "Everybody, please listen up! His and Her Highness have heard your pleas. As of now, Her Highness is developing a cure that will be unveiled today. Please allow His and Her Highness to fulfill their individual obligations. Do not turn to the cult of Daji. His and Her Highness need your worship and gifts now more than ever. If you turn to Daji, you will be left with one feeble god rather than two strong ones to save you . . ."

Wei was deep into the battlefield now, relieved of his burden to the people but not from the anxiety that plagued him. At once, the Zhou troops began to retreat in fear. The mere sight of Wei was enough to send dozens of them sprinting for their lives and left hundreds more frozen on the battlefield. Civilians collapsed out of relief before they began to sob at the combination of Yang's speech and Wei's pending victory.

I returned into the tent, confident that Yang had the situation handled. Yue was sitting up now, watching as Meihua gingerly poked around with a variety of sharp tools. She hadn't fully healed yet; just using Magician's Hand earlier took a heavy toll on her.

Yue looked at me, her gaze hard.

"Peijin, I can feel her. Daji."

"I know. She's everywhere," I said.

Hindsight activated!

The entire interior of the tent was covered in her voyeuristic eyes. It wasn't worth getting rid of them anymore.

"So, Yue, you can sense Daji?" Meihua said. Her perception was sharp as ever.

"Yes. I'm basically the best watchdog Peijin could get."

Meihua gave an unsurprised and sweet smile. Yue immediately tensed up, sensing she messed up.

"So, you're demonic? Only demons can sense each other so keenly. I can't believe I used to admire Daji's grace, thinking she was a divinity. What a fool I was," Meihua said.

Yue nervously hiccupped and looked away.

"Don't worry. I don't usually kill demons for fun," Meihua insisted with a perfectly soothing tone.

> **Divinity Spirit of the Jade Moon turns away from the scene.**

> **Divinity Spirit of the Jade Moon is overwhelmed by her emotions.**

> **Divinity One Who Fights in Front is comforting Spirit of the Jade Moon.**

Meihua froze, staring at a bubbling purple liquid before her. She then stood up and smiled at me. "Peijin, may we talk outside for a moment? There's this pretty spot I like to go to when I need to clear my head."

"Of course, Your Highness," I answered.

CHAPTER FORTY-FIVE

Hey, hey, what about me?" Yue interjected.

"You watch the kids," I ordered.

"Huh? Seriously?!"

Meihua and I headed outside, and I followed her to a small patch of grass that had a single blooming flower. She walked in circles around the small area.

"Peijin, I think my cure will work this time."

I could feel a rush of excitement course through me. "I think so, too."

Meihua looked dazed as she stared at the ground, her once soft hands fiddling with each other. "You're quite the idealist," she said softly. "To assume that if the plague stops, everything will work itself out with Daji and the civilians. That the rumors Daji spread will end, that Emperor Di Xin will allow Wei to keep his position, and that the citizens will care for him . . ."

"Eh?! Me, an idealist?!"

"Yes . . . I think so," she whispered before smiling at me again and pulling me into a tight hug. Taken aback, I didn't return it. Her words lingered in my head even after she pushed herself back.

She laughed weakly, but her crow's feet were now visible beside her eyes. "I guess that makes the two of us idealists, then, right? What a bad match."

Meihua stared far ahead at something I couldn't see. Her eyes were slightly glazed over now. The sun was at the top of the sky, and the large, white clouds gently rolled over the scenery with a childlike innocence. Down at the ground, however, the fog of blood persisted and tainted the forest.

"Peijin," Meihua began, her voice slightly wavering now. "When I first met you, I thought you were selfish."

My eye twitched.

2,634 observers have burst out laughing!

[Observers Chat]
Socrates: She laid that out very bluntly, Jia Li.

My brow furrowed. "Hey, if you called me out here to—"

"Peijin," she said, "I wish I were more like you."

Meihua blurted out the words, not meeting my eyes: "I wish I lived a little bit more like you."

I snorted, pushing my hair back and out of my face. "You don't mean that."

A character like Meihua saying such a thing caught me massively off guard. So far, characters like Yue or Feiyu matched the exact description I'd given them. Sure, there were differences like Yue's fear changing, but there were no drastic changes.

But this? Meihua was becoming a new person before me.

"I thought about what you said," Meihua continued, no longer walking. "About saving everybody with the serpent's eye."

"Yeah, I was pretty brilliant with that, right?" I said in a cocky tone, trying to dispel the strange energy that weighed down on us.

She ignored my attempt and slightly looked over her shoulder. I could make out the gentle slope of her features now, and I hated to admit it, but they lost their charm. All I saw now was an exhausted woman before me.

"I . . . I think you know me very well, Peijin. It's strange. I haven't known you for a long time, but every time I catch you staring at me, I feel . . . exposed?" Her intonation rose at the last word like she was searching for the right word.

". . . Don't make me sound like some kind of pervert now."

"But, Peijin, when you finally told me about the serpent's eye, I realized something about myself," Meihua said with a rising voice, finally turning around to face me. "Peijin, I don't want to save these people."

This was impossible.

"At first, I was thrilled. I thought I could finally get over the fact I was a failure. You just arrived, Peijin, but this whole time . . . I really thought I was going crazy. I'd never hated myself more for being so useless. But when I heard the civilians curse out Wei . . . Peijin, I think I found a cure, but I don't want to use it on them."

Meihua's voice grew more panicked, and she clutched at the fabric of her chest. "I don't want to save any of them if this is how they repay His Highness!

I'd rather use it to kill Daji and leave things be, however they turn out. I'm not an optimist. I can't stand this! I can't stand to see Wei—"

"Hey, hey, hey!" I exclaimed, grabbing her shoulders.

Finally, she let out a cry and tears began to fall down her face. "If Wei is going to go through all of this just to be used by the people he dedicated his life to, I'd rather leave this all behind. I'll leave Anyang to Daji or Emperor Di Xin. I don't care. But I can't stand to see Wei like this!

"Burn my temples and use me. Stab me a million times with the most cursed blade. Banish me and send me to hell for an eternity. I don't care what it is, but I can't bear to see Wei sad for even a minute! No, not even a second!"

I stared at her with a pained expression. More and more tears fell down her pretty face, and she looked up at me, pleading for some kind of answer.

Meihua would have never had a breakdown like this in *Surviving My First Run*, and a small look of satisfaction crossed my face before it vanished.

So, characters weren't cemented to what I had written. Even if this was just a ghost acting, the ghosts were meant to strictly follow the characters they portray when in a dungeon.

Scathing Reviewer activated!

The last thing I wanted was for Meihua to become as pitiful as I was. There was nothing to be gained from Meihua if she turned her back on her morals.

But . . .

"I-I'm sorry, Peijin. I'm ashamed that you have to see me like this," Meihua apologized, looking deeply distraught as she lowered her head to the ground before both me. "Peijin, please tell me that I'm wrong. That I'm being terrible, and that I should've never said such things."

I looked at her for a moment, the sad, pitiful expression on her face. Such a perfect woman was envious of someone like me.

"Meihua," I said firmly, placing the serpent's eye in her hand. "Be selfish. Whatever you decide, I'll stay by your side and fight with you. Whether or not you cure them or choose to go after Daji directly doesn't matter to me, as long as you don't abandon Wei."

Meihua looked like a massive weight had been lifted off her shoulders, and she embraced me. "Then . . . if we go after Daji with the extract, that'll be settled. It'll probably cause the plague to vanish, too. Wei and I may not be as powerful as we once were, but at least it's a life I can be proud of.

"I want to live for Wei . . . and for myself, too! I want to take care of the people I love, and I won't let anyone tell me otherwise," Meihua firmly declared, tightening her grip on me and actually suffocating me this time.

I would be lying if I said it wasn't incredible to watch this scene take place before me. I watched it play out with the fascination a toddler held when witnessing something for the first time. It was a complete altering of the storyline done by my very own characters.

Meihua was like an unfinished pot still on the potter's wheel. She'd been torn down, pummeled, cracked; and in the end, she came out as something completely different—something I never intended on creating.

So, my characters did have free will after all. I smiled at the thought, my mind clouded with images of my party members.

I hugged her back, my chin hooked around the soft slope of her shoulder. "Don't thank me for being a selfish bitch."

Ha, that was definitely a cool line. *Yeah, for sure.*

[Observers Chat]
Socrates: End my suffering. This broke my heart.

"His Highness will be back soon, so let us return," Meihua said, her eyes soft and gentle. I followed just beside her.

A chill ran down my entire body. The hairs on the back of my neck stood up. My entire body straightened and Zhige's red eye spun wildly.

A childish but familiar voice seemed to play just in my ear, but no one was standing beside me other than Meihua.

"Do you really think you can get out of this room without a single sacrifice? You're a fool. You created the very system that damns you," Karma said, her tone sneering and dripping with venom.

"It would look bad that just the author has special privileges, right? Especially since nobody knows your true identity. Maybe if you told all of them, I wouldn't have to nag you so. Oh, but then again, you're too much of a coward! You're going to fail! Ha ha ha!" Karma trailed off, getting lost in her own convoluted fantasies.

My blood was boiling with rage.

"Is the future set? Our futures?"

"I only know what I have to change."

I remembered the conversation I'd had with Meihua.

"Meihua." My voice trembled with a feeling of hopelessness and utter frustration.

"Then are we on the right track?"

My chest swelled with a terrible foreboding.

"I'll do my best, believe me."

CHAPTER FORTY-SIX

Not long after we returned, Wei began the trek back from the front lines. His once white robes were so soaked in blood that they looked like they were meant to be red, but he kept his white hair ribbon pristine. He resembled a horrific demon.

At the sight of him, cries and shouts erupted from the people all around.

"Your Highness, is it really true that there's a cure?"

"Your Highness, I need more spiritual energy, please! It's spreading again!"

"Ha, you seriously think he even cares about us? His Highness is gone all day!"

"They promise that today would be the day we got the cure! We just need to worship him more!"

Despite the shouts of everyone around him, as soon as Wei spotted Meihua, his brow immediately furrowed and he stumbled into the tent, collapsing on the ground beside her. His arms hung around her neck like he was a drowning man.

She instantly supported his weight and gently led him inside a station and laid him down on some straw. For a moment, a furious expression crossed her face—one that was completely foreign on her—before Wei's voice snapped her out of her trance.

"Meihua," he cried weakly. "I'm so tired . . ."

I couldn't bear to look at Wei and promptly turned away.

"Shh," Meihua shushed him as he mumbled incoherently for a bit. Grabbing a wet rag, she did her best to wipe the dried blood off his pale skin. For Wei, killing such a large number of people always took a toll on him—he was a man who upheld justice as if it were the only value in the world, and this was how he was being repaid.

"It's okay," Meihua whispered soothingly. "You worked hard. More than hard enough. Rest now, okay? I'll take care of everything."

Careful not to disturb him, Meihua leaned down and gently pressed her lips against his forehead as if he were the most vulnerable being in the world to her.

Wei and Meihua were the type of people to vehemently deny having a favorite person. But, if anyone looked at the scene playing out before me, they would know that these two were the most important people in the world to one another.

"Ah," I sighed, stepping back and leaving Wei and Meihua alone. "I'm jealous."

[Observers Chat]
Socrates: Jia Li would punch anyone who tried to comfort her.

Snorting, I rolled my eyes. "I wish I could punch you."

I stood right outside and drew the curtain closed again. My foot tapped on the ground, crunching against the gravel, as I surveyed everything around me.

Yang had done a good job of quelling the people's anxieties. He was now resting just a few feet away, trying to hide from the bright sun. He offered me a wave and smiled.

Yue peeked out from behind the curtains and stood beside me. "So, what did you two talk about?"

I looked ahead aimlessly. "She doesn't want to cure the civilians. She plans on killing Daji directly."

Yue's eyes widened. "Is that going to work?"

"It's riskier. Curing the civilians is a passive way to uproot Daji versus facing her directly . . . either way, we would probably upset Wei. If something goes wrong with curing the civilians, they'll blame him, and his faith in humanity will be lost. If something goes wrong when Meihua faces Daji, he'll also blame humanity."

"So, we're just fucked is what you're trying to say."

"I think Meihua could pull it off. She's going to tell Wei her plan now. He just needed a moment to catch his breath."

Yue perked up. "Hey, do you sense that?"

Hindsight activated!

I looked around the crowd and spotted who Yue was referring to. Yang, sensing something was up, followed my gaze to the same, mysterious man. He was glowing with a terrifying aura of demonic energy. Sporting a familiar black uniform and mask . . .

"Shit," I murmured.

It was Daji's disciple.

"Everyone!" the man announced. "I have found the cure to the plague! Daji has led me to it!"

"For fuck's sake, I'm going to kill that bast—!" My words were cut off when I was swarmed by a group of Daji soldiers disguised as citizens. They tackled Yang, Yue, and me to the ground.

I whipped Zhige up into the air, impaling one of the soldiers and tossing his body to the side as he dissipated into ash.

Daji's disciple continued speaking. "Look there, now!" he cried, pointing straight at me. "His Highness's lackies don't want me to tell you the truth. They're trying to stop me!"

Immediately, I froze, realizing what was going on. By confronting us in public, none of us could do anything to him. If we tried to, the situation would automatically turn on Wei for the worse, since people would think that Wei was quelling dissenting civilians. My blood was boiling with rage, but I held myself back.

Wei and Meihua emerged from the tent. Amelia and Ailun were peeking out, but I shook my head, signaling for them to stay back.

The man tore off the top of his uniform. "Do you see this? My scarred figure? I've been cured of the disease!" His body was scarred with where the demonic limbs used to be, but now, it had healed over. His skin was splotchy and red where the figures once were, but it wasn't anything like the moving parts we saw earlier.

"Could this really be?"

"Then did Daji have the cure the entire time?"

"Have we put our trust in the wrong divinity?"

"Dammit, I knew His Highness was just trying to get prayer money from us!"

The man smirked. "This—this is the power of Daji!" he declared, spinning around so people could see him. "This is what happens when a real divinity, someone who listens to our prayers, is worshipped!"

His hands trailed all over his body, touching his healed skin like he couldn't get enough of it.

The disguised Daji soldiers now charged toward Wei and Meihua, but to the average citizen, it looked like a refugee uprising. At once, I gripped Zhige, but Wei shook his head for me to stop, not wanting to betray his people.

Ha, even now, he was just brimming with morality. Meihua's face twisted in pain, unsure of what to do. To her, living selfishly meant taking control of her own life—but to intentionally turn all of Wei's people against him? She couldn't make that choice for him.

Daji's disciple snickered at the setup. "There is only one way to stop this disease from ravaging you and your loved ones. It is to take someone else's life."

My breath hitched in my throat, and I could sense my party having a similar reaction. That was never the cure in *Surviving My First Run*. I never even discussed a cure because after Meihua and Ailun's death, Wei went mad. There was no need for a cure.

There was only one answer: Karma. Karma permitted this cure because the room needed to be fair. It needed sacrifice.

"But how cruel would it be if we all started killing one another? And why would we, when . . ." He paused, pointing at the two divinities strung up on the wall. "There are two divinities just before us? We could save all of us by killing them, and they'll just revive.

"Don't you see it now, everybody? The reason Meihua and Wei never provided a cure sooner was because they knew the only solution was murder, and all of you would ask them to make that sacrifice. The selfish wenches they are, they prioritized themselves over all their people!"

"Is this true, Your Highness? Did you really keep this secret from us?"

"Hang him! Kill him now!"

"That fucking bastard!"

Vomit rose in my throat, leaving its signature burning sensation, and I could barely keep myself from completely throwing up everywhere. This couldn't be happening. This wasn't real. I never wrote this, no, it wasn't possible.

"W-wait," Wei stammered, looking defeated and frail as the soldiers tied him down. Having just returned from his battle, he was already low on spiritual energy, but now that the people's trust in him was shattered, he had barely any strength left. "This isn't right! There is a cure being worked on, I promise you!"

The civilians stormed toward Wei and Meihua now, screaming and shouting and throwing pebbles while the disguised soldiers continued to tie him up. Wei's eyes flickered with shock, and for once, he looked like he regretted his decision to protect his people before himself.

"Don't you dare touch her!" Wei screamed when the soldiers began to tie up Meihua. At once, he let out a small burst of spiritual energy, but it was still enough to blow back several civilians.

"Did he really just strike us?!"

"His Highness betrayed us!"

"He's willing to kill us!"

"Zhige!" I shouted. "Get—mmph!" A foot smashed my head into the ground, against the rocks. "Let go of—!"

Yue and Yang were struggling just beside me, trying to break free but overwhelmed by the number of soldiers. They even raided the tent, grabbing hold of Ailun and Amelia.

"Your Highness," cooed Daji's disciple, "shouldn't you make this sacrifice for your people? I'm sure you don't want them to go for Meihua next if you put up a fight."

Wei's eyes widened and his body went limp. Meihua gave him a mortified look.

"Don't do this for me, Wei," she pleaded. "You don't need to do this. Please."

There was nothing we could do. If we fought back, it would mean the death of Wei, as he would be entirely abandoned by everyone. If we didn't, he would be stabbed by all of the infected.

Wei made the decision for us.

"Go. If someone has to suffer, it should only be one of us."

Meihua's face steeled at his words, but her body thrashed against the guards. She couldn't stand the sight for a moment longer, but the moment she whipped out her sword, countless officers sprung on her and began to beat her into the ground.

Soon, all of us would face the same treatment by both the soldiers and civilians.

Although the civilians felt like nothing more than ants, the soldiers possessed incredible power thanks to them receiving the growing spiritual support of Daji.

I could feel my ribs get kicked, causing me to vomit on myself. My head was pressed into it, and I began choking on my own filth. People trampled our limbs and pinned us down, and all I could do was crawl over to Amelia and Ailun, shielding them with my body.

[Observers Chat]
KWrap: PEIJIN BREAK FREE YOU GOT THIS
MoldyBlanket: Oh my god I can't even watch anymore
Sapling123: PLEASE PLEASE YOU HAVE TO HELP WEI
CannedWorms: This room is cursed. There's just no happy ending for Wei.

More and more people lined up just before Wei, comically in single file. Swords were strewn out all before them as the first woman stumbled forward, wielding it.

"I-I'm sorry. I'll burn a candle for you later. Thank you for sacrificing yourself for your people!"

She stabbed Wei through the heart, and he let out an agonizing scream, thrashing and trying to break away from the searing pain. Immediately, however, the giant black marks that covered her skin shrank and vanished.

"It's true . . . It's true! It really does work! Oh, thank you, thank you!"

"Fuck—!" I screamed in rage. This "cure" shouldn't even have worked. The only reason it worked was because this was a dungeon, and although Wei was temporarily given elevated powers to properly relive his memories, he didn't have a spiritual core because he was, after all, a banished divinity.

So, Wei was trapped in this middle ground. The dungeon room assumed he had a spiritual core and kept him alive after each "kill," despite him not having one.

"You knew this!" I shouted at Karma in between attacks. "You planned this perfectly, didn't you?!"

Just behind the woman was a small child. The trembling mother placed the blade in the child's hands and guided him to Wei's trembling body. She shut his eyes with one of her hands while her other helped him thrust the sword through Wei's heart.

"It hurts! It hurts!" Wei cried, tears streaming down his face as a sob tore through his throat. If he looked exhausted before, he looked ruined now. Blood gushed out of his chest, but there would never be relief for an immortal man.

The woman cried, pulling her child back and bowing deeply before Wei. "Thank you, Your Highness! You're saving us!"

Meihua stared at the sight from the ground without making a sound. Her eyes were so wide, so filled with heartbreak and turmoil, that they looked like two blank disks taking in the world for the very first time.

"It hurts! It hurts!" More and more people ran forward and stabbed him through the heart relentlessly, clamoring to kill him and rid themselves of their pain. The more people who were cured, the more who seemed to grow frantic and seek their own relief.

"IT HURTS! IT HURTS! IT HURTS IT HURTS IT HURTS *IT HURTS—*"

The disciple of Daji clamped a wad of soiled cloth over Wei's face to silence him. Wei squeezed his eyes shut, and for the moment just before they closed, he seemed to be looking out into the world, begging for anyone to end his suffering.

Meihua's gaze was half-lidded and completely blank.

CHAPTER FORTY-SEVEN

Meihua turned toward me, not even fazed by the people stomping on her anymore. When I looked into those cold eyes, I knew what she planned to do.

She was going to kill Daji.

It wasn't revenge against the civilians that Meihua wanted. Despite all the feelings of regret and spite that consumed her, she wasn't going to stoop so low as to make her last move be one to end everyone's life. She didn't want Wei to hate her—that would have been true death.

Meihua hoped that they would leave Wei be. That was her only wish.

Wei's pained screams could no longer be heard, but it wasn't because of the rag that had been shoved into his mouth. So many people had picked up their swords by now and stabbed it through his heart, killing him over and over, that his entire abdomen had been reduced to no more than a bloody pile of gore and slush.

More and more people also missed—no longer able to even detect where Wei's heart was. Some people stabbed into his stomach, his neck, or his nearly amputated arms and legs.

Yang tried to move toward the crying Yue to shield her, but he couldn't do so without being pummeled. By now, his body was covered in bruises.

Both children were still beneath me. It was difficult not to crush them when so many people were parading on my back, but I protected them with all my might. I could hear Amelia's sobs coming from below me.

Finally, as the civilians finished their brutal stabbings of Wei, they withdrew.

They scrambled toward the Anyang wall, trying to make it inside and escape the havoc of war. Slowly, the surrounding area dissipated.

[Observers Chat]
Socrates: Jia Li, you have to get up. Please.

My blue robes tugged me back onto my feet but couldn't stop me from stumbling forward as I held Zhige, trying to steady myself.

Although a cure now existed and I had altered the previous storyline, everything was just as miserable. For the self-proclaimed god of fate, I totally fucked up my job. This was an indirect battle between Karma and me, and it was serving as a bad omen for my upcoming fate.

With a deep breath, Meihua finally shoved off the last few Daji soldiers and killed the rest, including the ones pinning my party down. She was no longer worrying about the few citizens who were still there to witness it.

Ailun screamed and sobbed, but Amelia wrapped her small arms around him. Just to their left, Yang stretched out his arms to catch Yue as he tried to get her to stand, cupping her cheek and lightly shaking her head.

Wei, however, remained lifeless. One of his eyes was lying beside his entrails on the ground, already regenerating. It looked around, speaking for a mute Wei. It locked eyes with me for a moment before spinning around, frantic and pitiful.

Meihua? Ailun? Peijin? Yang? Help me, it hurts. It hurts.

The eye asked all of those things with an innocent sense of loss.

[Observers Chat]
Socrates: Jia Li, get up! Meihua is leaving! You're so lucky that Archangel Michael isn't watching this play out. You'd be on his hit list right now!

"Shut up! You don't think I'm trying to get up?!"

Blue screens were lit up all around me as I was trying to level up whatever stats I could. Physique? Agility? Strength? Goddammit, was there anything I could even do?!

Meihua landed on the ground and dust flew all around her. A look of determination had crossed her once-delicate face, and though her lower lip trembled, she looked at me with a kind smile. Her pink lips curled up slightly at the ends, and her eyes closed into thin crescent lines. Her long lashes glistened in the smokey light before she opened those ink-colored eyes.

She laid the serpent's eye beside me, having already taken some of the extract. "Thank you, Peijin."

Meihua made her way to the Anyang wall and scaled it. Civilians, now cured, had already begun to flood into Anyang.

"Move over! Let me in!"

"Thank God! This is what we needed, and that twisted divinity was keeping us from this!"

"We should've stabbed him more times. If it's His Highness, it's deserved!"

Meihua had entrusted me with Wei's current body. She knew I would do everything I could to reunite them.

I bagged the serpent's eye, and I looked around at my bruised and battered party on the ground. "Everybody, get up now!" I ordered. "Meihua is going to defeat Daji, so we need to move fast and support her!"

I turned to Ailun. "Ailun, you and Yue work together to find out where Meihua and Daji are. We need to catch up to them as soon as possible."

I approached the muddied pool of guts and limbs that greeted me. Wei's limbs were still tied—more accurately, his feet and hands were still tied, but the rest of his body was missing.

I picked up what I thought resembled his head. His lips and mouth were barely visible, but it would have to be good enough.

As I scurried through my bag, I turned around and ordered the rest of the party, "Buy whatever is left in the Azure Dragon Store and worship Wei. Make it count."

"The best options are all in the higher-tier subscriptions," Yang called back, looking utterly defeated. His orange eyes had dimmed significantly, and it looked like at any moment, he would descend into some unforeseen emotion.

Goddammit. "Chang!" I screamed, pulling out all the elixirs from the earlier dungeon rounds. I was going to use them on Wei now—if anyone could stop Daji, it would be him. I wasn't stupid enough to take on battles I couldn't win.

I would have to severely skew Karma in my favor to do that, and Karma would probably only be pleased if I died.

Chang hesitantly appeared before me, clinging onto his tail and rocking back and forth anxiously. "Are you going to blackmail me again?"

"Chang, give me your scales. I need them to worship."

"Huh?! No way! These are precious, sacred treasures!" he refuted, his voice shrill and more annoying than usual.

"Why do you think I'm asking for them? I'm not looking for a souvenir."

Chang clung to his tail and pulled it even closer to his body.

I sighed in annoyance before barking, "Yang, get a few of Chang's scales and offer them to Wei. Meihua is only a ghost, so prioritize Wei."

Chang shouted in a mixture of protest and anxiety. "No! I seriously won't fall for your schemes this time, Peijin! There's a hierarchy, and you're below me."

Yang's stormy eyes locked with Chang's, and his scales immediately stood up in fear.

I was gently pouring the regeneration elixirs into Wei's mouth, but most of it seemed to spill out, since he resembled an anatomical figure in a biology textbook more than an actual human.

The skin around his mouth was missing, and I could see the contours of his facial muscles. But as more of the elixir was drunk, it immediately began to heal his wounds as healthy skin returned.

I stared at the sight with incredible interest and intent. I had written about these very same injuries in *Surviving My First Run*, but seeing them in person was an entirely different experience. I wondered if I were to rewrite this scene how much better my descriptions could be.

Scathing Reviewer activated!

"Your Highness, when we make it out of this, you're really going to owe me a lot," I grumbled. "Do you know how expensive these elixirs are? And here you are, using all of it. Just one man, too!" My voice trembled slightly from the adrenaline.

I unwaveringly poured more of the elixirs into his mouth, and he began to gulp it down greedily as his body seemed to recreate itself. He looked like a feral dog lapping up water for the first time in days.

"Slow down. I'm not taking it from you. If you choke right now, you'll probably die for real."

Wei grabbed my hand firmly and sat up, chugging the elixir as fat beads dripped down his face. When his eyes met mine . . . How could I describe them?

Wei was broken—no, he had been a broken man. He was a man who just realized that he could sacrifice his entire life for those around him, and they would still be cowards. There was no greater monster than his worshippers, and what did that mean for a god so righteous and moral as Wei?

But now, he was being nurtured. Specifically by me, a woman who spat cruel words at him and didn't seem to care about him at all if it weren't for the fact I was wiping the elixir off his face with utmost tenderness.

Wei's eyes welled with tears, and I pulled back, unsure of where my sudden attentiveness came from.

Wei's demeanor instantly changed in a moment, as if he was suddenly deeply preoccupied. Getting up, he searched for his sword and wielded it confidently, grabbing the hilt with fresh hands.

"Peijin, I'll properly thank you after," he said with complete anxiety.

"Wait, let us help you," I blurted out. "If you're confronting Daji right now, you'll need all the help you can get."

His face twisted into an unreadable expression. His entire sense of morality had just been completely destroyed, yet standing before him was an odd group of people who shared an innate bond but also seemed like they sometimes hated each other. The sight felt familiar to him, but he didn't know any of these people.

Keeping my eyes glued on his face, I added awkwardly, "And you also need a set of clothes, Your Highness." I was already extending the new white cultivator robes out to him.

Wei didn't have the energy for any embarrassed reaction as he took the robes from my hand and tied the belt around his thin waist.

I heard Chang yelp behind me and smack Yang firmly on the back of his head—now, Yang was holding one scale. He whispered into his hands and sent the spiritual offering to Wei. Instantly, Wei seemed to grow taller as a glowing aura resembling a halo appeared all around him.

Chang's scales were technically divine objects as they belonged to an Azure Dragon, one of the Four Auspicious Beasts of China.

"Peijin, there are no words I can use to thank you enough." Wei's voice cracked, and I could've sworn I saw tears beneath his fluttering lashes. "But if you hadn't . . . if you hadn't helped me, I think I really would've lost it, ha ha ha . . .

"When I was out, for some reason, you appeared in my memories. You had short hair. I don't know what I saw, Peijin, but I can feel that you're important to me."

He paused, and I could only stare at him with a flummoxed expression. Wei was recalling his current memories.

The tips of my ears were a slight red as I awkwardly tried to thank him, avoiding his gaze and turning to the side. "W-well, um . . . it's just how things should be?"

He smiled curtly before, with utmost sincerity, adding onto his previous statement.

"Please, catch up with me soon."

Wei ran so fast toward Meihua that it looked like he was flying, and he left all of us in the dust.

CHAPTER FORTY-EIGHT

Hissing through his teeth, Wei rested his violently throbbing forehead against his hand. Recently, Wei was constantly overtaken by powerful headaches that only got worse.

Who are you? Wei asked himself when he turned his back on Peijin and ran toward Meihua.

When he had been stabbed, gored, and murdered repeatedly at the hands of his very own worshippers, the very same people he devoted his life to protecting, he could only think of the overbearing pain.

But in the silence when he had been nothing more than long strands of human skin and organs, he thought of two things—his family and the weird, rude, and crass cultivator who suddenly appeared and sided with him.

Except, Peijin wasn't a cultivator in his memories—she was a woman with a short bob, blue hoodie, and that same glaring expression.

"Do exactly as I say, because if you don't, Wei will die at my hand."

"As soon as the room starts, you'll lose all your memories."

That voice echoed in his mind, but Wei couldn't pinpoint where he would have even heard such a phrase—nor what context they would be spoken in.

Had Peijin not offered a hand to both Meihua and him, what would have happened?

Wei groaned, grabbing onto his head as more thoughts or memories—he didn't even know what they were anymore—flashed before him. It didn't matter right now; he needed to find Meihua and help her defeat Daji.

He managed to grab hold of his bloodied white ribbon from the puddle of his organs and bones and tied his hair back up with it. One could hardly tell it was white anymore, but with a wave of his hand and just a bit of spiritual energy, it returned to its pristine state.

Without an ounce of hesitation, Wei stabbed into his forearm with his blade, blood trickling out. He thrust the tip of his sword into the ground to steady it as he dragged his index and middle fingers through the wound, coating them in the thick scarlet liquid.

His blood seemed to glimmer with spiritual energy from Chang's scale. He had no clue why such a low-ranking gremlin would be here, but he didn't question it.

Wei squatted down on the ground and elegantly tucked in his new white robes as he dragged his fingers on the ground, forming a seal. The quickening beat of his heart made him feel like he was suffocating, barely able to breathe due to his anxiety.

A week ago, His Highness could have gone head-to-head with Daji and come out victorious.

Now? Wei would be lucky to walk away with his life spared.

He bit down on his tongue as he finished drawing the teleportation seal to Meihua's location. The two were so inseparable that they could always sense each other's presence no matter where they were. Tearing his sword from the ground, Wei promptly activated the seal.

The seal remained perfectly still on the ground, dull and inactive.

Wei's heart fell.

He'd have to get to her manually—and if Meihua was already fighting Daji, she'd be weak by the time he made it.

With a deep inhale, Wei redirected his spiritual energy to his legs, feeling it swirl and move all around as his body heated up and tingled.

He sprang forward at godly speeds, bursting straight through the wall and past all the civilians who had completely forgotten their half-hearted promises about lighting him candles.

Wei was moving so fast that he was nothing but a passing breeze that disturbed a few strands of their hair.

Except to a familiar man in front of the crowd, who turned, his eyes following Wei.

Wei's form darted and weaved through trees, flattening out the grass beneath him as he seemed to fly through.

What did "justice" or "fairness" even mean to Wei anymore? Was it the utter abandonment of his people for his family? Was it justice for Wei's people to take matters into their own hands after his mortifying failures to stop the Zhou Army or the demonic plague?

Was this his retribution?

Meihua's bright smile and flowing chocolate hair appeared in his mind before the illusion was shattered by the drab, lifeless expression that filled her face when she watched him get stabbed through the heart thousands of times.

Tears welled up in his reddening eyes, but he blinked them away, bringing up a white sleeve to wipe at his face as his lower lip trembled. A sob rose in his throat, but he held it back, the only sign of his overwhelming pain in the tremble of his lashes.

Wei had always been an emotional man—too sympathetic and empathetic for his own good. It was what made him the greatest divinity, but it was also what made him weak enough to be trampled.

Even if this was how Wei would be repaid, and even if he would be stripped of all his divine powers in the end, he couldn't hate these people. Because if Meihua and Ailun and all the others were alive, then there must be other good people left in the world, too.

At least, that's what Wei wanted to cling to.

The forest path became more and more familiar as he could make out the tip of the shrine peeking out through the trees before he came to a halt.

The green grass below him was colored a deep red.

His eyes tracked the bloody mess on the ground into a cluster of looming, dark trees, and Wei felt his heart tighten in his chest. The scent of peach blossoms and lilies filled the air, giving the scene a light, iridescent glow.

If Meihua released this powerful of a skill, she must've been gravely injured.

"Daji . . . I'll kill you!" Wei swore, darting into the forest and leaping through it, his feet no longer touching the ground as he flew toward the end of the bloody path. His heart was beating relentlessly in his suffocating chest, his face growing more and more red as he could no longer stop for breath.

The buzzing in his ears grew louder and louder; Wei readjusted his grip on the hilt of his sword, trying to hide how much he was trembling.

What if what he found at the end of the trail wasn't Meihua? What if all he saw was the bloodied and mutilated corpse of his most beloved?

He finally reached the end of the path, eyes wide and crazed.

Before Wei, a vile, grotesque sight met him; bile rose immediately in his throat, burning him.

A towering white fox with nine flapping tails met him, its long and snarled teeth coated in both dry and wet blood. Its face was nimble and thin, almost beautiful, apart from its muzzle stained in crimson and its jeering yellow eyes. Its sharp, pearly white teeth had pieces of pink flesh stuck between.

"Y-you . . ." Wei stammered, his vision going red. "How dare you?!" Wei roared, his cultivation robes flying around him in a flurry of violent, dangerous, and uncontrollable spiritual energy.

A small whimper behind him caught his attention. It was barely audible and carried away by the breeze of spiritual energy.

Meihua's body clawed toward Wei. A trail of blood was behind her, growing as she dug her hands into the ground and moved forward one grueling bit at a time. Clutched in her arms was the serpent's extract in a vial, glowing with demonic energy.

Her robes seemed to fall flat just after her torso, and they were soaked in blood. As Meihua pushed herself up, flashing Wei that warm smile, he noticed it.

One of her legs was completely torn off.

"I'm really sorry, Wei," she whispered, bright tears streaming down her face now. They pooled at her lashes before they fell like bright orbs, splattering on the ground below her. "I really . . . I really . . ."

Daji's tails suddenly grew, waving all around her until they hid the glowing sun with their thick fur. At once, they shot forward—straight at Meihua.

Wei leapt forward and with flicks of his sword deflected the tails relentlessly; they were never ending, pushing him further and further back until he slammed into a tree. He picked up Meihua into one of his arms, shielding her body as they both were thrown into the ground.

"Don't waste your breath trying to talk to me!" Wei screamed, his voice hoarse as he held back his tears. "Heal yourself! Heal yourself!" he repeated frantically.

Meihua grabbed a hold of her pink ribbon sword again and whipped it against the ground—but for whatever reason, it didn't seem to respond to her nearly as well. In fact, its base was turning black.

A mixture of horror, frustration, and utter despair bloomed in Wei's chest. Blood soaked all of Meihua's robes, and she looked like a fragment of the woman she was.

"Stop it! Conserve your energy, Meihua!"

Meihua gently shut her eyes, her lashes twinkling from moisture as a few more tears slid down her cheeks. "I am," she whispered softly. The only time in her life that she had made a decision for herself and her family, it ended like this.

Carrying Meihua in one arm and his sword in the other, Wei darted forward and shot for Daji's back. He landed a hit, twisting his blade as he forced it into Daji's flesh deeper and deeper until a spray of blood shot at his face.

Daji roared out of pain and anger as she whipped around, swiping at him and forcing him to retreat. She steadied herself on her feet—the gash had torn the tendon in one of her hind legs, leaving her stagnant and crippled.

"Daji, if it's power you want, if it's money you want, whatever it is, you can have it all!" Wei screamed, wiping the blood off his sword. More and more of Meihua's pink sword was turning black, and Wei couldn't stop the anxiety overtaking him. "But leave my family out of this!"

Daji glared at him with her fox eyes. Her lips curled into a snarl, and she spoke with a deep, sultry voice.

"As long as people with the same values as yours exist, people like me will never thrive."

"Then I'll tear you down right here, and you won't have to worry about any 'values' anymore."

Blood erupted from Wei as a bronze sword pierced straight through his chest.

Blood pooled in Wei's mouth as he coughed, causing it to spray out.

Wei's grip on Meihua slackened as she fell to the ground. Sweat covered her forehead; Meihua was practically panting now as her entire body trembled out of pain. Despite being one of the greatest divine healers, she was in riveting pain and could do nothing but collapse on the ground.

The serpent's extract slid from her grasp.

The man behind Wei stepped forward, sliding his blade out of Wei in a clean movement. It was the man from the Anyang wall—the one who led the massacre against Wei.

At the sight of him, Wei's heart filled with immediate fear as he clutched his chest. It was in the very same place that he had stabbed Wei earlier . . . right through the heart.

"What do you think of my disciple, Wei? Isn't he impressive?" Daji called out, her ears pinned back and tails swirling in the air in a playful manner.

Daji's disciple walked forward and placed a foot on the vial of serpent's eye extract. Meeting eyes with Meihua, he crushed it fully and twisted his foot so it would be no more than ash mixed into the bloody dirt.

Meihua let out a loud cry as she watched the vial shatter beneath him. She hollered and cried before another wave of pain tore through her, causing her to fall limp.

She hid her face and weapon from him, but he kicked her back and jostled her face forward, staring right at her.

"Didn't I tell you to stay at the wall?"

Wei focused his spiritual energy on reviving himself, but it would still take some time to recover from a fatal wound. Daji was laid-back, looking like she had no care in the world as she licked the wound on her leg.

"Meihua," Daji said nonchalantly, "you're a fool if you think such a meager demonic object would affect me. Especially when you guard it so weakly. It has no more power than the lowest goblin. This is really how one of the heavenly realm's strongest divinities tries to save the world? Look at all the people you let die."

After a painstaking amount of time, Meihua's body finally stopped trembling. She navigated herself until she was standing and turned to face Wei. Miraculously, it seemed like she had healed or repaired her leg—Wei couldn't make it out from beneath her bloodied robes. Her lashes were lowered and hid her eyes as she spoke to both Wei and Daji.

"The only world I wish to save is him."

Meihua erupted into the air with a flash of blinding lightning as she whirled the black sword in the air, whipping it as the forest around her seemed to awaken and burst out of the soil.

CHAPTER FORTY-NINE

An incomprehensible amount of spiritual energy erupted through the forest as all of the plants and flora seemed to tear out of the ground, twisting and turning into the air before shooting straight toward the man and Daji.

Daji's eyes widened in complete disbelief as her nimble body leapt onto its feet and dodged the attack.

Wei's expression was twisted into fear and terror; did Meihua . . . have this kind of power?

As she swirled in the air, her black sword slicing and tearing into Daji's skin, she resembled a primal, terrifying beast. But still, to Wei, it almost looked like she was trying to hold back. This newfound power tapped into an endless pond of spiritual energy, but Meihua wasn't using all of it.

Realizing the new threat that Meihua posed, Daji darted behind her disciple before she unhinged her jaw, fire bursting out and causing all of the neighboring trees to light on fire.

Meihua coughed, covering her mouth with her already bloodied robes but not once did she slow her endless attack.

Wei gripped his chest, blood trickling out from the hole in his heart.

Please, please, please, please.

He begged and pleaded, tears welling up in his eyes as he tried to recover. He gripped onto his sword as Daji's disciple stormed straight at him, killing energy blazing from him.

Wei beat back against the man, who approached with even more ferocity. Wei channeled all his spiritual energy into each swing, slashing at the man, but the man perfectly matched his tempo, nearing Wei.

At the sight of the man's murderous intent, Meihua turned all her power to him, watching as branches erupted through his entire body before they spun and tore him into pieces.

Daji's tails suddenly seemed to multiply, turning into dozens behind her as they all shot straight at a distracted Meihua.

"No!" Wei screamed, darting forward, blood spilling out of the gaping wound in his chest, his hands sweating, his eyes welling with tears, his entire body trembling in complete horror and fear and devastation.

Meihua whipped her head back around and attempted to cut through the tails but to no avail—they pierced through her before erupting into bright red flames.

She created a vortex with her sword, whipping it in the air to quell the raging fire, but it couldn't fix the wounds littering her already wrecked body. Whatever power she had used to heal her leg, she now held it back.

With a faint smile, she thrashed her sword one last time before letting it go; its long black blade buried into Daji's entire body like shackles before she was seized.

"No!" Wei cried, his hands digging into the ground in disgust of his weakness. A martial god? Really? How could he have ever called himself a martial god?! How could he call himself anything other than a useless fucker?!

"No! Please, I'll do anything! Daji, please, you can do whatever you want to me but leave Meihua out of this! Please! Torture me for centuries, banish me for a millennium, but let her go!" Wei screamed, feebly slashing his sword as tears streamed down his face. "Please!"

"Wei," Meihua said softly, looking at him as the tails crushed her body. Her eyes were bright red, and little tears trickled down her face as she gave him a wide grin. "I'll die without regrets."

"Please!" Wei screamed, feeling no shame or dishonor at his pitiful state.

Meihua didn't bother bracing herself as Daji's jaw unhinged, her claws and tails holding Meihua down as they dug into her small body.

Meihua let out a small sob through her endlessly bright smile. "At least that's what I'd like to say," she choked. "But, I do have one. I wish I could've spent the rest of eternity with you."

"MEIHUA!"

Daji's jaw snapped shut on Meihua's head before tearing her entire spine out of her body, her spiritual core being pulled out. Crimson blood erupted as Meihua finally fell limp, completely lifeless. Meihua's beautiful features were lost in the hungry snaps of Daji's mouth as she hungrily chewed and swallowed her body, blood covering her lips. Wei could hear the grotesque sound of her spiritual core crunching.

Wei collapsed and stared at the sight before him in utter silence. He couldn't hear anything other than one repeating phrase.

I wish I could've spent the rest of eternity with you.

I wish . . .

I . . .

"Ah . . ." Wei gasped, staring at the ground as his nails gripped the dirt, digging into it. "Aghhh," he wailed, crying and screaming as he shouted louder and louder, pounding into the ground as hard as he could but hardly making a dent.

He gripped his head and screamed, the sound of Meihua's body crunching beside him. There would be no funeral. There would be no worship or candles burned or a goodbye. There would never be a sendoff, never be another portrait illustrated, never be . . .

Meihua was dead.

"Meihua, please, I can't! I can't!" Wei continued screaming, curling up into his small body like a pathetic abandoned dog.

Daji let out a satisfied sigh before cackling wildly, Meihua's blade still digging into her skin. Even after her death, her sword refused to let go.

A spiritual weapon without its owner was wild and lost.

Daji grabbed onto Wei's ruined body and hoisted him into the air, her face and claws covered with the scraps of Meihua.

She smiled at him, licking her chops as she gently undid his hair ribbon, tying it to both his hands instead. Instead of thrashing or attempting to escape, Wei hung there, completely limp. He was no more human than Meihua now.

"You really are a dumb dog," Daji said with her sly voice. "To let your emotions take such a hold over you. That's why fools like you end up abandoned on the streets.

"But, Your Highness," Daji continued, "I don't fall victim to such foolish emotions. I don't stop just because someone dies." Her ears flicked toward her dead disciple's body still bleeding out on the ground. She released Wei from her grasp.

Wei tumbled toward the ground, slamming against the sharp rocks and landing awkwardly. His limbs were entangled with the bloodied ribbon still wrapped around his wrists, yet he made no effort to set himself upright.

"Ah . . ."

A pitiful groan was all Wei could muster.

Meihua was dead.

Wei let out an anguished and animalistic moan, pressing the back of his hands against his shut eyes, which were riddled with tears as they streamed down his face. "Agh . . . I—" he stammered, "I . . . I . . ."

I can't.

Those were the only words His Highness wanted to say, and Wei couldn't even do that.

Because for someone who had fallen from such a dazzling height, Wei realized he couldn't do a lot of things.

No matter how strong he was, he couldn't save his people. No matter how loyal he was, it didn't mean whoever he protected wouldn't leave him in the dust, with no regard or care for him.

No matter how much he loved Meihua, he couldn't save her. No matter how strong Wei was, no matter how many worshippers he had, no matter how many soldiers he killed before returning to Meihua in complete tears every day, Wei still couldn't do anything.

In the end, Wei became nothing more than a stray dog kicked to the curb, tail tucked, and clinging onto memories of the generosity he once experienced.

And no one would even bother to throw him a scrap.

Daji sneered above him, her lips curled over her stained-red teeth, and her fox eyes were slanted and menacing, full of malice and raging fire. Nine white tails flicked behind her as if Daji were deeply entertained by the sight before her, and she lifted a slim paw to humorously shove and pull on Wei.

She batted him with his foot, and he accepted it.

How could any of this be fair? It wasn't. It definitely wasn't. But Wei was only a boy, freshly eighteen, and one who thought that the world was righteous as long as he worked hard enough. And he could always work hard enough—who could stop him?

The horrible reality of the world and people around him sank in.

"I thought I could change something," Wei cried softly, Daji's paw knocking him around on the ground as he clung onto the ribbon firmly, holding it against his chest in a feeble effort to protect it like it was his only thing left. It became a symbol of his height as a divinity and his disastrous downfall.

Protect it from what? Why did he even care? There was blood on his hands. There had always been blood on Wei's hands. Wei was no saint, and he was no pinnacle of morality—how many families had he torn apart as he slaughtered their sons and daughters on the battlefield?

His piercing headache only became worse and worse as it brought a fresh set of tears to his reddened eyes; it was accompanied by the bright flashing images of Peijin's face and the face of a young blond girl who had clung to Ailun.

Fairness? Fairness?! Was this how he was supposed to be repaid for all he had done?! Was this all people ever wanted from him? And now, after he had lost it all, the rest of his days would be spent in prison.

What a sick, twisted, cruel joke—and the undeniable truth. Just like how Meihua was only leftover scraps of meat and skin behind him.

"I'm really sorry, Peijin. I hope that your end is better than mine," Wei prayed before grabbing the hilt of his sword.

Suddenly, Daji burst out laughing, cackling with pleasure.

"And here I thought you were the darling of the heavens!" she cried, her voice rising and falling with each word like the shrill calls of a fox. "Dream on.

"You think it's your fault, Your Highness? You're wrong," Daji spat, lowering her face so she was level with Wei's dead and cold eyes. "The world has failed you. There is no justice or salvation, and you, with all your foolish thoughts, never recognized that.

"Do you think your people would've left you otherwise? Do you think they would've stabbed you in the heart thousands of times until you were nothing more than a puddle of flesh that stuck to the bottom of their shoes as they walked away?! Are you really that much of a fool?!

"The only one who has ever wronged you are all of the people you ever believed in," Daji finished, her voice jeering and eyes slitted.

Anger flared in Wei's heart, beginning as a small seed before it became a roaring fire in his chest. Normally, His Highness would have never reacted so strongly to provocative words—it clashed with the Four Books and Five Classics, which he preached to everyone around him. Lead a good life, become a strong leader, cultivate a moral and righteous character . . .

But weren't *his* people to blame? Wasn't there some truth in Daji's words, even if she was a cruel and unforgiving beast?

With a growing shout, Wei stood up and lifted his sword, swinging it toward Daji's head, his emotions bursting and overflowing out from his ruined body.

Wei tumbled forward, his blow missing as he landed on all fours again, clutching the ribbon like a crazed man. He left himself completely exposed.

Blood splattered all around him.

Wei lifted his lowered eyelashes, bringing a hand up to his chest.

It wasn't his blood.

Daji let out a wretched scream as Meihua's black sword suddenly tightened, digging right through Daji's fur and skin. The spiritual weapon seemed to have one last eruptive burst of energy as it sliced into her large body, causing blood to spray out.

Reeling back, Daji clawed at her own body, trying to get the sword to loosen as it returned to its original light pink color and fell off her—the black energy that once possessed the blade began seeping into Daji's body instead.

Without warning, Daji's entire body began to twist as mysterious black forms pushed out of her body. Inky vomit erupted from her mouth as her eyes widened, bloodshot and trembling.

"Wei, you fucker!" Daji roared, latching her tails onto the nearby trees in a feeble attempt to steady herself. Her claws dug into the ground, but more and more black figures erupted from her face and resembled the tails of a snake.

"You fucking dog! You were married to a demon this entire time?! Ha ha ha, to think that even someone like His Highness would do such a thing!" Daji's screams became more and more frantic as figures resembling serpents grew from her body.

In futile, desperate attempts, Daji lit herself on fire in an attempt to stop the overflow of demonic energy. Her demonic energy was clashing with someone else's—Wei stared in utter disbelief.

Meihua? A demon? Never.

"I'll kill you! I'll really fucking kill you this time, Wei! You would let your wife die just to kill me?! I never took you to be that kind of man, Wei, you fucking womanizer! You're just as twisted as the rest of us are!"

Daji's physical form alternated between her countless disguises. Suddenly, she was a beautiful woman with long white flowing hair, a seductive concubine, a small and tattered fox.

With a heinous bellow, she returned to the massive demonic fox and shrunk her paw, sticking it straight down her throat and into her stomach. The sight was horrific as Daji fished around her body, trying to fish out Meihua's demonic core.

Finally, she pulled out Meihua's decapitated head and spine and threw it onto the ground.

Both Wei and Daji immediately noticed her piercing red eyes, and the black slits for her pupils.

Wei froze, no longer trembling. Nothing moved except for the steady stream of tears down his face. Finally, he understood.

Earlier, the serpent eye extract that was so easily crushed was a fake. The real one? Meihua had consumed it.

"Meihua," Wei whispered, clutching his sword until his knuckles were white, "You stupid, stupid, stubborn woman."

Consuming a demon's core, in this case the serpent eye extract, was a way to absorb all of their demonic energy. If it was powerful enough, it would turn that person, or divinity, into a demon, though not without massive complications. Of course, a divinity consuming a demon's core was a catastrophic clash of energy.

It was just as bad for demons consuming another demon's core. Demons never worked together. They were just as bad with people or divinities as they were with each other, and any attempt to murder another was always taken. Consuming another demon's core would still assimilate all their power, however, that energy would fight against and try to overtake their demonic consumer.

As a solution, anyone who ever consumed a demonic core would go into isolation for days, weeks, or months, until the assimilation was complete.

For Meihua, a divinity, to have hidden as many signs of her transformation as she did was an impossible feat. It would have been completely grueling—one of the most painful experiences.

"You're such a dummy, Meihua," Wei faintly muttered, wiping his tears again as he turned away from Meihua's corpse and jumped backward, his heart filled with tumultuous emotions ranging from frustration to anger, pity, spite, admiration, and undying sorrow.

As the serpent's demonic energy flowed throughout Daji's body, her white fur coat turned gray and black; she made a last-ditch effort to transform her body, making it bigger and bigger as her limbs became contorted and bloated.

"This will be the last thing you ever see!" Daji roared, her face brutish and completely disproportionate. "Don't forget that you're still being persecuted!"

Her teeth were terrifyingly massive, one of her eyes was double the size of the other, and her lower jaw hung awkwardly from her mouth as she lunged straight toward Wei.

Filled with fresh anger, Wei's eyes narrowed, and his brows furrowed as he stood up, bringing his sword across his bloody body to defend himself, when suddenly two arms slammed into his back and lifted him into the air.

"Who told you to go running off like that?!" Peijin barked, straining to lift Wei's heavy body onto the soaring Zhige. She slipped from the side of the sword and awkwardly fell, shouting as she fell onto Zhige's hilt. "Where's Meihua? We're only a few seconds away from the party so—"

Peijin immediately stopped speaking when she saw the look in Wei's eye. In one moment, everything clicked.

"Peijin," Wei began.

Peijin cut him off. "Whatever you're worrying about, stop."

Wei only repeated himself. "Peijin."

"What?"

"You knew this would happen."

CHAPTER FIFTY

Peijin

Before I could even respond, Wei slammed into me, sending me flying into the ground just a few meters from where my party was waiting.

"Mph—!" I crashed through countless trees with a sharp cry, and Wei leapt down easily, meeting me at the bottom and hoisting me up by my robes.

"I remember now. I remember it all clearly," Wei said, his voice low. "Was this all part of your plan, Peijin? Did you want me to make a fool of myself? How did you make things worse?!" Wei roared, punching me straight in the stomach and sending me flying through the entire forest.

"Peijin?" I heard Yang's voice call out. "Are you all right?"

"Yang! Get out of here!" I shouted, but Wei instantly locked eyes on Yang and laughed bitterly.

"Is this what's going to happen to me every time I open my heart? Two thousand years. Two thousand years I spent rotting in that prison cell, and I still didn't learn my lesson!"

Wei appeared just before Yang and smashed his leg into Yang's side. Yang couldn't even react in time to defend himself before he slammed into the ground.

"Wei, calm down. We're on your side. We were trying to get you through the room, okay? You're fighting the wrong people!" I exclaimed.

There was a wild glint in Wei's eyes that I had never seen. He looked rabid, wild, and uncontrollable, and for the first time, I was scared of him.

"You expect me to believe that? You knew everything about me, Peijin. Is that why you approached me on the freeway? Or asked me about my ribbon and younger brother? You knew all along, and you didn't say a thing!" Wei roared.

He tore the ribbon from his hair and held it in his hands. "You must think I'm a total idiot, don't you, Peijin? Asking me where I got this ribbon, when you knew all along it was my spiritual weapon. And do you know how it was my spiritual weapon? Because Ailun fucking died the first time around, and his spirit haunted this ribbon! And in Yang's room, you used it to protect us because you knew it all along!"

My heart was pounding so hard I could hear it in my ears. "Wei, please, hear me out."

Amelia, Yue, and Ailun emerged from the forest. Without a moment's hesitation, Wei moved just before Ailun's ghost and stabbed him, turning him into ash.

Amelia let out a small cry of horror, and Wei's gaze flicked to her.

3,492 observers are expressing their horror!
312 gods are staring in horror!

[Observers Chat]
Socrates: GET OUT OF THERE
BMely: Oh my god
MoldyBlanket: You can't stop him! He'll kill you at this rate!
CactusLiver: It's not worth it Peijin leave him behind! He's mad!

Disciple Yue activated Magician's Hand!

Before Wei could even step toward Amelia, she vanished from his vision and behind the protective veil of Yue's illusion. His face twisted into a betrayed expression, and he searched for me, tearing through Yue's illusion.

"What, you trust me so little, you think I'd even kill Amelia? Ha! I'm really a monster now, aren't I? Go ahead, try and kill me!" Wei cried out, tears threatening to spill out from his face.

Amelia was crying now, trying to grab onto the ashes of Ailun to no avail.

Wei ripped through the illusion, already familiar with Yue's tricks. When he faced us, all of us were armed, ready to attack him—Amelia's dire wolf was snarling at him, Yue's spear was pointed straight for his throat, Yang's staff was ready to crush him, and Zhige's eye was flickering like mad.

"Wei," I said firmly, "this is between you and me, so leave them out of this. They had no idea, okay?"

"Very well."

Wei sprinted toward me, not even bothering to use his sword. His fists pummeled me, never once letting me catch my breath. I gasped in shock, and it felt like he was crushing all my bones easily.

I whipped Zhige before me to block his attacks, but I wasn't moving to retaliate. Each punch sent me flying back, and tears brimmed in my eyes.

"Wei, please! Listen to me!"

My pleas fell on deaf ears. Wei punched my face, and I could feel my eardrum burst as I collapsed onto the ground, coughing and hacking.

"Wei, things are different now than they were all that time ago. I can promise you, no one in this party ever plans on leaving you! History won't repeat itself this time. It's over, Wei!"

He walked to me, hovering above my body while I lay feebly on the ground. He was tall, but I never noticed our height difference until now. He towered over me, and his dark eyes fell upon me. The ribbon, his spiritual weapon—it floated around his wrist now, threatening to strike me like a snake.

"And? You think that overrides what I've learned about foolish people over the last two thousand years?"

I quivered before him, completely stunned by the flip in attitude. Of course, I expected it. I knew it would happen the moment I laid my eyes on him at the freeway. But to witness it was entirely different.

Here was a man who lost everything that ever mattered to him all because he wanted to try to help others. How could I ever expect him to open his heart to me, especially since I'd been deceiving everyone this whole time?

You have sufficiently understood Disciple Wei.

Card Dealer activated!

Before me, Wei's entire life, his emotions, and his beliefs lay stretched out, categorized into four suits and fifty-six cards. The suits were composed of the wands, the cups, the swords, and the pentacles, which dealt with actions, emotions, relationships, and work respectively.

Most of the cards before me were in color, depicting certain events in Wei's life, while parts I was yet to understand remained black and white. The one that instantly drew me was the Three of Swords, which symbolized sorrow and an accidental death. On it was a beautiful image of Meihua, covered in flower petals, being torn apart by vicious foxes.

I reached out and touched this card, and Wei froze before me.

How would you like to alter this card?

I stared at the card for a moment, dumbfounded. If I wanted to, I could so easily change Wei's entire perspective on Meihua's death. At once, I could make it so he never even remembered it, and he wouldn't need to seek out such violent revenge against the world. His entire being was laid out in front of me, just like that.

I looked into Wei's eyes and swallowed. In the end, I was left in the same spot as Feiyu.

But I couldn't do this. Not to my own characters. Not after I learned that they did have free will, that they could change into entirely different beings than the ones I originally created.

You have canceled this skill.

Wei seemed to have some knowledge of what I was doing, looking up at me with a bewildered expression and grabbing onto his head.

I reached up and wrapped my arms around Wei tightly. "It's different now. You know that too, don't you?"

My words were honest and unfiltered, demonstrating true compassion for Wei and his situation. For the first time, there couldn't be a derived double meaning from what I was saying.

Wei reached for his sword to stab into my side, but I jumped back, blocking him with Zhige. Still, his sword sliced into my side. I winced, but I held his eyes, my smile twisting in pain.

"You know it just as well as I do, Wei!" I shouted. "It's entirely different! This time, Meihua's death was from her free will and her decision to save you, not because of some stupid sense of morality she held. You need to live without tainting that sacrifice, Wei. It's nothing like it was the first time around!"

Wei's face only grew more pained, and I could see tears welling up in his eyes as he swung at me again. This time, he sliced through a part of my forearm.

"You can change things. Your fate isn't sealed. There are people out there who are willing to die for you again. We all are, so please, come back to the station with us!"

My entire party was involved in the fight now, but there was no intention to hurt Wei. Amelia's dire wolf drove him back without snapping or snarling. Yue's Demonic Fire didn't even burn Wei when it touched his skin. Yang only used his spear to defend the party members.

Zhige forced back Wei's sword until it finally flew from his hands. I stood, breathless in front of him. I could hear the rumbling of the train as it finally approached. He switched to his fists, throwing weak and frenzied punches at me. Some of them landed, others didn't.

Tears spilled down his cheeks. Wei fell to the ground before me, sobbing and reaching out for anything to hold on to like a drowning man. Instead of being met with nothing but his catastrophic thoughts, my entire party was there, wrapping their arms around him.

Amelia sniffled loudly, crying just as loud as Wei was. "Wei-shushu, please don't hurt us."

Yue, who always disagreed with Wei's sense of justice, now clung to him, burying her face against his chest and whispering something I couldn't hear.

I hated to admit it, absolutely despised it, but I could almost understand Karma for a moment. Why had I written like this? Dumping endless misfortunes on Wei, even if he were only a character . . . someone who was so endlessly kind, forgiving, and selfless.

I'd written it because I was bitter. Bitter and mad at the entire world around me because I felt as if I'd been dealt an unfair hand ever since I was born. So, I wrote. And I wrote and wrote and wrote to create a world where I'd never be dealt an unfair hand because I was the dealer.

I pulled back, extending my hand to Wei.

"Wei. Let's go home."

CHAPTER FIFTY-ONE

Wei looked up at me, his shoulders slumped. His lip quivered when he looked down at the ground, ashamed, before he took my hand and pulled himself up. He wiped his face clean with his white sleeve. I shot him a reassuring smile, and my party headed for the train.

The ground beneath me began to shake violently. I stumbled and grabbed onto Wei to keep myself steady before I searched for the culprit.

A horrifically large, corrupted Daji had lumbered her way to the temple. Her fur was spotted with massive black spots, entire snakes pouring out of the gaping holes before burrowing in her abdomen.

Her eyes came to mimic that of a serpent, but they were blinking independently, as if fighting within her for control.

"Wei!" she roared, the sound of it grating and horrific, "I'll fucking kill you!" As she spoke, pools of black blood poured out of her mouth, and she choked on it when speaking.

Daji slammed her tails on the ground. Her skin rippled and looked like scales before it was covered in fur then scales again. She lunged straight for Wei, but I intercepted, shoving Wei back and slicing through Daji's decaying body with Zhige.

A flurry of yellow sparks erupted out of Daji's body, and my eyes grew wide. Those yellow sparks could only mean one thing: Karma.

Instead of the groaning voice from the beast, I heard that familiar childish one.

"Ha ha ha, you know what you did, you know what you did! You broke the rules!"

I stared at my party, barking orders. "All of you, back up! Head toward the train. Let me take care of this one," I ordered.

"But, Peijin—" Yang began.

"I'm not telling you to leave me! Just let me handle this one!"

I was yet to tell my party about Karma, and now wasn't the time.

Daji's body suddenly fell limp and collapsed to the ground before yellow sparks took over it. Her body became reanimated, but this time, by Karma.

Karma sprinted toward me and smashed her paws down on the ground. "You know it just as well as I do. Somebody had to lose in Wei's room, whether it was your party or Wei. That's fate! You can never escape it!"

Karma lunged at me, her claws outstretched, but I leapt back, stabbing Zhige into part of her fleshy arm.

"Fuck your fate. I'll do things my own way!" I shouted, digging Zhige into the beast. It pierced through Daji's body, but Karma was unaffected, slamming one of her nine tails straight at me.

"You can't break your own rule, Peijin, not as long as I exist," Karma cackled. "Don't you get it? I'm going to instill your fate every step of the way."

Karma's long black claws grabbed onto me and forced me into the ground. I cried out in pain as one pierced through my shoulder. Once pinned by Karma, I couldn't get out from her grasp.

Zhige slashed into her fingers and tore them apart, but Karma lifted a hand and slapped the blade away, causing an explosion of yellow sparks at her interference.

Just before Karma's vile teeth could tear into me, a glowing ball burst down from the sky, light erupting out from it.

Blue, pink, and white robes swirled in the air alongside red flowers that sprinkled down from the sky in a flurry of gold karmic sparks.

"M-Meihua?!" I exclaimed, staring at the glowing ball of spiritual energy in the sky.

She twisted with stunning grace, raising her pink sword before whipping it right at Karma, her robes blowing back up against her body. They slid up her arms, revealing the large tattoo with large black characters beneath:

The World.

Another tarot card—and I had no fucking clue what it meant.

I let out a pained grunt at the feeling of the massive injury on my side, and I was upgrading my Physique level until I could handle the pain—but I was still frugal, and I needed as many stars as I could for the next chapter.

A burst of spiritual energy erupted from Meihua's sword as it landed straight on Karma's body.

Karma led out a gruesome, animalistic howl and immediately shrunk, trying to avoid her piercing sword, but there was no use.

"The Major Arcana, huh?!" Karma exclaimed, her expression wild. For the first time, she lost her composure. "I never thought you would come to Liu Peijin's defense of all people!"

The World smiled at Karma cruelly, even though such an expression was beautiful on Meihua's face. "A lonely being like you doesn't have many friends."

What I was witnessing, however, was a fight between two gods—Karma and the Major Arcana.

Because the World certainly wasn't the Meihua I knew.

[Observers Chat]
Socrates: The World tarot: Fulfillment and harmony or emptiness and incompletion. It's about reaping the fruits of your labor after a tumultuous event.

These two gods lunged at each other viciously. Karma with claw and tooth, the World with sword and grace. So, did the Major Arcana just take the forms of different characters the way Karma took my form?

The World was being pushed back by an explosion of yellow sparks that strove to drive her out. She whipped her sword in the air, and it crackled like a firework. She wrapped it around Karma's form, but Karma instantly tore it apart with the sparks.

What was Karma fighting so hard to ruin me for?

I smirked, looking at the two gods crash together in the air in a beautiful flurry of light. "I get it now, Karma. You're just an extension of everything I've written, aren't you? You can't stand me changing the story, because you loved it the way it was."

You have sufficiently understood Karma.
Card Dealer activated!

Fifty-six cards appeared before me. Most of them were in black and white, but the Ten of Swords was lit up beautifully. The card showed an illustration of me getting gored and disemboweled by Karma, who was using my appearance.

I had no clue what tarot cards stood for, but with this skill, I innately understood all the Minor Arcana cards. This one represented obsession.

How would you like to alter this card?

Karma's head instantly snapped toward me. "You're in my head." Her eyes were wide and terrifying, staring through my very existence.

I felt goose bumps appear all over me. Using this skill meant I could lose one of my own Minor Arcana cards, too, and all of them seemed to be of great importance.

Luckily, just peeking into Karma's brain was enough.

The World dug her ribbon straight through Karma's flesh, and Karma cried out in pain. The World hit her. Hit Karma.

Like a coward, Karma evaporated into millions of yellow sparks, escaping the situation. But I knew things would only get worse for me. Now that Karma knew I could influence her thinking . . . I'd created a more formidable opponent for myself.

The World let out a heavy sigh and descended toward me with a friendly look in her eye.

I raised Zhige firmly toward Meihua, my eyes like slits as I glared at her.

"You're not Meihua," I spat.

She turned toward me and bowed deeply, her hands folded together in a formal greeting. "The Tower. It's very nice to meet you for the first time. I wish it would have been under better circumstances."

Meihua then gestured toward Zhige, giving the blade a faint smile. "And, Haimo, it's always a joy to see you. I do believe your new name suits you more, but your creator might have some protests."

Zhige's eye spun wildly; the blade tried to jerk away from her, but I held it firm.

I grabbed Meihua by the collar and pulled her near, sliding the sleeve of her robes up to expose her pale arm.

The World was scribbled there, just like *the Tower* was on mine, except hers depicted a woman in long white robes standing atop a blooming lotus flower. The lovely woman held a vase of gushing water, and white foam swirled around at her feet.

I shoved her arm back firmly. Yellow sparks were springing out from Meihua's feet, but she suppressed them.

"So," I remarked, "you're part of the Major Arcana, aren't you? I could recognize those damned tattoos and red boxes anywhere. You're the one who descended at the start of the arc."

"I must apologize." She bowed again, and my face twisted into a look of disgust. I had to confirm my suspicions now. She looked identical to Meihua, but there was no way this could be the same woman I'd gotten so close to.

"Who are you?" I questioned.

She looked at me simply, her long lashes glistening in the light and her lips bright and red. "The World."

"That's not what I'm asking you. You look just like her," I protested, referencing the Meihua *I* knew.

The World nodded slightly, closing her eyes to avoid Wei's stare. "I'm not the Meihua you met earlier."

"Then are you just using her form? You're sick."

She laughed. "No, nothing like that. Once upon a time, I thought of myself as Meihua more than I thought of myself as the World."

I froze before her. "Are you from a different timeline?"

"I don't think of it that way."

"Ha," I laughed cruelly. "So, it's really like that then, right?"

I stood there for a moment, dozens of thoughts swarming through my head. There was one rule—only one—that I held to myself ever since I began *Surviving My First Run*.

No matter what, without any exception, in any universe, would I ever fuck around with time. I couldn't understand it, and as soon as it was brought up, nothing was ever set in stone.

If multiple timelines existed, there were suddenly infinite possibilities for this story and an infinite number of influences, and I didn't know any of them.

"Fuck!" I screamed, digging Zhige into the ground before turning around, taking in a deep breath.

This messed up everything. The Major Arcana was some time-traveling cult that could rival Karma? Bullshit. That wasn't possible. This world had gotten so much bigger and so much farther away from me.

The World stood there silently, watching me pensively. I hated the feel of her stare on me; it felt so alien and inhuman, and I thought about tearing her down, but I knew that would be stupid.

Meihua looked over at Amelia and then back at me.

"What's her name?"

I scoffed. "So, what, you don't know everyone here? Or has no one saved Amelia before me?"

"Amelia is a lovely name."

"Don't play dumb with me!" I shouted, holding back my anger and frustration. "If we're both part of this Major Arcana, then don't speak down on me! I don't fucking care who you are! The World is a stupid fucking name, and you come off as a total narcissist!"

Suddenly, I noticed a blue glint in her eyes, and she was staring too intently at me.

Scathing Reviewer activated!

The World winced and drew a hand before her eyes. "You have a strong skill to block me like that. That hasn't happened to me in a long, long time."

"Oh, are you fucking kidding me?! Really?! You're really fucking trying to use a skill on me right now?!" I roared, infuriated at her attempt to read my profile.

"I'm sorry. I'll be straight with you now," Meihua said honestly. "I don't have much time left before Karma overpowers me." Karma had retreated physically, but she continued as a force. Yellow sparks were already emerging at Meihua's feet.

A burst of jealousy and desire spread through me as I recalled my first interaction with Karma. The utter humiliation; the complete ruin of me with a few simple words. I craved the power that could put me on the same level as Karma.

Meihua cleared her throat but never broke eye contact. "I'm impressed by the work of the Tower. For such an abysmal arcana, you surprised me. We share a common enemy. Karma. Though, I'll say she's taken a particular liking to you," she confessed.

Abysmal?!

This World continued to talk, however, and I could see her struggle to control the growing yellow sparks beneath her. To have influenced the scenario this much and to have integrated . . . she was wickedly powerful.

Probably more than most gods I've written.

"This is the first time I've seen you," the World continued. "To answer your question, no, I've never met most of you. In fact, the only ones I recognize here are Wei and Yue."

Then only the characters, huh?

I bit my tongue. She didn't know I was the author then or who was or wasn't a character.

Sick and tired of her droning and growing increasingly mad at the air of superiority she carried, I cut her off, asking questions instead.

"How many runs has it been?"

She shook her head slightly. "I'm the youngest known member." She trailed off, staring at my arm. "Except for you. I've been around for . . . maybe a hundred?"

A hundred runs? *Oh, I'm really fucked. Surviving My First Run* was 3,649 chapters with just one incomplete run.

I thought back to the start of this arc, when I had tried to get on the train first with my party. Back then, Feiyu's party somehow entered, and on the front of the car were the words *Twenty-Two*. Now I confirmed that they knew about the Major Arcana.

More importantly, there was that one obstructed figure at the back of the car with flowing white hair.

"Fuck," I muttered. So, one of the disciples must have gone through the past runs too.

"Who is it?" I demanded, stepping toward Meihua and closing the distance. "Who the fuck is this goddamn disciple?!"

"You'll meet them in the next arc when you compete with the top three parties."

My eye twitched out of frustration at her useless answer, but I took a step back.

"Have you ever tried to destroy the system in any of the past runs?"

"Ah." Meihua smiled wistfully for a moment. "I'm not supposed to tell you this. In the run just before this, we made it. But right at the end, this unknown rogue skill sent us ba—"

She winced, a flurry of yellow sparks biting into her ankles. Karma was throwing a complete tantrum, and her spiritual energy could only hang on for so long.

"Rogue skill?" I grabbed onto her, shaking her. "What do you mean? What was it called?! What about the Eternal Wish?!"

"The Tower," she urged. "I don't have much time, so let me say this. Your future is destruction and revelation. That's why you've been picked as the Tower. Back in your dungeon room, something blocked me, blocked all of us, from watching your fight with Karma.

"You claim to be the god of fate and fortune, but none of us have ever seen you before this run. Yet here you are, predicting all of it. So, I need you to get to the end!" Meihua hurriedly exclaimed, cutting her arm and letting blood flow out as flowers erupted all around her.

"Wait!" Wei called out, gently reaching out a trembling hand toward Meihua's fluttering pink and blue robes. His jaw trembled like he was in freezing temperatures.

Before he could say anything, she got the first word in, cutting him off before he could come to any ill conclusions.

She bowed deeply before him, practically kowtowing.

"Your Highness. I apologize for all the hardships you have faced." Her tone was sympathetic and civil, but it remained a little distant, not holding any sort of intimacy or affection for Wei.

"So, you're a different Meihua, right? From some other timeline?"

She nodded.

"That means I must have saved you at some point, right? There was a way?" Wei asked.

She gave a weak smile. "I'm the youngest of all the Arcana because my survival meant ruin for many others. None of us can avoid Karma."

She reached out to Wei, covered in a flurry of yellow sparks now. "If you ever lose meaning in life, find meaning in Peijin until you can find meaning in your own. You must survive. Once you return to the arcs, you'll return to being a divinity, but your powers will be limited by Karma."

Yellow sparks covered her entire body now, but she let out one final call. "I will see you again in the future. When Karma permits, we can properly introduce ourselves."

Wei stood there, staring at the ground with tears in his eyes. I could only imagine the whirlwind of emotions he was going through right now.

Yue, Amelia, and Yang finally appeared behind us.

"Different timelines, huh?" Yang said, scratching his head. "How bad is that?"

"What's all this Karma nonsense, too?" Yue said, cocking her head.

I sighed. "Let's talk in the train."

My entire party gathered on the train, and I sat down, clutching Wei's sleeve. I looked at my reflection in the train window. Around me were characters—no, people—who I'd grown so close to. I could see their images in the tinted window, comforting me and Wei, but I couldn't focus on them.

I saw my own reflection twist into a childish smile, and I stared at it, my reflection not matching my own expression.

Karma was pissed.

Divinity Supreme Commander of the Heavenly Hosts has rejoined Channel #IS-2948.

CHAPTER FIFTY-TWO

Divinity Supreme Commander of the Heavenly
Hosts is announcing his return from prison!

Divinity Supreme Commander of the Heavenly
Hosts uses confetti screen effect!

Divinity Spirit of the Jade Moon is pleading with Divinity
Supreme Commander of the Heavenly Hosts to read the room.

Divinity Great Sage Equaling Heaven is snickering.

Divinity The One Who Fights in Front has smacked the Divinity
Supreme Commander of the Heavenly Hosts in the back of his head.

Demon Abyssal Kraken of Black Seas is deeply embarrassed.

Divinity Supreme Commander of the Heavenly Hosts is
scrambling to catch up on the broadcast stream at max speed.

Divinity Supreme Commander of the Heavenly Hosts screams in terror
at Disciple Yang's room, Disciple Peijin's room, and Disciple Wei's room!

Divinity Supreme Commander of the Heavenly
Hosts is attempting to descend into the arc!

> **Thousands of observers and gods immediately disable him!**

> **Divinity Supreme Commander of the Heavenly Hosts is begging for Divinity Blessed Martial Guard of Salvation to forgive him.**

> **Divinity Supreme Commander of the Heavenly Hosts sponsors every member of Peijin's World Dominion with 100,000 stars!**

> **Divinity Supreme Commander of the Heavenly Hosts is coughing blood at the injustice to Divinity Blessed Martial Guard of Salvation.**

> **Divinity Supreme Commander of the Heavenly Hosts calls for the eradication of all demons.**

> **Demon Abyssal Kraken of Black Seas awkwardly blushes.**

"It's strange to see myself addressed as a divinity now," Wei said softly. He was sitting up himself now, his hands politely folded in his lap like he was a timid child in a new classroom.

> **[Observers Chat]**
> **Nipon23:** what a total mess.

> **Divinity Supreme Commander of the Heavenly Hosts is applauding Wei's strength through tears.**

> **Divinity Supreme Commander of the Heavenly Hosts is urging observers to give Divinity Blessed Martial Guard of Salvation a five-star review to boost his spiritual energy.**

Archangel Michael proceeded to blow up the chat and surrounding area with blue boxes before Chang opened up a one-on-one between him and his disciple.

Something Archangel Michael said must have been very emotional because Wei's eyes welled up with tears again, but Yang comforted him as I stared, my lips slightly agape.

"Peijin," Wei said softly, "could you help me pick my skill?"

Before him hovered the familiar board, and I read the options.

> **POTENTIAL SKILLS LIST**
> **Judgment**

Thirty Aethyrs
Divine Right

Judgment would allow Wei to determine someone's morality, and if they were beneath his own moral code, he would gain immense stat boosts against them. It was a good skill for someone as righteous as him.

But the Thirty Aethyrs would allow Wei to enter the Enochian plane and contact all Judeo-Christian divinities with ease while also accessing secrets of the universe. It was a complicated skill that overwhelmed most of its users, but given Wei's long background as a divinity, I felt confident in his ability to use it.

Divine Right was the skill previously offered to me, and with the next arc where party dominance would be determined, it wasn't as necessary.

"Wei, would you be all right pursuing a different method of cultivation? If so, I'd pick Thirty Aethyrs."

He nodded and clicked it, giving me a slight bow of his head. "It's the one Archangel Michael wanted me to pick too." He gave me a reassured smile. "I'm glad you both said the same. I'm lucky to have you two looking out for me again."

"Peijin!" Chang suddenly cried out, appearing and grabbing onto my face and practically crawling all over me. His long claws dug into my hoodie and he would grab my skin, pinching and tugging and pulling at it until I firmly slapped him back.

"What is it with you?!"

He handed me an orange lollipop, and I shut up temporarily, listening to him.

"Peijin, do you think I'm going to get fired from my job? If they find out that some extinct goddess just entered my arc, I'm going to be murdered. I'll be put in the Hall of Shame for every dragon to mock."

I shot him a judgmental look. "You're fine. The higher-ups will call an emergency meeting if they haven't already. You're at the bottom of the pyramid, so they can't blame you for not being strong enough to stop it."

"I'm serious, Peijin!" Chang shouted, pulling at his whiskers at my glare. "I'm going to get skinned. They're going to make a fashion line out of my scales, and you'll probably buy the whole collection just to pawn me off to some church or cult for worshipping."

". . . You think so lowly of me."

[Observers Chat]
Socrates: I mean, he's not wrong . . .

"Of course I do!" Chang retorted. "Do you want to go over every lie you've told?"

"Hey, I—"

"Let's start with the first arc. The first! In the tutorial, you already—"

I grabbed Chang and squeezed him until he squeaked, and he vanished in a flurry of sparks.

"I hate that stupid dragon," Yue spat.

I popped the orange lollipop out of my mouth. "Don't shit on him like that. He's been good to us. Once we land and get a short break, I'll explain what happened with the Major Arcana and Karma."

Yang looked at me. "We all heard the conversation. But what's going on with Karma?"

"It turns out Karma isn't just the system that serves as checks and balances. It's also a being, and it hates me. Wants me dead."

"Then that makes the Major Arcana good. They're the only thing I've seen rival Karma at all, and if Karma hates you, then you should befriend the Major Arcana."

I scoffed loudly. "The moment I figure out how to bring both down, we're having a team meeting."

Yue gave me a disappointed, disgruntled, and dismayed look before she nodded toward Amelia, who was sitting across from me, her short legs dangling and unable to touch the floor beneath her.

"You know she wants you to talk to her, right?" Yue said. "You're so bad with kids. You're just bad with people in general."

My eye twitched as I held myself back from punching her. She seemed to recover just fine, so what the hell was I worried about?

I looked at Amelia, but she avoided my gaze. She pretended to finally look up accidentally, and I gestured for her to come sit by me. At once, she leapt toward me and wrapped her arms around my neck.

She remained silent, but I knew what she wanted to say.

I let out a heavy sigh, unsure of how to tell her about what she had missed and what Wei had just gone through. But, when it was me with my own mother and father, had I not wanted to know?

But maybe Amelia was too young to know. Maybe she was too young to be in these scenarios at all, and so was Ailun, but that hadn't held me back when I was the one holding the pen.

When I explained the deaths of Ailun and Meihua to Amelia, she didn't cry at all.

It felt like this train ride was going to go on for an eternity.

"Are you okay?" I asked her softly, gently running my hands through her hair with my good hand. The other was still injured, but the wrapped bandage was doing a good enough job holding it together.

She nodded and opened her mouth to speak, but she held herself back and blinked repeatedly. I could tell that the moment she opened her mouth, she would burst into tears.

"You can cry if you want to," I reassured her, still combing through her hair before pulling it over her shoulder.

She shook her head. "I'm not crying."

I gave her my best smile. Amelia was like an open book, and I viewed her as a bit of a crybaby—not that that was a bad thing. Since I met her, I thought that she had reminded me of someone or something. I wondered if that had been myself.

"All right," I said simply.

While I stroked the back of her head, I noticed it was rather flat. Her parents must not have held her much when she was a kid and let her lie in her crib most of the time.

Thinking about this made me feel a little bit better. I thought that maybe I could treat her sweetly without having to feel so bad about my role in her parents' deaths.

Wei sat beside me, and I felt like I couldn't quite face him. He was turned toward Yang, who comforted him relentlessly.

I wished I could have said something to Wei that would have made him feel better the way Yang could. But that was why Yang was always a star, even if he worked at a pest control company.

I thought if I was reborn, I would want to be someone like him. I wanted to be well liked, approachable, and comforting. It was silly that I could write characters like Feiyu perfectly, but I myself could never fill any of those roles.

With Amelia in my arms, I moved until I was standing before Wei, my hurt hand gripping the pole to balance myself in the moving car.

"Wei," I stated, "I hope you can forgive me for not doing better."

The band around his arm floated up and around me, gently pressing against me curiously before pulling back and twisting and turning like a newborn kitten in the grass for the first time.

Wei looked surprised, but his gaze softened. "Peijin, thank you for not leaving."

For some reason, his words caused my chest to swell up, and my expression faltered for a moment. Back in Yue's room, I was someone she could never rely on, but here, I was relieved to find that at least someone could look at me differently.

"Wei, be my sword," I suddenly declared. "I want you to stay by my side until this apocalypse is over. In a few moments, we'll be off this train. Whether or not you agree, I will end this. But, when I reach the end, I want you to be there too."

His eyes widened as he blinked at me before he stood up and laughed lightly. "You make it sound so transactional, Peijin. I'd do it for you regardless."

He took my hand and shook it. I stood in front of the train doors, and before they opened, I turned back toward my party. "The next arc begins with us fighting against the top parties. I want all of you to take some time off. By the time you all wake up from your kiddy naps, I'll have dissected the Arcana," I said in a cocky tone, smiling widely to seal their doubts.

And so, the poor dog was back in service—maybe it was out of a sense of guilt or obligation, but when the doors slid open, Wei grabbed his sword and walked out of the train first.

In front of us, Feiyu sat on a foldable chair that looked comically small beneath him. A long black blade was being sharpened in his hands, gleaming as the light reflected off it. The train rumbled and groaned before it left for its next destination.

"Welcome back," Feiyu said.

Arc #2—Dungeons of Great Turmoil has concluded!
Stars received: 10,000

Congratulations! You have completed the arc.

ABOUT THE AUTHOR

BananaDragon is the author of the Scathing Reviewer series, originally released on Royal Road. Adventurous at heart, she loves taking pictures of the vast outdoors with shaky hands and painting portraits with mere, scattered brushstrokes. She also enjoys sitting under her backyard's vast oak trees on a soft pink blanket with a pen and notebook in her hands, sipping a sweet iced coffee. BananaDragon lives in Chicago.

Podium

DISCOVER MORE

STORIES UNBOUND

PodiumEntertainment.com